VAL McDERMID

THE MERMAIDS
SINGING

HarperCollins*Publishers*

HarperCollins*Publishers*
77–85 Fulham Palace Road,
Hammersmith, London W6 8JB

www.fireandwater.com

This paperback edition 2000

5 7 9 8 6

First published in Great Britain by
HarperCollins*Publishers* 1995

ISBN 0 00 649358 0

Set in Sabon

Printed and bound in Great Britain by
Bookmarque Ltd, Croydon, Surrey

Acknowledgements

It's always disturbing when life seems to imitate art. I started planning this book in the spring of 1992, long before the killings that shook the gay community in London. I sincerely hope that there is nothing in these pages that will cause grief or offence to anyone.

As ever, I have picked brains galore and thoroughly exploited my friends while researching and writing *The Mermaids Singing*. I'd particularly like to thank senior clinical psychologist and offender profiler Mike Berry of Ashworth Top Security Psychiatric Hospital in Liverpool for giving so generously of his time and expertise in the preparation of this book. The insights and information I gleaned from him have been invaluable, as well as stopping the conversation at dinner parties dead in its tracks.

Thanks too to Peter Byram of the Responsive College Unit in Blackburn, who gave me advice on the finer points of computer technology. Alison Scott and Frankie Hegarty provided helpful information on matters medical. Detective Superintendent Mike Benison of the Sussex Police generously made time in his busy schedule to fill me in on the handling of major murder enquiries. Jai Penna, Diana Cooper and Paula Tyler demonstrated yet again that some lawyers are generous with their time and knowledge.

For their support, patience and advice throughout, I'd particularly like to thank Brigid Baillie and Lisanne Radice. It can't be easy putting up with someone who spends her days inside the head of a serial killer . . .

The northern city of Bradfield is entirely a creature of my imagination. In particular, the attitudes and behaviour attributed to assorted professionals, including police officers, were chosen for reasons of fictional necessity rather than verisimilitude. In Britain, we are fortunate to have few serial killers; that's because most of them are caught after their first murder. Let's hope the profilers and the police can keep it that way.

Val McDermid

Val McDermid grew up in a Scottish mining community then read English at Oxford. She was a journalist for sixteen years, spending the last three years as Northern Bureau Chief of a national Sunday tabloid. She is now a full-time writer and lives in South Manchester.

The Mermaids Singing won the 1995 CWA Gold Dagger Award for Best Crime Novel of the Year. *A Place of Execution*, her complex and disturbing stand-alone thriller, was published to great acclaim last year, and is now available in paperback.

She has written six crime novels featuring Manchester PI Kate Brannigan, and the latest in this much-praised series, *Star Struck*, won the Grand Prix des Romans d'Aventure in France.

A further five novels feature journalist-sleuth Lindsay Gordon.

For Tookie Flystock, my beloved serial insect killer.

I have heard the mermaids singing, each to each.
I do not think that they will sing to me.

'THE LOVE SONG OF J. ALFRED PRUFROCK'
T. S. ELIOT

The soul of torture is male

COMMENT ON EXHIBIT CARD
*THE MUSEUM OF CRIMINOLOGY AND TORTURE,
SAN GIMIGNANO, ITALY.*

All chapter epigraphs are taken from
'On Murder considered as one of the fine arts'
by Thomas De Quincey (1827)

You always remember the first time. Isn't that what they say about sex? How much more true it is of murder. I will never forget a single delicious moment of that strange and exotic drama. Even though now, with the benefit of experience and hindsight, I can see it was an amateurish performance, it still has the power to thrill, though not any longer to satisfy.

Although I didn't realize it before the decision to act was forced upon me, I had been paving the way for murder well in advance. Picture an August day in Tuscany. An air-conditioned coach whisking us from city to city. A busload of Northern culture vultures, desperate to fill every moment of our precious fortnight's package with something memorable to set against Castle Howard and Chatsworth.

I'd enjoyed Florence, the churches and art galleries filled with strangely contradictory images of martyrdom and Madonnas. I had scaled the dizzy heights of Brunelleschi's dome surmounting the immense cathedral, entranced by the winding stairway that leads up from the gallery to the tiny cupola, the worn stone steps tightly sandwiched between the ceiling of the dome and the roof itself. It was like being inside my computer, a real role-playing adventure, working my way through the maze to daylight. All it lacked were monsters to slay on the way. And then, to emerge into bright day and amazement that up here, at the end of this cramped ascent, there was a postcard and souvenir seller, a small, dark, smiling man stooped from years of lugging his wares aloft. If it had really been a game, I would have been able to purchase some magic from him. As it was, I bought more postcards than I had people to send them to.

After Florence, San Gimignano. The town rose up from the green Tuscan plain, its ruined towers thrusting into the sky like fingers clawing upwards from a grave. The guide burbled on about 'a medieval Manhattan', another crass comparison to add to the list we'd been force-fed since Calais.

As we neared the town, my excitement grew. All over Florence, I'd seen the advertisements for the one tourist attraction I really wanted to see. Hanging splendidly from lampposts, gorgeous in rich red and gold, the banners insisted that I visit the Museo Criminologico di San Gimignano. Consulting my phrasebook, I'd confirmed what I'd thought the small print said. A museum of criminology and torture. Needless to say, it wasn't on our cultural itinerary.

I didn't have to search for my target; a leaflet about the museum, complete with street plan, was thrust upon me less than a dozen yards inside the massive stone gateway set in the medieval walls. Savouring the pleasure of anticipation, I wandered around for a while, marvelling at the monuments to civic disharmony that the towers represented. Each powerful family had had its own fortified tower which they defended against their neighbours with everything from boiling lead to cannons. At the peak of the city's prosperity, there were supposedly a couple of hundred towers. Compared to medieval San Gimignano, Saturday night down the docks after closing time seems like kindergarten, the seamen mere amateurs in mayhem.

When I could no longer resist the pull of the museum, I crossed the central piazza, tossing a bicoloured 200-lire coin in the well for luck, and walked a few yards down a side street, where the now familiar red and gold hangings adorned ancient stone walls. Excitement buzzing in me like a blood-crazed mosquito, I walked into the cool foyer and calmly bought my entrance ticket and a copy of the glossy, illustrated museum guide.

How can I begin to describe the experience? The physical reality was so much more overwhelming than photographs or videos or books had ever prepared me for. The first exhibit was a ladder rack, the accompanying card describing its function in loving detail in Italian and English. Shoulders would pop out of their sockets, hips and knees separate to the sound of rending cartilage and ligament, spines stretch out of alignment till vertebrae fell apart like beads from a broken string. 'Victims,' the card said laconically, 'often measured between six and nine inches taller after the rack.' Extraordinary minds the inquisitors had. Not satisfied with interrogating their heretics while they were alive and suffering, they had to seek further answers from their violated bodies.

The exhibition was a monument to the ingenuity of man. How could anyone not admire the minds that examined the human body so intimately that they could engineer such exquisite and finely calibrated suffering? With their relatively unsophisticated technology, those medieval brains devised systems of torture so refined that they are still in use today. It seems that the only improvement our modern post-industrial society has been able to come up with is the additional frisson provided by the application of electricity.

I moved through the rooms, savouring each and every toy, from the gross spikes of the Iron Maiden to the more subtle and elegant machinery of pears, those slender, segmented ovoids which were inserted into vagina or anus. Then, when the ratchet was turned, the segments separated and extended till the pear had metamorphosed into a

3

strange flower, petals fringed with razor-sharp metal teeth. Then it was removed. Sometimes the victims survived, which was probably a crueller fate.

I noticed unease and horror on the faces and in the voices of some of my fellow visitors, but recognized it for the hypocrisy it was. Secretly, they were loving every minute of their pilgrimage, but respectability forbade any public display of their excitement. Only the children were honest in their ardent fascination. I would have happily bet that I was far from the only person in those cool, pastel rooms who felt the surge of sexual desire between their legs as we drank in the exhibits. I have often wondered how many holiday sexual encounters have been spiced and salted by the secret recollection of the torture museum.

Outside, in a sun-drenched courtyard, a skeleton crouched in a cage, bones clean as if stripped by vultures. Back in the days when the towers stood tall, these cages would have hung on the outer walls of San Gimignano, a message to inhabitants and strangers alike that this was a city where the law exacted a harsh penalty if it was not respected. I felt a strange kinship with those burghers. I too respect the need for punishment after betrayal.

Near the skeleton, an enormous metal-shod spoked wheel leaned against the wall. It would have looked perfectly at home in an agricultural museum. But the card fixed to the wall behind it explained a more imaginative function. Criminals were bound to the wheel. First, they were flayed with scourges that ripped the flesh from their bones, exposing their entrails to the eager crowd. Then, with iron bars, their bones were broken on the wheel. I found myself thinking of the tarot card, the wheel of fortune.

When I realized I was going to have to become a killer, the memory of the torture museum rose before me like a muse. I've always been good with my hands.

After that first time, part of me hoped I wouldn't be

4

forced to do it again. But I knew that if I had to, the next time it would be better. We learn from our mistakes the imperfections of our actions. And luckily, practice makes perfect.

1

Gentlemen, I have had the honour to be appointed by your committee to the trying task of reading the Williams' Lecture on Murder, considered as one of the Fine Arts; a task which might be easy enough three or four centuries ago, when the art was little understood, and few great models had been exhibited; but in this age, when masterpieces of excellence have been executed by professional men, it must be evident, that in the style of criticism applied to them, the public will look for something of a corresponding improvement.

Tony Hill tucked his hands behind his head and stared up at the ceiling. There was a fine web of cracks around the elaborate plaster rose which surrounded the light fitting, but he was oblivious to it. The faint light of dawn tinged with the orange of sodium streetlamps filtered in through a triangular gap at the top of his curtains, but he had no interest in that either. Subconsciously, he registered the central-heating boiler kicking in, readying itself to take the edge off the damp winter chill that seeped in round door and window frames. His nose was cold, his eyes gritty. He couldn't remember the last time he'd had a straight night's sleep. His concerns about what he had to get through that day was part of the reason for the night's interrupted dreams, but there was more than that. Much more.

As if today wasn't more than enough to worry about. He knew what was expected of him, but delivering it was another story. Other people managed these things with nothing more than a short-lived flutter in the stomach, but not Tony. It required all his resources to maintain the façade he'd need to get through the day. In circumstances like these, he understood how much it took out of method actors to produce the fraught, driven performances that captivated their audiences. By tonight, he'd be good for nothing except another vain attempt at eight hours' sleep.

He shifted in bed, pulling one hand out and running it through his short dark hair. He scratched the stubble on his chin and sighed. He knew what he wanted to do today, but equally, he was well aware it would be professional suicide if he did. It didn't matter that he knew there was a serial killer loose in Bradfield. He couldn't afford to be the one to say it first. His stomach clenched on emptiness and he winced. With a sigh, he pushed the duvet back and got out of bed, shaking his legs to unfurl the concertina folds of his baggy pyjamas.

Tony trudged off to the bathroom and snapped on the light. As he emptied his bladder, he reached out with his free hand and switched on the radio. Bradfield Sound's traffic announcer was revealing the morning's projected bottlenecks with a cheerfulness that no motorist could have equalled without large doses of Prozac. Thankful that he wouldn't be driving that morning, Tony turned to the sink.

He gazed into his deep-set blue eyes, still bleary with sleep. Whoever said the eyes were mirrors of the soul was a true bullshit merchant, he thought ironically. Probably just as well, or he wouldn't have an intact mirror in the house. He undid the top button of his pyjama jacket and opened the bathroom cabinet, reaching out for the shaving foam. The tremor he spotted in his hand stopped him short. Angrily, he slid the door shut with a loud crack and reached up for his electric razor. He hated the shave it produced, never leaving him with the fresh, clean feeling that came from a wet shave. But better to feel vaguely scruffy than to turn up looking like a walking illustration of the death of a thousand cuts.

The other disadvantage of the electric razor was that he didn't have to concentrate so hard on what he was doing, leaving his mind free to range over the day ahead. Sometimes it was tempting to imagine that everybody was like him, getting up each morning and selecting a persona for the day. But he had learned over years of exploring other people's minds that it wasn't so. For most people, the available selection was severely limited. Some people would doubtless be grateful for the choices that knowledge, skill and necessity had brought Tony. He wasn't one of them.

As he switched off the razor, he heard the frantic chords that preceded every news summary on Bradfield Sound. With a sense of foreboding, he turned to face the radio, tense and alert as a middle-distance runner waiting for the starting pistol. At the end of the five-minute bulletin, he sighed with relief and pushed open the shower curtain. He'd expected a revelation that would have been impossible for him to ignore. But so far, the body count was still three.

On the other side of the city, John Brandon, Bradfield Metropolitan Police's Assistant Chief Constable (Crime) stooped over the washbasin and stared glumly into the bathroom mirror. Not even the shaving soap covering his face like a Santa Claus beard could give him an air of benevolence. If he hadn't chosen the police, he'd have been an ideal candidate for a career as a funeral director. He was two inches over six feet, slim to the point of skinny, with deep-set dark eyes and prematurely steel-grey hair. Even when he smiled, his long face managed to sustain an air of melancholy. Today, he thought, he looked like a bloodhound with a head cold. At least there was good reason for his misery. He was about to pursue a course of action that would be as popular with his Chief Constable as a priest in an Orange Lodge.

Brandon sighed deeply, spattering the mirror with foam. Derek Armthwaite, his Chief, had the burning blue eyes of a visionary, but there was nothing revolutionary in what they saw. He was a man who thought the Old Testament a more appropriate handbook for police officers than the Police And Criminal Evidence Act. He believed most modern police methods were not only ineffective but also heretical. In Derek Armthwaite's frequently aired opinion, bringing back the birch and the cat-o'-nine-tails would be far more effective in reducing crime figures than any number of social workers, sociologists and psychologists. If he'd had any idea of what Brandon had planned for that morning, he'd have had him transferred to Traffic, the present-day equivalent of Jonah being swallowed by a whale.

Before his depression could overwhelm his resolve, Brandon was startled by a banging on the bathroom door. 'Dad?' his elder daughter shouted. 'You going to be much longer?'

Brandon snatched up his razor, dunked it in the basin and scraped it down one cheek before replying. 'Five minutes, Karen,' he called. 'Sorry, love.' In a house with three teenagers and only one bathroom, there was seldom much opportunity for brooding.

Carol Jordan dumped her half-drunk coffee on the side of the washbasin and stumbled into the shower, nearly tripping headlong over the black cat that wound himself round her ankles. 'In a minute, Nelson,' she muttered as she closed the door on his interrogative miaow. 'And don't waken Michael.'

Carol had imagined that promotion to detective inspector and the concomitant departure from the shift rota would have granted her the regular eight hours' sleep a night that had been her constant craving since the first week she joined the force. Just her luck that the promotion had coincided with what her team were privately calling the Queer Killings. However much Superintendent Tom Cross might bluster to the press and in the squad room that there were no forensic connections between the killings, and nothing to suggest the presence of a serial killer in Bradfield, the murder teams thought differently.

As the hot water cascaded over Carol, turning her blonde hair mouse, she thought, not for the first time, that Cross's attitude, like that of the Chief Constable, served his prejudices rather than the community. The longer he denied that there was a serial killer attacking men whose respectable façade hid a secret gay life, the more gay men would die. If you couldn't get them off the streets any longer by arresting them, let a killer remove them. It didn't much matter whether he did it by murder or by fear.

It was a policy that made a nonsense of all the hours she and her colleagues were putting in on the investigation. Not to mention the hundreds of thousands of pounds of taxpayers' money that these enquiries were costing, particularly since Cross insisted each killing be treated as an entirely separate entity. Every time one of the three teams came up with some detail that seemed to link the killings, Tom Cross dismissed it with five points of dissimilarity. It didn't matter that each time the links were different and the dissimilarities the same tired quintet. Cross was the boss. And the DCI had opted out of the strife completely, taking sick leave with his opportunistic bad back.

Carol rubbed the shampoo to a rich lather and felt herself gradually wake under the warm spray. Well, her corner of the investigation wasn't going to run aground on the rock of Popeye Cross's bigoted prejudice. Even if some of her junior officers were inclined to grasp at the boss's tunnel vision as an excuse for their own uninspired investigations, she wasn't going to stand for anything less than one hundred per cent committed action, and in the right direction. She'd worked her socks off for the best part of nine years, first to get a good degree and then to justify her place on the promotion fast track. She didn't intend her career to hit the buffers just because she'd made the mistake of opting for a force run by Neanderthals.

Her mind made up, Carol stepped out of the shower, shoulders straight, a defiant glint in her green eyes. 'Come on, Nelson,' she said, shrugging into her dressing gown and scooping up the muscular bundle of black fur. 'Let's hit the red meat, boy.'

Tony studied the overhead projection on the screen behind him for a final five seconds. Since the majority of his audience had expressed their lack of commitment to his lecture by pointedly not taking notes, he wanted at least to give their subconscious minds the maximum opportunity to absorb his flow chart of the criminal profile generating process.

He turned back to his audience. 'I don't have to tell you what you already know. Profilers don't catch criminals. It's bobbies that do that.' He smiled at his audience of senior police officers and Home Office officials, inviting them to share his self-deprecation. A few did, though most remained stony faced, heads on one side.

However he dressed it up, Tony knew he couldn't convince the bulk of the senior police officers that he wasn't some out-of-touch university boffin there to tell them how to do their jobs. Stifling a sigh, he glanced at his notes and continued, aiming for as much eye contact as he could achieve, copying the casual body language of the successful stand-up comics he'd studied working the northern clubs. 'But sometimes we profilers see things differently,' he said. 'And that fresh perspective can make all the difference. Dead men do tell tales, and the ones they tell profilers are not the same as the ones they tell police officers.

'An example. A body is found in bushes ten feet away from the road. A police officer will note that fact. He'll check the ground all around for clues. Are there footprints? Has anything been discarded by the killer? Have any fibres been snagged on the bushes? But for me, that single fact is only the starting point for speculations that, taken in conjunction with all the other information at my disposal, may well lead me to useful conclusions about the killer. I'll ask myself, was the body deliberately placed there? Or was the killer too knackered to carry it further? Was he hiding it or dumping it? Did he want it to be found? How long did he expect or want it to stay hidden? What is the significance of this site for him?' Tony lifted his shoulders and held out his hands in an open, questioning gesture. The audience looked on, unmoved. God, how many tricks of the trade was he going to have to pull out of the hat before he got a response? The prickle of sweat along the back of his neck was becoming a trickle, sliding down between his skin and his shirt collar. It was an uncomfortable sensation that reminded him of who he really was behind the mask he'd assumed for his public appearance.

Tony cleared his throat, focused on what he was projecting rather than what he was feeling, and continued. 'Profiling is just another tool that can help investigating officers to narrow the focus of their investigation. Our job is to make sense of the bizarre. We can't give you an offender's name, address and phone number. But what we *can* do is point you in the direction of the kind of person who has committed a crime with particular characteristics. Sometimes we can indicate the area where he might live, the kind of work we'd expect him to do.

'I know that some of you have questioned the necessity for setting up a National Criminal Profiling Task Force. You're not alone. The civil libertarians are screaming about it too.' At last, Tony thought with profound relief. Smiles and nods from the audience. It had taken him forty minutes to get there, but he'd finally cracked their composure. It didn't mean he could relax, but it eased his discomfort. 'After all,' he went on, 'we're not like the Americans. We don't have serial killers lurking round every corner. We still have a society where more than ninety per cent of murders are committed by family members or people known to the victims.' He was really taking them with him now. Several pairs of legs and arms uncrossed, neat as a practised drill-hall routine.

'But profiling isn't just about nailing the next Hannibal the Cannibal. It can be used in a wide variety of crimes. We've already had notable success in airport anti-hijacking measures, in catching drug couriers, poison-pen writers, blackmailers, serial rapists and arsonists. And just as importantly, profiling has been used very effectively to advise police officers on interview techniques for dealing with suspects in major crime enquiries. It's not that your officers lack interviewing skills; it's just that our clinical background means we have developed different approaches that can often be more productive than familiar techniques.'

Tony took a deep breath and leaned forward, gripping the edge of the lectern. His final paragraph had sounded good in front of the bathroom mirror. He prayed it would hit the right spot rather than stamp on people's corns. 'My team and I are now one year into a two-year feasibility study on setting up the National Criminal Profiling Task Force. I've already delivered an interim report to the Home Office, who confirmed to me yesterday that they are committed to forming this task force as soon as my final report is delivered. Ladies and gentlemen, this revolution in crime fighting is going to happen. You've got a year to make sure it happens in a form that you feel comfortable with. My team and I have all got open minds. We're all on the same side. We want to know what you think, because we want it to work. We want violent, serial offenders behind bars, just like you do. I believe you could use our help. I know we can use yours.'

Tony took a step backwards and savoured the applause, not because it was particularly enthusiastic, but because it signalled the end of the forty-five minutes he'd been dreading for weeks. Public speaking had always been firmly outside the boundaries of his comfort zone, so much so that he'd turned his back on an academic career after achieving his doctorate because he couldn't face the constant spectre of the lecture theatre. The ability to perform was not a reason in itself for doing so. Somehow, spending his days poking around in the distorted recesses of the minds of the criminally insane was far less threatening.

As the short-lived clapping died away, Tony's Home Office minder bounced to his feet from his front-row chair. While Tony provoked a wary distrust in the police section of his audience, George Rasmussen generated more universal irritation than a flea bite. His eager smile revealed too many teeth and a disturbing resemblance to George Formby that was at odds with the seniority of his Civil Service post, the elegant cut of his grey pinstripe suit and the yammering bray of a public-school accent so exaggerated that Tony was convinced Rasmussen had really been educated in some inner-city comprehensive. Tony half listened as he shuffled his notes together and replaced his acetates in their folder. Grateful for fascinating insight, blah, blah . . . coffee and those absolutely delicious biscuits, blah, blah . . . opportunity for informal questions, blah, blah . . . remind you all submissions to Dr Hill due by . . .

The sound of shuffling feet drowned out the rest of Rasmussen's spiel. When it came to a choice between a civil servant's vote of thanks and a cup of coffee, it was no contest. Not even for the civil servants. Tony took a deep breath. Time to abandon the lecturer. Now he had to be the charming, well-informed colleague, eager to listen, to assimilate and to make his new contacts feel he was really on their side.

John Brandon stood up and stepped aside to allow the other people in his row to move out of their seats. Watching Tony Hill's performance hadn't been as informative as he'd hoped. It had told him a lot about psychological profiling, but almost nothing about the man, except that he seemed self-assured without being arrogant. The last three quarters of an hour hadn't made him any more certain that what he was planning was the right course of action. But he couldn't see any alternative. Staying close to the wall, Brandon moved forward against the flow until he was level with Rasmussen. Seeing his audience vote with its feet, the civil servant had sharply wound up his speech and switched off his smile. As Rasmussen gathered up the papers he'd dumped on his seat, Brandon slipped past him and crossed the floor towards Tony, who was fastening the clasps on his battered Gladstone bag.

Brandon cleared his throat and said, 'Dr Hill?' Tony looked up, polite enquiry on his face. Brandon swallowed his qualms and continued. 'We haven't met before, but you've been working on my patch. I'm John Brandon . . .'

'The ACC Crime?' Tony interrupted, a smile reaching his eyes. He'd heard enough about John Brandon to know he was a man he wanted on his side. 'I'm delighted to meet you, Mr Brandon,' he said, injecting warmth into his voice.

'John. It's John,' Brandon said, more abruptly than he'd intended. He realized with a spurt of surprise that he was nervous. There was something about Tony Hill's calm assurance that unsettled him. 'I wonder if we can have a word?'

Before Tony could reply, Rasmussen was between them. 'If you'd excuse me,' he interjected without any note of humility, the smile back in place. 'Tony, if you'd just come through now to the coffee lounge, I know our friends in the police will be eager to chat to you on a more intimate basis. Mr Brandon, if you'd like to follow us.'

Brandon could feel his hackles rising. He felt awkward enough about the situation without having to fight to keep their conversation confidential in a room full of coffee-swilling coppers and nosy Home Office mandarins. 'If I could just have a word with Dr Hill in private?'

Tony glanced at Rasmussen, noting the slight deepening of the parallel lines between his eyebrows. Normally, it would have tickled him to wind up Rasmussen by continuing his conversation with Brandon. He always enjoyed pricking pomposity, reducing the self-important to impotent. But too much hung on the success of his encounters with other police officers today, so he decided to forego the pleasure. Instead, he turned pointedly away from Rasmussen and said, 'John, are you driving back to Bradfield after lunch?'

Brandon nodded.

'Perhaps you could give me a lift, then? I came on the train, but if you don't mind, I'd rather not wrestle with British Rail on the way back. You can always drop me at the city limits if you don't want to be seen fraternizing with the Trendy Wendies.'

Brandon smiled, his long face creasing into simian wrinkles. 'I don't think that'll be necessary. I'll be just as happy to drop you at force headquarters.' He stood back and watched Rasmussen steer Tony to the doors, fussing all the way. He couldn't shake off the slightly disconcerted feeling that the psychologist had given him. Maybe it was simply that he'd grown so accustomed to being in control of everything in his world that asking for help had become an alien experience that automatically made him feel uncomfortable. There was no other obvious explanation. Shrugging, Brandon followed the crowd through to the coffee lounge.

* * *

Tony snapped the seat belt closed and savoured the comfort of the unmarked Range Rover. He said nothing as Brandon manoeuvred out of the Manchester force headquarters' car park and headed for the motorway network, unwilling to interfere with the concentration necessary to avoid missing the way in an unfamiliar city. As they cruised down the slip road and joined the fast-flowing traffic, Tony broke the silence. 'If it helps, I think I already know what it is you wanted to talk to me about.'

Brandon's hands tensed on the wheel. 'I thought you were a psychologist, not a psychic,' he joked. He surprised himself. Humour wasn't his natural mode; he normally resorted to it only under pressure. Brandon couldn't get used to how nervous he felt asking this favour.

'Some of your colleagues would take more notice of me if I was,' Tony said wryly. 'So, do you want me to have a guess and run the risk of making a complete fool of myself?'

Brandon snatched a quick look at Tony. The psychologist looked relaxed, hands palm down on his thighs, feet crossed at the ankles. He looked as though he'd be more at home in jeans and a sweater than in the suit which even Brandon recognized as well past its fashionable sell-by date. He could relate to that, remembering the scathing comments his daughters routinely passed on his own plain clothes. Brandon said abruptly, 'I think we've got a serial killer operating in Bradfield.'

Tony released a small, satisfied sigh. 'I was beginning to wonder if you'd noticed,' he said ironically.

'It's by no means a unanimous opinion,' Brandon said, feeling the need to warn Tony before he'd even asked for his help.

'I'd gathered as much from the press coverage,' Tony said. 'If it's any comfort to you, I'm as certain as I can be from what I've read that your analysis is right.'

'That's not entirely the impression you gave in those

quotes of yours I saw in the *Sentinel Times* after the last one,' Brandon said.

'It's my job to cooperate with the police, not to undermine them. I assumed you had your own operational reasons for not going public with the serial-killer angle. I did stress to them that what I was saying was no more than an informed guess based on the information that was in the public domain,' Tony added, his genial tone contradicting the sudden tensing of his fingers that ruched the material of his trousers into loose pleats.

Brandon smiled, aware only of the voice. 'Touché. So, are you interested in giving us a hand?'

Tony felt a warm rush of satisfaction. This was what he had craved for weeks now. 'There's a service area a few miles down the road. D'you fancy a cup of tea?'

Detective Inspector Carol Jordan stared at the broken chaos of flesh that had once been a man, determinedly forcing her eyes to remain out of focus. She wished she hadn't bothered to snatch that stale cheese sandwich from the canteen. Somehow, it was acceptable for young male officers to throw up when they were confronted with victims of violent death. They even got sympathy. But in spite of the fact that women were supposed to lack bottle anyway, when female officers chucked up on the margins of crime scenes they instantly lost any respect they'd ever won and became objects of contempt, the butts of locker-room jokes from the canteen cowboys. Pick the logic out of that, Carol thought bitterly as she clamped her jaws tighter together. She thrust her hands deep into the pockets of her trench coat and clenched her fists, the nails pressing into her palms.

Carol felt a hand on her arm, just above the elbow. Grateful for the chance to look away, she turned to find her sergeant looming above her. Don Merrick towered a good eight inches over his boss, and had developed a strange hunchbacked stoop when he spoke to her. At first, she'd found it amusing enough to regale friends with over drinks or the occasional dinner party when she managed to squeeze a night off. Now, she didn't even notice. 'Area's all cordoned off now, ma'am,' he said in his soft Geordie accent. 'Pathologist's on his way. What d'you think? Are we looking at number four?'

'Don't let the Super hear you say that, Don,' she said, only half joking. 'I'd say so, though.' Carol looked around. They were in the Temple Fields district, in the rear yard of a pub which catered primarily to the gay trade, with an upstairs bar that was lesbian three nights a week. Contrary to the jibes of the macho men she'd overtaken in the promotion stakes, it wasn't a bar Carol had ever had reason to enter. 'What about the gate?'

'Crowbar,' Merrick said laconically. 'It's not wired into the alarm system.'

Carol surveyed the tall rubbish dumpsters and the stacked crates of empties. 'No reason why it should be,' she said. 'What's the landlord got to say?'

'Whalley's talking to him now, ma'am. Seems he locked up last night about half past eleven. They've got bins on wheels behind the bars for the empties, and at closing time they just wheel them into the yard back there.' Merrick waved over towards the back door of the pub, where three blue plastic bins stood, each the size of a supermarket trolley. 'They don't sort them out till the afternoon.'

'And that's when they found this?' Carol asked, gesturing over her shoulder with her thumb.

'Just lying there. Open to the elements, you might say.'

Carol nodded. A shudder ran through her that was nothing to do with the sharp north-eastern wind. She took a step towards the gate. 'OK. Let's leave this to the SOCOs for now. We're only in the way here.' Merrick followed her into the narrow alley behind the pub. It was barely wide enough for a single vehicle to squeeze down. Carol looked up and down the alley, now closed off by police tapes and guarded at either end by a pair of uniformed constables. 'He knows his turf,' she mused softly. She walked backwards along the alley, keeping the gate of the pub in constant view. Merrick followed her, waiting for the next set of orders.

At the end of the alley, Carol stopped and swung round to check out the street. Opposite the alley was a tall building, a former warehouse that had been converted into craft workshops. At night, it would be deserted, but in midafternoon, almost every window framed eager faces, staring out from the warmth within at the drama below. 'Not much chance of anyone looking out of a window at the crucial time, I suppose,' she remarked.

'Even if they had, they wouldn't have taken any notice,' Merrick said cynically. 'After closing time, the streets round here are jumping. Every doorway, every alley, half the parked cars have got a pair of poofs in them, shagging the arse off each other. It's no wonder the Chief calls Temple Fields Sodom and Gomorrah.'

'You know, I've often wondered. It's pretty clear what they were up to in Sodom, but what do you suppose the sin of Gomorrah was?' Carol asked.

Merrick looked bewildered. It increased his resemblance to a sad-eyed Labrador to a disturbing degree. 'I'm not with you, ma'am,' he said.

'Never mind. I'm surprised Mr Armthwaite hasn't got Vice pulling them all in on indecency charges,' Carol said.

'He did try it a few years back,' Merrick confided. 'But the police committee had his bollocks barbecued for it. He fought them, but they threatened him with the Home Office. And after the Holmwood Three business, he knew he was already on thin ice with the politicians, so he backed down. Doesn't stop him slagging them off every chance he gets, though.'

'Yeah, well, I hope this time our friendly neighbourhood killer has left us a bit more to go on, or our beloved leader might just pick another target for his next slagging off.' Carol straightened her shoulders. 'Right, Don. I want a door-to-door of the businesses, now. And tonight, we're all going to be out on the streets, talking to the trade.'

Before Carol could complete her instructions, a voice from beyond the tapes interrupted. 'Inspector Jordan? Penny Burgess, *Sentinel Times*. Inspector? What have you got?'

Carol closed her eyes for a brief moment. Dealing with the recalcitrant bigots in the chain of command was one thing. Dealing with the press was infinitely worse. Wishing she'd stayed in the yard with the grisly corpse, Carol took a deep breath and walked towards the cordon.

'Let me get this straight. You want me to come on board for the duration of this murder enquiry, but you don't want me to tell anyone?' The look of amusement in Tony's eyes masked his anger at the reluctance of influential policemen to accept the value of what he could do.

Brandon sighed. Tony wasn't making it easy for him, but then, why should he? 'I want to avoid any suggestions in the press that you are helping us. The only chance I have of getting you formally involved with the investigation is to persuade the Chief Constable that you're not going to be stealing the limelight from him and his coppers.'

'And that it won't become public knowledge that Derek Armthwaite, the Hand Of God, is turning to the mumbo-jumbo men for help,' Tony said, an edge in his voice betraying more than he wanted to.

Brandon's face twisted in a cynical smile. It was good to see that it was possible to ruffle that smooth surface. 'If you say so, Tony. Technically, it's an operational matter, and he's not really supposed to interfere unless I'm doing something that's counter to force and Home Office policy.

And it is the policy of BMP to use expert assistance whenever it is appropriate.'

Tony snorted with laughter. 'And you think he'll accept me as "appropriate"?'

'I think he doesn't want another confrontation with the Home Office or the police committee. He's due to retire in eighteen months, and he's desperate for the knighthood.' Brandon couldn't believe what he was saying. He didn't even voice this kind of disloyalty to his wife, never mind to a virtual stranger. What was it about Tony Hill that had made him open up so swiftly? There must be something in this psychology lark after all. Brandon comforted himself that at least he had harnessed that something in the service of justice. 'So what do you say?'

'When do I start?'

Even that first time, I planned the event more carefully than a theatre director plans the first production of a new play. In my mind, I crafted the experience, till it was like a bright and shining dream, there every time I closed my eyes. I checked and rechecked every choreographed move, making sure I hadn't missed some vital detail that would endanger my freedom. Looking back on it now, the mental movie I created was almost as pleasurable as the act itself.

The first step was to find a place where I could safely take him, a place we could be private together. I immediately dismissed my home. I can hear my neighbours' squalid arguments, the barking of their hysterical German shepherd and the irritating thud of their stereo's bass; I had no desire to share my apotheosis with them. Besides, in my terraced street, there are too many curtain twitchers. I wanted no witnesses to Adam's arrival or his departure.

I considered renting a lock up garage, but rejected that for the same reasons. Besides, it seemed too seedy, too much of a cliché from the world of television and film. I wanted something in keeping with what was going to happen. Then I remembered my mother's Auntie Doris. Doris and her husband Henry used to farm sheep on the moors high above Bradfield. Then, about four years ago, Henry died. Doris tried to keep things going for a while, but when her son Ken invited her out last year for an extended holiday with his family in New Zealand, she sold the sheep and packed her bags. Ken had written to me at Christmas, saying his mother had suffered a mild heart attack and wouldn't be coming back for the foreseeable future.

That night, I took advantage of a lull in work to call Ken. At first, he sounded surprised to hear from me, then muttered, 'I suppose you're using the phones at work.'

'I've been meaning to ring for ages,' I said. 'I wanted to know how Auntie Doris was doing.' It's much easier to appear solicitous via satellite. I made the appropriate noises while Ken bored on about his mother's health, his wife, their three kids and their sheep.

After ten minutes, I decided I'd had enough. 'The other thing is, Ken, I was worried about the house,' I lied. 'It's so isolated up there, someone should keep an eye on the place.'

'You're not wrong,' he said. 'Her solicitor's supposed to be doing that, but I don't reckon he's been near it.'

'Do you want me to pop out and check it over? Now I'm back living in Bradfield, it would be no bother.'

'Would you? That'd be a hell of a load off, I don't mind telling you. Between ourselves, I'm not sure Mum's ever going to be well enough to go back home again, but I'd hate to think of anything happening to the family home,' Ken said eagerly.

Hate to think of anything happening to his inheritance, more like. I knew Ken. Ten days later, I had the keys. On my next day off, I drove out there to check the accuracy of my recollection. The rutted track leading to Start Hill Farm was much more overgrown than the last time I'd been there, and my four-wheel drive jeep struggled to climb the three miles from the nearest single-track lane. I cut the engine a dozen yards from the grim little cottage and sat listening for five minutes. The biting wind from the high moors rustled the overgrown hedges, occasional birds sang. But there were no human sounds. Not even the distant thrum of traffic.

I got out of the jeep and had a look round. One end of the sheep shed had collapsed into a random pile of millstone grit, but what pleased me was that there was no sign of casual human visitations; no picnic remains, no corroding beer cans, no crumpled newspapers, no cigarette butts, no used condoms. I walked back to the house and let myself in.

It was little more than a two-up, two-down. Inside, it was very different from the cosy farmhouse I remembered. All the personal touches – photographs, ornaments, horse brasses, antiques – were gone, packed up in crates in storage, a very Yorkshire precaution. In a way, I was relieved; there was nothing here that could trigger off memories that would interfere with what I had to do. It was a blank tablet, with all humiliations, embarrassments and pain erased. Nothing of my past lurked to surprise me. The person I had been was absent.

I walked through the kitchen towards the pantry. The shelves were empty. God knows what Doris had done with her serried ranks of jams, pickles and home-made wines. Maybe she'd shipped them to New Zealand as a hedge against being fed alien food. I stood in the doorway, and stared at the floor. I could feel a foolish grin of relief spread across my face. My memory hadn't let me down. There was a trapdoor in the floor. I squatted down and pulled the rusty iron ring. After a few seconds, the door swung back on creaking hinges. As I sniffed the air from the cellar, I grew more convinced that the gods were with me. I had feared it would be damp, fetid and stale. But instead, it was cool and fresh, slightly sweet.

I lit my camping gas lamp and carefully descended the flight of stone stairs. The lamp revealed a sizeable room, about twenty feet by thirty. The floor was flagged with stone slabs, and a broad stone bench ran the length of one wall. I held the lamp high and saw the solid beams of the roof. The lath and plaster ceiling was the only part of the cellar that showed any signs of disrepair. I could easily fix that with plasterboard, which would serve the double purpose of preventing any light escaping through the bare floorboards above. At right angles to the stone bench was a slop sink. I remembered the farm was served by its own spring. The tap was stiff, but when I finally managed to turn it, the water ran out pure and clear.

Near the stairs stood a scarred wooden workbench, complete with vices and G-clamps, Henry's tools hanging in neat rows above. I sat on the stone bench and hugged myself. A few hours' work was all that was needed to turn this into a dungeon far superior to anything the games programmers had ever come up with. For a start, I didn't have to think about creating an in-built weakness so my adventurers could escape.

By the end of the week, coming out to the farm in my time off, I had completed the job. Nothing sophisticated; I'd fixed padlock and internal bolts to the trapdoor, I'd repaired the ceiling, and covered the walls in a couple of coats of whitewash. I wanted the place as light as possible to improve the quality of the video. I'd even run a spur off the ring main to provide me with electricity.

I'd thought long and hard before I'd decided how to punish Adam. Finally, I'd fixed on what the French call the chevalet, the Spanish escalero, the Germans the ladder, the Italians veglia and the poetic English 'The Duke of Exeter's Daughter'. The rack got its euphemistic name from the resourceful John Holland, Duke of Exeter and Earl of Huntingdon. After a successful career as a soldier, the duke became Constable of the Tower of London and somewhere around 1420 he introduced that splendid instrument of persuasion to these shores.

The earliest version consisted of an open rectangular frame raised on legs. The prisoner was laid underneath it, fastened by ropes round his wrists and ankles. At each corner, the ropes were attached to a windlass operated by *a warder pulling on levers. This inelegant and labour-intensive device became more sophisticated over the years, ending up more like a table or a horizontal ladder, often incorporating a spiked roller in the middle so that, as the prisoner's body moved, his back was shredded on the spikes. Pulley systems had also been designed which linked all four ropes together, making it possible for the machine to be used by one person alone.*

Fortunately, those who have applied punishment through the ages have been thorough in their descriptions and drawing. I also had the photographs in the museum handbook to refer to, and with the assistance of a CAD program, I'd designed my very own rack. For the mechanism, I'd cannibalized an old-fashioned clothes wringer that I picked up in an antique shop. I'd also bought an old mahogany dining table in an auction. I took it straight up to the farm and dismembered it in the kitchen, admiring the craftsmanship that had gone into the solid timber. It took a couple of days to build the rack. All that remained was to test it.

2

Let the reader then figure to himself the pure frenzy of horror when in this hush of expectation, looking, and indeed, waiting for the unknown arm to strike once more, but not believing that any audacity could be equal to such an attempt as yet, whilst all eyes were watching... a second case of the same mysterious nature, a murder on the same exterminating plan, was perpetrated in the very same neighbourhood.

As soon as Brandon started the engine, the mobile phone mounted on the dashboard trilled. He grabbed the handset and barked, 'Brandon.' Tony could hear the computerized voice say, 'You have messages. Please call 121. You have messages...'

Brandon took the phone from his ear, hit the keys and jammed it back again. This time, Tony couldn't hear what was said. After a moment, Brandon dialled another number. 'My secretary,' he explained briefly. 'Sorry about this... Hello, Martina? John. You were looking for me?'

A few seconds into the answer, Brandon squeezed his eyes shut, as if in pain. 'Where?' he asked, his voice dull. 'OK, got it. I'll be there within the half-hour. Who's dealing?... Fine, thanks, Martina.' Brandon opened his eyes and ended the call. He carefully replaced the handset and twisted in his seat to face Tony. 'You wanted to know when you could start? How about now?'

'Another body?' Tony asked.

'Another body,' Brandon agreed grimly, turning back

and slamming the car into gear. 'How do you feel about scenes of crime?'

Tony shrugged. 'I'll probably lose my lunch, but it's a bonus for me if I get to see them in a fairly pristine state.'

'There's nothing pristine about the way this sick bastard leaves them,' Brandon growled as he shot on to the motorway and made straight for the outside lane. The speedo read ninety-five before he eased back on the accelerator.

'Has he gone back to Temple Fields?' Tony asked.

Taken aback, Brandon shot him a quick look. Tony was staring straight ahead, his dark eyebrows corrugated in a frown. 'How did you know?'

That was a question Tony wasn't prepared to answer. 'Call it a hunch,' he stalled. 'I think last time out he was scared that Temple Fields might be getting a bit too hot. Dumping the third body in Carlton Park shifted the focus, maybe stopped the police concentrating on one area, probably relaxed people's vigilance a bit. But he likes Temple Fields. Either because he knows the patch really well, or else it's important to his fantasy. Or maybe it makes some kind of statement for him,' Tony mused aloud.

'Do you always come up with half a dozen different hypotheses every time someone tosses you a fact?' Brandon asked, flashing his lights at a BMW that was reluctant to give up possession of the fast lane. 'Shift, you bastard, before I get Traffic out to you,' he snarled.

'I try,' Tony said. 'That's how I do the job. Gradually, the evidence makes me eliminate some of my initial thoughts. Eventually, some sort of pattern begins to form.' He fell silent, already fantasizing about what he would find at the scene of the crime. His stomach felt hollow, muscles fluttering like a musician before a concert. Normally, all he ever got to see were the second-hand, sanitized versions of crime scenes. No matter how good the photographer and the other forensic officers, it was always someone else's vision he had to translate. This time, he was going to be as close to a killer as he'd ever been. For a man who lived his life behind the shield of learned behaviours, penetrating a killer's façade was the only game in town.

Carol said, 'No comment,' for the eleventh time. Penny Burgess's mouth tightened and her eyes flicked round the scene, desperate for someone who would be less of a stone wall than Carol. Popeye Cross might be a male chauvinist pig, but in between the patronizing comments he always salted a few memorable quotes. Drawing a blank, she focused on Carol again.

'What happened to sisterhood, Carol?' she complained. 'Come on, give us a break. Surely there must be something you can tell me apart from "No comment".'

'I'm sorry, Ms Burgess. The last thing your readers need to hear is ill-informed off-the-cuff speculation. As soon as I've got anything concrete to say, I promise you'll be the first to know.' Carol softened her words with a smile.

She turned to walk away, but Penny grabbed the sleeve of her mac. 'Off the record?' she pleaded. 'Just for my guidance? So I don't end up writing something that makes me look a pillock? Carol, I don't have to tell you what it's like. I work in an office full of guys that are running a book on when I'll make my next cock-up.'

Carol sighed. It was hard to resist. Only the thought of what Tom Cross would make of it in the squad room kept her mouth closed. 'I can't,' she said. 'Anyway, as far as I'm concerned, you've been doing just fine so far.' As she spoke, a familiar Range Rover turned the corner. 'Oh shit,' she muttered, pulling her arm away from the reporter. All she needed was John Brandon deciding she was the police source behind the *Sentinel Times*'s serial-killer hysteria. Briskly, Carol walked towards Brandon's car as it jerked to a halt, waiting for someone to shift the tapes keeping the crowd at bay. She stopped and waited while the constables rushed to impress the ACC with their efficiency. The Range

Rover nosed forward, giving Carol the opportunity to spot the stranger in Brandon's passenger seat. As the two men climbed down, she scanned Tony, committing the details to the memory bank she'd trained herself to develop. You never knew when you'd need to come up with a photofit. Around five-eight, slim, good shoulders, narrow hips, legs and trunk in proportion, short dark hair, side parting, dark eyes, probably blue, shadows under the eyes, fair skin, average nose, wide mouth, lower lip fuller than upper. Shame about the dress sense, though. The suit was even more out of fashion than Brandon's. It didn't look worn, however. Deduction: this was a man who didn't spend his working life in a suit. Equally, he didn't like throwing money away, so the suit was going to be worn till it fell to bits. Second deduction: he probably wasn't married or in a permanent relationship. Any woman whose partner needed a suit occasionally would have pitched him into buying a timelessly classic style that wouldn't look so absurd five years after its purchase.

By the time she'd reached this conclusion, Brandon was by her side, gesturing to his companion to join them. 'Carol,' he said.

'Mr Brandon,' she acknowledged.

'Tony, I'd like you to meet Detective Inspector Carol Jordan. Carol, this is Dr Tony Hill from the Home Office.'

Tony smiled and held out his hand. Attractive smile, Carol added to her list of particulars as she shook the hand. Good handshake, too. Dry, firm without the macho need to crush the bones that so many senior officers exhibited. 'Pleased to meet you,' he said.

A surprisingly deep voice, faintly northern. Carol kept her own smile tight. You never knew with the Home Office. 'Likewise,' she said.

'Carol's heading up one of the murder teams we've got on these killings. Number two, is it, Carol?' Brandon asked, already knowing the answer.

'That's right, sir. Paul Gibbs.'

'Tony's in charge of the Home Office National Crime Profiling Task Force feasibility study. I've asked him to take a look at these murders, to see if his experience can give us any pointers.' Brandon's eyes bored into Carol's, making sure she realized there were lines to be read between.

'I'd appreciate any help Dr Hill can give us, sir. From the brief look I've had at the scene of the crime, I don't think we've got any more to go on than in the previous similar cases.' Carol signalled that she understood what Brandon was saying. They were both walking the same tightrope, but from different ends. Brandon could not be seen to undermine Tom Cross's operational authority, and if Carol wanted a tolerable existence in the Bradfield force, she couldn't openly contradict her immediate superior, even if the ACC agreed with her. 'Would Dr Hill like to see the crime scene?'

'We'll all have a look,' Brandon said. 'You can fill me in as we go. What have we got here?'

Carol led the way. 'It's in the back yard of the pub here. The scene of crime is obviously not the scene of death. No blood at all. We have a white male, late twenties, naked. ID unknown. He appears to have been tortured before death. Both shoulders seem to have been dislocated, and possibly his hips and knees. Some tufts of hair are missing from the scalp. He's lying on his front, so we've not had a chance to see the full extent of his injuries. I'd guess the cause of death is a deep wound to the throat. It also looks like the body had been washed before it was dumped.' Carol ended her flat recitation at the yard gate. She glanced back at Tony. The only difference her words had made was a tightening of his lips. 'Ready?' she asked him.

He nodded and took a deep breath. 'As I'll ever be,' he said.

'Stay outside the tapes please, Tony,' Brandon said. 'The

SOCOs will still have a lot to do, and they don't need us dumping forensic traces all over their murder scene.'

Carol opened the gate and waved the two of them through. If Tony had thought her words had prepared him for the sight inside, one look told him otherwise. It was grotesque, made all the more so by the unnatural absence of blood. Logic screamed that a body so broken should be an island in a lake of gore, like an ice cube in a Bloody Mary. He had never seen a corpse so clean outside a funeral parlour. But instead of being laid out calm as a marble statue, this body was twisted into a loose-limbed parody of the human frame, a disjointed puppet left lying where it fell when the strings were cut.

When the two men entered the yard, the police photographer stopped snapping and gave John Brandon a nod of recognition. 'All right, Harry,' Brandon said, seemingly undaunted by the sight before him. No one could see the hands clenched into tight fists in the pockets of his waxed jacket.

'I've done all the long- and medium-range stuff, Mr Brandon. I've just got the close-ups to go,' the photographer said. 'There's a lot of wounds and bruising; I want to make sure I've got it all.'

'Good lad,' Brandon said.

From behind them, Carol added, 'Harry, when you've done that, can you snap all the cars parked up in the immediate area?'

The photographer raised his eyebrows. 'The lot?'

'The lot,' Carol confirmed.

'Good thinking, Carol,' Brandon chipped in before the scowling photographer could say anything more. 'There's always the outside chance that me laddo left the scene on foot or in the victim's car. He might have left his here to collect later. And photographs are that much harder for the defence brief to argue with than a bobby's notebook.'

With a sharp snort of breath, the photographer turned

back to the corpse. The brief exchange had given Tony time to get a grip on his churning stomach. He took a step closer to the body, trying to glean some primitive understanding of the mind that had reduced a man to this. 'What's your game?' he said inside his head. 'What does this mean to you? What translations are going on between this broken flesh and your desire? I thought I was the expert in keeping things battened down, but you're something else, aren't you? You are truly special. You're the control freak's control freak. You are going to be one of the ones they write books about. Welcome to the big time.'

Recognizing that he was dangerously close to admiration for a mind so disturbingly complex, Tony forced himself to focus on the realities of what lay before him. The deep slash to the throat had virtually decapitated the man, leaving the head tilted as if hinged at the back of the neck. Tony took a deep breath and said, 'The *Sentinel Times* said they all died from having their throats cut. Is that right?'

'Yes,' Carol said. 'They were all tortured while they were still alive, but it's the throat wounds that have been fatal in each case.'

'And have they all been as deep as this?'

Carol shook her head dubiously. 'I'm only completely familiar with the second case, and that was nowhere near as violent a gash as this. But I have seen the photographs of the other two, and the last one was nearly this bad.'

Thank God for something recognizably textbook, Tony thought. He took a couple of steps back and scanned the area. The body aside, there was nothing to distinguish it from the back yard of any other pub. Crates of empties were stacked against the walls, the lids on the big industrial wheelie bins were firmly closed. Nothing obvious taken away, nothing obvious left behind except for the corpse itself.

Brandon cleared his throat. 'Well, everything seems to

be under control here, Carol. I'd better go and have a word with the press. I saw Penny Burgess trying to rip the sleeve out of your coat when I got here. No doubt the rest of the pack are baying at her heels by now. I'll see you back at HQ later. Drop by my office. I want to have a chat with you about Dr Hill's involvement. Tony, I'll leave you in Carol's capable hands. When you're finished here, maybe you can arrange a session with Carol so she can go through the case files.'

Tony nodded. 'Sounds good. Thanks, John.'

'I'll be in touch. And thanks again.' With that, Brandon was gone, closing the gate behind him.

'You do profiling, then,' Carol said.

'I try,' he said cautiously.

'Thank God the powers that be have finally seen sense,' she said drily. 'I was beginning to think they'd never get round to admitting we've got a serial killer on our hands.'

'You and me both,' Tony said. 'I was worried after the first one, but I've been convinced since the second one.'

'And I suppose it's not your place to tell them that,' Carol said wearily. 'Bloody bureaucracy.'

'It's a sensitive point. Even when we have a national task force set up, I suspect we're still going to have to wait for the individual police forces to come to us.'

Carol's reply was cut off by the banging of the yard gate as it was thrown open. They both swung round. Framed in the doorway was one of the biggest men Tony had ever seen. He had the solid brawn of a prop forward run to seed, his beer gut preceding his massive shoulders by a good half-dozen inches. His eyes protruded like boiled gooseberries from a fleshy face, the source of Detective Superintendent Tom Cross's nickname. His mouth, like that of his cartoon namesake, was an incongruously small cupid's bow. Mousey hair fringed a bald spot like a monk's tonsure. 'Sir,' Carol greeted the apparition.

Pale eyebrows furled in a discontented scowl. Judging by the deep lines between his brows, it was a familiar expression. 'Who the bloody hell are you?' he demanded, waving a stubby finger at Tony. Automatically, Tony noted the bitten nail. Before he could respond, Carol spoke smartly. 'Sir, this is Dr Tony Hill from the Home Office. He's responsible for the National Crime Profiling Task Force feasibility study. Dr Hill, this is Detective Superintendent Tom Cross. He's in overall charge of our murder enquiries.'

The second half of Carol's introduction was drowned out by Cross's booming response. 'What the hell are you up to, woman? This is a murder scene. You don't let any old Tom, Dick or Home Office penpusher walk all over it.'

Carol closed her eyes fractionally longer than a blink. Then she said in a voice whose cheerful tone astonished Tony, 'Sir, Mr Brandon brought Dr Hill with him. The ACC thinks Dr Hill can help us profile our killer.'

'What d'you mean, killer? How many times do I have to tell you? We've not got a serial killer loose in Bradfield. We've just got a nasty bunch of copycat queers. You know what the trouble is with you fast-track graduates?' Cross demanded, aggressively leaning towards Carol.

'I'm sure you'll tell me, sir,' Carol said sweetly.

Cross stopped momentarily, with the slightly baffled air of a dog who can hear the fly but can't see it. Then he said, 'You're all desperate for glory. You want glamour and headlines. You don't want the bother of proper coppering. You can't be arsed grafting on three murder enquiries so you try to knock 'em all into one to minimize the effort and maximize the press coverage. And you,' he added, wheeling round towards Tony. 'You can remove yourself from my crime scene right now. The last thing we need is bleeding-heart liberals telling us we're looking for some poor sod who wasn't allowed to have a teddy bear when

36

he were a lad. It's not mumbo jumbo that catches villains, it's police work.'

Tony smiled. 'I couldn't agree more, Superintendent. But your Assistant Chief Constable seems to think that I can help you target your police work more effectively.'

Cross was too old a hand to fall for civility. 'I run the most effective team in this force,' he retorted. 'And I don't need some bloody doctor telling me how to catch a bunch of homicidal poofters.' He turned back to Carol. 'Escort *Doctor* Hill off the premises, Inspector.' He managed to make her rank sound like an insult. 'And when you've done that, you can come back here and fill me in on what you've managed to find out about our last killer.'

'Very good, sir. Oh, by the way, you might like to join the ACC. He's giving an impromptu press conference round the front.' This time, the sweetness was tinged with acerbity.

Cross gave a perfunctory glance at the body lying exposed in the yard. 'Well, *he*'s not going any place, is he?' he remarked. 'Right, Inspector, I'll expect a report just as soon as I've finished with the ACC and the press.' He turned on his heel and stormed out as noisily as he'd arrived.

Carol put a hand on Tony's elbow and steered him out of the gate. 'This is going to be worth seeing,' she muttered in his ear as she ushered him down the alley in Cross's wake.

Half a dozen reporters had joined Penny Burgess behind the yellow plastic tapes. John Brandon faced them. As they grew closer, they could hear the cacophony of questions the press were hurling at the ACC. Carol and Tony hung back as Cross pushed past a constable standing at Brandon's shoulder and shouted, 'One at a time, ladies and gentlemen. You'll all get heard.'

Brandon half turned towards Cross, his face expressionless. 'Thank you, Superintendent Cross.'

'Have we got a serial killer loose in Bradfield?' Penny Burgess demanded, her voice cutting through the momentary quiet like the cry of some bird of ill omen.

'There's no reason to suppose . . .' Cross started.

Brandon cut across him icily. 'Leave this to me, Tom,' he said. 'As I said a moment ago, this afternoon we have found the body of a white male in his late twenties or early thirties. It's too soon to be one hundred per cent certain, but there are indications that this killing may be connected to three previous homicides that have taken place in Bradfield over the last nine months.'

'Does that mean you're treating these murders as the work of one serial killer?' asked a young man with a tape recorder thrust forward like a cattle prod.

'We are examining the possibility that one perpetrator is responsible for all four crimes, yes.'

Cross looked as if he wanted to hit someone. His hands were bunched into fists at his sides, his brows so low they must have cut his vision to a slit. 'Though it's only a possibility at this stage,' he said mutinously.

Penny chipped in ahead of the opposition again. 'How will this affect your approach to the investigation, Mr Brandon?'

'As of today, we will be amalgamating the three previous murder enquiries with this latest one into a single major incident task force. We will be making full use of the Home Office Large Major Enquiry System computer to analyse the available data, and we are confident that this will enable us to develop new leads,' Brandon said, his lugubrious face belying the optimism in his voice.

'Yo, go for it,' Carol muttered under her breath.

'Haven't you left it a bit late? Hasn't the murderer had a head start because you wouldn't acknowledge he was a serial killer?' a voice from the rear of the pack shouted angrily.

Brandon squared his shoulders and looked stern. 'We're

policemen, not clairvoyants. We don't theorize ahead of the evidence. Rest assured, we will be doing everything within our power to bring this killer to justice as swiftly as is humanly possible.'

'Will you be using a psychological profiler?' It was Penny Burgess again. Tom Cross shot Tony a look of pure hatred.

Brandon smiled. 'That's all for now, ladies and gentlemen. There will be a statement later from the force press office. Now, if you'll excuse us, we've got a lot of work to do.' He nodded benevolently towards the press, then he turned away, taking Cross firmly by the elbow. They walked back towards the alley, Cross's back rigid with fury. Carol and Tony followed a few paces behind. As they went, Penny Burgess's voice rang out behind them. 'Inspector Jordan? Who's the new boy?'

'God, that woman doesn't miss a trick,' Carol muttered.

'I'd better keep out of her way, then,' Tony remarked. 'Me ending up front-page news could be a serious health hazard.'

Carol stopped in her tracks. 'You mean the killer could target you?'

Tony grinned. 'No. I mean your Chief Constable would have an apoplexy.'

The irresistible urge to mirror his smile hit Carol. This man was unlike any Home Office Jobsworth she'd ever encountered. Not only did he have a sense of humour, he didn't mind being indiscreet. And close up, he definitely fell into the category her friend Lucy described as 'a bit chewy'. He was showing signs of being the first interesting man she'd met in the Job for a very long time. 'You could be right,' was all she said, managing to sound noncommittal enough for her words not to be held against her.

They reached the corner of the alley in time to see Tom Cross round on Brandon. 'With respect, sir, you just contradicted everything I've been telling them buggers since this sideshow started.'

'It's time for a different approach, Tom,' Brandon said coolly.

'So why not discuss it with me instead of making me look a dickhead in front of that mob? Not to mention my own men.' Cross leaned forward belligerently. His hand strayed upwards, index finger pointed, as if he were going to stab Brandon in the chest with it. But common sense careerism prevailed, and the hand dropped back by his side.

'You think if I'd had you in my office and suggested a different approach I'd have got one?' There was steel beneath the mildness in Brandon's voice, and Cross recognized it.

His lower jaw jutted. 'At the end of the day, operational decisions are down to me,' he said. Beneath the belligerence, Tony pictured a small boy, an aggressive bully resenting the adults who still had the power to sort him out.

'But I'm the ACC Crime and the buck stops with me. I make the policy decisions, and I've just made one that happens to impact on your sphere of operations. From now on, this is one single major incident enquiry. Is that clear, Tom? Or do you want to take it further?' For the first time, Carol saw for herself how John Brandon had climbed so far up the greasy pole. The threat in his voice was no empty posturing. He was clearly prepared to do whatever it took to achieve his ends, and he acted with all the assurance of a man used to winning. There was nowhere left for Tom Cross to go.

Cross rounded on Carol. 'Have you got nothing better to do, Inspector?'

'I'm waiting to make my report, sir,' she said. 'You told me to wait for you after the press conference.'

'Before you get into that ... Tom, let me introduce you to Dr Tony Hill,' Brandon said, motioning Tony to come forward.

'We've met,' Cross said, sullen as a schoolboy.

'Dr Hill has agreed to work closely with us in this investigation. He's got more experience in profiling serial offenders than just about anybody else in the country. He's also agreed to keep his involvement under wraps.'

Tony gave a self-deprecating, diplomatic smile. 'That's right. The last thing I want is to turn your enquiry into a sideshow. If there's any credit going when we nail this bastard, I want it to go to your team. They'll be the ones doing the work, after all.'

'You're not wrong there,' Cross muttered. 'I don't want you under our feet, getting in the road.'

'None of us want that, Tom,' Brandon said. 'That's why I've asked Carol to act as liaison officer between Tony and us.'

'I can't afford to lose a senior officer at a time like this,' Cross protested.

'You're not losing her,' Brandon said. 'You're gaining an officer with a unique overview of all the cases. Could prove invaluable, Tom.' He glanced at his watch. 'I better be off. The Chief's going to want a briefing on this one. Keep me posted, Tom.' Brandon sketched a wave and stepped back into the street and out of sight.

Cross pulled a packet of cigarettes out of his pocket and lit up. 'You know your trouble, Inspector?' he said. 'You're not as smart as you like to think you are. One step out of line, lady, and I'll have your guts for a jock strap.' He took a deep drag of his cigarette and leaned forward to blow smoke in Carol's direction. The gesture was ruined by the gust of wind that snatched the smoke away before it reached her. Looking disgusted, Cross turned on his heel and marched back to the scene of the crime.

'You meet a nice class of person in this job,' Carol said.

'At least I know now which way the wind blows,' Tony replied. As he spoke, he felt a drop of rain on his face.

'Oh shit,' Carol said. 'That's all we need. Look, can we meet tomorrow? I can grab the files tonight and skim them beforehand. Then you can get stuck in.'

'Fine. My office, ten o'clock?'

'Perfect. How do I find you?'

Tony gave Carol directions, then watched as she hurried back down the alley. An interesting woman. And attractive too, most men would agree to that. There were times when he almost wished he could find an uncomplicated response in himself. But he'd long since gone beyond the point where he would allow himself to be attracted to a woman like Carol Jordan.

It was after seven when Carol finally made it back to headquarters. When she rang John Brandon's extension, she was pleasantly surprised to find him still at his desk. 'Come on up,' he told her.

She was even more surprised when she walked through his secretary's door and found him pouring two steaming mugs from the coffee maker. 'Milk and sugar?' he asked her.

'Neither,' she said. 'This is an unexpected pleasure.'

'I gave up smoking five years ago,' Brandon confided. 'Now it's only the caffeine that holds me together. Come through.'

Carol walked into his office, fired with curiosity. She'd never been across the threshold before. The decor was regulation cream paint, the furniture identical to Cross's office, except that here the wood was gleaming, free from scuffs, scratches, cigarette burns and the telltale rings left by hot cups. Unlike most senior officers, Brandon hadn't decorated his walls with police photographs and his framed commendations. Instead, he'd chosen half a dozen reproductions of turn-of-the-century paintings of Bradfield street scenes. Colourful yet moody, often rain-soaked, they mirrored the spectacular view from the seventh-floor window.

The only item in the room that ran true to expectation was the photograph of his wife and children on the desk. Even that was no posed, studio shot, but an enlargement of a holiday snap on board a sailboat. Deduction: in spite of the impression Brandon strove to give as a bluff, straightforward, conventional copper, he was actually far more complex and thoughtful under the surface.

He waved Carol to a pair of chairs in front of his desk, then sat down in the other one. 'One thing I want to be clear about,' Brandon said without preliminary. 'You report to Superintendent Cross. He's in charge of this operation. However, I want to see copies of your reports and Dr Hill's, and I want to know any theories the pair of you come up with that you're not ready to commit to paper. Think you can handle that balancing act?'

Carol's eyebrows rose. 'There's only one way to find out, sir,' she said.

Brandon's lips twitched in a half smile. He'd always preferred honesty to bullshit. 'OK. I want you to make sure you are given access to everybody's files. Any problems with that, any sense that anyone's trying to stall you and Dr Hill, and I want to know about it, no matter who's responsible. I'll talk to the squad myself in the morning, make sure nobody's in any doubt about what the new rules of the game are. Anything you need from me?'

Another twelve hours in the day would be a start, Carol thought wearily. Loving a challenge was all very well. But this time, it looked like love was going to be an uphill struggle.

Tony closed his front door behind him. He dropped his briefcase where he stood and leaned against the wall. He'd got what he wanted. It was a battle of wits now, his insight against the killer's stockade. Somewhere in the pattern of these crimes there lay a labyrinthine path straight to a murderer's heart. Somehow, Tony had to tread that path, wary of misleading shadows, careful to avoid straying into treacherous undergrowth.

He shrugged away from the wall, feeling suddenly exhausted, and headed for the kitchen, pulling off his tie and unbuttoning his shirt on the way. A cold beer, and then he could go through his scanty collection of press clippings on the three previous murders. He had just opened the fridge to grab a can of Boddingtons when the phone rang. He slammed the door shut and snatched up the extension, juggling with the cold can. 'Hello?' he said.

'Anthony,' the voice said.

Tony swallowed hard. 'This isn't a good time,' he said, cutting coldly across the husky contralto coming down the line. He dumped the can on the worktop and popped the ring pull with one hand.

'Playing hard to get? Oh, well, that's part of the fun, isn't it? I thought I'd cured you of trying to avoid me. I thought we'd left all that behind us. Don't say you're going to regress and hang up on me again, that's all I ask.' The voice was teasing, laughter bubbling just beneath the surface.

'I'm not playing hard to get,' he said. 'It really isn't a good time.' He could feel the slow burn of anger rising from the pit of his stomach.

'That's up to you. You're the man. You're the boss. Unless, of course, you want things different for a change. If you catch my drift.' The voice was almost a sigh, teasing him with its elusive quality. 'After all, this is strictly between you and me. Consenting adults, as they say.'

'So don't I have the right to say no, not right now? Or is it only women who have that right?' he said, hearing the tension in his voice as the anger rose like bile in his throat.

'God, Anthony, your voice gets so sexy when you're angry,' the voice purred.

44

Nonplussed, Tony held the phone away from his ear, staring at it as if it were an artefact from another planet. Sometimes he wondered if what came out of his mouth were the same words that arrived in his listeners' ears. With a clinical detachment he couldn't bring to his caller, he noted that his grip on the phone was so tight his fingers were white. After a moment, he put the receiver back to his ear. 'Just listening to your voice makes me wet, Anthony,' she was saying. 'Don't you want to know what I'm wearing, what I'm doing right now?' The voice was seductive, the breathing more audible than it had been at first.

'Look, I've had a hard day, I've got a load of work to do and much as I enjoy our little games, I'm not in the mood tonight.' Agitated, Tony looked desperately round his kitchen as if searching for the nearest exit.

'You sound so tense, my darling. Let me soothe all that pressure away. Let's play. Think of me as a relaxation technique. You know you'll work better afterwards. You know I give you the best time you've ever had. With a stud like you and a sex queen like me, there's nothing we can't do. And for starters, I'm going to give you the dirtiest, sexiest, horniest phone call we've ever shared.'

Suddenly, his anger found a weakness in the dam and burst free. 'Not tonight!' Tony yelled, slamming the phone down so hard the can of beer jumped. Creamy froth swelled up through the triangular hole in the top. Tony stared at it in disgust. He picked up the can and threw it in the sink. The can clattered against the stainless steel, then rolled from side to side. Beer and foam spurted out in brown and cream gouts as Tony dropped into a crouch, head down, hands over his face. Tonight, faced with staring into the depths of someone else's nightmares, he absolutely did not want the inevitable confrontation with his own deficiencies that the phone calls always brought in their wake. The phone rang again, but he remained motionless, eyes squeezed shut. When the answering machine picked up, the caller disconnected the line. 'Bitch,' he said viciously. 'Bitch.'

When my neighbours go out to work in the morning, they leave their German shepherd loose in the back yard. All day long, he lopes restlessly up and down the yard, quartering the poured concrete with the diligence of a prison officer who really loves the work. He's heavy-set, black and brindle, with a shaggy coat. Whenever anyone enters the yards on either side of his, he barks, a long, deep-throated cacophony that lasts far longer than any intrusion. When the bin men come down the back alley to trundle our wheelie bins to their truck, the dog becomes hysterical, standing on his hind legs, forepaws scrabbling uselessly against the heavy wooden gate. I've watched him from the vantage point of my back-bedroom window. He's nearly as tall as the gate itself. Perfect, really.

Next Monday morning, I bought a couple of pounds of steak and cut it into one-inch cubes, like all the best recipes say. Then I made a small incision in each cube and inserted one of the tranquillizers my doctor insists on prescribing for me. I never wanted them, and certainly never use them, but I'd had the feeling they might come in useful one day.

I came out of my back door and listened cheerfully to the dog's salvo of barks. I could afford to be cheerful; it would be the last time I'd have to endure it. I plunged my hand into the bowl of moist meat, enjoying its cool, slippery feel. Then I tossed it over the wall in handfuls. I returned indoors, washed up and went upstairs to my vantage point by the computer. I chose the atmospheric world of Darkseed, calming my excitement with the gothic and macabre underworld I had come to know so well. In spite of my absorption in the game, though, I couldn't help glancing out of the window every few minutes. After a while, he slumped to the ground, tongue lolling out of his mouth. I exited from my game and picked up my binoculars. He seemed to be breathing, but wasn't moving.

I ran downstairs, picking up the holdall I'd prepared earlier, and got into the jeep. I reversed it down the alley till the tailgate was level with next-door's yard gate. I turned off the engine. Silence. I couldn't resist a certain smug satisfaction as I picked up my crowbar and jumped down. It took moments to force next-door's gate. As it swung open, I could see the dog hadn't stirred. I opened the holdall and crouched down beside him. I shoved his tongue back into his mouth and taped his muzzle shut with a roll of surgical tape. I bound his legs together, front and back, and dragged him to the jeep. He was heavy, but I keep myself in shape, and it wasn't too hard to manhandle him into the back.

His breath was coming in soft snores when we got to the farmhouse, but there was no flicker of consciousness, even when I thumbed back his eyelids. I tipped him into the wheelbarrow I'd left out there, wheeled him through the cottage and emptied him down the flight of steps. I switched on the lights and hauled the dog on to the rack like a sack of potatoes, then turned to study my knives. I'd fitted a magnetic strip to the wall, and there they hung suspended, each sharpened to a professional edge; cleaver, filleting knife, carving knife, paring knife and craft knife. I chose the craft knife, cut away the tape from the dog's legs and spread him out on his stomach. I fastened the strap round his middle to hold him tightly against the rack. That's when I realized I had a problem.

Sometime in the past few minutes, the dog had stopped breathing. I thrust my head against the rough hairs of his chest, searching for a heartbeat, but it was too late. I'd obviously miscalculated the drug dosage, and given him too much. I was furious, I have to admit. The dog's death wouldn't affect the practicalities of scientifically testing my apparatus, but I had been looking forward to his suffering; a small revenge for the dozens of times his demented barking had woken me up, especially when I'd come off a hard night shift. But he'd died without a moment's suffering. The last thing he'd known was a couple of pounds of steak. It didn't please me that he'd died happy.

That wasn't all; I soon discovered a second problem. The straps I'd fitted were fine for human ankles and wrists. But the dog didn't have hands or feet to stop his limbs slipping free.

I didn't puzzle for long. It was a far from elegant solution, but it served my purpose. I still had some six-inch nails left over from the repairs and modifications I'd made to the cellar. I carefully placed his left front paw so it straddled a gap in the timbers. I felt for the space between the bones and, with one blow of my club hammer, I drove the nail through at right angles to the paw, just above the last joint. I fixed the strap below the nail, and tugged at it. I reckoned it would hold for long enough.

I'd fixed the other legs within five minutes. Once he was securely strapped down, I was finally able to get started on the business of the day. Even with the bare prospect of a purely scientific experiment, I could feel the excitement rising in me till it was like a hard lump in my throat. Almost, it seemed, without conscious thought, my hand strayed to the handle of the rack. I watched it, detached, as if it were the hand of a stranger. It caressed the cogs, ran lightly over the wheel, and finally came to rest on the handle. The aroma of lubricating oil still hung lightly on the air, melding with the faint smell of paint and the stale, doggy smell of my assistant in the experiment. I took a deep breath, shivered in anticipation, and slowly began to turn the handle.

3

I do not stick to assert, that any man who deals in murder must have very incorrect ways of thinking, and truly inaccurate principles.

Don Merrick unzipped his flies. With a sigh of relief, he relaxed his muscles and let his bursting bladder empty. Behind him, the cubicle door opened. His pleasure was abruptly shattered when a heavy hand descended on his shoulder. 'Sergeant Merrick. Just the man I wanted to see,' Tom Cross boomed. Inexplicably, Merrick discovered he couldn't finish what he'd started.

''Morning, sir,' he said cautiously, shaking himself and quickly tucking his manhood out of Cross's sight.

'Told you about her new assignment, has she, your guv'nor?' Cross asked, all lads-together bonhomie.

'She mentioned it, yes, sir.' Merrick looked longingly at the door. But there was no escape. Not with Cross's hand still clamped on his shoulder.

'I hear you're planning on taking your inspector's exams,' Cross remarked.

Merrick's stomach clenched. 'That's right, sir.'

'So you'll be needing all the friends in high places you can find, eh, lad?'

Merrick forced his lips apart in what he hoped was a smile to match Cross's. 'If you say so, sir.'

'You've got the makings of a good officer, Merrick. As long as you remember where your loyalties lie. I know Inspector Jordan's going to be a very busy lady over the next few weeks. She might not always have time to keep me fully *abreast* of things.' Cross leered suggestively. 'I'll be relying on you to keep me informed of all developments. You understand, lad?'

Merrick nodded. 'Aye, sir.'

Cross dropped his hand and made for the door. Opening it, he turned back to Merrick and said, 'Especially if she starts shagging our doctor friend.'

The door sighed shut behind Cross. 'Fuck and bollocks,' Merrick said softly to himself as he moved to the washbasin and started scrubbing his hands vigorously under the hot tap.

Tony had been at his desk since eight. So far, all he'd done was make some photocopies of the Crime Analysis Report form he'd devised for the projected task force. Heavily based on the FBI's Violent Criminal Apprehension Program questionnaire, it aimed to produce a standard classification of every aspect of the crime, from the victim through to the forensic evidence. He shuffled the forms absently, then rearranged his newspaper cuttings into a neat pile. He justified his lack of activity by telling himself that until Carol arrived with the police files, there was little he could do. But that was merely an excuse.

The truth was, there was good reason why concentration was eluding him. She was in his head again. The mystery woman. At the start, he'd felt vulnerable, unwilling to take part in her games. Just like his patients, he thought ironically. How many times had he uttered the maxim that everybody was reluctant to cooperate with therapy at some level? He'd lost count of the number of times he'd slammed the phone down in the early days. But she had persisted, patiently continuing to administer her soothing persuasions till he had started to relax, even to join in.

She had completely thrown him off balance. She had seemed from the first to have an instinct for his Achilles heel, yet she never attacked it. She was everything anyone could desire in a fantasy lover, from gentle to raunchy. The key question for Tony was whether he was pathetic because he managed to relate to pornographic phone calls from a stranger, or whether he should congratulate himself on being so well adjusted that he understood what he needed and what worked for him. But he could not escape the fear that, if not yet dependent on the phone calls, he was at risk of succumbing to that danger. Already incapable of sustaining a normal sexual relationship, was he colluding in the worsening of his condition, or was he moving towards recovery? The only way to test which was correct was to attempt the shift from fantasy to reality. But he was still too wary of fresh humiliation for that. For now, it seemed he'd have to settle for the mysterious stranger who managed to make him feel like a man for long enough to drive the demons underground.

Tony sighed and picked up his mug. The coffee was cold, but he drank it anyway. In spite of himself, he began replaying past conversations in his mind. As if he hadn't run through it enough during the early hours of the morning when sleep had been as elusive as the Bradfield serial killer. The woman's voice buzzed in his ears, inescapable as someone else's Walkman in a train carriage. He tried to close off his emotions and treat the calls with the intellectual objectivity he brought to his work. All he had to do was shut himself off, the way he did when he was examining the perverse fantasies of his patients. He'd certainly had enough experience of refusing to recognize echoes in himself.

Stop the voice. Analyse. Who was she? What drove her? Maybe, like him, she simply enjoyed digging around in messy heads. That at least would explain how she'd wormed her way through his barricades. She was certainly a different animal from the women who worked for the sleazy telephone sex chatlines. Before he'd started this study for the Home Office, he'd been engaged in a piece of research into those chatlines. A significant number of the recently convicted offenders he had dealt with had admitted they were regular callers to the premium-rate phone lines where they could pour their sexual fantasies, however bizarre, obscene or perverse, into the ears of dismally paid women who were encouraged by their bosses to indulge the callers for as long as they were prepared to pay. He'd actually phoned some of the lines himself, just to sample what was on offer, and to discover, using the transcripts of some of his interviews, just how far it was possible to go before disgust overcame the profit motive or the desperate need to earn a living.

Finally, he'd interviewed a selection of the women who worked the phones. The one thing they all held in common was a sense of being violated and degraded, however some of them dressed it up in the contempt they voiced for their clients. He'd come to several conclusions, but the paper he'd subsequently written hadn't included all of them. Some he'd left out because they were too off the wall, others because he feared they might reveal too much about his own psyche. That included his conviction that the response of a man who had previously called a chatline to a dirty phone call from a member of the opposite sex would be radically different to that of a woman in the same situation. Instead of slamming down the receiver, or reporting it to Telecom, most of these men would be either amused or aroused. Either way, they'd want to hear more.

All he had to work out now was why, unlike the chatline workers, this woman found telephone sex with a stranger so appealing. What he needed was to satisfy the intellectual curiosity that was at least as strong as his urge to explore the sexual playground she had opened up for him. Maybe he should consider suggesting a meeting. Before he could go any further, the phone rang. Tony started, his hand stopping halfway in its automatic journey to the receiver. 'Oh, for God's sake,' he muttered impatiently, shaking his head like a high-diver surfacing. He picked up the phone and said, 'Tony Hill.'

'Dr Hill, it's Carol Jordan here.'

Tony said nothing, relieved that his thoughts had failed to conjure up the mystery woman.

'Inspector Jordan? Bradfield Police?' Carol continued into the silence.

'Hello, yes, sorry, I was just trying to . . . clear a space on my desk,' Tony stumbled, his left leg starting to jitter like a cup of tea on a train.

'I'm really sorry about this, but I'm not going to be able to make it for ten. Mr Brandon's called all the squad together for a briefing, and I don't think it would be politic to miss it.'

'No, I can see that,' Tony said, his free hand picking up a pen and unconsciously doodling a daffodil. 'It's going to be hard enough for you to act as go-between without making it look like you're not part of the team. Don't worry about it.'

'Thanks. Look, I don't think this briefing is going to last that long. I'll be with you as soon as I can. Probably around eleven, if that doesn't interfere with your schedule.'

'That's fine,' he said, relieved he wouldn't have too long to brood before they could get down to work. 'I've no meetings in the diary for today, so take your time. You're not putting me out.'

'OK. See you then.'

Carol replaced the phone. So far, so good. At least Tony Hill didn't seem a prisoner of his professional ego, unlike several of the experts she'd had dealings with. And, unlike most men, he'd perceived her potential difficulty, sympathized without patronizing her, and had happily gone along with a course of action that would minimize her problems.

Impatiently, she pushed away the memory of the attraction she'd felt for him. These days, she had neither the time nor the inclination for emotional involvement. Sharing a flat with her brother and finding the time to sustain a few close friendships took as much of her energy as she could spare. Besides, the ending of her last relationship had dealt her self-esteem too serious a blow for her to enter on another one lightly.

The affair with a casualty surgeon in London hadn't survived her move from the Met to Bradfield three years before. As far as Rob was concerned, it was Carol's decision to move to the frozen north. So travelling up and down motorways to spend time together was down to her. He had no intention of wasting any of his valuable off-duty time putting unnecessary mileage on his BMW just to go to a city whose only redeeming feature was Carol. Besides, nurses were a lot less stroppy and critical, and they understood long hours and shift work just as well as a copper, if not better. His brutal self-interest had shaken Carol, who felt cheated of the emotion and energy she'd invested in loving Rob. Tony Hill might be attractive, charming, and, if his reputation was correct, intelligent and intuitive, but Carol wasn't about to risk her heart again. Especially not with a professional colleague. If she was finding it hard to get him out of her mind, it was because she was fascinated by what she could learn from him about the case, not because she fancied him.

Carol ran a hand through her hair and yawned. She'd been home for precisely fifty-seven minutes in the previous twenty-four hours. Twenty of those had been spent in the shower in a futile attempt to inoculate herself against the effects of no sleep. She'd spent a large chunk of the evening out on the knocker with her CID team, pursuing fruitless enquiries among the nervous inhabitants, workers and regular customers of Temple Fields and its gay businesses. The men's reactions had ranged from total noncooperation to abuse. Carol felt no surprise. The area was seething with a mass of contradictory feelings.

On the one hand, the gay businesses didn't want the area swarming with police because it was bad for cash flow. On the other hand, the gay activists were angrily demanding proper protection now the police had belatedly decided that there was a gay serial killer on the loose. One group of customers were horrified to be questioned, since their gay life was a deep secret from wives, friends, colleagues and parents. Another group were happily playing macho men, boasting that they'd never get into a situation where they were slaughtered by some glassy-eyed maniac. Yet another group were eager for details, obscurely and, in Carol's eyes, obscenely excited by what could happen when one man went out of control. And there was a handful of hardline lesbian separatists who made no secret of their glee that this time, men were the targets. 'Maybe now they'll understand why we were so outraged during the Yorkshire Ripper hunt when men suggested single women should have a curfew,' one had sneered at Carol.

Exhausted by the turmoil, Carol had driven back to headquarters to begin her trawl of the files of the existing enquiries. The murder room was strangely quiet, since most of the detectives were out in Temple Fields, pursuing different lines of enquiry or taking advantage of a few hours off to catch up on their drinking, their sex lives or their sleep. She'd already had a quick word with her opposite numbers on the other two murder investigations, and they had reluctantly agreed to give her access to their files provided she had the material back on their desks first thing in the morning. It was exactly the response she'd expected; superficially cooperative, but, in real terms, calculated to cause her even more problems.

When she'd walked through her office door, she'd been appalled by the sheer volume of paper. Stacks of interview statements, forensic and pathology reports, files of photographs virtually buried her office. Why, in God's name, hadn't Tom Cross decided to use the HOLMES computer system for the earlier murders? At least then all the material would be accessible in the computer, indexed and cross-referenced. All she'd have had to do then was to persuade one of the HOLMES indexers to print out the relevant stuff for Tony. With a groan, she closed her door on the mess and walked through the empty corridors to the uniform sergeant's office. The time had come to test the ACC's instruction to all ranks to cooperate with her. Without another pair of hands, she'd never get through the night's work.

Even with the grudgingly granted help of a PC, it had been a struggle to get through the material. Carol had skimmed the investigation reports, extracting everything that seemed to hold the possibility of significance and passing it on to the constable for copying. Even so, there was a daunting pile of material for Tony and her to work through. When her assistant knocked off at six, Carol wearily loaded the photocopies into a couple of cardboard cartons and staggered down to her car with them. She helped herself to full sets of photographs of all the victims and scenes of crime, filling in a form to requisition fresh copies for the investigating teams to replace the ones she'd taken.

Only then had she headed home. Even there, she had no respite. Nelson waited behind the door, miaowing crossly as he wove his sinuous body round her ankles, forcing her to head straight for the kitchen and the tin opener. When she dumped the bowl of food in front of him, he stared suspiciously at it, frowning. Then hunger overcame his desire to punish her and he wolfed down the whole bowl without pause. 'Nice to see you missed me,' Carol said drily as she made for the shower. By the time she emerged, Nelson had clearly decided to forgive her. He followed her around, purring like a dialling tone, sitting down on every garment she selected from the wardrobe and placed on the bed.

'You really are the pits,' Carol grumbled, pulling her black jeans out from under him. Nelson carried on adoring her, his purr not disrupted in the slightest. She pulled on the jeans, admiring the cut in her wardrobe mirror. They were Katharine Hammett, but she'd only paid £20 for them in a seconds shop in Kensington Church Street, where she went on a twice-annual trawl for the designer clothes she loved but couldn't afford, even on an inspector's wages. The cream linen shirt was French Connection, the ribbed grey cardigan from a chain store men's department. Carol picked a few black cat hairs from the cardigan and caught Nelson's reproachful stare. 'You know I love you. I just don't need to wear you,' she said.

'You'd get a shock if he answered you,' a man's voice said from the doorway.

Carol turned to face her brother, who leaned against the doorjamb in his boxer shorts, blond hair tousled, eyes bleary with sleep. His face had a strange congruence with Carol's, as if someone had scanned her photograph into a computer and subtly altered the features away from the feminine and towards the masculine. 'I didn't wake you, did I?' she asked anxiously.

'Nope. I've got to go to London today. The money man cometh.' He yawned.

'The Americans?' Carol asked, crouching down and scratching the cat behind the ears. Nelson promptly rolled over on to his back, displaying his full stomach to be stroked.

'Correct. They want a full demo of what we've done so far. I've been telling Carl that nothing looks very impressive right now, but he says they want some reassurance that they're not just pouring their development money into a black hole.'

'The joys of software development,' Carol said, rumpling Nelson's fur.

'Leading-edge software development, please,' Michael

said, self-mockingly. 'How about you? What's happening down the murder factory? I heard on the news last night that you'd copped for another one.'

'Looks like it. At least the powers that be have finally admitted that we've got a serial killer on the loose. And they've brought in a psychological profiler to work with us.'

Michael whistled. 'Fuck me, Bradfield police enter the twentieth century. How's Popeye taking it?'

Carol pulled a face. 'He likes it about as much as a poke in the eye with a sharp stick. He thinks it's a total waste of bloody time,' Carol said, dropping her voice and affecting Tom Cross's Bradfield accent. 'Then when I was appointed liaison officer with the profiler, he perked up.'

Michael nodded, a cynical expression on his face. 'Two birds with one stone.'

Carol grinned. 'Yeah, well, it'll need to be over my dead body.' She stood up. Nelson gave a small miaow of protest. Carol sighed and headed for the door. 'Back to work, Nelson. Thanks for taking my mind off the bodies,' she said.

Michael swung out of the doorway to let her pass and gave her a hug. 'Take no prisoners, sis,' he said.

Carol snorted. 'I don't think you've quite grasped the principle of policing, bro.'

By the time she was behind the wheel, the cat and Michael were forgotten. She was back with the killer.

Now, a couple of hours and a stack of overnight murder team reports later, home seemed a memory as distant as her summer holiday in Ithaca. Carol forced herself out of her chair, picked up the paperwork and walked into the main CID office.

It was standing room only by the time she arrived, detectives normally based in other stations jockeying for position in the crowd. A couple of her detective constables shifted to make room for her, one offering his chair.

'Fucking brown nose,' a voice said audibly from the other side of the room. Carol couldn't see who had spoken, but recognized it wasn't one of her own team. She smiled and shook her head at her junior officer, choosing instead to perch on the edge of his desk beside Don Merrick, who nodded a morose greeting. The clock read nine-twenty-nine. The room smelled of cheap cigars, coffee and damp coats.

One of the other inspectors caught Carol's eye and started to move towards her. But before they could speak, the door opened and Tom Cross barrelled in, followed by John Brandon. The superintendent looked disturbingly benign as he marched in. The troops parted automatically before him, leaving a clear path for him and Brandon to walk to the whiteboard at the far end of the room.

''Morning, lads,' Cross said genially. 'And lasses,' he added as an obvious afterthought. 'There's nobody here that doesn't know we've got four unsolved murders on our hands. We've got IDs for the first three bodies – Adam Scott, Paul Gibbs and Gareth Finnegan. So far, we've not made any progress on the fourth victim. The lads down the path lab are working on him now, trying to come up with a face that won't frighten the horses when we release the picture to the press.'

Cross took a deep breath. If anything, his expression became even more benevolent. 'As you all know, I'm not a man given to theorizing ahead of the evidence. And I've been reluctant officially to connect these killings because of the media hysteria that would bring down about us. Judging by this morning's papers, I was right about that.' He pointed to several of the newspapers the detectives held.

'However, in the light of this latest killing, we're going to have to revise our strategy. As of yesterday afternoon, I have amalgamated the four murder enquiries into one major investigation.'

There was a murmur of support. Don Merrick leaned

forward and murmured in Carol's ear, 'Changes his tune more often than a juke box.'

She nodded. 'I wish he changed his socks as often.'

Cross glared in their direction. He couldn't have heard the remarks, but seeing Carol's lips move was enough of an excuse. 'Settle down,' he said sternly. 'I'm not finished yet. Now, it doesn't take much in the way of detective abilities to see that this place is too small for us *and* the normal activities of the station, so as soon as we're finished here this morning, we'll be moving this operation to the former station in Scargill Street, which some of you will remember was mothballed six months ago. Overnight, there's been a team of maintenance workers, computer whizz kids and British Telecom engineers getting it back to temporary operational status.'

A groan went up. No one had shed a tear when the old Victorian building in Scargill Street had been closed down. Draughty, inconvenient, short of parking spaces, ladies' toilets – everything except cells – the building had been earmarked for demolition and redevelopment. Typically, there hadn't been enough money in the budget to push ahead with the project. 'I know, I know,' Cross said, cutting across their complaints. 'But we'll all be under one roof, so I'll be able to keep an eye on you. I will be in overall charge of the enquiry. You'll have two inspectors to report to – Bob Stansfield and Kevin Matthews. They'll be sorting out your assignments in a minute. Inspector Jordan will be otherwise engaged on an initiative of Mr Brandon's.' Cross paused. 'Which I'm sure you'll all want to cooperate with.'

Carol kept her head high and looked around. The faces she could see mostly showed open cynicism. Several heads turned towards her. There was no warmth in their stares. Even those who might support the profiling initiative were brassed off that the prime job had gone to a woman rather than one of the lads.

'So Bob will take over Inspector Jordan's operational responsibilities for Paul Gibbs and Adam Scott, and Kevin will handle yesterday's body as well as Gareth Finnegan. The HOLMES team have been called in, and they'll be starting to input their data just as soon as the boffins have got the wires in place. Inspector Dave Woolcott, who some of you will remember from when he was a sergeant here, will be the enquiry manager in charge of the HOLMES team. Over to you, Mr Brandon.' Cross stepped back and waved the ACC forward. His gesture was only just on the right side of the border between insolence and politeness.

Brandon took a moment to look around the room. He'd never had to make a more important pitch. Most of the detectives in the room were jaded and frustrated. Many of them had been working on one of the previous murders for months now, with precious little to show for it. Tom Cross's powers of motivation were legendary, but even he was facing an uphill struggle, not least because of his pig-headed refusal to admit before now that the crimes were connected. It was time to beat Tom Cross at his own game. Bluntness had never been Brandon's strong suit, but he'd been practising all morning. In the shower, in front of the shaving mirror, in his head while he ate his egg on toast, in the car on the way to the station. Brandon thrust one hand in his trouser pocket and crossed his fingers.

'This is probably the toughest task of any of our careers. As far as we're aware, this guy is only operating in Bradfield. In a way, I'm glad about that, because I've never seen a better bunch of detectives than we've got here. If anyone can nail this bastard, it's you lot. You've got a hundred and ten per cent support from your senior officers, and all the resources you need are going to be made available, whether the politicians like it or not.' Brandon's note of belligerence won a murmur of agreement from the room.

'We're going to be blazing a trail here in more ways than one. You all know about the Home Office plans for a national task force for profiling repeat offenders. Well, we're going to be the guinea pigs. Dr Tony Hill, the man who's going to be telling the Home Office what to think, has agreed to work with us. Now, I know there are some amongst you who think that profiling is a load of crap. But like it or not, it's part of our future. If we cooperate and work with this guy, we're a lot more likely to see this task force end up something like we want it to be. If we piss him off, we're liable to be lumbered with a bloody great millstone round our neck. Is that clear to everyone here?'

Brandon looked sternly round the room, not missing out Tom Cross. The nods varied from enthusiastic to barely perceptible. 'I'm glad we all understand one another. Dr Hill's job is to assess the evidence we provide him with and to come up with a profile of the killer to help us focus our enquiries. I've appointed Inspector Carol Jordan as the liaison officer between the murder squad and Dr Hill. Inspector Jordan, can you just stand up a minute?'

Startled, Carol scrambled to her feet, dropping her files on the way. Don Merrick immediately got down on his knees and grabbed the spilling papers. 'For those of you from other divisions who don't know Inspector Jordan, there she is.' Nice one, Brandon, thought Carol. As if there were squads of female detectives to choose from.

'Inspector Jordan is to have access to each and every piece of paper on this enquiry. I want her kept fully informed of any developments. Anyone who is pursuing a promising lead should discuss it with her as well as with their own inspector, or Superintendent Cross. And any requests from Inspector Jordan must be treated as urgent enquiries. If I hear that anybody's being a smartarse, trying to freeze Inspector Jordan or Dr Hill out of the investigation, I won't be taking prisoners. The same goes for anybody who leaks anything about this aspect of the investigation to the media. So think on. Unless you've got a burning ambition to climb back into uniform and walk the streets of Bradfield in the rain for the rest of your career, you'll do everything in your power to help her. This isn't a competition. We're all on the same side. Dr Hill isn't here to catch the killer. That's your –'

Brandon stopped in mid-sentence. No one had noticed the door opening, but the words of the communications room sergeant captured everyone's attention faster than a gunshot. 'Sorry to interrupt, sir,' he said, his voice tight with suppressed emotion. 'We've got an ID on yesterday's victim. Sir, he's one of ours.'

It was an American journalist who said, 'I have seen the future and it works.' I know just what he meant. After the dog, I knew Adam wouldn't be any problem.

I spent the rest of the week in a state of nervous tension. I was even tempted to try one of the tranquillizers myself, but I resisted. This wasn't the time to give in to weakness. Besides, I couldn't afford to be anything less than completely in control of myself. My years of self-discipline paid off; I doubt if any of my colleagues noticed anything unusual in my behaviour at work, except that I couldn't bring myself to do the weekend overtime I usually volunteer for.

By Monday morning, I was at a peak of readiness. I was primed and polished, the perfect killer-in-waiting. Even the weather was on my side. It was a crisp, clear autumnal morning, the kind of day that brings a smile even to the lips of commuters. Just before eight, I drove past Adam's home, a new terraced three-storey town house with integral garage on the ground floor. His bedroom curtains were closed, the milk bottle still sitting on his doorstep, half a Daily Mail *protruding from his letter box. I parked a couple of streets away outside a row of shops and retraced my journey. I walked down his street, satisfied that so far I was right on time. His bedroom curtains were drawn back, the milk and newspaper gone. At the end of the street, I crossed to the little park opposite and sat on a bench.*

I opened my own Daily Mail *and imagined Adam reading the same stories that I was staring at unseeingly. I shifted my position so I could see his front door without craning round the paper, and put my peripheral vision on alert. Right on schedule, the door opened at eight-twenty, and Adam appeared. Casually, I folded up my paper, dumped it in the litter bin by the bench and strolled off down the street in his wake.*

The tram station was less than ten minutes' walk away, and I was right behind him as he strode on to the crowded platform. The tram glided into the station moments later and he moved forward with the flow of passengers. I hung back slightly and let a couple of people come between us; I was taking no chances.

He was craning his head as he entered the carriage. I knew exactly why. When their eyes met, Adam waved and squirmed through the crowd so they could chatter mindlessly all the way into town. I watched him as he leaned forward. I knew every expression on his face, every angle and gesture of his lean, muscular body. His hair; the little curls in the nape of his neck still damp, his skin pink and glowing from his shave, the scent of his Aramis cologne. He laughed aloud at something in their conversation, and I felt the sour taste of bile rise in my mouth. The taste of betrayal. How could he? It should have been me talking to him, making his face light up, bringing that beautiful smile to his warm lips. If my fixity of purpose had ever wavered, the sight of the pair of them enjoying their Monday-morning encounter would have turned my resolve to granite.

As usual, he left the tram in Woolmarket Square. I was less than a dozen yards behind him. He turned back to wave to his soon-to-be bereaved lover. I swiftly turned away, pretending to read the tram timetable. The last thing I wanted right then was for him to notice me, to realize I was dogging his steps. I gave it a few seconds, then took up the pursuit. Left into Bellwether Street. I could see his dark hair bobbing among the shop and office workers crowding the pavements. Adam cut down an alley to his right, and I emerged in Crown Plaza just in time to see him enter the Inland Revenue building where he worked. Satisfied that this was just another Monday, I carried on through the plaza, past the squat glass and metal office block, and into the newly restored Victorian shopping arcades.

I had time to kill. The thought brought a smile to my lips.

I went off to do some studying in the Central Library. They had nothing new in, so I settled for an old favourite, Killing for Company. Dennis Nilsen's case never ceases both to fascinate and repel me. He murdered fifteen young men without anyone even missing them. No one had the faintest idea that there was a gay serial killer stalking the homeless and rootless. He befriended them, took them home, gave them drink, but he could only cope with them once they had been perfected in death. Then, and only then, could he hold them, have sex with them, cherish them. Now that is sick. They'd done nothing to deserve their fate; they had committed no betrayal, no act of treachery.

The only mistake Nilsen made was in the disposal of the bodies. It's almost as if subconsciously he wanted to be caught. Chopping them up and cooking them was fine, but flushing them down the toilet? It must have been obvious to a man as intelligent as he was that the drains wouldn't be able to handle that volume of solids. I've never understood why he didn't just feed the meat to his dog.

However, it's never too late to learn from the mistakes of others. The blunders of killers never cease to amaze me. It doesn't take much intelligence to understand how the police and forensic scientists operate and to take appropriate precautions, especially since the men who earn their living trying to catch the killers have obligingly written *detailed textbooks about the precise nature of their work. On the other hand, we only ever hear about the failures. I knew I was never going to appear in those catalogues of incompetence. I had planned too well, every risk minimized and balanced against the benefits it would bring. The only account of my work will be this journal, which will not see printer's ink until my last breath is a distant memory. My only regret is that I won't be around to read the reviews.*

I was back at my post by four, even though I'd never known Adam leave work before a quarter to five. I sat in the window of Burger King on Woolmarket Square, perfectly placed to watch the mouth of the alley leading to his office. Right on cue, he emerged at 4.47 and headed for the tram stop. I joined the knot of people waiting on the raised platform, smiling quietly to myself as I heard the tram hoot in the distance. Enjoy your tram ride, Adam. It's going to be your last.

4

The fact was, I 'fancied' him, and resolved to commence business upon his throat.

When Damien Connolly failed to turn up at the start of his shift as local information officer in F Division's station on the south side of the city, the duty sergeant hadn't been unduly worried. Although PC Connolly was one of the best collators in the force, and a trained HOLMES officer, he was a notoriously bad timekeeper. At least twice a week, he came hurtling through the doors of the station a good ten minutes after his shift was due to start. But when he still hadn't shown up half an hour after he was due on duty, Sergeant Claire Bonner felt a twinge of irritation. Even Connolly had enough sense to realize that if he was going to be more than fifteen minutes late, he had to phone in. Today of all days as well, when headquarters were demanding a full turnout of HOLMES officers on the serial-killer investigation.

Sighing, Sgt Bonner checked Connolly's home number in her files and dialled it. The phone rang and rang, till finally it was automatically disconnected. She felt a prickle of concern. Connolly·was something of a loner outside the job. He was quieter and maybe more thoughtful than most of the officers on Sgt Bonner's relief, always keeping his distance when he joined in the social life of the station. As far as she was aware, there was no girlfriend in whose bed Connolly might have overslept. His family were all up in Glasgow, so there were no relatives to try locally. Sgt

Bonner cast her mind back. Yesterday had been a day off for the relief. When they'd knocked off from the previous night shift, Connolly had come for breakfast with her and half a dozen of the other lads. He'd not said anything about having plans for his time off other than catching up on his kip and working on his car, an elderly Austin Healey roadster.

Sgt Bonner went through to the control room and had a word with her opposite number, asking him to have one of the patrol cars swing round by Connolly's house to check he wasn't ill or injured. 'See if they can check the garage, make sure that bloody car of his hasn't come off the jack with him underneath,' she added as she went back to her desk.

It was after eight when the control room sergeant appeared in her office. 'The lads have checked Connolly's house. No answer to the door. They had a good scout round, and all the curtains were open. Milk on the door-step. No sign of life as far as they could make out. There was only one thing a bit odd that they could see. His car was parked on the street, which isn't like him. I don't have to tell you, he treats that motor like the crown jewels.'

Sgt Bonner frowned. 'Maybe he's got somebody stopping with him? A relative, or a girlfriend? Maybe he's let them stick their car in the garage?'

The control room sergeant shook his head. 'Nope. The lads had a look in the garage window, and it was empty. And don't forget the milk.'

Sgt Bonner shrugged. 'Not a lot more we can do, then, is there?'

'Well, he's over twenty-one. I'd have thought he'd have more sense than to go on the missing list, but you know what they say about the quiet ones.'

Sgt Bonner sighed. 'I'll have his guts for garters when he shows his face. By the way, I've asked Joey Smith to stand in for him in the collator's office for this shift.'

The control room sergeant cast his eyes upwards. 'You really know how to make a man's day, don't you? Couldn't you have got one of the others? Smith can barely manage the alphabet.'

Before Sgt Bonner could argue the toss, there was a knock at the door. 'Yeah?' she called. 'Come in.'

A PC from the control room entered hesitantly. She looked faintly sick. 'Skip,' she said, the worry in her voice obvious from the single word. 'I think you'd better have a look at this.' She held out a fax, the bottom edge ragged where it had been torn hastily off the roll.

Being nearer, the control room sergeant took the flimsy sheet and glanced at it. He drew in his breath sharply, then closed his eyes for a moment. Wordlessly, he handed the fax to Sgt Bonner.

At first, all she saw was the stark black and white of the photograph. For a moment, her mind automatically protecting her from horror, she wondered why someone had gone over her head and reported Connolly missing. Then her eyes translated the marks on the paper into words. *Urgent fax to all stations. This is the unidentified murder victim discovered yesterday afternoon in the back yard of the Queen of Hearts public house, Temple Fields, Bradfield. Photograph to follow later this a.m. Please circulate and display. Any information to DI Kevin Matthews at Scargill Street Incident Room, ext. 2456.*

Sgt Bonner looked bleakly at the other two officers. 'There isn't any doubt about it, is there?'

The PC looked at the floor, her skin pale and clammy. 'I don't think so, skip,' she said. 'That's Connolly. I mean, it's not what you'd call a good likeness, but it's definitely him.'

The control room sergeant picked up the fax. 'I'll get on to DI Matthews right away,' he said.

Sgt Bonner pushed her chair back and stood up. 'I'd

better go round to the morgue. They're going to need a formal identification as soon as possible so they can get weaving.'

'This makes it a whole new ball game,' Tony said, his face sombre.

'It certainly ups the stakes,' Carol said.

'The question I'm asking myself is whether or not Handy Andy knew he was giving us a bobby,' Tony said softly, swinging round in his chair to stare out of the window at the city rooftops.

'Sorry?'

He gave a twisted smile and said, 'No, it's me who should apologize. I always give them a name. It makes it personal.' He swung back to face Carol. 'Does that bother you?'

Carol shook her head. 'It's better than the station nickname.'

'Which is?' Tony asked, eyebrows raised.

'The Queer Killer,' Carol said, her distaste clear.

'That begs a lot of questions,' Tony said noncommittally. 'But if it helps them deal with their fear and anger, it's probably no bad thing.'

'I don't like it. It doesn't feel personal to me, calling him the Queer Killer.'

'What does make it personal to you? The fact that he's taken one of yours now?'

'I felt like that already. As soon as we got the second murder, the one I was handling, I was convinced we were dealing with a serial offender. That was when it got personal for me. I want to nail this bastard. I need to. Professionally, personally, whatever.' The cold vehemence in Carol's voice gave Tony confidence. This was a woman who was going to pull out all the stops to make sure he had what he needed to do his job. Her tone of voice and the words she'd chosen were also a calculated challenge, showing him she didn't give a damn what he made of her desire. She was just what he needed. Professionally, at any rate.

'You and me both,' Tony said. 'And together, we can make it happen. But only together. You know, the first time I got directly involved in profiling, it was a serial arsonist. After half a dozen major fires, I knew how he was doing it, why he was doing it, what was in it for him. I knew exactly the kind of mad bastard he was, yet I couldn't put a name or a face to him. It drove me crazy with frustration for a while. Then I realized it wasn't my job to do that. That's your job. All I can do is to point you in the right direction.'

Carol smiled grimly. 'Just point, and I'll be off like a gun dog,' she said. 'What did you mean when you said you wondered whether he knew Damien Connolly was a bobby?'

Tony ran a hand through his hair, leaving it spiky as a punk's. 'OK. We've got two scenarios here. Handy Andy may not have known Damien Connolly was a bobby. It may be nothing more than a coincidence, a particularly unpleasant coincidence for his colleagues, but a coincidence nevertheless. That's not a scenario I'm happy with, however, because my reading, based on the little I know so far, is that these aren't random victims snatched by chance. I think he chooses his victims with care, and plans thoroughly. Would you agree with that?'

'He doesn't leave things to chance, that's obvious,' Carol said.

'Right. The alternative is that Handy Andy knows full well that his fourth victim is a policeman. That in itself leads to two further possibilities. One: Handy Andy knew he'd killed a copper, but that fact is supremely irrelevant to the meaning of the killing for him. In other words, Damien Connolly fulfilled all the other criteria that Andy needs from his victims, and he would have died at this point whether he was a bobby or a bus driver.

'The other scenario is the one I like best, though. The fact that Damien was a copper is a crucial part of the reason why Handy Andy *chose* him as his fourth victim.'

'You mean he's thumbing his nose at us?' Carol asked.

Thank God she was quick. That was going to make the job so much simpler. She'd done well to get as far up the ladder as she had, given she had looks as well as brains. Either attribute without the other would have made promotion easier. 'That's certainly a possibility,' Tony acknowledged. 'But I think it's more likely to be about vanity. I think he'd started to get pissed off with Detective Superintendent Cross's refusal to acknowledge his existence. In his own eyes, he's very successful at what he does. He's the best. And he deserves recognition. And that desire for recognition has been thwarted by the police's refusal to admit there's only one offender behind these killings. OK, so the *Sentinel Times* has been speculating about a serial killer since the second victim, but that's not the same as being given the official accolade by the police themselves. And I may have unwittingly added fuel to the fire after the third killing.'

'You mean, the interview you did with the *Sentinel Times*?'

'Yeah. My suggestion that it was possible there were two killers at work will have made him angry that he wasn't being acknowledged as the master of his craft.'

'Dear God,' Carol said, torn between revulsion and fascination. 'So he went out and stalked a police officer so we'd take him seriously?'

'It's a possibility. Of course, it can't have been just any police officer. Even though making his point to the powers that be is important to Handy Andy, the prime directive is still to go for victims who fulfil his very personal criteria.'

Carol frowned. 'So what you're saying is that there's something about Connolly that makes him different from most other coppers?'

'Looks like it.'

'Maybe it's the sexuality thing,' Carol mused. 'I mean, there aren't many gays in the force. And those that there are tend to be so deep in the closet you could mistake them for a clothes hanger.'

'Whoa,' Tony laughed, holding up his hands as if to fend her off. 'No theorizing without data. We don't know yet whether Damien was gay. What might be useful, though, is to find out what shifts Damien worked recently. Say, the last two months. That'll give us some idea of the times he was at home, which might help the officers who'll be questioning his neighbours. Also, we should be asking around the other officers on his relief, to check out whether he always left alone, or if he ever gave anyone a lift home. We need to find out everything there is to know about Damien Connolly both as a man and as a bobby.'

Carol pulled out her notebook and scribbled a reminder to herself. 'Shifts,' she muttered.

'There's something else this tells us about Handy Andy,' Tony said slowly, reaching for the idea that had just swum into his consciousness.

Carol looked up, her eyes alert. 'Go on,' she said.

'He's very, very good at what he does,' Tony said flatly. 'Think about it. A police officer is a trained observer. Even the thickest plod is a lot more alert to what's going on around them than the average member of the public. Now, from what you've told me, Damien Connolly was a bright lad. He was a collator, which means he was even more on the ball than most officers. As I understand it, a collator's job is to act like the station's walking encyclopaedia. It's all very well having all the local information about known villains and MOs on file cards, but if the collator isn't sharp, then the system's worthless, am I right?'

'Spot on. A good collator is worth half a dozen bodies on the ground,' Carol said. 'And by all accounts, Connolly was one of the best.'

Tony leaned back in his chair. 'So if Handy Andy stalked Damien without setting any alarm bells ringing, he must be bloody good. Face it, Carol, if somebody was tailing you on a regular basis, you'd pick them up, wouldn't you?'

'I bloody hope so,' Carol said drily. 'But I'm a woman. Maybe we're just a bit more on our guard than the blokes.'

Tony shook his head. 'I think a copper as smart as Damien would have noticed anything other than a very professional tail.'

'You mean we might be looking for someone who's in the Job?' Carol demanded, her voice rising as she spoke the unthinkable.

'It's a possibility. I can't pitch it more strongly than that till I've seen all the evidence. Is that it?' Tony asked, nodding towards the cardboard box Carol had deposited by the door of his office.

'That's some of it. There's another box and some folders of photographs still in the car. And that's after some serious editing.'

Tony pulled a face. 'Rather you than me. Shall we go and fetch it, then?'

Carol stood up. 'Why don't you get started while I go and get the rest?'

'It's the photographs I want to look at first, so I might as well come and help,' he said.

'Thanks,' Carol said.

In the lift, they stood on opposite sides, both conscious of the other's physical presence. 'That's not a Bradfield accent,' Tony remarked as the doors slid shut. If he was going to work successfully with Carol Jordan, he needed to know what made her tick, personally as well as professionally. The more he could find out about her, the better.

'I thought you said you left the detective work to us?'

'We're good at stating the obvious, us psychologists. Isn't that what our critics on the force say?'

'Touché. I'm from Warwick, originally. Then university at Manchester and into the Met on the fast track. And you? I'm not great on accents, but I can spot you're a Northerner, though you don't sound like Bradfield either,' Carol replied.

'Born and bred in Halifax. London University, followed by a DPhil at Oxford. Eight years in special hospitals. Eighteen months ago, the Home Office head-hunted me to run this feasibility study.' Give a little to get a lot, Tony thought wryly. Who exactly was probing whom?

'So we're both outsiders,' Carol said.

'Maybe that's why John Brandon chose you to liaise with me.'

The lift doors slid open and they walked through the underground car park to the visitors' parking area where Carol had left her car. Tony hefted the cardboard box out of the boot. 'You must be stronger than you look,' he gasped.

Carol picked up the folders of photographs and grinned. 'And I'm a black belt in Cluedo,' she said. 'Listen, Tony, if this maniac is in the Job, what sort of stuff would you expect to find?'

'I shouldn't have said that. I was theorizing ahead of data, and I don't want you to place any weight on it, OK? Strike it from the record,' Tony panted.

'OK, but what would the signs be?' she persisted.

They were back in the lift before Tony answered her. 'Behaviour that exhibits a familiarity with police and forensic procedure,' he said. 'But in itself, that proves nothing. There are so many true-crime books and TV detectives around these days that anyone could know that sort of stuff. Look, Carol, please put it out of your head. We need to keep an open mind. Otherwise the work we do is valueless.'

Carol stifled a sigh. 'OK. But will you tell me if you still think that way after you've seen the evidence? Because if it's more than a slim possibility, we might need to rethink the way we're dealing with the enquiry.'

'I promise,' he said. The lift doors slid open, as if placing their own full stop on the conversation.

Back in the office, Tony slid the first set of photographs out of their folders. 'Before you start, could you fill me in on how you want to pursue this?' Carol asked, notebook at the ready.

'I'll go through all the pictures first, then I'll ask you to take me through the investigation so far. When we've done that, I'll work through the paperwork myself. After that, what I usually do is draw up a profile of each of the victims. Then we have another session with these,' he said, brandishing his forms. 'And then I walk out on the high wire and do a profile of the offender. Does that sound reasonable to you?'

'Sounds fine. How long is all that likely to take?'

Tony frowned. 'It's hard to say. A few days, certainly. However, Handy Andy seems to work on an eight-week cycle, and there's no sign that he's accelerating. That's unusual in itself, by the way. Once I've studied the material I'll have a better idea of how in control he is, but I think we've probably got a bit of time to spare before he kills again. Having said that, he may well have already selected his next victim, so we've got to make sure that we keep any progress we make well away from the press. The last thing we want is to be the catalyst for him speeding up the process.'

Carol groaned. 'Are you always this optimistic?'

'It goes with the territory. Oh, and one more thing? If you develop any suspects, I'd prefer not to know anything about them at this stage – there's a danger that my subconscious will alter the profile accordingly.'

Carol snorted. 'We should be so lucky.'

'That bad, is it?'

'Oh, we've pulled in anybody who's got form for

indecent assault or violent offences against gay men, but none of them looks even a remote possibility.'

Tony pulled a sympathetic face then picked up the photographs of Adam Scott's corpse and slowly started going through them. He picked up a pen and moved his A4 pad nearer to him. He glanced up at Carol. 'Coffee?' he asked. 'I meant to ask earlier, but I was too interested in what we were talking about.'

Carol felt like a co-conspirator. She had been enjoying their conversation too, in spite of a twinge of guilt that multiple murders shouldn't be a source of pleasure. Talking with Tony was like talking to an equal who had no axe to grind, whose primary concern was finding a path to the truth rather than a way to boost the ego. It was something she'd missed on this case so far. 'Me too,' she admitted. 'I'm probably approaching the point where coffee is a necessity. Do you want me to go and fetch some?'

'Good God, no!' Tony laughed. 'That's not what you're here for. Wait there, I'll be right back. How do you take yours?'

'Black, no sugar. In an intravenous drip, preferably.'

Tony took a large Thermos jug out of his filing cabinet and disappeared. He was back inside five minutes with two steaming mugs and the jug. He handed Carol a mug and gestured towards the Thermos. 'I filled it up. I figured we might be some time. Help yourself as and when.'

Carol took a grateful sip. 'Will you marry me?' she asked, mock romantic.

Tony laughed again, to cover the lurch of apprehension that shifted his stomach, a familiar response to even the most idle of flirtations. 'You won't be saying that in a few days' time,' he said evasively, turning his attention back to the photographs.

'Victim number one. Adam Scott,' he said softly, making a note on his pad. He went through the photographs one by one, then went back to the beginning. The first picture showed a city square, tall Georgian houses on one side, a modern office block on a second and a row of shops, bars and restaurants on the third. In the centre of the square was a public garden, crossed by two diagonal paths. In the middle was an ornate Victorian drinking fountain. The park was surrounded by a three feet high brick wall. Along two sides of the garden was deep shrubbery. The ambience was slightly seedy, the stucco of the houses peeling in places. He imagined himself standing on the corner, taking in the view, smelling the fumid city air mixed with the stink of stale alcohol and fast food, hearing the night sounds. The rev of engines, the sound of high heels on pavements, occasional laughs and cries borne on the wind, the twitter of starlings, conned out of sleep by the sodium light of streetlamps. Where did you stand, Andy? Where did you watch your ground from? What did you see? What did you hear? What did you *feel*? Why here?

The second photograph showed a section of the wall and the shrubbery from the street side. The photograph was clear enough for Tony to make out the little iron squares on the top of the wall, which were all that remained of railings that had presumably been removed during the war to make guns and shells. A section of the bushes showed broken branches and crumpled leaves. The third shot showed the body of a man, face down on the earth, his limbs splayed at strange angles. Tony let himself be drawn into the picture, trying to put himself in Handy Andy's shoes. How did it feel, Andy? Were you proud? Were you scared? Were you exultant? Did you feel a spasm of regret at abandoning the object of your desire? How long did you allow yourself to drink in this sight, this strange tableau that you created? Did the sound of foot-steps move you on? Or did you not care?

Tony looked up. Carol was watching him. To his sur-prise, for once he didn't feel uncomfortable to have a woman's eyes on him. Perhaps because their relationship had so firm a professional base, but without direct competition. The tension in him relaxed a notch. 'The place where the body was found. Tell me about it.'

'Crompton Gardens. It's at the heart of Temple Fields, where the gay village and the red-light district overlap. It's poorly lit at night, mostly because the streetlights are always being vandalized by the sex vendors who want a bit of darkness to cover their activities. There's a lot of sex goes on in Crompton Gardens, in the bushes and on the park benches under the trees, in the office doorways, in the basement areas of the houses. Rent, prostitution and casual pick-ups. There are people around throughout the night, but they're not the sort who are going to come forward about anything unusual they might have seen, even if they noticed it,' Carol explained while Tony took notes.

'The weather?' he asked.

'Dry night, though the ground was pretty damp.'

Tony returned to the photographs. The body was shot from various angles. Then, following the removal of the body, the dumping ground was pictured in close-up sections. There were no visible footprints, but some scraps of black plastic were lying under the body. He pointed at them with the tip of his pen. 'Do we know what these are?'

'Bradfield Metropolitan Council bin bags. Standard issue to businesses, blocks of flats . . . anywhere wheelie bins are inappropriate. That grade of bag has been in use now for the last two years. There's apparently nothing to indicate whether they were already there or if they were dumped at the same time as the body,' Carol said.

Tony raised his eyebrows. 'You seem to have assimilated a helluva lot of detail since yesterday afternoon.'

Carol grinned. 'It's tempting to pretend I'm Superwoman, but I have to confess that I'd already made a point of finding out what I could about the other two enquiries. I was convinced they were linked, even if my boss wasn't. And in fairness to my colleagues, the inspectors leading the other two enquiries had an open mind. They didn't object to me making the occasional trawl through their stuff. Ploughing through it all overnight just refreshed my memory, that's all.'

'You've been up all night?'

'Like you said, it goes with the territory. I'll be fine till about four this afternoon. Then it'll hit me like a sledge-hammer,' Carol admitted.

'Message received and understood,' Tony replied, turning back to the photographs. He moved on to the series of shots from the postmortem. The body lay on its back on the white slab, the hideous wounds visible for the first time. Tony went slowly through the whole sequence of pictures, sometimes flicking back to previous shots. When he closed his eyes, he could picture Adam Scott's intact body, slowly breaking out in wounds and bruises like alien blooms. He could almost conjure up the slo-mo vision of the hands that brought flesh to such a pass. After a few moments, he opened his eyes and spoke again. 'These bruises on the neck and chest – what did the pathologist say?'

'Suck marks. Like love bites.'

A head descending, predatory, a bizarre parody of love. 'And these sections of the neck and chest. Three places where the flesh has been cut away?' Tony asked distantly.

'They were removed postmortem. Maybe he likes to eat them?'

'Maybe,' Tony said doubtfully. 'Was there any trace of bruising in the remaining tissues, can you remember?'

'I think there was.' Carol's surprise showed in her voice.

Tony nodded. 'I'll check the pathologist's report. He's a clever lad, our Handy Andy. My first reaction is that these aren't souvenirs, or indications of cannibalism. I think they might have been bite marks. But Handy Andy knows enough about forensic dentistry to realize that identifiable bite marks would be enough to put him away. So once the frenzy's spent, he's cooled down and removed the evidence. These cuts to the genitals – pre or postmortem?'

'Post. The pathologist remarked that they seemed quite tentative.'

Tony gave a small smile of satisfaction. 'Did the pathologist say what has caused the trauma to the limbs? The shots at the site look like a rag doll.'

Carol sighed. 'He didn't want to be pushed to an official conclusion. All four limbs were dislocated, and some of his vertebrae were out of alignment. He said . . .' She paused and imitated the pathologist's portentous delivery, ' "Don't quote me, but I'd expect to see injuries like this after the Spanish Inquisition had put someone on the rack." '

'The rack? Shit, we're really dealing with a messy mind here. OK. Next set. Paul Gibbs. This one's yours, I think?' Tony asked as he replaced Adam Scott's photographs and took out the contents of the second folder. He repeated the process he'd gone through before. 'So where is this scene in relation to the first one?' Tony asked.

'Hang on a minute. I'll show you.' Carol opened one of the boxes and picked out the large-scale map she'd thought to bring with her. She unfolded it and spread it out on the floor. Tony got up from his desk and crouched down beside her. She was instantly aware of the smell of him, a mixture of shampoo and his own faint, animal scent. No macho aftershave, no cologne. She watched his pale, square hands on the map, the short, almost stubby fingers, with their neatly trimmed nails and a sparse scattering of fine black hairs on the bottom section of each finger. Appalled, she felt a stirring of desire. You're pathetic as an adolescent, she savagely chided herself. Like a teenager who fancies the first teacher who says anything nice about your work. Grow up, Jordan!

Under the guise of pointing out the sites on the map, Carol inched away. 'Crompton Gardens is here,' she said.

'Canal Street is about half a mile away, over here. And the Queen of Hearts pub is just along here, about midway between the two.'

'Is it safe to assume he knows the area well?' Tony asked, making his own mental map of the murder sites.

'I think so. Crompton Gardens is a pretty obvious dumping ground, but the other two imply quite a high degree of familiarity with Temple Fields.' Carol sat back on her haunches, trying to work out if the pattern of sites implied an approach from one specific direction.

'I need to take a look at the scenes. Preferably around the time the bodies were dumped. Do we know when that was?' Tony said.

'We don't know about Adam. Estimated time of death is an hour either side of midnight, so not before then. With Paul, we know the doorway was clear just after three a.m. Gareth's time of death is estimated at between seven and ten p.m. the evening before his body was found. And with Damien, the yard was clear at half past eleven,' Carol recited, closing her eyes to recall the information.

Tony found himself staring at her face, glad of the freedom her shuttered eyelids gave him. Even without the animation of her blue eyes, he could see that she'd be classified beautiful. Oval face, broad forehead, clear pale skin, and that thick blonde hair, cut slightly shaggy. A strong, determined mouth. A furrow that appeared between her brows when she concentrated. And his appreciation was as clinical as if she were a photograph in a casebook. Why was it that, faced with a woman any normal man would regard as attractive, something in him closed down? Was it because he refused to allow himself to feel the first stirrings that might lead him to a place where he was no longer in control, where humiliation lurked? Carol's eyes opened, registering surprise when she saw him watching her.

He felt his ears tingle with a blush and turned back to the map. 'So he's a night owl,' he said abruptly. 'I'd like to take a look at the area tonight, if I can. Maybe you can get someone else to show me round so you can catch up on your sleep.'

Carol shook her head. 'No. If we can get through here by five, I'll go home and grab a few hours' shut-eye. I'll pick you up around midnight and we can go then. Is that OK?' she asked, belatedly.

'Perfect,' Tony said, getting to his feet and retreating behind his desk. 'As long as you don't mind.' He picked up the photographs and forced himself back behind Handy Andy's eyes. 'He's made a real mess of this one, hasn't he?'

'Paul's the only one who's been beaten up like this. Gareth has cuts to his face, but nothing as extreme. Paul's face has been smashed to a pulp – broken nose, broken teeth, broken cheekbone, dislocated jaw. The anal injuries are horrendous as well; he's been partially disembowelled. The degree of violence is one of the reasons why the Super felt we were looking at a different perpetrator. Also, none of his limbs are dislocated, unlike the other three.'

'This is the one the papers said was covered up with bin bags?'

Carol nodded. 'Same variety as the scraps found under Adam's body.'

They moved on to Gareth Finnegan. 'I'm going to have to give some serious thought to this one,' he said. 'He's changed his pattern in at least two significant ways. First, the dumping ground moves from Temple Fields to Carlton Park. It's still a gay cruising area, but it's an aberration.' He stopped himself short and gave a hollow laugh. 'Listen to me. As if his whole behaviour isn't wildly aberrant. The second thing is his letter and video to the *Sentinel Times*. Why did he decide to announce this body and none of the others?'

'I've been thinking about that,' Carol said. 'And I wondered if it had something to do with the fact that it could have lain there for days, even weeks, otherwise.'

Tony made a note on his pad and gave her the thumbs-up sign with the other hand. 'These wounds to the hands and feet. I know it sounds off the wall, but it almost looks like he was crucified.'

'The pathologist wasn't crazy about going on the record with that one either. But the hand wounds, coupled with the dislocation of both shoulders, makes crucifixion a conclusion that's hard to resist, especially when you remember this probably happened on Christmas Day.' Carol got to her feet, rubbing the sleep out of her eyes. She couldn't manage to stifle a jaw-cracking yawn. She paced round the small office, shrugging her shoulders to loosen the taut muscles. 'Sick bastard,' she muttered.

'The genital mutilations are getting more severe,' Toby observed. 'He's virtually castrated this one. And the fatal wounds, the cutting of the throat. That's getting deeper too.'

'Does that tell us anything?' Carol asked, almost unintelligible through another yawn.

'Like your pathologist, I'm reluctant to speculate just yet,' Tony said. He moved on to the final set of pictures. For the first time, Carol saw his professional mask slip. Horror swept across Tony's face, widening his eyes, drawing his lips back in a hissed intake of breath. She wasn't surprised. When they'd turned Damien Connolly over, a six-foot rugby-playing detective had keeled over in a dead faint. Even the experienced police pathologist had turned away momentarily, visibly struggling not to be sick.

Rigor mortis had frozen Damien Connolly's limbs in a parody of human gesture. The dislocated joints stuck out at crazy angles. But there was more, and worse. His penis had been severed and thrust into his mouth. His torso was branded from chest to groin in a bizarre, random pattering of starburst burns, none more than half an inch across.

'Dear God,' Tony breathed.

'He's really getting the hang of this, isn't he?' Carol said bitterly. 'Takes a pride in his work, doesn't he?'

Tony said nothing, forcing himself to study the appalling photographs as closely as he'd done with the previous sets. 'Carol,' he eventually said. 'Has anybody come up with any theories as to what he's used to make these burn marks?'

'Not a one,' she said.

'They're odd,' he said. 'The patterns vary. It's not like he's used some random object and kept on using it. There are at least five different shapes. Have you got anybody who can do computer pattern analysis? To see if there's any hidden message here? There must be dozens of these bloody burns!'

Carol rubbed her eyes again. 'I don't know. Me and computers are about as compatible as the Prince and Princess of Wales. I'll ask when I go back to the office. And if we don't have someone, I'll ask my brother.'

'Your brother?'

'Michael's a computer genius. He works in games software development. You want a pattern analysed, manipulated, turned into a shoot-'em-up arcade game, he's your man.'

'And he can keep his mouth shut?'

'If he couldn't, he wouldn't be doing the job he does. Millions of pounds depend on his company getting on the next rung of the ladder before anybody else. Believe me, he knows when to button his lip.'

Tony smiled. 'I didn't mean to sound offensive.'

'You didn't.'

Tony sighed. 'I wish to God I'd been brought in sooner on this. Handy Andy's not going to stop here. He's too much in love with his work. Look at these pictures. This bastard's going to carry on capturing and torturing and killing until you catch him. Carol, this guy's a career killer.'

*I walked boldly up the path and pressed Adam's doorbell.
In the seconds before he answered the chime, I composed
my face into what I believed was an apologetic smile. I
could see the fuzzy outline of his head and shoulders as he
walked down the hall. Then the door opened and we were
face to face. He half smiled quizzically. As if he'd never
noticed me before in his life.*

*'I'm sorry to bother you,' I said. 'Only my car's broken
down, and I don't know where there's a pay phone, so I
wondered if I might use your phone to call the AA? I'll
pay for the call, of course . . .' I let my voice trail away.*

*His smile broadened and relaxed, his dark eyes crinkling
at the corners. 'No problem. Come in.' He stepped back
and I moved inside the door. He gestured down the hall.
'There's a phone in the study. Just on the right there.'*

*I moved slowly down the hall, ears alert for the sound
of the front door closing behind me. As the lock snapped
back into place, he added, 'There's nothing worse, is there?'*

*'I'll just look up the number,' I said, pausing in the
doorway to reach in my backpack. Adam kept on walking,
so that when I pulled out the Mace spray, he was only a
couple of feet away from me. It couldn't have been more
perfect. I let him have it full in the face.*

*He roared in pain and stumbled back against the wall,
hands clawing at his face. I moved in swiftly. One foot
between his ankles, hands on his shoulders, a quick twist*

and down he went, face crushed into the carpet, gasping for breath. I was down on top of him in seconds, gripping one wrist and twisting his arm up his back while I snapped the handcuff over it. He was struggling against me by now, tears streaming down his face, but I managed to grab his other flailing arm and snap the other half of the cuffs on it.

His legs were thrashing under me, but my weight was enough to keep him pinned to the floor while I took a ziplock plastic bag from my backpack. I opened it, extracted a pad soaked in chloroform and clamped it over his nose and mouth. The sickly odour drifted upwards into my nostrils, making me feel slightly light-headed and queasy. I hoped the chloroform hadn't gone off; I'd had the bottle for a couple of years, ever since I'd stolen it from the dispensary on a Soviet ship where I'd spent the night with the first officer.

Adam struggled even harder when he felt the cold compress cut off his access to the air, but within minutes his legs stopped their pointless thrashing. I waited a little longer, just to be on the safe side, then I rolled off and fastened his legs together with surgical tape. I returned the chloroform pad to its secure bag, then I taped Adam's mouth shut.

I stood up and took a deep breath. So far, so good. Next, I pulled on a pair of latex gloves and took stock. I am familiar with the theory of the French forensic scientist Edmond Locard, first demonstrated in a murder trial in 1912, that every contact leaves a trace; a criminal will always take something away from the scene of his crime and leave something behind. With this in mind, I had carefully chosen my wardrobe for today. I was wearing Levi 501s, the same brand I'd seen Adam wear often. I'd topped it with a baggy V-necked cricket sweater, the exact double of one I'd watched him buy in Marks and Spencer a couple of weeks before. Any stray fibres I left behind would inevitably be ascribed to the contents of Adam's own wardrobe.

I took a quick look round the study, pausing by his answering machine. It was one of the old-fashioned ones, with a single cassette tape. I opened the machine and helped myself to the tape. It would be nice to have a memory of his voice sounding normal; I knew that the soundtrack on the video wouldn't have that same relaxed quality.

The door to the garage was locked. I headed off up the stairs, where I found the jacket of his suit tossed over the back of a chair in the kitchen diner. The bunch of keys was in the left-hand pocket. Back downstairs, I opened the garage door and unlocked the hatchback of his two-year-old Ford Escort. Then I went back for Adam. He had, of course, come round. His eyes were filled with panic, muffled grunts came from behind the gag. I smiled down at him as I pressed the chloroform pad over his nose again. This time, of course, he couldn't struggle effectively at all.

I pulled him into a sitting position, then brought a chair through from the study. I managed to get him on to the chair, and from there I was able to sling him over my shoulder and stagger through into the garage. I dumped him in the luggage space, and slammed the tailgate shut. Not a trace of his body was visible.

I checked my watch. Just after six. It would be another hour till it was dark enough to be certain none of the neighbours passing casually would notice a stranger driving out of Adam's garage. I filled the time by browsing through his life. Packets of photographs revealed friends, a family Christmas dinner. I would have fitted into this life perfectly. We could have had it all, if he hadn't been such a fool.

I was startled out of my reverie by the phone. I let it ring, and went through to the kitchen. I helped myself to a bottle of creme cleanser and a cloth and carefully washed down all the paintwork in the hall. I put the used cloth in my backpack, then fetched the vacuum cleaner. I went over the entire hall slowly and carefully, erasing all traces of the struggle from the hard-wearing Berber carpet. I trailed the vac behind me, right into the garage, where I left it in a corner, looking as if it had always lived there. Satisfied I'd removed all traces of me, I climbed into Adam's car, pressed the remote-control button on his key-ring and started the engine as the garage door rose smoothly before me.

I shut the door behind me, and drove off. I could hear muffled noises from the back of the car. I raked around in the glove box till I found a Wet, Wet, Wet cassette. I shoved it into the player and turned the volume up high. I sang along with the music as I drove out of the city and on to the moors.

I'd been worried that Adam's car might not make it all the way up the track, and I'd been right. About half a mile from home, the road became too overgrown and rutted. With a sigh, I got out and walked up to collect the wheelbarrow. When I opened the tailgate to tip him into the barrow, his eyes were wide and staring. His muffled calls were wasted on me, however. I dragged him unceremoniously out of the car and into the barrow. It was a hard half-mile up the track, since his constant struggling made steering more difficult. Luckily, Auntie Doris had had the foresight to buy a proper builder's barrow, one with two wheels in front.

When we reached the farmhouse, I opened the trapdoor. The cellar below looked dark and welcoming. Adam's eyes widened in terror. I stroked his soft hair and said, 'Welcome to the pleasure dome.'

5

As to ... the mob of newspaper readers, they are pleased with anything, provided it is bloody enough. But the mind of sensibility requires something more.

After he'd seen Carol to her car, Tony walked across the campus to the general stores and bought a copy of the evening paper. If publicity was what Handy Andy craved, he'd finally achieved it. Fear and loathing stalked the pages of the *Bradfield Evening Sentinel Times*. Five of them, to be precise. Pages 1, 2, 3, 24 and 25, plus an editorial, were devoted to the Queer Killer. If the nickname was anything to judge by, the police were already leaking like a Cabinet committee.

'You're not going to like being called the Queer Killer, are you, Andy?' Tony said softly to himself as he walked back to his office. Back behind his desk, he studied the paper. Penny Burgess had had a field day. The front page screamed, QUEER KILLER STRIKES AGAIN! in banner headlines. In smaller headline type, readers were told, POLICE ADMIT SERIAL KILLER STALKS CITY. Beneath was a lurid account of the discovery of Damien Connolly's body, and a photograph of him at his passing-out parade. The turnover on pages two and three was a sensationalist summary of the three previous cases, complete with sketch map. 'Bricks without straw, right enough,' Tony said to himself as he flicked through to the centre spread. GAYS TERRIFIED BY QUEER KILLER MONSTER left the reader in no doubt who the *Sentinel Times* had decided were at risk. The copy focused on the supposed hysteria gripping Bradfield's gay community, complete with interior shots of cafés, bars and clubs that made the scene look seedy enough to pander to the readers' prejudices.

'Oh boy,' Tony said. 'You're really going to hate this, Andy.' He turned back to the editorial.

'At last,' he read, 'police have admitted what many of us have believed for some time. There is a serial killer on the loose in Bradfield, his target the young, single men who frequent the city's sordid gay bars.

'It's a disgrace that the police have not warned the city's homosexuals to be on their guard before now. In the twilight world of anonymous pick-ups and casual sex, it cannot be difficult for this predatory monster to find willing victims. The police's silence can only have made it easier for the killer.

'Their reluctance to speak out has probably increased the gay community's existing suspicion of the police, making them fear that the authorities value the lives of gay men less than those of other members of the community.

'Just as it took the murders of "innocent" women rather than prostitutes to make the police pay full attention to the Yorkshire Ripper, it is wrong that a police officer has had to be murdered before Bradfield Metropolitan Police takes this Queer Killer seriously.

'In spite of this, we urge the gay community to cooperate fully with the police. And we demand that the police investigate these horrific killings diligently and with compassion for the concerns of Bradfield's homosexuals. The sooner this vicious killer is caught, the safer we all will be.'

'The usual mixture of self-righteousness, indignation and unrealistic demands,' Tony said to the Devil's Ivy on his windowsill. He clipped the articles and spread them across the desk. He switched on his micro-cassette recorder and spoke.

'*Bradfield Evening Sentinel Times*, February 27th. At last, Handy Andy has made the big time. I'm wondering how important that is to him. One of the tenets of profiling serial offenders is that they crave the oxygen of publicity. But this time, I'm not so sure he's too bothered about that. There were no messages after the first two killings, neither of which received that much publicity after the initial discovery of the bodies. And although there was a message directing the police to the third body via a newspaper, that note made no claims about the earlier killings. I had puzzled over that until Inspector Carol Jordan offered an alternative explanation for the note and accompanying video, namely that without direction, the body may have lain undiscovered for some time. So, while Handy Andy may not be obsessive about creating headlines and panic, it's clear he wants the bodies found while they are still recognizably his work.' He switched off the cassette with a sigh. Although he'd turned his back on the academic circus years before, he couldn't escape his training; every stage of the process had to be on record. The prospect of this investigation providing the raw material for articles or even a book was something Tony found hard to resist.

'I'm a cannibal,' he said to the plant. 'Sometimes I disgust myself.' He shovelled the clippings together and tucked them into his press-cuttings folder. He opened the boxes and took out the stacks of document wallets they contained. Carol had labelled them all neatly. Fluent capitals, Tony noted. A woman comfortable with the written word.

Each victim had a pathology report and a preliminary forensic report. The witness statements were divided into three groups: Background (victim), Witness (scene of crime) and Miscellaneous. Selecting the Background (victim) files, he walked his wheeled chair across to the table where his personal computer stood. When he'd arrived at Bradfield, the university had offered him a terminal linked into their network. He'd declined, not wanting to waste time learning a new set of protocols when he was perfectly at home with his own PC. Now, he was glad he didn't have to add data security to the list of worries that kept him awake at nights.

Tony called up the customized software that would allow him to make comparisons between the victims, and started the long slog of inputting the data.

Five minutes in the Scargill Street station was enough to make Carol wish she'd gone straight home. To get to the office she'd been allocated for the duration of the investigation, she had to walk the length of the main squad room. Copies of the evening paper were strewn over half the desks, mocking her with their thick black headlines. Bob Stansfield was standing with a couple of DCs halfway down the room and he called to her as she passed. 'The good doctor knocked off already, has he?'

'From what I've seen of the good doctor, Bob, he could give some of our bosses a few lessons in working overtime,' Carol said, wishing she could think of some sharper put-down. Doubtless it would come to her hours later in the shower. On the other hand, maybe it was as well she hadn't come up with something too devastating. Better not alienate the lads any more than her assignment had already done. She stopped and smiled. 'Anything new?' she asked.

Stansfield detached himself from his juniors, saying, 'Right, lads, get on with it.' He moved over to Carol's side and said, 'Not as such. The HOLMES team are working flat out, smacking all we've got so far into the computer, see what correlations they can come up with. Cross has ordered us to pull in all the nonces again. He's convinced one of them's our best bet.'

Carol shook her head. 'Waste of time.'

'You said it. This bastard's not got form, I'd put money on it. Kevin's got a team going out tonight to try something a bit different, though,' he added, taking out and lighting his last cigarette. He tossed the packet in a nearby bin, an expression of disgust on his face. 'If we don't get a fucking break soon, I'm going to have to put in for a raise to cover my bloody nicotine consumption.'

'Me, I'm drinking so much coffee I've got a permanent case of the jitterbug boogies,' Carol said ruefully. 'So what's this idea of Kevin's?' Gently does it. First the rapport, then the question. Funny how getting information out of colleagues followed the same rules as interrogating suspects.

'He's got an undercover team going out on the gay scene, concentrating on the clubs and pubs with a reputation for S&M.' Stansfield snorted. 'They've all been down Traffic this avvy, scrounging leather trousers off the bike boys.'

'It's worth a try,' Carol said.

'Yeah, well let's hope Kevin's not sending in a bunch of closet pansies like Damien Connolly turned out to be,' Stansfield said. 'Last thing we want is a bunch of CID fairies ending up wearing their own handcuffs.'

Carol refused to dignify the comment with a reply and moved off towards her office. She'd got her hand on the door when Cross's voice boomed down the room. 'Inspector Jordan? Get your body in here.'

Carol closed her eyes and counted to three. 'Coming, sir,' she said cheerfully, turning back and walking the length of the room to Cross's temporary office. He'd only been in there a day, but already he'd marked it like a tomcat spraying his territory. The room reeked of cigarette smoke. Half-drunk polystyrene cups of coffee strategically placed on window ledge and desk top had butts floating in them. There was even a girlie calendar on the wall, proof that sexism was alive and well and working in the advertising industry. Hadn't they realized *yet* that it was the women who stood in the supermarkets deciding which brand of vodka to buy?

Leaving the door open in a bid for air, Carol walked into Cross's office and said, 'Sir?'

'What's Wonder Boy come up with then?'

'It's a bit early for conclusions, sir,' she said brightly. 'He's got to read through all the reports I copied for him.'

Cross grunted. 'Oh aye, I forgot he's a bloody professor.' He spat the word out sarcastically. 'Everything in writing, eh? Kevin's got some more stuff on the Connolly business; you'll have to catch up with him. Was there anything else, Inspector?' he asked belligerently, as if she were the one who had imposed herself on him.

'Dr Hill has a suggestion, sir. About the burn marks on PC Connolly's body. He wondered if there was anyone on the HOLMES team who could do statistical pattern analysis.'

'What the bloody hell is statistical pattern analysis?' Cross said, dumping the end of his cigarette into a coffee cup.

'I think it means –'

'Never mind, never mind,' Cross interrupted. 'Go and see if anybody down there knows what the hell you're on about.'

'Yes, sir. Oh, and sir? If we can't do it here, my brother works in computers. I'm sure he could do it for us.'

Cross stared at her, his expression unreadable for once. When he spoke, he was all affability. 'Fine. Go ahead. Mr Brandon gave you carte blanche, after all.'

So that's what a passing buck sounds like, Carol thought as she headed downstairs to the HOLMES room. A five-minute conversation with a harassed Inspector Dave Woolcott confirmed what she'd already suspected. The HOLMES team had neither the software nor the expertise to carry out the analysis Tony wanted. As Carol walked down to the canteen in search of Kevin Matthews, she hoped Michael could deliver in complete confidence. Keeping quiet about technological developments was very different from resisting the urge to gossip about a high-profile murder enquiry. If he let her down, she could kiss goodbye to a future outside Personnel.

Kevin was hunched alone over a cup of coffee, a plate with the remains of a fry-up next to him. Carol pulled out the chair opposite him. 'Mind if I join you?'

'Be my guest,' Kevin said. He looked up and gave her the ghost of a grin, pushing his unruly ginger curls back from his forehead. 'How's it going?'

'Probably a lot easier than it is for you and Bob.'

'What's this Home Office boffin like, then?'

Carol considered for a moment. 'He's cautious. He's quick, he's sharp, but he's not a know-all, and he doesn't seem to want to tell us how to do our job. It's really interesting watching him work. He looks at things from a different perspective.'

'How do you mean?' Kevin asked, looking genuinely interested.

'When we look at a crime, we look for physical clues, leads, things that point us to who we might want to talk to or where we might want to look. When *he* looks at a crime, he's not interested in all that stuff. He wants to know why the physical clues happened the way they did so he can work out who did it. It's as if we use information to move us forward and he uses it to move him backwards. Does that make sense?'

Kevin frowned. 'I think so. You think he's got what it takes?'

Carol shrugged. 'It's early days yet. But yeah, on first impressions, I'd say he's got something to offer.'

Kevin grinned. 'Something to offer the investigation or something to offer you?'

'Piss off, Kevin,' Carol said, tired of the innuendo that

followed her round the job. 'Unlike some, I never shit on my own doorstep.'

Kevin looked momentarily uneasy. 'Only joking, Carol, honest.'

'Jokes are supposed to be funny.'

'OK, OK, sorry. What's he like to work with, though? Nice bloke, or what?'

Carol spoke slowly, measuring her words. 'Considering he spends his working life getting inside the minds of psychopaths, he seems pretty normal. There's something quite ... closed off about him. He keeps his distance. Doesn't give much away. But he treats me like an equal, not like some thick plod. He's on our side, Kevin, and that's the main thing. I'd guess he's one of those work-aholics who's more interested in getting the job done than anything else. And speaking of getting the job done, Popeye says you've turned something up on PC Connolly?'

Kevin sighed. 'For what it's worth. One of the neigh-bours came home from work at ten to six. She knows the time because the shipping forecast had just started on the car radio. Connolly was on his drive, closing the bonnet of his car. He had overalls on. The neighbour says he must have been working on the car, he was always at it. By the time the neighbour got out of her car and into the house, Damien was reversing his car into the garage. The same neighbour came out about an hour later on her way to a game of squash, and she noticed Connolly's car parked on the street. She was a bit surprised, because he never left the car sitting out, especially after dark. She also noticed that the light was on in Connolly's garage. And that's about the size of it.'

'Is it an integral garage?' Carol asked.

'No, but it's attached to the house, and there's a door from the garage leads into the kitchen.'

'So it looks like he was snatched from the house?'

Kevin shrugged. 'Who knows? There's no sign of a

struggle. I spoke to one of the SOCOs who turned the place over, and he said not to hold our breath.'

'Sounds just like the first two.'

'That's what Bob says.' Kevin pushed his chair back. 'I better get weaving. We're going out on the town tonight.'

'I might bump into you later,' Carol said. 'Dr Hill wants a tour of the crime scenes at the sort of time when the bodies were dumped.'

Kevin got to his feet. 'Just don't let him talk to any strange men.'

Tony took the plastic container of lasagne out of the microwave and sat down at the breakfast bar in his kitchen. He'd input all the data that he could find on the four victims, then he'd transferred the files to a floppy disk so he could work on it at home while he waited for Carol to arrive. As soon as he'd reached the tram stop, he'd realized he was ravenous. Then he remembered he'd eaten nothing since his breakfast cereal. He'd been working with such concentration, he hadn't even noticed. He found the hunger curiously satisfactory. It meant he was too involved in what he was doing to be conscious of himself. He knew from long experience that his best work came when he lost self-consciousness, when he could immerse himself in the patterns of another human being, locked into that other's idiosyncratic logic, in tune with a different set of emotions.

He attacked the food with gusto, shovelling it down as quickly as possible so he could get to his computer and carry on with his victim profiles. There were still a couple of forkfuls left in the dish when the phone rang. With no pause for thought, Tony snatched up the phone. 'Hello?' he said cheerfully.

'Anthony,' the voice said. Tony dropped the fork, tipping the pasta out on the worktop.

'Angelica,' he said. He was back in his own world, anchored within his own head at the sound of her voice.

'Feeling more sociable today?' the sweet huskiness asked.

'I wasn't feeling anti-social yesterday. I just had things to do I couldn't ignore. And you distract me,' Tony said, wondering why he bothered to justify himself to her.

'That's the general plan,' she said. 'But I missed you, Anthony. I was so horny for you, and when you discarded me like an old sock, all my pleasure in the day was over.'

'Why do you do this with me?' he demanded. It was a question he'd asked before, but she had always deflected him.

'Because you deserve me,' the voice said. 'Because I want you more than anyone in the world. And because you don't have anyone else in your life to make you happy.'

It was the same old story. Cut off the question with some flannel. But tonight, Tony wanted answers, not flattery. 'What makes you think that?' he asked.

The voice chuckled softly. 'I know more about you than you can possibly dream. Anthony, you don't have to be alone any more.'

'What if I like being alone? Isn't it fair to assume that I'm alone because I want to be?'

'You don't look like a happy boy to me. Some days, you look like you need a hug more than anything in the world. Some days, you look like you haven't slept for more than a couple of hours. Anthony, I can bring you peace. Women have hurt you before, we both know that. But I won't. I can stop it hurting. I can make you sleep like a baby, you know that. All I want is to make you happy.' The voice was soothing, gentle.

Tony sighed. If only . . . 'I find that hard to believe,' he stalled. Right from the start of these conversations, part of him had wanted to slam the phone down on this exquisite torture. But the scientist in him wanted to hear what she had to say. And the damaged man inside had enough self-awareness to know he needed to be cured, and that this might just be the way. He reminded himself of his earlier resolve not to let her get under his skin, so that when the time came, he could walk away without pain.

'But you let me try.' The voice was so self-assured. She was confident of her power over him.

'I listen, don't I? I join in. I haven't put the phone down yet,' he said, forcing artificial warmth into his voice.

'Why don't you do just that? Why don't you put down this phone and go upstairs to your bedroom and pick up the extension there? So we can be comfortable?'

A cold stab of fear hit Tony in the chest. He struggled to frame the question professionally. Not, 'How do you know that?', but, 'What makes you think I've got a phone in the bedroom?'

There was a pause, so brief that Tony couldn't be certain he wasn't imagining it. 'Just guessing,' she said. 'I've got you sussed. You're the kind of man who has a phone by the bed.'

'Well guessed,' Tony said. 'OK. I'm going to put the phone down and I'll pick up in the bedroom.' He replaced the receiver and hurried through to his study, where he switched the answering machine over to 'record' mode. Then he picked up the phone again. 'Hello? I'm back,' he said.

'Are we sitting comfortably? Then I'll begin.' Again that low, sexy chuckle. 'We are going to have some real fun tonight. Wait till you hear what I've got lined up for you tonight. Oh, Anthony,' she said, her voice dropping almost to a whisper. 'I've been dreaming about you. Imagining your hands on my body, running your fingers over my skin.'

'What are you wearing?' Tony asked. It was, he knew, the standard question.

'What would you like me to be wearing? I have an extensive wardrobe.'

Tony bit back the crazy urge to say, 'Fishermen's waders,

a tutu and a rainmate.' He swallowed hard and said, 'Silk. You know how I like the feel of silk.'

'That's why you love my skin. I take a lot of trouble to keep myself in perfect condition. But just for you, I've covered some of my skin with silk. I'm wearing a pair of black silk French knickers and a sheer black silk camisole. Oh, I love the feeling of silk against my body. Oh, Anthony,' she groaned. 'The silk's rubbing against my nipples, gently, like your fingers would. Oh, my nipples are hard as rocks, sticking up, inflamed with you.'

In spite of himself, Tony began to feel the stirrings of interest. She was good, no two ways about it. Most of the women he'd heard on the chatlines had sounded stale and bored, their responses predictable and stereotypical. Nothing in their conversations had aroused anything other than scientific interest in him. But Angelica was different. For one thing, she sounded like she meant it.

She moaned softly. 'God, I'm wet,' she breathed. 'But you can't touch me yet, you've got to wait. Just lie back, that's a good boy. Oh, I love to undress you. I've got my hands under your shirt, my fingers are running over your chest, stroking you, touching you, feeling your nipples under my fingers. God, you're wonderful,' she sighed.

'That's nice,' Tony said, enjoying the caress of her voice.

'That's just the beginning. Now I'm straddling you, unbuttoning your shirt. I'm leaning over you, my nipples inside the silk brushing against your chest. Oh, Anthony!' her voice exclaimed in pleasure. 'You really are pleased to see me, aren't you? You're hard as a rock underneath me. Oh, I can't wait to get you inside me.'

Her words froze Tony. The erection he'd felt hardening inside his trousers died like a snowflake in a puddle. They were there again. 'I think I'm going to disappoint you,' he said, his voice cracking.

That sexy chuckle again. 'No way. You're already more

than I dreamed. Oh, Anthony, touch me. Tell me what you want to do to me.'

Tony could find no words.

'Don't be shy, Anthony. There are no secrets between us, nowhere we can't go. Close your eyes, let the feelings flow. Touch my breasts, go on, suck my nipples, eat me, let me feel your hot wet mouth all over me.'

Tony groaned. This was almost more than he could bear, even in the interests of science.

Angelica's voice was more breathy now, as if her words were arousing her as much as they should have been arousing him. 'That's right, oh God, Anthony, that's wonderful. Oh-oh-oh,' she said in a shuddering moan. 'See, I told you I was wet. That's right, plunge your fingers deep into my cunt. Oh God, you're the best ... Let me ... let me, oh God, let me get at you.'

Tony heard the sound of a zipper down the phone line. 'Angelica ...' he started to say. It was falling apart again, just as it always did, spiralling out of control like a wounded bird.

'Oh, Anthony, you're beautiful. That's the most beautiful cock I've ever seen. Oh, let me taste you ...' Her voice tailed off with the sound of sucking.

The blood rushed to Tony's face in a sudden wave of shame and anger. He slammed the phone down and immediately took it off the hook again. Jesus, what kind of a man couldn't even get it up over the phone? And what kind of scientist couldn't divorce his own pathetic failings from the exercise of objective data collection?

The worst of it was, he recognized his own behaviour. How many times had he sat across the table from a multiple rapist, arsonist or killer and watched them reach the point in their reliving of events where they could no longer face themselves. Just like him, they closed down. They couldn't disconnect a phone, but they closed down just the same. Eventually, of course, with the right therapy, they breached the walls and managed to confront what had brought them there. That was the first step towards recovery. Part of Tony prayed that Angelica knew enough about the theory and practice of psychology to stick with him till he too could break down the barriers and stare into the face of whatever it was that had bred this sexual and emotional cripple.

But the other part of him hoped she'd never call again. Never mind 'no pain, no gain'. He just wanted no pain.

John Brandon scrupulously wiped his plate with the last piece of nan bread and smiled at his wife. 'That was great, Maggie,' he said.

'Mmm,' his son Andy agreed through a mouthful of lamb and aubergine curry.

Brandon shifted awkwardly in his chair. 'If it's all right with you, I think I'll pop back down to Scargill Street for an hour. Just to see how things are going.'

'I thought ranking officers like you didn't have to work evenings,' Maggie said good-humouredly. 'I thought you said the troops didn't need you breathing down their necks?'

Brandon looked sheepish. 'I know. But I just want to see how the lads are going on.'

Maggie shook her head, a resigned smile on her face. 'I'd rather you went down and got it out of your system than you sat all night fidgeting in front of the telly.'

Karen perked up. 'Dad, if you're going back into town, can you drop me at Laura's? So we can work on our history project?'

Andy snorted. 'Work on how you're going to get off with Craig McDonald, more like.'

'You know nothing,' Karen huffed. 'Will you, Dad?'

Brandon got up from the table. 'Only if you're ready now. And I'll pick you up on my way back.'

'Oh, Dad,' Karen complained. 'You said you were only

going to be gone an hour. That's not nearly long enough for us to do all we want to.'

It was Maggie Brandon's turn to snort with laughter. 'If your father's back before half past nine, I'll make Scotch pancakes for supper.'

Karen looked at each parent in turn, the anguish of choice written on her fourteen-year-old face. 'Dad?' she said. 'Can you pick me up by nine o'clock?'

Brandon grinned. 'Why do I feel like I've been stitched up?'

It was just after half past seven when Brandon arrived in the HOLMES room. Even that late, every terminal was occupied. The sound of fingers hitting keyboards clicked away under the quiet conversations taking place at a few of the desks. Inspector Dave Woolcott sat beside one of the collators, who was pointing out some detail on the screen. No one looked up when Brandon entered.

He walked over behind Woolcott and waited till he had finished talking to the constable on the terminal. Brandon suppressed a sigh. It was definitely time he started thinking about retirement. It wasn't just the bobbies that looked young to him now; even the inspectors didn't look old enough to be out of probationer's cap bands. 'Keep trying for a match, Harry, cross-ref with the CROs,' he heard Woolcott say. The lad on the keyboard nodded and stared into his screen.

''Evening, Dave,' Brandon said.

Woolcott swung round in his chair. Registering who the newcomer was, he got to his feet. ''Evening, sir.'

'I was on my way home, and I thought I'd swing by and see how you were doing,' Brandon lied smoothly.

'Well, sir, it's early days. We'll have teams working round the clock for the next couple of days, feeding in all the statement details from the earlier cases as well as PC Connolly's. I'm also liaising with the team manning the hot-line phones. Most of it's the usual spite, vengeance and paranoia, but Sergeant Lascelles is doing a good job of prioritizing the messages.'

'Anything coming out yet?'

Woolcott rubbed his bald spot in the reflex gesture which his second wife claimed had caused the problem in the first place. 'Bits and pieces. We've got a few names of blokes who were out and about in Temple Fields on at least two of the nights in question, and those are being actioned. We've also been hammering the PNC with car index numbers that have shown up regularly around the times of the killings. Luckily, ever since the second killing, Inspector Jordan's had somebody clocking car numbers round the gay village. It's a long job, sir, but we'll get there.'

If he's in there, Brandon thought. It was he who had been adamant that this was a case for the HOLMES team. But this killer was unlike any he'd seen or read about. This killer was careful.

Brandon didn't know much about computers. But one adage had stuck: garbage in, garbage out. He hoped fervently that he hadn't given his men a job that should have gone to the Cleansing Department.

Carol's eyes snapped open, heart pounding. In her dream, a heavy cell door had slammed shut, leaving her a prisoner of cold, sweating windowless walls. Still groggy from sleep, it took her a moment to realize that the familiar weight of Nelson's body wasn't lying across her feet. She heard footsteps, the rattle of keys being thrown on a table. A narrow sliver of light spilled through the few inches of open door Nelson required for his comings and goings. She rolled over with a groan and grabbed the clock. Ten past ten. Robbed of twenty minutes' precious sleep by Michael's noisy return.

Carol stumbled out of bed and pulled on her heavy towelling bathrobe. She opened her bedroom door and walked into the enormous room that made up most of the third-floor flat she shared with her brother. Half a dozen floor-mounted up-lights of different heights cast a warm and elegant glow on the room. Nelson appeared from the kitchen doorway, bouncing lightly on the stripped-wood flooring. Then he crouched and, in a leap that seemed to defy gravity, bounded into the air, touching briefly on a tall thin speaker before landing delicately on top of a blond wood bookcase. From there, he stared supercili-ously across the room at Carol, as if to say, 'I bet you can't do that.'

The room was about forty feet by twenty-five. At one end, a group of three two-seater sofas covered with quilted throws surrounded a low coffee table. At the opposite end stood a dining table with six chairs in the style of Rennie Mackintosh. Near the sofas was a TV and video on a black trolley. About half of the back wall was occupied by shelves crammed with books, videos and CDs.

The walls were painted a cool dove-grey, except for the far wall, which was exposed brickwork, with five high arched windows looking out over the city. Carol walked across the room till she could just see the edge of the black ribbon of the Duke of Waterford canal below. The city lights glittered like a cheap jeweller's window. 'Michael?' she called.

Her brother stuck his head out of the narrow galley kitchen, looking surprised. 'I didn't realize you were home,' he said. 'Did I wake you?'

'I was getting up soon anyway. I've got to go back to work. I was just grabbing a few hours,' she said resignedly. 'Is the kettle on?' She walked across to the kitchen and perched on a high stool while Michael made tea and carried on building himself a sandwich with ciabatta, beef tom-atoes, black olives, spring onions and tuna.

'Eat?' he asked.

'I could handle one of those,' Carol admitted. 'How was London?'

Michael shrugged. 'You know. They like what we're doing, but could we have it finished yesterday.'

Carol pulled a face. 'Sounds just like the *Sentinel Times*'s editorials about the serial killer. What exactly is it you're doing at the moment anyway? Is it explainable in words of one syllable to a techno-illiterate?'

Michael grinned. 'The next big thing is going to be computer adventure games with the same quality as videos. You film real stuff and digitize it and manipulate it to produce gameplay that's as real as a movie. So we're on to the next, next big thing. Imagine you're playing a computer adventure, but all the characters are people you know. You're the hero, but not just in your imagination.'

'You've lost me now,' Carol said.

'OK. When you install the game on your computer, you'll plug in a scanner and scan photographs of yourself and anybody else you want in your game. The computer reads that information, and translates it into screen images. So instead of Conan the Barbarian leading the quest, it's Carol Jordan. You can import pics of your best friends or your lust objects to be your companions in the game. Anybody you don't like, you turn into the baddies. So, you could have an adventure with Mel Gibson, Dennis Quaid and Martin Amis, and fight enemies like Saddam Hussein, Margaret Thatcher and Popeye,' Michael explained enthusiastically as he stuffed the ingredients into the bread. He dumped the sandwiches on plates and together they walked back into the living room and sat staring out over the canal as they ate.

'Clear?' he asked.

'As it needs to be,' Carol said. 'So once you've got this software up and running, presumably you could use it to put people in compromising positions? Like blue movies?'

Michael frowned. 'Theoretically. Your average computer nerd wouldn't even know where to begin. You'd need to know what you were doing and you'd also need seriously expensive hardware to get decent quality stills or videos off your computer.'

'Thank God for that,' Carol said, with feeling. 'I was beginning to think you were creating a Frankenstein's monster for blackmailers and tabloid journalists.'

'No chance,' he said. 'Anyway, close analysis would show it up. So what about you? How's your quest coming along?'

Carol shrugged. 'I could do with a few superheroes to help out, to be honest.'

'What's this profiler like? He going to shake things up a bit?'

'Tony Hill? He already has. Popeye's going around with a face like a melted wellie. But I'm hopeful we might get something constructive out of him. I've had one session with him already, and he's bursting with ideas. He's a nice guy as well, no hassle to work with.'

Michael grinned. 'That must be a refreshing change.'

'You're not kidding.'

'And is he your type?'

Carol pulled a piece of crust off her bread and threw it at Michael. 'God, you're as bad as the sexist pigs I work with. I haven't got a type, and even if I did and Tony Hill was it, you know I won't mix work with pleasure.'

'Given the fact that you work all hours and spend all your spare time asleep, I guess you're looking at a lifetime of celibacy,' Michael replied drily. 'So is he gorgeous, or what?'

'I hadn't noticed,' Carol said stiffly. 'And I doubt whether he's even noticed I'm female. The man's a work-aholic. In fact, he's the reason I'm working again tonight. He wants to see the scenes of crime at around the time the bodies were dumped so he can get a feel for it.'

'Shame you've got to go out again,' Michael said. 'It's ages since we've had a night in with the telly and a few bottles of wine. We see so little of each other just now, we might as well be married.'

Carol smiled ruefully. 'The price of success, eh, bro?'

'I guess so.' Michael got up. 'Oh well, if you're going to work, I might as well do a couple of hours before I sack out.'

'Before you go . . . I need a favour.'

Michael sat down again. 'As long as it doesn't involve doing your ironing.'

'What do you know about statistical pattern analysis?'

Michael frowned. 'Not a lot. I did a little bit when I was doing part-time jobbing work while I was doing my PhD, but I don't know what's state of the art right now. Why? You want something looking at?'

Carol nodded. 'It's a bit grisly, I'm afraid.' She outlined the sadistic injuries to Damien Connolly. 'Tony Hill has an idea they might yield some kind of a message.'

'Sure, I'll have a look for you. I know a bloke who's almost certainly got the latest software in the field. I'm sure he'd let me have some time on his machine to fiddle about with this,' Michael said.

'Not a word to anybody what it's about,' Carol said.

Michael looked offended. 'Of course not. What do you take me for? Listen, I'd rather get on the wrong side of a serial killer than you. I'll keep my mouth shut. Just get the stuff to me tomorrow, and I'll do my best, OK?'

Carol leaned over and rumpled her brother's blond hair. 'Thank you. I appreciate it.'

Michael grabbed her in a quick hug. 'This is seriously weird territory, little sis. Be careful out there, huh? You know I can't afford the mortgage on this place alone.'

'I'm always careful,' Carol said, ignoring the small voice inside her warning not to tempt fate. 'I'm a survivor.'

'I wanted you the first time I saw you,' I said softly. 'I've wanted you for so long.'

Adam's lolling head straightened slightly. I pressed the remote record button on the tripod-mounted video camera. I didn't want to miss a thing. Adam's eyelids, heavy from all that chloroform, struggled open to a slit, then suddenly snapped wide as memory kicked in. His head thrashed from side to side as he tried to see where he was, how he was restrained. As he took in his nakedness, spotted the details of the soft leather wrist and ankle cuffs, and realized that he was fastened to my rack, a moan of what sounded like panic escaped from behind the tape over his mouth.

I stepped out of the shadows behind him and moved into his line of vision, my body oiled and shining in the bright lights. I had stripped down to my underwear, carefully chosen to show off my superb body to its best advantage. When he saw me, his eyes opened even wider. He attempted to speak, but all that came out was a strained mumble.

'But you decided you couldn't allow yourself to want me, didn't you?' I said, my voice hard and accusing. 'You betrayed my love. You didn't have the courage to choose a love that would have exalted us both. No, you ignored your real self and went for a stupid little bimbo, that trashy tart. Don't you realize? I'm the only one in the world who understands, really understands, what you need. I could

*have given you ecstasy, but you chose the safe, pathetic
option. You didn't have the nerve for a marriage of true
minds and bodies, did you?'*

*Drops of sweat were trickling down his temples, in spite
of the coolness of the cellar. I moved forward and stroked
his body, running my hand over his pale, muscular chest,
fluttering my fingers over his groin. He flinched convulsively, his dark-blue eyes pleading. 'How could you betray
what I know is in your heart?' I hissed, digging my
nails into the soft flesh above the wiry curls of his dark
pubic hair. He tensed against me. I thrilled to the
sensation. I took my hand away and admired the scarlet
half-moons my nails had left in his skin. 'You know you
belong to me. You told me. You wanted me, we both know
you did.'*

*Another groan from behind the gag. Now the sweat had
spread to his chest, droplets matting the thick dark hair
that tapered down his abdomen into a thin line pointing
to his cock lying curled and useless as a slug between his
legs. Even though it was obvious that he didn't want me,
the very sight of his vulnerable nakedness aroused me. He
was beautiful. I could feel the blood flowing faster, feel
my flesh expanding, ready to take him, ready to explode.
I hated myself for that weakness, and I turned away before
he could see the effect he was having.*

*'All I wanted was to love you,' I said quietly. 'I didn't
want it to be like this.' My hand strayed to the handle of
the rack and caressed the smooth wood. I turned my head
and gazed at Adam's beautiful face. Slowly, infinitely
slowly, I started to turn the handle. His body, already taut,
tightened against the pull of the straps. His effort was
wasted. The gears on the winding mechanism multiplied
my small exertion till it equalled the strength of several
men. Adam was no match for my machine. I could see the
muscles of his arms and legs bulge, his chest heaving as he
struggled for breath.*

'It's not too late,' I said. 'We could still be lovers. Would you like that?'

Desperately, he moved his head. There was no mistaking it, it was a nod. I smiled. 'That's more like it,' I said. 'Now all you have to do is show me you mean it.'

I ran one hand over his damp chest, then rubbed my face against the fine dark hairs. I could smell his fear, taste it in his sweat. I buried my head in his neck, sucking and biting, nibbling his ears. His body stayed rigid, but I felt no trace of an erection beneath me. Frustrated, I pulled away. I leaned over him and, in one swift agonizing movement, I yanked the tape away from his mouth.

'Aagh!' he yelled as the adhesive ripped his skin, rasping on the faint stubble. He licked dry lips. 'Please, let me go,' he whispered.

I shook my head. 'I can't do that, Adam. Maybe if we were really lovers . . .'

'I won't tell anyone,' he croaked. 'I promise.'

'You betrayed me once,' I said sadly. 'How can I trust you now?'

'I'm sorry,' he said. 'I didn't realize . . . I'm sorry.' But there was no penitence in his eyes, only desperation and fear. I'd played this scene so many times in my head. Part of me exulted that I'd predicted the shape of it so well, that the dialogue was almost identical to the scenario I'd conjured up. Part of me felt an inexpressible sadness that he was exactly as weak and faithless as I'd feared. And yet another part of me was almost uncontrollably excited by what lay ahead, whether love or death, or both.

'It's too late for words,' I said. 'It's time for actions. You said you wanted us to be lovers, but that's not what your body's saying. Maybe you're scared. But there's no need to be. I'm a generous person, a loving person. You could find that out for yourself. I'm going to give you one last chance to atone for your betrayal. I'm going to leave you now for a while. When I come back, I expect you to be able to control your fear and show me how you really feel about me.'

I let him go and walked over to the camcorder. I took out the tape that had been recording our encounter and replaced it with a fresh one. At the top of the stairs, I turned back. 'Otherwise, I'll be forced to administer punishment for your treachery.'

'Wait!' he howled desperately as I disappeared from sight. 'Come back,' I heard as I dropped the trapdoor into place. I expect he carried on yelling. But I couldn't hear him. I went upstairs to Auntie Doris and Uncle Henry's bedroom. I slotted the video into the player I'd set up on the chest at the end of the bed, switched on the TV and climbed between the cold cotton sheets. Even if Adam didn't want me, I couldn't escape my desire for him. I watched him on his rack, my hand stroking me, touching myself with all the skill and ingenuity I wanted from him, imagining his beautiful cock swelling in my mouth. Every time I reached the point of orgasm, I stopped, gripping myself tight, forcing myself not to come, to save myself for what lay ahead. After I'd gone through the video for the fourth time, I decided he'd had long enough.

I slipped out of bed and went back downstairs. I looked at him spread-eagled on the rack. 'Please,' he said. 'Let me go. I'll do anything you want, but let me go. I'm begging you.'

I smiled and gently shook my head. 'I will take you back to Bradfield, Adam. But first, it's time to party.'

6

People begin to see that something more goes to the composition of a fine murder than two blockheads to kill and be killed – a knife – a purse – and a dark lane. Design, gentlemen, grouping, light and shade, poetry, sentiment, are now deemed to be indispensable to attempts of this nature.

Work might not solve anything, but it was a great diversionary tactic. Tony stared into the screen, scrolling down through the tabulated information he'd gleaned from the police reports. Satisfied that he'd incorporated everything useful, he switched on the printer. While it chattered and stuttered its way through the print-out, Tony opened another file and started to sketch out the conclusions he had drawn from the raw data. Anything, anything to keep her at bay.

He was so absorbed in his work he barely registered the doorbell's first peal. When it rang out a second time, he looked up, startled, at the clock. Five past eleven. If it was Carol, she was earlier than he'd anticipated. They'd already agreed that there was little point in beginning their trip before midnight. Tony got to his feet, uncertain. Since she knew his phone number, it wouldn't be too hard for Angelica to discover his address too. He arrived at the front door just as the bell rang for the third time. Wishing he'd installed a peephole, Tony cautiously inched the door open.

Carol grinned. 'You look like you're expecting Handy Andy,' she said. When Tony said nothing, she added, 'Sorry

I'm a bit early. I did try ringing, but you were engaged.'

'Sorry,' Tony mumbled. 'I must have accidentally left it off the hook from earlier. Come on in, it's no problem.' He found a smile from somewhere and led Carol into his study. As he reached his desk, he slid the phone back on the hook.

Carol registered that the phone's engaged signal had been no accident. Deduction: he didn't want to be disturbed, not even by the answering machine. Probably, like her, he couldn't resist a ringing phone. She glanced at the sheets of paper sitting on the printer table. 'You've obviously been busy,' she said. 'And there was me thinking you were taking your time answering the door because you'd gone for a quick zizz.'

'Did you get some sleep?' Tony asked, noting that she looked more clear-eyed than she had done earlier.

'Four hours. Which is about ten too few. I've got a couple of bits of information for you, by the way.' She filled him in succinctly on the results of her visit to Scargill Street, leaving out Cross's hostility.

Tony listened carefully, making a couple of notes on his pad. 'Interesting,' he said. 'I don't think there's a lot of point in pulling in the sex offenders again, though. If Handy Andy's got form, it's more likely to be juvenile offences, petty burglary, minor violence, that sort of thing. Still, I've been wrong before.'

'Haven't we all? By the way, I checked with the HOLMES room, and there's no one there who knows anything about statistical pattern analysis, so I've asked my brother to see what he can do for us. Should I just give him a set of the photographs, or is there some other way of presenting the raw data?'

'I suppose there's less chance of a mistake if he works directly from the photographs,' Tony said. 'Thanks for sorting that out for me.'

'No sweat,' Carol said. 'Secretly, I think he's quite

chuffed to be asked. He thinks I don't take him seriously. You know, he writes games software, I do the real thing.'

'And do you?' Tony asked.

'What? Take him seriously? You bet I do. I respect anybody that understands something as far beyond my grasp as computers. Besides, he earns about twice what I do. That has to be serious.'

'I don't know about that. Andrew Lloyd Webber probably earns more in a day than I do in a month, but I still don't take him seriously.' Toby stood up. 'Carol, do you mind if I abandon you for ten minutes? I need a quick shower to wake me up.'

'Fine, feel free. It's me that's early.'

'Thanks. D'you want a brew while you're waiting?'

Carol shook her head. 'I'll pass, thanks. It's cold out there, and there aren't many places a woman can have a pee in Temple Fields in the early hours.'

Almost shyly, Tony picked up the sheaf of a print-out and proffered it to Carol. 'I've started the work on the victims. Maybe you'd like to take a look while I'm gone?'

Eagerly, Carol took the paper. 'I'd love to. I'm fascinated by this whole process.'

'This is just very preliminary,' Tony stressed, backing towards the door. 'I mean, I've not drawn any conclusions yet. I'm working on that.'

'Relax, Tony, I'm on your side,' Carol said as he left the room. She stared after him momentarily, wondering what it was that had unsettled him. By the time they parted in the afternoon, they had built up an easy camaraderie, she'd thought. But now, he was edgy, abstracted. Was it that he was tired, or was it that he was uncomfortable to have her sitting in his home? 'God, does it matter?' she muttered to herself. 'Concentrate, Jordan. Pick the man's brains.' She focused on the first sheet and studied the data.

	Adam S.	Paul G.	Gareth F.	Damien C.
Victim No.	1	2	3	4
Date of crime	6/7.9.93	1/2.11.93	25/26.12.93	20/21.2.94
Bradfield resident?	Yes	Yes	Yes	Yes
Sex	M	M	M	M
Ethnic origin	Caucasian	Caucasian	Caucasian	Caucasian
Nationality	British	British	British	British
Age	28	31	30	27
Star sign	Gemini	Cancer	Scorpio	Capricorn
Height	5'10''	5'11''	5'11''	6'
Weight	147lb	136lb	151lb	160lb
Build	Medium	Slim	Medium	Medium
Musculature	Good	Average	Average	Excellent
Hair length	Abv collar	Collar	Abv collar	Abv collar
Hair colour	Brown	Dark brown	Brown	Reddish brown
Hair type	Wavy	Straight	Straight	Curly
Tattoos	No	No	No	No
Clothing	None	None	None	None
Occupation	Civil servant	University lecturer	Solicitor	Police officer
Place of work	City centre	South of city centre	City centre	Southern suburbs
Car owned	Ford Escort	Citroën AX	Ford Escort	Classic Austin Healey
Hobbies	Working out, angling	Walking	Working out, theatre, cinema	Car restoration
Residence	Modern terraced town house; integral garage	Edwardian terraced house; no garage	Thirties semi; no garage	Modern detached estate house; attached garage
Relationship status	Divorced Lived alone NCP RP	Single Lived alone NCP NRP	Single Lived alone CP NRP	Single Lived alone NCP NRP
Personal items missing?	Wedding ring, watch	Watch	Signet ring, watch	Watch
Items missing from home?	Answering-machine tape	Answering-machine tape	None known	None known

Known sexual history	Hetero	Hetero	Hetero	Not known
Last seen by previous acquaintance	Tram home from work, 6 p.m. approx.	Leaving work, 5.30 p.m. approx.	Home, 7.15 p.m.	Home, 6 p.m.
Criminal record	None	None	None	None
Connection to scene of crime	None known	None known	None known	None known
Status of body-recovery site	Urban	Urban	Suburban/ rural	Urban
Site of first contact with killer	Unknown	Unknown	Unknown	Unknown
Site of death	Unknown	Unknown	Unknown	Unknown
Disposition of body	Semi-hidden to cause short delay before discovery	Semi-hidden to cause short delay before discovery	Hidden; note to police via newspaper required	Openly displayed but in area unattended until specific time
Body posed?	No	No	No	No
*Has the body been washed?	Yes	Yes	Yes	Yes
Cause of death	Throat cut	Throat cut	Throat cut	Throat cut
**Ligatures?	Wrists Ankles Adhesive gag	Wrists Ankles Adhesive gag	Wrists Ankles Adhesive gag	Wrists Ankles Adhesive gag
Bite marks	No	No	No	No
Putative bite marks (i.e., flesh removed)	Yes	Yes	Yes	Yes
Location of marks	Neck (2) Chest (1)	Neck (2)	Neck (3) Abdomen (4)	Neck (3) Chest (2) Groin (4)

Signs of torture or unusual assault?	Yes (see A)	Yes (see B)	Yes (see C)	Yes (see D)

*BODY WASHING: No fragranced materials appear to have been used, suggesting that the offender is not using the washing process as a means of denial; rather, in line with the rest of his cautious behaviour, I suggest that this washing is intended to obliterate forensic clues, especially since the killer appears to have taken particular care with the fingernails. Scrapings on all four victims showed nothing except traces of unperfumed soap.

**LIGATURES: None were found on bodies, but postmortems reveal bruising consistent with handcuffs on wrists, slight traces of adhesive, missing hairs and bruising round ankles consonant both with parcel tape and with separate ligatures, and traces of adhesive on face around mouth. No traces of blindfolds.

A: *Adam Scott.* Dislocation of ankles, knees, hips, shoulders, elbows and several vertebrae. Consistent with being stretched on a rack. Tentative postmortem cuts to penis and testicles.

B: *Paul Gibbs.* Severe lacerations to rectum, virtual destruction of anal sphincter and partial disembowelment. Suggestive of spiked object repeatedly inserted via anus. Also some burnt tissue internally, suggesting the possibility of heat or electric shock. Face badly beaten before death; bruising, broken facial bones and teeth. Postmortem cuts to genitals, more pronounced than in A.

C: *Gareth Finnegan.* Irregular pierce wounds to hands and feet, ½" diameter approx. Lacerations to left cheek and nose, suggestive of glass or bottle being broken across face by right-handed assailant. Shoulders dislocated. ?Possible crucifixion? Postmortem wounds to genitals, virtually castrated.

D: *Damien Connolly.* Dislocations similar to A, but no major spinal trauma, ruling out the idea of a rack. Large number of small, star-shaped burns to torso. Penis severed postmortem and inserted in victim's mouth.
Query: Were Damien Connolly's handcuffs still in his home or police locker?

Query: Why are the bodies always dumped Monday night/ Tuesday morning? What happens on Monday that allows him to be free? Does he work nights and have Monday off? Is he perhaps a married man who has Monday free because his wife does things with friends, e.g., girls' night out? Or is it that Monday isn't a traditional 'going out' night and he can be more sure of finding his victims at home?

Carol was aware that Tony had returned, but she carried on reading, simply raising one hand and waving her fingers to indicate she knew he was there. When she reached the end of the report, she took a deep breath and said, 'Well, Dr Hill, you *have* been busy.'

Tony smiled and shrugged himself away from the door-jamb he'd been leaning against. 'I can't believe there's anything in there that you didn't already have filed neatly away in your head.'

'No, but seeing it laid out like that somehow makes it clearer.'

Tony nodded. 'He has a very specific type.'

'Do you want to talk about it now?'

Tony looked down at the floor. 'I'd rather leave most of it for now. I need to let it sink in, and I need to go through all the rest of the witness statements before I can think about a profile.'

Carol couldn't help feeling disappointed. 'I understand,' was all she said.

Tony smiled. 'Were you expecting more?'

'Not really.'

His smile broadened. 'Not even a smidgen?'

The smile was infectious. Carol grinned back. 'Hoping, maybe. Expecting, no. By the way, there was one thing I didn't understand. NCP? CP? NRP? I mean, we're not talking National Car Parks and the Communist Party here, are we?'

'No current partner. Current partner. No recent partner. Acronymitis. It's the disease that afflicts all of us in the soft sciences like psychology, sociology. We have to mystify the uninitiated. Sorry about that. I try to keep things as jargon-free as possible.'

'So you don't confuse us thick plods, eh?' Carol teased.

'It's more about self-preservation. The last thing I want is to give the sceptics another big stick to hit me with. It's hard enough getting people to accept that my reports are even worth reading without alienating them with all that unnecessary pseudo-scientific mumbo jumbo.'

'I believe you,' Carol said ironically. 'Shall we go?'

'Sure. There is one thing I would like to bounce off you now,' Tony said, suddenly serious again. 'The victims. Everybody's assuming this killer is targeting gay men. Now, there are hundreds, probably thousands of openly gay men in Bradfield. We've got the biggest gay scene in the country outside London. Yet every one of those victims has no known history of homosexuality. What does that say to you?'

'He's in the closet himself and he only goes for men who are closeted too?' Carol hazarded.

'Maybe. But if they're all busily passing as straight, how does he meet them?'

Carol straightened the edges of the papers to give herself a moment. 'Contact magazines? Small ads? Multi-user phone chatlines? The Internet?'

'OK, all possibilities. But there was no evidence of any of those interests, according to the reports of the officers who searched their houses. Not in one single case.'

'So what are you trying to say here?'

'I don't think Handy Andy gets turned on by gay men. I think he likes them straight.'

Sergeant Don Merrick decided he'd never felt more fed up. As if it wasn't bad enough that he had Popeye on his back over the guv'nor's new assignment, he was now a servant of three masters. He was supposed to make sure that Inspector

Jordan's orders were carried out when she wasn't around, and he was also supposed to be working for Kevin Matthews on the Damien Connolly case as well as liaising with Bob Stansfield on the work that he and Inspector Jordan had already completed on the Paul Gibbs case. To top it all, he was spending his evening in the Hell Hole.

Never, in his opinion, was a club more aptly named. The Hell Hole advertised itself in the gay press as 'The club that dominates Bradfield. One visit and you'll be enslaved. You're *bound* to have the time of your life in the Hell Hole!' All of which was a coy way of saying that the Hell Hole was the place to go to pick up partners if sado-masochism and bondage was how you got your rocks off.

Merrick felt like Snow White at an orgy. He didn't have a clue how he was supposed to behave. He wasn't even sure if he looked right. He'd opted for an old, ripped pair of Levis that normally only saw the light of day when he was doing odd jobs around the house, a plain white T-shirt and the battered leather jacket he used to wear on his motorbike in the days before the kids came along. In his back pocket were his official handcuffs, there in the hope they'd lend some verisimilitude to his pose. Looking round the dimly lit bar, Merrick spotted so much distressed denim and leather that he expected to see an SOS flare rising above the dance floor. Superficially, at least, he thought he might just look the part. Which was worrying in itself. As his eyes grew accustomed to the low lighting, he caught sight of a few of his colleagues. Mostly, they looked as uncomfortable as he felt.

The club had been virtually empty when he'd first arrived just after nine. Feeling incredibly conspicuous, Merrick had asked for a pass-out and gone back on to the streets. He'd wandered round Temple Fields for the best part of an hour, stopping in a café-bar for a cappuccino. He'd wondered why some of the gay clientele had been giving him strange looks until he realized that he was the only customer wearing leather and denim. Clearly he'd transgressed some unwritten dress code. Uncomfortable, Merrick had swallowed the scalding coffee as quickly as he could and got back out on to the streets.

He felt seriously vulnerable, alone on the pavements and walkways of Temple Fields. The men who passed him, either singly, in couples or in groups, all eyed him up and down speculatively as he passed, most glances pausing at his crotch. He squirmed inside, wishing he'd picked a pair of jeans that didn't hug his body quite so tightly. As a couple of black youths walked past, arms entwined, he heard one say loudly to the other, 'Great ass for a white guy, huh?' Merrick felt the blood rise to his cheeks, unsure whether it was anger or embarrassment. In a moment of dreadful clarity, he realized what women meant when they complained of being treated as objects by men.

He returned to the Hell Hole, relieved that the place had filled up now. Loud disco music throbbed, the beat so strong Merrick seemed to feel it inside his chest. On the dance floor, men in leather adorned with chains, zips and peaked caps moved energetically, showing off their Nautilus-hardened muscles, thrusting their groins into empty air in bizarre parodies of sex. Stifling a sigh, Merrick pushed his way through the crowd to the bar. He ordered a bottle of American beer that tasted unbelievably insipid to a palate trained to expect the nutty sweetness of Newcastle Brown.

Turning round to face the dance floor again, Merrick leaned against the bar and surveyed the room, desperately trying to avoid eye contact with anyone in particular. He'd been standing like that for about ten minutes when he became aware that the man standing next to him wasn't actually trying to be served. Merrick glanced round to discover the man's eyes fixed on him. He was almost as tall as the detective, but with a broader, more muscular build. He wore tight black leather trousers and a white vest. His blond hair was cut short at the sides, longer on top, and his body was as tanned and smooth as a Chippendale. He raised his eyebrows and said, 'Hi. I'm Ian.'

Merrick grinned weakly. 'Don,' he replied, raising his voice to combat the music.

'I've not seen you in here before, Don,' Ian said, moving closer so that his naked arm pressed against the worn leather of Merrick's sleeve.

'It's my first time,' Merrick said.

'You new in town, then? You don't sound local.'

'I'm from the North East,' Merrick said carefully.

'That explains it. A bonny laddie from Geordieland,' Ian said, with a bad imitation of Merrick's accent.

Merrick felt his smile grow sick and die. 'You a regular here, then?' he asked.

'Never miss it. Best bar in town for the kind of guy I like.' Ian winked. 'Can I buy you a drink, Don?'

The sweat trickling down Merrick's back had nothing to do with the warmth of the bar. 'I'll have another one of these,' he said.

Ian nodded and turned round to the bar, using the crowd around him as an excuse to thrust himself against Merrick. Merrick stared across the room, his jaw set. He noticed one of the other murder squad detectives watching him. His colleague gave a grotesque wink and mimed one finger pumping into the closed fist of his other hand. Merrick turned away, coming face to face with Ian, who had been served. 'There you go, bonny laddie,' Ian said. 'So, you looking for a bit of fun tonight, Geordie?'

'Just checking out the scene,' Merrick said.

'What's the scene like up in Newcastle, then?' Ian asked. 'Bit lively? Cater for all tastes, does it?'

Merrick shrugged. 'I don't know. I'm not from Newcastle. I come from a little village up on the coast. It's not the kind of place where you can be yourself.'

'I get you,' Ian said, laying a hand on Merrick's arm.

'Well, Don, if you want to be yourself, you've come to the right place. And you've found the right guy.'

Merrick prayed he didn't look as terrified as he felt. 'It's certainly busy enough,' he tried.

'We could go somewhere quieter, if you like. There's another room through the back there, where the music isn't so loud.'

'No, I'm fine here,' Merrick said quickly. 'I like the music, if I'm honest.'

Ian moved forward so his torso leaned against Merrick's. 'What is it you're into, Don? Top or bottom?'

Merrick choked on his beer. 'I'm sorry?' he gasped.

Ian laughed and rumpled Merrick's hair. His light-blue eyes glinted wickedly, holding Merrick's stare. 'You really are an innocent abroad, aren't you? What I'm saying is, what do you like best? Handing it out or taking it?' His hand strayed down to Merrick's trousers. Just when the detective thought he was going to be groped in a way that no one apart from his wife had ever done, Ian's hand slid to one side and moved round to stroke Merrick's buttock.

'That depends,' Merrick croaked.

'On what?' Ian asked suggestively, moving so close that Merrick could feel the other man's erection against his leg.

'On how much I trust the person I'm with,' Merrick replied, trying not to let his revulsion show in voice or expression.

'Oh, I'm very trustworthy, me. And you look like the reliable kind too.'

'Are yez not a bit worried, like, about strangers? With this serial killer doing the rounds?' Merrick asked, using the opportunity of putting his empty bottle back on the bar to move away slightly from Ian's insistent body.

Ian's smile was cocky. 'Why should I be? These guys that are getting topped don't hang out in places like this. Stands to reason that this isn't where this mad bastard's picking them up.'

'How do you know that?'

'I've seen the pictures in the papers, and I've never spotted a single one of them out on the scene. And believe me, I know the scene. That's how I knew you were the new kid in town.' Ian moved closer again and thrust a hand in Merrick's back pocket. He ran his fingers over the hard outline of the handcuffs. 'Hey, that feels interesting. I'm starting to get a picture of what you and me could be like.'

Merrick forced a laugh. 'For all you know, I could be the killer.'

'So what if you are?' Ian said, all self-assurance. 'I'm not the type this fucking nutter goes for. He likes closet queens, not macho men. If he picked me up, he'd want to fuck, not commit murder. Besides, a good-looking guy like you doesn't need to kill somebody to get a fuck.'

'Yeah, well, maybe so, but how do I know you're not the killer?'

'Tell you what, just to prove I'm not, I'll let you top tonight. You'll be in charge. I'll be the one with handcuffs on.'

Carry on like this and you won't be wrong, Merrick thought to himself. He reached down and gripped Ian's wrist hard, removing his hand from the pocket. 'I don't think so,' he said. 'Not tonight. Like you said, I'm the new kid in town. I'm not going home with anybody till I know a bit more about them.' He released Ian's wrist and stepped back. 'Nice talking to you, Ian. Thanks for the drink.'

Ian's face altered in an instant. His eyes narrowed and the smile changed to a snarl. 'Wait a minute, Geordie. I don't know what sort of poxy Watch With Mother clubs you're used to, but in this city, you don't get into a clinch with somebody and take drinks off him if you're not prepared to come across.'

Merrick tried to get away, but the press of bodies round the bar made any movement difficult. 'I'm sorry if there's been a misunderstanding,' he said.

Ian's arm shot out and gripped Merrick firmly just below his bicep. The pain was excruciating. Merrick found a moment to wonder what sort of person actively sought out pain like this as part of their sexual pleasure. Ian thrust his face so close that Merrick could smell the bad breath he'd learned to associate with amphetamine abuse. 'It's not a misunderstanding,' Ian said. 'You came here tonight for sex. There's no other reason to be here. So sex is what we're going to do.'

Merrick swivelled on the balls of his feet and jabbed his elbow sharply underneath Ian's ribcage. His breath burst out of him in a sudden 'whoosh', and he doubled over, letting go of Merrick's arm in the reflex of clutching at his solar plexus. 'No, we're not,' Merrick said mildly, moving away through the space that had cleared around him as if by magic.

On his way across the room, one of the other undercover officers fell into step beside him. 'Nice one, Sarge,' he said out of the corner of his mouth. 'You did what we've all been wanting to do ever since we got in here.'

Merrick stopped and smiled at the constable. 'You're supposed to be doing an undercover. Either fucking dance with me or fuck off and let one of these poofters chat you up.'

Leaving the constable open mouthed, Merrick walked over to the far side of the dance floor and leaned against the wall. The commotion he'd left at the bar had died down. Ian pushed his way through the crowd, still holding his stomach, and left the club, shooting venomous glares at Merrick.

Before long, Merrick had company again. This time, he recognized his companion as a detective constable from one of the other divisions who had only joined the murder squad that day. He was sweating under the weight of heavy leather jacket and trousers that looked suspiciously like standard police motorcycle issue. He leaned close to

Merrick, so he wouldn't be overheard in the crowd round the dance floor and said urgently, 'Skip, there's a guy I think we should take a look at.'

'Why?'

'I overheard him mouthing off to a couple of blokes that he knew the dead guys. He was boasting about it. Reckoned there weren't many that could say that. And I heard him say that the killer must be a body-builder like him, on account of lugging bodies around. He was saying he bet there were people here tonight who didn't know they knew a murderer. Boasting, like, all the way.'

'Why don't you bring him in yourself?' Merrick asked, his interest quickened by what he'd heard, but reluctant to deprive the constable of the credit of pulling in a suspect.

'I tried to strike up conversation with him, but he gave me the brush-off.' The constable gave a wry smile. 'Maybe I'm not his type, skip.'

'And what makes you think I am?' Merrick demanded, not sure whether he was being subtly insulted here.

'He's wearing the same kind of gear as you.'

Merrick sighed. 'You better point him out to me.'

'Don't look now, sir, but he's standing over by the disco speakers. IC1 male, five foot six, short dark hair, blue eyes, clean shaven, heavy Scottish accent. Dressed like you. Drinking a pint of lager.'

Merrick leaned back against the wall and slowly scanned the room. He got the suspect on the first pass. 'Got him, I think,' he said. 'OK, son, thanks. Look fucked off when I go.'

He shrugged away from the wall and left the constable practising his depressed look. Slowly, Merrick moved round the room until he found himself next to the man who'd been pointed out to him. He had the bulky build of a weightlifter and the face of a boxer. His outfit was almost identical to Merrick's, save that his jacket had more buckles and zips. 'Busy in here tonight,' Merrick said.

'Aye. Lots of new faces. Half of them probably polis,' the man said. 'See that jerk you were just talking to? He might as well have come in his Panda car. Did you ever see a more obvious busy in all your born days?'

'That's why I fucked him off sharpish,' Merrick replied.

'I'm Stevie, by the way,' the man said. 'Busy night you're having with the unwanted solicitations. I saw you sort that toerag out earlier. Nicely done, pal.'

'Thanks. I'm Don.'

'Nice to meet you, Don. You new about here, then? Accent like that, you're obviously not a local.'

'Does everybody know everybody else here?' Merrick asked with a wry smile.

'Pretty much. It's a real village, Temple Fields. 'Specially the S&M scene. Let's face it, if you're gonnae let somebody tie you up, you want to know what you're getting into.'

'You're not wrong, Stevie,' Merrick said with feeling. 'Even more so when there's a killer on the loose.'

'My point exactly. I mean, I don't suppose these guys that got themselves killed thought they were up for anything more than a bit of rough. I knew them, you know. Adam Scott, Paul Gibbs, Gareth Finnegan and Damien Connolly. Every last one of them, and let me tell you, I wouldn't have had them pegged for that sort of scene. Just shows you, doesn't it? You can never tell what goes on in people's heads.'

'How come you knew them, then? I thought the paper said they weren't known on the scene,' Merrick said.

'I run a gym,' Stevie said proudly. 'Adam and Gareth, they were members. We used to go out for a drink now and again. That Paul Gibbs, I knew him through a mate of mine, used to have a pint with him and all. And that copper, Connolly, he came round the gym after we had a burglary.'

'I bet there's not many around here that can say they knew all the poor sods,' Merrick said.

'You're right there, pal. Mind you, I don't suppose the killer had anything more in mind than a wee bit of fun.'

Merrick's eyebrows rose. 'You think it's fun to murder folk?'

Stevie shook his head. 'Naw, you're no' following me. See, I don't think he sets out to kill these guys. Naw, it's kind of an accident, if you get my meaning. They're playing their games, and your man just gets carried away, and it all gets out of hand. He's obviously strong, he carts these bodies about and dumps them in the middle of the city, for God's sake. He's not going to be a seven-stone weakling, now is he? If he's a real body-builder like me, he maybe doesn't know his own strength. Could happen to anybody,' he added after a moment's pause.

'Four times?' Merrick demanded incredulously.

Stevie shrugged. 'Maybe they asked for it. Know what I mean? Prick teases and that? Promising what they didnae want to deliver when push came to shove? I've been there, Don, and let me tell you, there've been times when I've wanted to strangle the wee bastards.'

The detective in Merrick was straining at the leash. Carol Jordan wasn't the only Bradfield copper who'd been reading up on the psychology of the serial killer. Merrick had read cases where killers got off on this kind of justification, swaggering in front of a third party. The Yorkshire Ripper, he knew, had boasted to his male cronies about 'doing' prostitutes. He wanted Stevie in an interview room. The only problem was how to get him there.

Merrick cleared his throat. 'I suppose the only way to avoid that is to get to know the people you go to bed with before you get there.'

'My point exactly. You fancy getting out of here? Maybe going for a cup of coffee down the diner? Getting to know each other a wee bit better?'

Merrick nodded. 'Sure,' he said, dumping the remains of his beer on a nearby table. 'Let's go.' Soon as they got outside, he could switch his radio to 'transmit only' and one of the back-up teams would pick them up. Then they could test Stevie's bravado in Scargill Street.

Although it was after midnight, the street outside the Hell Hole was far from deserted. 'This way,' Stevie said, pointing to his left. Merrick slid his hand into his jacket and adjusted the radio switch.

'Where is it we're going?' he asked.

'There's an all-night diner in Crompton Gardens.'

'Great. I could murder a bacon butty,' Merrick said.

'Very bad for your health, all that grease,' Stevie said seriously.

As they rounded the corner into the alley leading into the square, Merrick sensed someone stepping out of a darkened doorway behind him. He started to turn towards the sound of footsteps.

Just like Bonfire Night, was his last conscious thought as a starburst of light erupted behind his eyes.

It didn't last as long as I'd expected. Surprisingly, Adam proved more fragile than the German shepherd. Once he'd lapsed into unconsciousness following the dislocation of his limbs, he proved impossible to rouse. I waited for hours, but nothing seemed to bring him round; not pain, not cold water, not warmth. I was disappointed, I admit it. His pain had been a mere shadow of mine, his punishment not enough for the betrayal that occasioned it.

I finished what I had to do, neatly and swiftly, just after midnight. Then I took him off the rack and folded him into a heavy-duty garden rubbish sack. I put that inside a black Bradfield Metropolitan Council bin bag. It was a struggle to get the dead weight back up the cellar steps and into the wheelbarrow, but my hours pumping iron paid off.

I couldn't wait to get home to my computer, to transform the evening into something transcendent. But I still had work to do before I could relax and indulge myself. I drove into the city centre just above the legal speed limit – not so fast I'd get pulled for speeding, and not so slow that I'd be stopped on suspicion of being a careful drunk driver. I made for the gay cruising area behind the university. Temple Fields used to be a student area, filled with small cafés, restaurants, shops and bars with low prices and standards. Then, about ten years ago, a couple of the bars became gay. Our left-wing city council responded to *pressure and funded a gay and lesbian centre, which moved into the basement of an Indian restaurant. That seemed to trigger a domino effect, and within a year or two, Temple Fields had become Cruising City and the straight students had moved over to Greenholm on the far side of campus. Now, Temple Fields was home to gay bars, clubs, chichi bistros, shops selling leather and bondage gear, and a nightly rent rack right along the canal.*

By half past one on a Tuesday morning, there were still quite a few men out on the streets. I drove around a couple of times, concentrating on the area round Crompton Gardens. The square was dark; most of the streetlights had been vandalized for reasons of sexual privacy, and the council was too strapped for cash to repair them. Besides, none of the local businesses was complaining; the darker the square, the more desirable the area, the bigger their profits.

I looked around cautiously. Nothing stirred. I wrestled the bag to the lip of the boot, then half rolled, half carried it on to the low wall. I tipped it over the edge with a rustling thud and closed the tailgate as quietly as I could. I took a penknife out of my pocket, leaned over the wall and slit the bags open. I pulled them free of the body and crumpled them into a ball.

Just after two, I parked Adam's car a couple of streets away from his house then walked back to my jeep, stuffing the bags in a litter bin on the way. I was in bed by three. In spite of my burning desire to carry on with my work, I was overwhelmed with exhaustion. Not surprising, considering the effort I'd expended. I was asleep as soon as I switched off the light.

When I woke, I rolled over and looked at the clock. Then I checked with my watch. I had to accept its corroboration. I'd been asleep for thirteen and a half hours. I don't think I've ever slept for that length of time, not even after general anaesthetic. I was furious with myself. I'd been looking forward to sitting down at my computer to relive and rebuild my encounter with Adam till it more closely resembled my deepest fantasies. But now I barely had enough time to shower and eat.

On my way into work, I picked up a late city final edition of the Bradfield Evening Sentinel Times. I'd made page two of the paper:

NAKED BODY FOUND

The mutilated body of a naked man was found in Bradfield's gay village early this morning.

Council worker Robbie Greaves made the grisly discovery as he made a routine rubbish collection in the Crompton Gardens area of Temple Fields.

Now the city's gay community fears this may be the first act of a gay serial killer like the man who recently terrorized London's homosexuals.

The body was found among shrubs behind a wall in the park, a notorious night-time meeting place for gay men looking for casual sex.

The man, said to be in his late twenties, has not yet been identified. Police describe him as white, 5ft 10ins, muscular build, with short dark wavy hair and blue eyes. He has no distinguishing marks or tattoos.

A police spokesman said, 'The man's throat had been cut and his body mutilated. Whoever committed this callous crime is a violent and dangerous man. The nature of the victim's injuries mean the killer must have been covered in blood.

'We believe the man was killed elsewhere and the body dumped in the park sometime during the night.

'We would urge anyone who was in the Crompton Gardens area of Temple Fields last night to come forward for the purposes of elimination. All information will be treated in the strictest confidence.'

Robbie Greaves, 28, the council worker who discovered the body, said, 'I'd only just started work. It was just after half past eight. I was using my grab to pick up litter. When it touched the body, I thought at first it was a dead cat or dog. Then I lifted up the bushes and saw the body.

'It was horrible. I threw up, then I ran to the nearest phone box. I've never seen anything like it in my life and I hope I never do again.'

Well, at least they'd got one thing correct. The body was killed somewhere else and dumped in Crompton Gardens. As for the rest of it ... If this was any indication of the police's skills, I didn't think I'd have too much to worry about. That was fine by me. The last thing I wanted was to be arrested, since I'd already chosen Adam's successor. Paul, I knew, was going to be different. This time, it wouldn't have to end in death.

7

All his acquaintances afterwards described his dissimulation as so ready and so perfect, that if, in making his way through the streets . . . he had accidentally jostled any person, he would . . . have stopped to offer the most gentlemanly apologies: with his devilish heart brooding over the most hellish of purposes, he would yet have paused to express a benign hope that the huge mallet, buttoned up under his elegant surtout, with a view to the little business that awaited him about ninety minutes further on, had not inflicted any pain on the stranger with whom he had come into collision.

Carol turned off the main drag and cut through the back doubles to emerge in Crompton Gardens. 'Adam Scott was found just there,' she said, pointing to a spot halfway down one side of the shrubbery.

Tony nodded. 'Can you drive slowly round the square, then park up against the wall where the body was found, please?'

Carol did as he asked. As they cruised round the square, Tony gazed out intently, swinging round in his seat a couple of times to snatch a second look. When the car stopped, he got out. Without waiting for Carol, he crossed to the pavement and prowled round the edge of the square. Carol got out of the car and followed in his wake, trying to see what Tony saw.

Neither the murders nor the freezing weather had changed the habits of those who frequented Temple Fields.

Doorways and basement areas still held grunting couples, heterosexual and homosexual alike. A few froze momentarily at the sound of Carol's heels on the pavement, but most ignored it. A great place to hang out if you were into voyeurism, Carol thought cynically.

Tony reached the end of the houses and crossed the street to the shop and bar fronts. Here, there were no copulating couples. The city's crime rate dictated heavy shutters and grilles for windows and doors. Ignoring them, Tony looked over towards the gardens in the centre of the square, matching what he'd seen on the photographs with the reality. There were no bushes on this side, only the low wall. He barely noticed two men walking past, wrapped round each other like competitors in a three-legged race. He wasn't interested in anyone else but Handy Andy.

'You've been here,' he said to himself. 'This isn't a place you just happened on, is it? You've walked this pavement, watched these parodies of love and affection that people pay for. But that's not what you were after, was it? You wanted something different, something a lot more intimate, something you didn't have to pay for.' How had they felt, those voyeuristic adventures of Handy Andy? Tony concentrated.

'You've never had a normal relationship with another person,' he thought. 'The prostitutes don't bother you, though. Or the rent boys. You're not killing them. You're not interested in what you can do with them. It's the couples that get to you, isn't it? I know, you see, I know that for myself. Am I projecting? I don't think so. I think you're looking for coupledom, the perfect relationship, the one where you can be yourself, the one that will value you as highly as you think you should be valued. And then it will be all right. The past won't matter. But it does matter, Andy. The past is what matters most of all.'

He was suddenly aware of Carol standing by his side, looking at him curiously. Probably his lips were moving.

He'd better be careful, or she'd be consigning him to the bin marked 'nutter' too. He couldn't afford that, not if he was to keep her on his side long enough to achieve the result he needed.

The last building on that side was an all-night diner, its windows opaque with condensation. In the bright light inside, shapes moved like creatures of the deep. Tony moved forward and pushed open the door. A handful of customers glanced up at him before returning to their fry-ups and chat-ups. Tony stepped back on to the street and let the door sigh shut behind him. 'I don't think you go in there,' he decided. 'I don't think you want to be seen to be alone in a place that's meant for companionship.'

The third side of the square consisted of a couple of modern office blocks. In the doorways, a clutch of homeless teenagers slept, bundled in clothes, newspapers and cardboard boxes. By now, Carol had caught up with him. 'Have they been interviewed?' Tony asked.

Carol pulled a face. 'We tried. My dad used to do a bit of folk singing. When I was a kid, he used to sing me a song with the chorus, "Oh, but I may as well try and catch the wind." Now I know what it means.'

'That good, eh?'

They crossed to the houses on the fourth side of the square, passing a pair of hookers on the corner. 'Hey, gorgeous!' one of them shouted. 'I could give you a better time than that tight-arsed bitch.'

Carol snorted with laughter. 'Now there's a triumph of hope over experience,' she said wryly.

Tony said nothing. The words had barely penetrated his reverie. He continued slowly down the pavement, pausing every few steps to drink in the atmosphere. Conflicting music filtered out faintly into the night from the flats and bedsits. The smell of curry wafted on the breeze that rustled the litter and sent polystyrene fast-food trays tumbling along the gutters. The square was never entirely empty, he noted. 'You despise their messy lives, don't you?' he said to himself. 'You like things clean and neat and orderly. That's partly why you wash the bodies. That's at least as important to you as erasing the forensic traces.' He turned the final corner and walked across to the rear of Carol's car, feeling the first stirrings of confidence that he was capable of mapping this complex and fatally skewed mind.

'He probably had to sit here for a few minutes to make sure he wasn't being watched,' Tony said. 'Depending on what kind of vehicle he's using, it could have taken as little as a minute to get the body out and over the wall. But he'd want to be sure no one was watching.'

'We did a full door-to-door across the street, but nobody admitted to seeing anything out of the ordinary,' Carol replied.

'Let's face it, Carol, when you look at what's ordinary round here, it leaves plenty of scope for a serial killer. OK, I've seen enough. Shall we go?'

Cross bounded into the squad room, surprisingly light on his feet as fat people often are, as if somehow moving lightly negates the bulk of their body. 'All right, then, where is the scumbag?' he bellowed. Then he caught sight of the thin figure leaning against the wall, his conversation with Kevin Matthews interrupted by Cross's entrance.

'Sir?' Cross said, stopping in his tracks. 'I wasn't expecting you in.' He threw a look of pure venom at Kevin Matthews.

Brandon straightened up. 'No, Superintendent, I don't suppose you were.' He took a couple of steps towards Cross. 'I left instructions with the control room that if any arrests were made in connection with the serial killings I was to be informed at once. This is going to be a high-profile case when it comes to court, Tom. I want us to be seen to be squeaky clean.'

'Yes, sir,' Cross said mutinously. However Brandon

dressed it up, what he was saying was that he didn't believe Cross was the man to make sure that over-zealous detectives didn't go too far. With Brandon pacing the corridors, no serial-killer suspects were going to have unfortunate accidents in custody. Cross turned to Kevin Matthews. 'What exactly happened?'

Kevin, so pale with tiredness and stress that his freckles stood out on milk-white skin like some vicious pox, said, 'As far as we can make out, Don Merrick came out of the Hell Hole with some bloke. One of the back-up teams saw them. Don switched his radio on to transmit, so we're assuming he wanted this bloke picked up for questioning. They were heading for the all-night diner in Crompton Gardens, according to the back-up boys. There's an alley that's a short cut through to the gardens, and they went down there. Next thing the back-up hear is a scuffle going on. They leg it round there and find Don on the floor and two blokes slugging it out. They arrested the pair of them and they're kicking their heels in the cells.'

'What about Merrick?' Cross demanded. For all his faults, Cross was a copper's copper. His men were almost as important to him as his own career.

'He's down Casualty getting stitches in a sore head. He came round in the ambulance. I've got one of my lads down there with him taking a statement.' Kevin glanced at his watch. 'He should be back any time now.'

'So what are we looking at here?' Cross demanded. 'Have we got a suspect, or what?'

Brandon cleared his throat. 'I think we can assume that Merrick thought the man he was with was worth a chat. As for the man who attacked them, I suspect we'll need to wait for Merrick's statement. I suggest Inspector Matthews and one of his team talk to the attacker while you and I have a preliminary chat with Merrick's target. That OK with you, Tom?'

Cross nodded, disgruntled. 'Yes, sir. And as soon as your

lad gets back from Casualty, Kevin, I want to see him.'
He moved towards the door, looking over his shoulder
expectantly at Brandon.

Brandon said, 'Before we go, Tom, I think we need
Inspector Jordan and Dr Hill in here.'

'With respect, sir, it's the middle of the night. Do we
really need to bugger up the man's sleep?'

'I don't want to get into questioning anyone about the
murders until I've had the chance to take Dr Hill's advice
about how the interview should proceed. Besides, the two
of them are probably still out working. DI Jordan was
planning to show Dr Hill the crime scenes tonight. Can
you fix that, Inspector?'

Kevin glanced at Cross, who nodded slightly. 'No problem, sir. I'll page Inspector Jordan right away. I'm sure
she'll be delighted to lend a hand.'

Brandon smiled and walked past Cross into the corridor.
'Just shows what happens to your bottle when you get
behind a desk,' Cross muttered, shaking his head in mock-
sorrow. 'You get so's you need a bloody psychologist to
tell you how to interview some scumbag off the streets.'

Canal Street was still busy. People came in and out of
clubs, taxis dropped off and picked up, couples shared
their kebabs and chips on street corners, rent boys and
hookers watched the slow-moving traffic, pouncing on the
least opportunity. 'Interesting, isn't it, how areas become
defined?' Tony said to Carol as they walked briskly along
the street.

'You mean this is the zone for public encounters, while
Crompton Gardens is for the dark side?'

'And ne'er the twain shall cross over,' Tony said. 'It's
really quite lively for the time of night, isn't it? Are Monday
nights quieter?'

'A bit,' Carol said. 'A couple of the clubs shut on Mondays. And one of the others has a women-only night.'

'So there's probably not as much street traffic,' Tony mused. As they'd driven round the streets, speculating on Handy Andy's approach route, Tony had been struck by how very public an area he'd chosen for his first two victims. Almost as if he were setting himself challenges. Now, at the corner of the alley leading to the side door of Shadowlands, he looked along the street and mused. 'He's desperate to be the best,' he said softly.

'Sorry?'

'Handy Andy. He just doesn't go for the easy options. His victims are all in the high-risk category. His dumping grounds aren't obscure, deserted hiding places. The bodies are cleaned of forensic clues. He's smarter than us, he thinks, and he has to keep proving it to himself. I'd hazard a guess that the next body's going to be dumped somewhere very, very public.'

Carol felt a shiver run through her that was nothing to do with the cold. 'Don't talk about the next body as if we're not going to find him before then,' she pleaded. 'It's just too depressing to think about.'

Carol led the way into the short dark cul-de-sac. 'Now, the second body, Paul Gibbs, was found just down here. All there is down here is the fire exit for the Shadowlands club.'

'It's dark enough,' Tony complained, stumbling over the edge of a disintegrating cardboard carton.

'We did suggest to the manager that a security light would be a good idea, if only to prevent him being mugged when he's locking up at night, but you can see how seriously he's taken the idea,' Carol replied, raking through her handbag to find her mini-torch. She snapped it on and the narrow beam revealed Tony silhouetted against a hooker in a red rubber dress giving a blow-job to a bleary-eyed businessman in the fire-exit doorway.

'Hoy!' the outraged man shouted. 'Bugger off, Peeping Tom!'

Carol sighed. 'Police. Zip your dick or you're nicked.' Before she'd even finished the sentence, the hooker was on her feet and heading for the mouth of the alley as fast as her stilettoes would let her. Realizing it wasn't worth arguing now the whore had gone, the man quickly fastened his trousers and pushed past Tony. As he turned the corner, he shouted, 'Frigid cunt!' back at her.

'You all right?' Tony asked, his genuine concern obvious.

Carol shrugged. 'When I started in the job, it really shook me when punters abused me like that. Then I realized it was them that had the problem, not me.'

'The theory's sound. How does it work in practice?'

Carol pulled a face. 'Some nights I go home and stand in the shower for twenty minutes and I still don't feel clean.'

'I know exactly what you mean. Some of the messy heads I have to poke about inside leave me feeling like I'll never have a normal relationship with another human being again.' Tony turned away, not wanting his face to betray him. 'So this is where you found Paul?'

Carol moved forward to stand beside him. She shone her torch into the doorway. 'He was lying there, with a couple of bin bags tucked around him so he wasn't immediately obvious. Judging by the condoms lying around, the working girls had been screwing the night away smack bang next to a corpse.'

'I take it you've talked to the girls?'

'Yes, we've had them all in. The one that scuttled out of here like a cockroach when the light goes on uses this spot most nights. She says she had a punter some time around four in the morning. She knows it was then because this bloke is a regular who comes off his shift at the newspaper-printing plant about then. Anyway, she was going to bring him down here, but there was a car in the way.' Carol sighed. 'We thought we'd cracked it, because she could remember the make, model and the numbers on the licence plate, because it was the same as the number of her house. Two-four-nine.'

'Don't tell me. Let me guess. It was Paul Gibbs's car.'

'Got it in one.'

The insistent bleep of Carol's pager cut into the conversation, demanding as a baby's cry. 'I have to find a phone,' Carol said.

'What is it?'

'One thing you can always say for sure,' Carol said, hurrying back out of the alley. 'It's never good news.'

'Look, I've told youse all I know. I'd just met this guy Don in the Hole, we was going for a cup of tea and suddenly there's footsteps and Don hits the ground like Vinny Jones just tackled him and I turn round and there's this bampot with a brick. So I give him the citizen's arrest with the left hook, and that's when your boys turn up mob-handed, and here I am.' Stevie McConnell spread his hands out in front of him. 'Youse should be giving me a commendation, no' the third degree.'

'And you expect us to believe this . . .' Cross consulted his notes. 'This Ian attacked this Don just because he'd turned him down earlier in the evening?'

'That's about the size of it. Look, this Ian, he's known about the town. He's a heidbanger. He gets out of his brain on speed and thinks he's God Almighty. This Don gave him a right showing up, you know, made him look like a big jessie instead of macho man, so your man was for getting his own back. Look, you gonnae let me go, or what?'

Cross was spared from replying by a knock on the door. Brandon shrugged away from the wall he'd been leaning against and opened the door. He exchanged a few murmured words with the constable outside then came back in. 'Interview suspended at 1.47 a.m.,' he said, leaning past

Cross to turn off the tape recorder. 'We'll be back shortly, Mr McConnell,' Brandon promised.

Outside the interview room, Brandon said, 'Inspector Jordan and Dr Hill are upstairs. And DS Merrick has come back from Casualty. Apparently, he says he's well enough to run through the evening's events himself.'

'Right. Well, we'd better hear what he's got to say, and then we can have a proper go at Jock.' Cross marched upstairs to the squad room, where a concerned Carol was hovering over Merrick. Tony sat a few feet away, feet propped up on the rim of a wastepaper bin.

'Bloody hell, Merrick!' Cross roared, seeing the dramatic bandage that turbanned his head. 'You've not turned into one of them bloody Sikhs, have you? Christ, I knew it was a risk sending a team into poofterville undercover, but I wasn't expecting religious mania.'

Merrick smiled weakly. 'I figured that way you couldn't send me back into uniform for cocking up, sir.'

Cross gave a grudging smile in return. 'Let's be hearing it, then. Why have I got a bolshie little sporran-sucker in my nick?'

Brandon, standing a couple of feet behind Cross, interrupted. 'Before DS Merrick runs through the evening's events for us, I just want to explain to Dr Hill why we've dragged him in here at this time of night.' Tony straightened up in his chair and pulled a sheet of paper towards him. 'When you were giving your lecture the other day,' Brandon continued, moving past Cross and sitting on the edge of a desk, 'you mentioned that psychologists can often give pointers to detectives about interview approaches. I wondered if you could apply that to this situation.'

'I'll do my best,' Tony said, uncapping his pen.

'How do you mean, interview approaches?' Cross said suspiciously.

Tony smiled. 'A recent example from my own experience. A force I'd been advising had arrested a suspect in two rape cases. He was the macho type, all bluster and muscle. I suggested that they send in a woman CID officer to interview him, preferably a small, very feminine woman. That made him angry right from the start, because he held women in contempt and thought he wasn't being treated with the appropriate respect. I'd briefed her in advance to suggest in her line of questioning that he couldn't possibly be the rapist since, frankly, she didn't think he had it in him. The result was, he blew his stack and coughed to the two rapes they had him in the frame for, as well as three other offences they didn't even know about.'

Cross said nothing. 'DS Merrick?' Brandon asked.

Merrick took them through his experiences in the bar with frequent pauses for thought. At the end of his recital, Brandon and Carol looked expectantly towards Tony. 'What do you think, Tony? Are either of them a possible?' Brandon asked.

'I don't think Ian Thomson is a starter. This killer is far too careful to get involved in something as ridiculously high profile as a street brawl. Even if Don hadn't been a police officer, the chances are that Thomson would have ended up in trouble for going after someone with a half-brick. Even in a city where attacks on gays are not noted for their high priority in policing terms,' he added drily.

Cross scowled. 'Gays get treated same as everybody else by the lads,' he blustered.

Tony wished he'd kept his mouth shut. The last thing he wanted was to get into a head-to-head with Tom Cross on Bradfield police's 'gays and blacks don't count' policy. He decided to ignore the comment and forged on. 'Also, there's nothing in what we know about the killer's behaviour to suggest that he's an upfront S&M gay man. It's clearly not from the gay scene that he's selecting victims. However, McConnell sounds more interesting from your point of view. Do we know what he does for a living?'

'He's the manager of a gym in the city centre. The same gym that Gareth Finnegan used,' Cross said.

'Hasn't he been questioned before?' Brandon asked. Cross shrugged.

'One of Inspector Matthews's team has spoken to him,' Carol butted in. 'I noticed the report when I was preparing the material for Dr Hill,' she added hastily, when she saw the beginnings of a scowl on Cross's face. God forbid he should think she was trying to undermine him. 'My dustbin memory,' she continued, trying to make a joke of it. 'As far as I can remember, it was simply a routine enquiry, checking up on whether Gareth had had any particular buddies or contacts at the gym.'

'Do we know McConnell's domestic arrangements?' Tony asked.

'He shares a house with another couple of shirt-lifters,' Cross said. 'He says they're both in the body-building game too. So, is he in the frame or not?'

Tony doodled in the margin of his notes. 'It's possible,' he said. 'What are the chances of getting a search warrant?'

'On what we've got at the moment? Not good. And we've no grounds for a search without one. Not even in our wildest dreams can we claim that a street assault gives us grounds to search McConnell's house for evidence relating to serial killings,' Brandon said. 'What would we be looking for in particular?'

'A camcorder. Any indication that he has access to somewhere isolated and deserted like an old warehouse, factory, derelict house, lock-up garage.' Tony ran a hand through his hair. 'Polaroid photographs. Sado-masochistic pornography. Souvenirs of his victims. The jewellery missing from the bodies.' He looked up and met Tom Cross's sneer. 'And you should check the deep freeze just on the off chance that he's kept the pieces of flesh he removed from the bodies.' He felt a moment's gratification when Cross's expression changed to disgust.

'Charming. But first we have to get something more to go on. Any suggestions?' Brandon asked.

'Send DS Merrick and Inspector Jordan in to interview him. The realization that the man he tried to pick up is a police officer will unsettle him, make him feel that his instincts can't be trusted. There's a chance too that he has problems with women –'

'Of course he's got problems with women,' Cross interjected. 'He's a bloody arse bandit.'

'Not all gay men dislike women,' Tony said mildly. 'But a lot do, and McConnell may be one of them. At the very least, Carol will make him feel threatened. All-male situations offer him the opportunity for camaraderie, so we take that off him.'

'Let's try it, then,' Brandon said. 'If DS Merrick is up to it.'

'I'm game, sir,' Merrick said.

Cross looked as if he couldn't decide whether to hit Brandon or Tony. 'I might as well bugger off home, then,' he blustered.

'Good idea, Tom. You've had more than your fair share of all-nighters lately. I'll hang on here, see what comes out of McConnell's interview.'

Cross stomped out of the squad room, passing Kevin Matthews on the way. The atmosphere visibly lightened in Cross's absence. 'Sir?' Kevin said. 'Ian Thomson – it looks like he's out of the frame on the murders.'

Brandon frowned. 'I thought I told you not to bring the murders up? At this stage, all we want to front Thomson with is the assault.'

'I didn't bring up the murders, sir,' Kevin said defensively. 'But it emerged during the interview that Thomson works three nights a week as a DJ in Hot Rocks. That's a gay club in Liverpool. He does Monday, Tuesday and Thursday. It should be easy enough to check whether he was working on the nights of the murders.'

'OK, get someone on it,' Brandon said.

'Which leaves McConnell,' Carol said thoughtfully.

'Let's do it,' Brandon said.

'Any tips?' Carol asked Tony.

'Don't be afraid to patronize him. Stay sweetness and light, but make it clear that you're the ranking officer. And DS Merrick – you can afford to play the gratitude card a bit.'

'Thanks,' Carol said. 'OK, Don?'

They left Brandon and Tony together. 'How is it going?' Brandon asked, getting up and stretching.

Tony shrugged. 'I'm starting to get a feel for his victims. There's a definite pattern there. He's a stalker, I'm sure of it. I should have a rough profile in a day or two. It's just bad timing that you've pulled in a suspect now.'

'How do you mean, bad timing?'

'I understand why you wanted my input. But I don't like knowing about suspects before I draw up my profile. The danger is that I skew the profile subconsciously so that it's a better fit for the suspect.'

Brandon sighed. He'd always found it hard to be optimistic in the small hours. 'We'll cross that bridge when we come to it. By this time tomorrow, our suspect might just be a distant memory.'

Getting to know Paul was somehow more exciting than Adam had been. Partly, I suppose, because I knew now I could handle it if things didn't work out the way I wanted. Even if Paul didn't have the insight to see that I could give him more than anyone else, even if he rejected my love, even if he went as far as Adam and actually betrayed the inevitability of our partnership with someone else, I knew that there was an alternative scenario that could give me almost as much satisfaction as the achievement of what I deserved.

But this time, I felt sure that I would get what I wanted. Adam, I now saw, had been immature and weak. Paul was neither of those, I could tell at once. For a start, he hadn't chosen to live in the yuppie part of town like Adam. Paul lived on the south side of the city in Aston Hey, a leafy suburb beloved of university lecturers and alternative therapists. Paul's house was in one of the more inexpensive streets. Like mine, it was terraced, though his two-up and two-down rooms were obviously far bigger. Unlike mine, he had a small garden at the front, and his back yard was twice the size, scattered with terracotta planters and tubs filled with flowers and dwarf shrubs. The perfect place to sit together for a preprandial drink after work on summer evenings.

Now with Paul, I'd have the chance to live in Aston Hey, to enjoy those quiet streets, to walk in the park together, to be just like other couples. He had an interesting job, too – lecturer at Bradfield Institute of Science and Technology, specializing in CAD programs. We already had so much in common. It was a shame I'd never be able to show him what I'd achieved with Adam.

One of the major advantages of having no mortgage is that I have virtually all of my salary to play with. It's a substantial disposable income for someone of my age and with my lack of dependants. That means I can afford a state-of-the-art computer system, with regular upgrades to keep me out there at the leading edge. Given that one software program alone cost me nearly three thousand pounds, it's just as well I don't have anyone leeching off me. With my new CD-ROM system, video digitizer and special-effects software, it took me less than a day to import the videos into my computer. Once they were digitized and installed there, I could manipulate and morph the images to tell any story I wanted to see. Thanks to other video erotica I'd already installed on my system, I was even able to give Adam the erection he'd failed to achieve in life. Finally, I could fuck him, suck him, fist him, and watch him do the same to me. But the knowledge that I would be able to do that still hadn't been enough to save him. Not even my computer and my imagination could give me the joy and satisfaction he could have done if he'd only been honest with himself about his desire for me. And so, every day he had to die all over again. The ultimate fantasy, constantly changing, shaped to fit my every mood and whim. At last, Adam was performing everything he could ever have fantasized about. It was a shame he couldn't share in my pleasure.

It wasn't perfect, but at least I was having more fun than the police. From what I read, it was clear they were getting nowhere. Adam's death barely merited a mention in the national media, and even the Bradfield Evening Sentinel Times gave up after five days. Adam's body was identified *after four days, when anxious colleagues reported him missing after failing to get any reply from his phone or his doorbell. I was interested in their tributes (popular, hard-working, well liked, etc.) and I felt a moment's regret that his stupidity had deprived me of their friendship. The* Sentinel Times's *crime reporter had even managed to track down Adam's ex-wife, a mistake he'd made at twenty-one which he'd extricated himself from by his twenty-fifth birthday. Her comments made me laugh out loud.*

Adam Scott's ex-wife Lisa Arnold, 27, fought back the tears as she said, 'I can't believe this could have happened to Adam.

'He was a friendly man, really sociable. But he wasn't a big drinker. I can't imagine how this weirdo managed to get hold of him.'

Lisa, a primary-school teacher who has since remarried, went on, 'I've no idea what he was doing in Crompton Gardens. He never showed any gay tendencies when we were married. Our sex life was quite normal. If anything, it was a bit boring.

'We married too young. Adam's mother had brought him up to expect a wife who waited on him hand and foot, and that just wasn't me.

'Then I met someone else and I told Adam I wanted a divorce. He was really upset, but I think it was more that his pride was hurt.

'I haven't seen him since the divorce, but I heard he was living on his own. I know he's had a few affairs over the last three years, but nothing serious as far as I know.

'I just can't get used to the idea that he's dead. I know we hurt each other, but I'm still devastated that he's been murdered like this.'

I didn't rate the chances of Lisa's second marriage lasting the course if she still had as little insight into the workings of the male mind. Boring? Lisa was the only reason sex with Adam could be boring.

And as for calling me a weirdo! She was the one who had turned her back on a charming, handsome man who loved her so much that he was still talking about her to complete strangers three years after she'd rejected him. I knew all about it; I'd listened to him. If anyone was a weirdo, it was Lisa.

8

No unpractised artist could have conceived so bold an idea as that of a noon-day murder in the heart of a great city. It was no obscure baker, gentlemen, or anonymous chimney-sweeper, be assured, that executed this work. I know who it was.

Stevie McConnell ran both hands through his hair in a gesture of desperation. 'Look, how many times do I have to tell you? I was telling porkies. I was trying to make myself sound the big man. I wanted to cop off, I was trying to make myself interesting. I never knew Paul Gibbs or Damien Connolly. I never saw either of them in my life.'

'We can prove you knew Gareth Finnegan,' Carol said coldly.

'OK, I admit I knew Gareth. He was a member down the gym, I can't pretend I'd never met him before. But Christ, woman, the man was a lawyer. He must have known thousands of people in the city,' McConnell said, thumping the table with a solid fist.

Carol didn't even flinch. 'And Adam Scott,' she went on relentlessly.

'Yeah, yeah,' he said wearily. 'Adam Scott had a trial one-month membership down the gym about two years ago. He never joined up. I bumped into him a couple of times in my local pub, we had a jar together, that's all there was to it. I have a drink with a lot of people, you know. I'm not a bloody hermit. Christ, if I killed everybody

I've ever stood at a bar with, youse bastards would be busy from now till the next century.'

'We will prove you knew Paul Gibbs and Damien Connolly. You know that, don't you?' Merrick chimed in.

McConnell sighed. His hands clenched, forcing the muscles in his powerful forearms into sharp relief. 'If you do, you'll have to make it up, because you can't prove what isn't true. You're not going to do a Birmingham Six on me, you know. Look, if I was really this mad bastard, do you think I'd have hung around to help you? First sign of trouble, I'd have legged it. Stands to reason.'

Sounding bored, Carol said, 'But you didn't know then that Sergeant Merrick was a police officer, did you? So give us your alibi for Monday night.'

McConnell leaned back in the chair and stared at the ceiling. 'Mondays is my day off,' he recited. 'Like I said, the guys that share my house are on their holidays, so I was on my tod. I got up late, went down the supermarket for my messages, then I went for a swim. About six o'clock, I drove out to the multi-screen off the motorway, and I went to see the new Clint Eastwood film.'

Abruptly, he lurched forward in the chair. 'They'll be able to confirm it. I paid by credit card, and their system's all computerized. They can prove I was at the pictures,' he said triumphantly.

'They can prove you bought a ticket,' Carol said laconically. From the cinema to Damien Connolly's house would take no more than half an hour round the motorway, even allowing for rush-hour traffic.

'I can tell you the whole plot, for fuck's sake,' McConnell said angrily.

'You could have seen it any time, Stevie,' Merrick said gently. 'What did you do after the pictures?'

'I went home. Cooked myself a steak and some vegetables.' McConnell paused and stared at the table. 'Then

I went into town for the last hour. Just for a quick drink with a few mates.'

Carol leaned forward, sensing McConnell's reluctance. 'Where in town?' she demanded.

McConnell said nothing.

Carol leaned further forward, the tip of her nose an inch from his. Her voice was quiet but icy cold. 'If I have to stick your face on the front page of the *Sentinel Times* and send a team into every pub in the city, I'll do it, Mr McConnell. Where in town?'

McConnell breathed in heavily through his nose. 'The Queen of Hearts,' he spat.

Carol leaned back, satisfied. She stood up. 'Interview terminated at 3.17 a.m.,' she said, leaning over to switch off the tape recorder. She looked down at McConnell. 'We'll be back, Mr McConnell.'

'Wait a minute,' he protested as Merrick got up and the two of them made for the door. 'When am I going to get out of here? You've got no right to keep me!'

Carol turned back in the doorway, smiled sweetly and said, 'Oh, I have every right, Mr McConnell. You've been arrested for assault, let's not forget. I have twenty-four hours to make your life a misery before I even have to think about charging you.'

Merrick gave an apologetic smile as he backed out of the room in Carol's wake. 'Sorry, Stevie,' he said. 'The lady's not wrong.'

He caught up with Carol as she was asking the custody sergeant to return McConnell to the cells. 'What do you think, ma'am?' Merrick asked as they walked off together.

Carol stopped and eyed Merrick critically. His skin was pale and clammy, his eyes feverishly bright. 'I think you need to go home and get some sleep, Don. You look like shit on a stick.'

'Never mind me. What about McConnell, ma'am?'

'We'll see what Mr Brandon has to say.' Carol set off for the stairs, Merrick trailing behind her.

'But what do *you* think, ma'am?'

'On the face of it, he could be our man. He's got nothing approaching an alibi for Monday night, he runs the gym where Gareth Finnegan worked out, he knew Adam Scott and by his own admission he was in the Queen of Hearts on Monday night for the last hour. He's certainly strong enough to have carted the bodies in and out of a car. He's got form, even if it is only a couple of breaches of the peace and a Section 18 wounding. And he's into S&M. But that's all circumstantial. And I still don't think we've got grounds for a search warrant,' Carol rattled off. 'What about you, Don? Got a feeling in your water about this one?'

They turned down the corridor towards the murder squad room. 'I kind of like him,' Merrick said grudgingly. 'I can't imagine that I'd take a liking to the bastard that's been doing these murders. But then, I suppose that's a pretty daft reaction. I mean, he's not the two-headed man, is he? He's got to have something about him that lets him get close enough to his victims to do the business. So maybe it *is* Stevie McConnell.'

Carol opened the door to the squad room, expecting to find Brandon and Tony still sitting there, fuelled by coffee and canteen sandwiches. The room was empty. 'Where's the ACC got to now?' Carol said, tiredness lending her voice a note of exasperation.

'Maybe he's left a message at the front desk,' Merrick suggested.

'And maybe he's done the sensible thing and buggered off home to bed. Well, that's us for tonight, Don. McConnell can stew for a bit. See what the bosses have to say in the morning. Maybe we can try for a search warrant now we know McConnell was in the Queen of Hearts. Now, get out of my sight and go home to bed before your Jean accuses me of leading you off the straight and narrow. Get some sleep. I don't want to see you before noon, and if your head's hurting, stay in bed. That's an order, Detective Sergeant.'

Merrick grinned. 'Yes, ma'am. See you.'

Carol watched Merrick walk back down the corridor, worried at the slow deliberation of his movements. 'Don?' she called. Merrick turned enquiringly back to her. 'Get a taxi. My authorization. I don't want you wrapped round a lamppost on my conscience. And that's an order, too.' Merrick grinned, nodded and disappeared down the stairs.

With a sigh, Carol walked down the squad room to her temporary office. There was no message on her desk. Bloody Brandon, she thought. And bloody Tony Hill. Brandon at least should have waited till she'd finished her interrogation of McConnell. And Tony might have left some indication of when he expected them to meet to discuss his profile. Muttering under her breath, Carol followed Merrick out of the building. As she reached the foyer, the officer minding the front desk called, 'Inspector Jordan?'

Carol turned back. 'I'm what's left of her.'

'The ACC left a message for you, ma'am.'

Carol approached the desk and took the envelope the constable handed her. She ripped it open and pulled out a single sheet of paper. 'Carol,' she read. 'I have taken Tony off on a little mission. I'll drop him at home afterwards. Please be in my office for ten this morning. Thanks for your hard work. John Brandon.'

'Great,' Carol said bitterly. She gave the constable a tired smile. 'I don't suppose you know where Mr Brandon and Dr Hill were headed?'

He shook his head. 'Sorry, ma'am. They didn't say.'

'Wonderful,' she muttered sarcastically. Turn your back for a minute and they were off playing their boys' games. Little mission, indeed. Bollocks to that, Carol thought as she marched back to her car. 'Three can play at that game,' she said as she turned the ignition key.

Tony flicked through the last of the magazines and returned it to the box file in the bedside storage cube. 'S&M always leaves me feeling faintly queasy,' he remarked. 'And this lot's particularly nasty.'

Brandon agreed. McConnell's collection of hard-core pornography consisted mostly of magazines crammed with glossy colour pictures of well-muscled young men torturing each other and masturbating. A few were even more disturbing, with their graphic shots of male couples indulging in full sex with an array of sado-masochistic trappings. Brandon couldn't remember seeing nastier examples, even when he'd done a six-month attachment with Vice.

They were sitting on the bed in Stevie McConnell's room. As soon as Carol and Merrick had left for their interrogation, Brandon had said, 'Would it be helpful to you to see where McConnell lives?'

Tony picked up his pen again and started to doodle on the sheet of paper. 'It might give me some insight into the man. And if he is the killer, there could be evidence that ties him into the crimes. I don't mean murder weapons, or anything like that. I'm thinking more of the souvenirs. Photographs, newspaper clippings, as well as the stuff I was talking about before. But it's academic, isn't it? You said there was no chance of getting a search warrant.'

Brandon's melancholy face lit up in a strange smile, almost a leer. 'When you've got a suspect in custody, there are things you can do to circumvent the rules. You game?'

Tony grinned. 'I'm fascinated.' He followed Brandon downstairs to the cells. The custody sergeant hastily dropped the Stephen King novel he'd been reading and jumped to his feet.

'It's all right, Sergeant,' Brandon said. 'If I only had a couple of prisoners to think about, I'd be enjoying a good read, too. I'd like to have a look at McConnell's property.'

The sergeant unlocked the property cupboard and handed the transparent plastic bag to Brandon. There was a wallet, a handkerchief and a bunch of keys inside. Brandon opened it and removed the keys. 'You haven't seen me, have you, Sergeant? And you won't see me when I come back in a couple of hours, will you?'

The sergeant grinned. 'You couldn't possibly have been here, sir. I'd have been bound to notice.'

Twenty minutes later, Brandon was parking the Range Rover outside McConnell's terraced house. 'Lucky for us McConnell happened to mention that the two blokes he shares the house with are away on holiday.' He took a cardboard box out of the glove compartment and gave Tony a pair of latex gloves. 'You'll need these,' he said, slipping a pair over his own hands. 'If we do get a search warrant, it would be a bit embarrassing when the finger-print team turn up you and me as prime suspects.'

'There's one thing I'm curious about,' Tony said as Brandon inserted the key in the mortice lock.

'What's that?'

'This is an illegal search, right?'

'Right,' Brandon said, opening the door and stepping into the hall. He groped for the light switch, but didn't turn it on when he found it.

Tony followed him, closing the door behind him. Only then did Brandon snap the light on, revealing a carpeted hall and stairs. There were a couple of framed posters of body-builders on the walls. 'So if we find any evidence, presumably it's inadmissible?'

'Also right,' said Brandon. 'But there are ways round that. For example, if we find a bloodstained cut-throat razor under McConnell's bed, it will mysteriously find its way on to the kitchen table. Then we go to the magistrate, explain that we went to McConnell's house to check he was telling the truth when he said his house-mates were on holiday, and we happened to look through the windows and we spotted what we have reason to believe is the weapon used to kill Adam Scott, Paul Gibbs, Gareth Finnegan and Damien Connolly.'

Tony shook his head in amusement. 'Bent? Us? Never, your honour!'

'There's bent and there's bent,' Brandon said grimly. 'Sometimes you need to give things a shove in the right direction.'

Tony and Brandon moved through the house, room by room. Brandon was intrigued by Tony's method. He would walk into a room, stand in the middle of the floor and slowly scan the walls, the furniture, the floor coverings, the shelves. He almost sniffed the air. Then, meticulously, he opened cupboards and drawers, lifted cushions, examined magazines, checked titles of books, CDs, cassettes and videos, handling everything he touched with the care and precision of an archaeologist. Within seconds, his mind was busy, analysing everything he saw and touched, slowly building a picture in his mind of the men who lived here, constantly matching it against the embryonic picture of Handy Andy that was developing in his mind like a photographic print in developer fluid.

'Have you been here, Andy?' he asked himself. 'Does this feel like you, smell like you? Would you watch these videos? Are these your CDs? Judy Garland and Liza Minnelli? The Pet Shop Boys? I don't think so. You're not camp, I know that much about you. And there's nothing camp or chichi about the house. This place is so aggressively masculine. A living room furnished in eighties chrome and black. But it's not a straight man's house, is it? No girlie magazines, not even car magazines. Just body-building periodicals stacked under the coffee table. Look at the walls. Men's bodies, oiled and shining, muscles like carved wood. The men who live here know who they are, they know what they like. I don't think this is you,

Andy. You're controlled, Andy, but not this controlled. It's one thing to keep yourself buttoned up, it's another thing altogether to be strong enough to project so coherent an image. I should know, I'm the expert. If you were as firmly rooted in your identity as the guys who live here, you wouldn't have to do what you do, would you?

'Look at the books. Stephen King, Dean R. Koontz, Stephen Gallagher, Iain Banks. Arnold Schwarzenegger's biography. A couple of paperbacks about the Mafia. Nothing soft, nothing gentle, but nothing off the wall either. Would you read these books? Maybe. I think you'd like to read about serial killers, though, and there's none of that here.'

Tony turned slowly towards the door. It was a small shock to see Brandon standing there. He'd become so absorbed in his scrutiny that he'd lost all sense of being in company. Watch yourself, Tony, he warned himself. Stay inside your head.

In silence, they trooped through to the kitchen. It was spartan, but well equipped. In the sink there was a dirty soup bowl and a mug half full of cold tea. A small shelf of cookery books testified to the occupants' obsession with healthy eating. 'Fart city,' Tony observed wryly, opening a cupboard filled with jars of pulses. He opened the drawers, noting the kitchen knives. There was a small vegetable knife with a blade worn thin from sharpening, a bread knife whose blade was pitted with age, and a cheap carving knife, the handle bleached from the dishwasher. 'These are not your tools, Andy,' Tony said to himself. 'You like knives that do their work properly.'

Without consulting Brandon, he walked out of the kitchen and up the stairs. Brandon watched him stick his head round the first bedroom door and reject it. As he passed, he saw that it was obviously the couple's room. He followed Tony through the door across the landing. In McConnell's bedroom, Tony seemed to drift away altogether into a world of his own. The room was simply furnished with modern pine bed, chest of drawers and wardrobe. An array of weightlifting trophies sat on the deep windowsill. A tall bookcase was crammed with pulp science fiction and a handful of gay novels. On a small table, there was a games computer and a television monitor. On a shelf above was a collection of games. Tony browsed through Mortal Kombat, Streetfighter II, Terminator 2, Doom and a dozen other games whose keynote was violent action.

'This is more like it,' he murmured. He stood by the chest of drawers, hand poised to open one. 'Maybe it's you after all,' he thought. 'Maybe you leave the living room to the other two. What if this is your only domain? What would I expect to find here? I'd want your souvenirs, Andy. You need to keep something by you, otherwise the memory disintegrates too fast. We all need something tangible. The discarded perfume spray that holds her fragrance and summons her before my eyes like a hologram; the theatre programme from the night we first made love and it was all right. Keep the good memories, throw away the bad. What have you got for me?'

The first three drawers were disappointingly innocuous: underwear, T-shirts, socks, jogging suits and shorts. When Tony opened the bottom drawer, he sighed in satisfaction. The drawer contained McConnell's S&M gear – handcuffs, leather restraint straps, cock rings, whips, and a clutch of items that looked to Brandon as if they ought to be in some kind of laboratory or mental institution. As Tony calmly took them out and examined them, Brandon shuddered.

Tony sat down on the bed and looked around. Slowly, cautiously, he tried to construct a picture of the man who lived in this room. 'You like to exercise power through violence,' he thought. 'You enjoy the flow of pain in your sexual experience. But there's no subtlety here. No sign that you're a man who plans things with care and detail.

You worship your body. It's a temple to you. You've achieved things, and you're proud of that. You're not socially inadequate. You manage to share a house with two other men, and you're not obsessive about your privacy, since there's no lock on the door. You don't have a problem with your sexuality, and you're comfortable with the idea of picking up a man in a club, provided you have the chance to get to know him a bit first.'

His picture-building was interrupted by Brandon. 'Look at this, Tony!' he said excitedly. The ACC had been painstakingly going through a shoebox full of papers, mostly receipts, electrical guarantees, bank and credit-card statements. The box was almost empty, but now, he held out a flimsy slip of paper.

Tony took it. It was some kind of official police form. He frowned. 'What's this?'

'It's the form you get when an officer stops you in a car and you haven't got your documents with you. You have to take them to a police station within a fixed period, so they can check everything's in order. Look at the name of the officer,' Brandon urged.

Tony looked again. The name that had at first seemed a scrawled jumble suddenly resolved itself into 'Connolly'.

'I recognized his number,' Brandon said. 'You can hardly make out the name.'

'Shit,' Tony breathed.

'Damien Connolly must have stopped him for some minor traffic offence, or just on a spot check, and asked him to produce his documents,' Brandon said.

Tony frowned. 'I thought Connolly was a local information officer? What was he doing dishing out a traffic ticket?'

Brandon looked over Tony's shoulder at the slip of paper. 'It was nearly two years ago. Connolly obviously wasn't a collator then. Either he was doing a stint with Traffic or he was on duty in the area car when he saw

McConnell doing something he shouldn't have been.'

'Can you check that out discreetly?'

'No problem,' Brandon said.

'You've cracked it, then, haven't you?'

Brandon looked astonished. 'You mean ... you think that clinches it? McConnell's the man?'

'No, no,' Tony said hastily. 'Not at all. All I meant was that if you can track that back from the other end, you should be able to get a magistrate to grant you an official search warrant on the basis that McConnell knew three of the four victims, which goes beyond mere coincidence.'

'Right,' Brandon said, sighing. 'So you're still not convinced McConnell's the killer?'

Tony stood up and paced to and fro across the carpet, its jagged geometric pattern of grey, red, black and white reminding him of the one and only migraine he'd ever had. 'Before you found this, I'd come to the conclusion you'd got the wrong man,' he said after a few moments. 'I know I've not had time to sit down and write out a full profile yet, but I felt like I was beginning to get a sense of what this killer's like. And there are too many things here that don't fit that picture. But this is a hell of a coincidence. This is a big city. We've established that Stevie McConnell knew or at least had met three out of the four victims. How many people are going to be in that position?'

'Not many,' Brandon said grimly.

'I still don't like McConnell for the killer, but it's possible that the killer is someone he knows, someone who's met Adam Scott and Gareth Finnegan through him,' Tony said. 'Maybe even somebody who was with him when he got that traffic ticket, or someone that he pointed Damien out to. You know the kind of thing: "That's the bastard who nicked me for speeding." '

'You really don't think it's him, do you?' Brandon said flatly, disappointment in his voice. 'I suppose it's thin. After all, there's no evidence as such to connect the house to the killings,' he said cautiously. 'But you said yourself, he's more likely to be doing his killing somewhere else. That might be where he keeps his souvenirs.'

'It's not just the absence of souvenirs,' Tony said. 'Putting it crudely, John, serial murderers kill to turn their fantasies into reality. Typically, they have fantasies developed to the point where they are more real to them than the world around them. There's nothing here to suggest McConnell is that type of personality. Sure, he's got a stack of porn mags. But so have most single men of his age, regardless of sexual orientation. He's got violent computer games, but so have thousands of teenagers and grown men too. What there is is plenty of evidence to suggest that Stevie McConnell isn't a sociopath. Look around you, John. This whole house reeks of normality. The kitchen calendar has dates for people coming round for dinner. Look at that pile of Christmas cards on his bookshelf. There must be fifty there. Look at his holiday snaps. He was obviously with the same partner for four or five years, judging by the locations and hairstyle changes. Stevie McConnell doesn't seem to have problems forming relationships with people. OK, so there doesn't seem to be anything relating to his family, but a lot of gay people get cut off by their families when they come out. It doesn't mean that his family were dysfunctional in the ways that typically lead to the development of a serial killer. I'm sorry, John. I wasn't sure at first, but the more I've seen, the more this guy just doesn't smell right to me.'

Brandon got to his feet and carefully replaced the slip of paper exactly where he'd found it. 'It grieves me to say so, but I think you're right. When I interviewed him earlier, I thought he was way too calm to be our man.'

Tony shook his head. 'Don't let that mislead you. Chances are when you do pull the right guy, he'll be calm too. Don't forget, this is something he's planned carefully. Although he thinks he's the best, he'll still have made contingency plans. He'll expect to be brought in for questioning sooner or later. He'll be ready for you. He'll be reasonable, pleasant. He won't look like a con. He'll be bland, helpful, and he won't ring alarm bells with your detectives. His alibi will be no alibi. He'll probably say he's been with a tart, or been to an away football match on his own. He'll end up being eliminated from your enquiries because other suspects will be superficially far more appealing.'

Brandon managed to look even more depressed than normal. 'Thanks, Tony. You've really cheered me up now. So what do you suggest?'

Tony shrugged. 'Like I said, it's a possibility that he knows the killer. He may even have his own suspicions. I'd hang on to him for a bit longer, sweat him for what and who he does know. But I wouldn't call off the team. Get a warrant. Do a proper search, under the floorboards, in the loft. You never know what you might turn up. Don't forget, I could be completely wrong.'

Brandon glanced at his watch. 'Right. I'd better get these keys back before the end of the custody sergeant's shift. I'll drop you off on the way.'

With a last look to check they'd left nothing out of place, Brandon and Tony left McConnell's house. As they approached the Range Rover, a voice from the shadows said, 'Good morning, gentlemen. You're nicked.' Carol stepped forward into the light of the streetlamp. 'Dr Anthony Hill, and Assistant Chief Constable John Brandon, I am arresting you on suspicion of breaking and entering. You do not have to say anything . . .' At that point, the giggles took over.

Brandon's heart had thudded into his throat at her first words. 'Hellfire, Carol,' he protested. 'I'm too old for tricks like that.'

'But not for ones like this, I see,' Carol said drily, gesturing with her thumb towards McConnell's house.

'Unauthorized search, and with a civilian? Just as well for you I'm off duty, sir.'

Brandon gave a weary smile. 'So why are you loitering with intent around the suspect's house?'

'I'm a detective, sir. I thought I might find you and Dr Hill here. Any joy?'

'Dr Hill thinks not. What about your interview?' Brandon asked.

'Your suggestions worked really well, Tony. McConnell's got no alibi to speak of for Damien Connolly's murder, apart from one hour late on in the evening, by which time Damien could have been dead already. The significant thing is where he was for that hour. Sir, he was drinking in the pub where the body was dumped.'

Tony's eyebrows climbed and he sucked his breath in sharply. Brandon turned to him. 'Well?'

'It's exactly the cheeky sort of thing Handy Andy could pull. You might want to get someone to check if he's a regular in there. If he isn't, it makes it significant,' Tony said slowly. Before he could say more, he was overwhelmed by a huge yawn. 'Sorry,' he yawned. 'I'm not a night bird.'

'I'll drive you home,' Carol said. 'I think the ACC has something to drop off at the station.'

Brandon looked at his watch. 'Fine. Make it eleven, not ten, Carol.'

'Thank you, sir,' Carol said with feeling as she unlocked her car for Tony. He slumped into the passenger seat, unable to stop the wave of yawns that had engulfed him.

'I'm really sorry,' she made out through a jaw-cracker. 'I can't stop yawning.'

'Did you find anything to make it worthwhile?' Carol said, her tone more sympathetic than her words.

'Damien Connolly nicked him a couple of years ago for a traffic offence,' Tony said heavily.

Carol whistled. 'Gotcha! We've caught him in a double lie, Tony! McConnell originally told Don Merrick he'd met

Connolly after a burglary at the gym. Then in the interview he denied ever having seen him. He said he'd been lying to make himself seem interesting. But now it turns out he really had met him! What a break!'

'Only if you believe he's the killer,' he said. 'I'm sorry to disappoint you, Carol, but I don't think he's the one. I'm too tired to go through it all now, but once I've drawn up my profile and we go through it, you'll see why I can't get excited about Stevie McConnell.' He yawned again and leaned his head on his hand.

'When can we do that?' Carol asked, fighting the urge to shake his thoughts out of him.

'Listen, give me the rest of today to myself, and by tomorrow morning I'll have a draft profile for you. How's that?'

'Fine. Anything else you need in the meantime?'

Tony said nothing. Carol gave him a quick sidelong glance and realized he had dozed off. All right for some, she thought. Forcing herself to concentrate, she drove across town to Tony's house, a turn-of-the-century brick-built semi in a quiet street a couple of tram stops away from the university. Carol pulled up outside. The car's slow glide to immobility did nothing to disturb Tony, whose breathing had become audible.

Carol undid her seat belt and leaned over to shake him gently. Tony's head came up in a startled gesture, his eyes wide and frantic. He stared uncomprehendingly at Carol. 'It's all right,' she said. 'You're home. You fell asleep.'

Tony rubbed his eyes with his fists, muttering something unintelligible. He looked blearily at Carol and gave a sleepy, lopsided smile. 'Thanks for bringing me home.'

'No problem,' Carol said, still twisted round in her seat, fiercely aware of his closeness. 'I'll give you a ring this afternoon, we can fix up a time to meet tomorrow.'

Tony, awake now, felt claustrophobic. 'Thanks again,' he said, retreating hastily, opening the car door and almost tumbling on to the pavement, thanks to the combination of haste and sleepiness.

'I can't believe I wanted him to kiss me,' Carol said to herself as she watched Tony open his gate and walk up the short path. 'Dear God, what is happening to me? First I treat Don like a mother hen, then I start fancying the expert witnesses.' She saw the front door open, stuffed a cassette in the stereo and drove off. 'What I need,' she told Elvis Costello, 'is a holiday.'

'You tease, and you flirt, and you shine all the buttons on your green shirt,' he sang back.

'Last night, we were practically sticking the champagne on ice. Now you're telling me you want to let McConnell go?' Cross shook his head in a gesture of exasperation so ancient it probably appeared on a Greek vase. 'What's happened to change everything? Come up with a cast-iron alibi, has he? Out on the razz with Prince Edward and his body-guards, was he?'

'I'm not saying let him go this minute. We need to question him closely about his associates, check if he introduced anyone to both Gareth Finnegan and Adam Scott. And after that, we have to let him walk. There's no real evidence, Tom,' Brandon said wearily. Lack of sleep had transformed his face into a grey mask that wouldn't have looked out of place in a Hammer Horror film. Cross, on the other hand, looked and sounded as fresh as a toddler who's just had a nap.

'He was in the Queen of Hearts that night. For all we know, he had Damien Connolly's body in the boot of his car, just waiting for closing time. It's got to be grounds for searching his gaff.'

'As soon as we've got enough evidence to get a search warrant, we'll do it,' Brandon said, reluctant to admit that he'd already taken that unorthodox step. Earlier, he'd asked Sergeant Claire Bonner to check all Damien

Connolly's arrests and traffic tickets, supposedly on the off chance of a connection to McConnell, but so far, she hadn't unearthed the crucial information that he knew was lurking there.

'I suppose this is all down to Boy Wonder,' Cross said bitterly. 'I suppose the shrink says McConnell's childhood wasn't unhappy enough.'

Carol bit her tongue. It was bad enough being the fly on the wall in this clash of the titans without reminding either of her bosses she was witnessing their conflict.

Brandon frowned. 'I have consulted with Dr Hill, and yes, he does feel that on the basis of what we've got so far, McConnell probably isn't our man. But that's not the main reason why I think we should let him loose. The lack of evidence is a hell of a lot more important to me.'

'And to me. That's why we need time to collect some more. We need to interview these poofters he was drinking with on Monday night, to see what kind of state he was in. And we need to take a look at what McConnell's got under his mattress,' Cross said forcefully. 'We've had him in custody for less than twelve hours, sir. We're entitled to keep him till gone midnight. Then we can charge him with the assault for now, and ask the magistrates for a lie-down in police custody, which gives us another three days. That's all I'm asking for. I'll have nailed him by then. You can't say no to that, sir. You'll have the lads up in arms.'

Wrong, Carol thought. You were doing fine up till then, but the emotional blackmail just scuppered you.

Brandon's ears flushed scarlet. 'I hope no one thinks that because we are questioning someone the work stops,' he said, a dangerous edge in his voice.

'They're dedicated, sir, but they've been working on this a long time without a break in the case.'

Brandon turned away, staring out of the window at the city below. His instincts said to let McConnell go after they'd had one last attempt at digging his contacts out of him, but he had known without Cross's clumsy comments that having a suspect had given the murder squad a new lease of energy. Before he could make a decision, there was a knock at the door. 'Come in,' Brandon called, swinging round and dropping heavily into his chair.

Kevin Matthews's carrot curls appeared round the door. He looked like a kid who's been promised a trip to Disneyland. 'Sir,' he said. 'Sorry to interrupt, sir, but we've just had a report from Forensic on the Damien Connolly killing.'

'Come in and tell us, then,' Cross invited genially.

Kevin gave an apologetic smile and slid his slim frame round the door. 'One of the SOCOs found a scrap of torn leather caught on a nail on the gate,' he said. 'It's a secure area, the public can't just walk in, so we thought it might be significant. Obviously, we had to eliminate the people who work at the pub, and the draymen who deliver there. Anyway, it turns out that the yard was whitewashed and the gates were painted only a month ago, so we didn't have to chase too many bodies. Bottom line is, no one admitted owning anything made from leather like this, so we sent it off to Forensic and asked them to look at it double urgent. The report's just come back.' He proffered the report to Brandon, eager as a Boy Scout.

The relevant passage had been highlighted in yellow. It leapt off the page at Brandon. 'The fragment of dark-brown leather is extremely unusual. For a start, it appears to be deerskin of some sort. More significantly, analysis indicates that it has been cured in sea water rather than a specialist chemical-curing medium. I know of only one source of such leather: the former Soviet Union. Because regular supplies of the correct chemicals are difficult to come by, many tanners there still use the old method of curing with sea water. I would guess that the fragment has come from a leather jacket that originated in Russia. Leather like this is not available commercially elsewhere, since it does not meet the quality levels required by Western retail outlets.' Brandon read it, then tossed it across the desk towards Cross.

'Bloody hell!' Cross said. 'You mean we're looking for an Ivan?'

I read somewhere that murder enquiries cost a million pounds a month. When Paul demonstrated he was every bit as stupid and treacherous as Adam, I began to realize the actions I'd been forced to take might start to have a significant impact on local taxes. Not that I minded a few extra pence a year on my council-tax bills; it was a small price to pay for the satisfaction I gained from dealing with their perfidy.

I was devastated by Paul's defection. Just as I'd set the scene for the triumphant celebration of our love, he turned his back on me and chose another. The night he made his first approach, I don't know how I got home. I can't remember a single detail of the journey. I sat in my jeep outside the farm, raging against his shallowness, his failure to recognize that I was the one he truly loved. My anger was so strong I'd lost all physical coordination. I virtually fell out of the driver's seat and staggered like a drunk towards the haven of my dungeon.

I climbed on to the stone bench and hugged my knees to my chest while the unfamiliar tears rolled down my cheeks and splashed on the raw stone, staining it dark as Adam's blood. What was wrong with them? Why couldn't they let themselves have what I knew they wanted?

I wiped my eyes. I owed it to both of us to make the experience as rich and as perfect as possible. It was time *for new toys. Adam had been the dress rehearsal. Paul was going to be the first night.*

The ploy of the car that wouldn't start had served me well with Adam, so I used it on Paul. It worked like a dream. Before I was three steps down the hall, he'd even invited me to have a drink while I was waiting for the AA man. But I didn't fall for his blandishments; he'd had his chance, and it was too late now for me to abort my plans for our union on my terms.

When he came round, he was strapped into a Judas chair. It had taken me a few days to construct it, since I'd had to start from scratch. The Judas chair was one of my San Gimignano discoveries. I'd only ever seen a couple of references to it in my books, none of which made it at all clear how exactly it was constructed. But there in the museum, they had their very own working model. I had taken a couple of photographs to augment the one in the museum catalogue, and equipped with those, I had worked out a practicable design on my computer.

It's not a machine that inquisitors have used much, though I can't quite see why. The San Gimignano museum puts forward a theory which frankly seems absurd to me. Coupled with some of the other descriptions on the cards, this daft theory convinces me that the cards have been written by some blinkered, obsessive feminist. The theory goes thus: it was OK to use implements of torture on women such as vaginal pears that shredded the cervix and vagina, so-called 'Chastity' belts which ripped their labia to a bloody pulp, implements that chopped nipples as efficiently as a cigar cutter, because women were a separate species from the inquisitors, and indeed were often creatures of the devil. On the other hand, so this demented theory goes, torture instruments used on men tend not to be directed against their sexual organs, in spite of the

tenderness of those areas, because – wait for it – the tor-
turers felt subconsciously connected to their victims and
therefore any mutilation inflicted on their cocks and balls
were unthinkable. Clearly, the caption writer in San Gimignano is far from au fait with the refinements of the Third
Reich.

My Judas chair, even if I say so myself, is a masterpiece
of the type. It consists of a square frame with a leg at each
corner, with arm supports for the forearms and a thick
plank up the back. Much like a primitive carving chair,
except that there is no seat. Instead, below the gap where
the seat should be, there is a sharply barbed conical spike,
attached to the chair legs at its base by a cross-brace of
strong wooden struts. For the spike, I'd used one of the
large cones that cotton yarn used to be wound round on
industrial looms. You can pick them up in the souvenir
shop of any outpost of the heritage industry. I'd covered
it with a thin, flexible sheet of copper, and fastened thin
strands of razor wire in a spiral round the outside. I'd
added my own refinement to the example in the torture
museum; my spike was wired up to the electrical supply
via a rheostat, allowing me to apply electric shocks of
varying intensity. The whole thing is bolted to the floor to
prevent accidents.

While he'd still been unconscious, Paul had been held
above the spike by a strong leather strap under his armpits,
binding him to the back of the chair. I'd also strapped each
ankle to one of the front legs of the chair. As soon as I
unfastened the strap, he'd be thrown on his own resources,
relying on the muscles in his calves and his shoulders to
keep him from the savage spike, carefully sited immediately
below his anus. Since the chair was so high that only his
toes could reach the floor, I didn't expect him to hold out
too long.

His eyes registered the same panic I'd already seen in
Adam. But his situation was entirely of his own making.

I told him so before I ripped the tape away from his mouth.

'*I had no idea, no idea,*' *he gabbled.* '*I'm sorry, I'm so sorry. You've got to let me make it up to you. Just let me out of this thing, and I promise we can make a fresh start.*'

I shook my head. '*Robert Maxwell got one thing right. He said trust is like virginity; you can only lose it once. You have a treacherous soul, Paul. How can I believe in you?*'

His teeth began chattering, though not, I suspect, from cold. '*I made a mistake,*' *he forced out.* '*I know that. Everybody makes mistakes. Please, all I ask is the chance to make it right. I can make it right, I promise.*'

'*Show me, then,*' *I said.* '*Show me you mean it. Show me you want me.*' *I stared at his shrivelled cock, dangling with his balls in the space where the seat should have been. I had looked forward to beauty, but he had failed me there, too.*

'*N-not here, not like this. I can't!*' *His voice rose in a pathetic wail.*

'*It's this or nothing. Here or nowhere,*' *I told him.* '*By the way, in case you're wondering, you're strapped into a Judas chair.*' *Carefully, I explained how the chair worked. I wanted him to make an informed choice. As I talked, his skin turned grey and clammy with fear. When I explained about the electricity, he lost it completely. Piss dribbled from his cock, splashing on the floor beneath him. The stink of warm urine rose and choked me.*

I slapped him so hard his head cracked against the back board of the Judas chair. He cried out, and tears sprang into his eyes. '*You dirty, filthy baby,*' *I shouted at him.* '*You don't deserve my love. Look at you, pissing and crying like some little girl. You're not a man.*'

Hearing my mother's words coming from my mouth shattered my self-control as nothing else could have done. I kept hitting him, revelling in the crunch of cartilage as his nose collapsed under my fist. I was beside myself with anger. He'd fooled me into thinking he was something he wasn't. I'd thought Paul was strong and brave, intelligent and sensitive. But he was just a stupid, cowardly, lecherous pig, a pathetic excuse for a man. How had I ever let myself imagine he could be a worthy partner? He wasn't even resisting, just sitting there mewing like a kitten, letting me hit him.

Panting with exertion and anger, I finally stopped. I stepped back and stared contemptuously at him, watching his tears wash lines through the blood on his face. 'You brought this on yourself,' I hissed. All my careful plans had gone up in smoke.

But now, I didn't want to give him the second chance I'd given Adam. I didn't want Paul's love, not under any circumstances. He didn't deserve me. I stepped round to the back of the chair and grasped the tongue of the strap. 'No,' he whimpered. 'Please, no.'

'You had your chance,' I said angrily. 'You had your chance and you blew it. You've no one to blame but yourself, coming here and pissing on the floor like a baby who can't control itself.' I pulled the strap, tightening it enough to let me slip it free of the buckle. Then I let it slide free.

Paul's muscles instantly clenched, holding him rigidly in place, a scant half-inch above the spike. I moved round into his line of vision and slowly stripped off, caressing my body, imagining what his hands would have felt like. His eyes bulged with effort as he tried to keep himself in place. I sat down and slowly, deliciously began to rub myself, irresistibly turned on by his fight to stay away from the agonizing spike.

'You could have been doing this,' I sneered, aroused still further by the quivering of his thighs and calves. 'You could have been making love instead of fighting to keep your arse in working order.'

If he'd worked out like Adam had, the pleasure would have lasted longer. As it was, his screams of agony mingled with my groans of pleasure. I came like a Guy Fawkes rocket, fire flashing through me and erupting in an orgasm that had me buckling at the knees.

He tried to pull free, but the barbs just cut deeper into his tender flesh. I lay back in the chair, savouring the waves of pleasure that flowed through me after my orgasm, Paul's moans and screams an extravagant counterpoint to my sexual satisfaction.

As time passed, he sank lower on the spike, and his screams moderated to whimpering groans. To my surprise, I felt sexual desire rise in me again. After the exquisite pleasure of my first orgasm, I wanted my excitement matched again. I reached for the control box for the electrical current to the spike, and pressed the button that completed the circuit. Even with a relatively low current, Paul's body convulsed in an arc that wrenched him almost clear of the spike, a fine spray of blood spattering the floor for a couple of feet around.

I matched the rhythms of our two bodies, the speed and intensity of our mutual excitement keeping perfect pace. I felt my muscles quiver like his as I thrust against my hand. As I came, my body arched in sync with his, my gasps echoed by his last agonized cries before unconsciousness came.

I have to confess I was surprised by how much I enjoyed Paul's punishment. Perhaps because he had deserved so much more than Adam, perhaps because I had had higher expectations of him in the first place, or perhaps simply because I was getting better at what I had to do. Whatever the reason, my second excursion into murder left me feeling as if I'd found my true vocation at last.

9

> We dry up our tears, and ... discover that a transaction
> which, morally considered, was shocking, and without a
> leg to stand upon, when tried by principles of Taste, turns
> out to be a very meritorious performance.

'OK, Andy, it's showtime,' Tony said to the blank screen
of his computer. After Carol had dropped him off, he'd
stumbled upstairs, kicking off his shoes and letting his
quilted baseball jacket lie where it fell on the landing. Pausing only to empty his bladder, he'd burrowed under the
duvet and fallen into the deepest sleep he'd known for
months. When he'd woken, it had been after noon. But for
once, he felt no guilt about the work he should have been
doing. He felt refreshed, excited, elated even. Searching
Stevie McConnell's house had given him a new certainty
that he really did understand what he was doing. He had
known, with absolute clarity, that Handy Andy did not
live like that. And although it wasn't something he could
admit to anyone outside the tight circle of fellow profilers,
there was a real rush in realizing that he could probably
find his way into Handy Andy's head and map a path
through the tortured labyrinth of his unique logic. All he
had to do now was find the key to the door.

In the office, Tony powered his way through the remaining piles of documents, making notes as he went along.
Then he closed the blinds and told his secretary to hold all
his calls. He moved his own chair round the desk so that
it faced the visitor's chair. On the desk to one side, he

placed his tape recorder, still switched off. He walked over to the door and stood with his back to it, contemplating the room. Some poem he'd once read echoed in his mind. Something about a road that divided in a wood, and the importance of choosing the branch less travelled by. For as long as he could recall, his fascinations had led him down the road less travelled by. It was the road that his patients walked, the dark path that led into the under-growth, away from the dappled sunshine of the broad path. 'I need to understand why you chose that road, Andy,' Tony murmured. 'This is what I do best, Andy. You see, I know what draws me to that road. But I'm not like you. I can go back when I want to. I can choose the sunny path. I don't have to be here. All I'm doing is studying your footsteps. Or at least, that's what I tell the world.

'But we know the truth, don't we? You can't hide from me, Andy,' he said softly. 'I'm just like you, you see. I'm your mirror image. I'm the poacher turned gamekeeper. It's only hunting you that keeps me from being you. I'm here, waiting for you. Journey's end.' He stood for a moment longer, savouring the admission he'd made to himself.

Finally, he sat down in his chair and leaned forward, elbows on knees, hands loosely linked. 'OK, Andy,' he said. 'It's just you and me. We're going to skip the prelimi-naries; all that stuff where we do the verbal arm wrestling and you eventually decide to talk to me. We're going straight for it. First off, I want to say how impressed I am. I've never seen a cleaner job. I don't just mean the bodies, I mean the whole thing. Sweet as a nut, you did it. Never a witness. Let me rephrase that. Never anybody seeing any significance in what they saw or heard, because there must have been people who saw or heard something, but they didn't make the connection. How did you manage to be so invisible?' He pressed 'record' on the cassette recorder, then stood up and stepped across to the other chair.

Tony took a deep breath and deliberately relaxed his body. He used breathing techniques to put himself into a light state of trance. He instructed his conscious mind to let go, to allow his higher self to access directly all he knew about Handy Andy and to answer for him. When he spoke, even his voice was different. The timbre was rougher, the tones deeper. 'I blended in. I took care. I watched and I learned.'

Tony swapped chairs again. 'You obviously did a good job of it,' he said. 'How did you choose them?'

Back into Andy's chair. 'I liked them. I knew it would be special with them. I wanted to be like them. They all had good jobs, a nice life. I'm good at learning things, I could have learned to be like them. I could have fitted into their lives.'

'So why kill them?'

'People are stupid. They don't understand me. I was the one they always laughed at, then they learned to be afraid of me. I don't like being laughed at, and I'm tired of people being wary of me, like I'm some animal that's going to go for them. I gave them a chance, but they didn't give me any choice. I had to kill them.'

Tony sank back in his own chair. 'And after you'd done it once, you realized that was the best thing in the world.'

'I felt good. I felt in control. I knew what was going to happen. I'd planned it all out, and it worked!' Tony surprised himself by the degree of enthusiasm that came out. He waited, but nothing more seemed to emerge.

He returned to his own chair. 'Didn't last for long, did it? The pleasure? The sense of power?'

In Andy's chair, he felt at a loss for the first time. Usually, he found role play loosened up his ideas, let his thoughts flow free. But something was clogging this up. That something was clearly at the heart of the issue. Tony moved back to his own seat and thought about it. 'Serial killers act out their fantasies in their crimes. The crime itself never lives up to the fantasy, so it has limited power. Its details are incorporated into the fantasies, which are then realized in a second, often more ritualistic killing. And so on. But as time goes by, the fantasies have less and less staying power. The killings have to get closer and closer together to keep the fantasies fuelled. But your killings don't get closer together, Andy. Why is that?'

He moved across, not hopeful. He allowed his mind to blank, letting his consciousness drift off, hoping it would come up with an answer that might satisfy his idea of Andy. After a few moments, Tony felt himself slipping away from consciousness. All at once, from what felt like a long way away, a deep chuckle rumbled through him. 'That's for me to know and you to find out,' his own voice mocked him.

Tony shook his head like a diver coming to the surface. Dazed, he got to his feet and snapped the blinds open. So much for alternative techniques. What was interesting, however, was the point at which his brain had snagged. This was one of the factors about Handy Andy that was unique. The gaps stayed constant. Even allowing for his use of a camcorder, it was still remarkable.

The line of thought restored Tony's earlier vigour and he decided to take a side trip to the university library's media-studies section where he went through the back numbers of the *Bradfield Evening Sentinel Times* for the appropriate dates. A careful scrutiny of the entertainments pages revealed little in common between the four evenings in question, unless he was prepared to consider that the local art cinema always showed classic British black-and-white comedies on Mondays. Somehow, he couldn't imagine *Passport to Pimlico* fuelling homicidal sexual fantasies. Finally, just after seven, he was ready to start on the profile.

He started with the usual caveat.

The following offender profile is for guidance only and shouldn't be regarded as an identikit portrait. The offender is unlikely to match the profile in every detail, though I would expect there to be a high degree of congruence between the characteristics outlined below and the reality. All of the statements in the profile express probabilities and possibilities, not hard facts.

A serial killer produces signals and indicators in the commission of his crimes. Everything he does is intended, consciously or not, as part of a pattern. Uncovering the underlying pattern reveals the killer's logic. It may not appear logical to us, but to him it is crucial. Because his logic is so idiosyncratic, straightforward traps will not capture him. As he is unique, so must be the means of catching him, interviewing him and reconstructing his acts.

Tony continued the profile with a detailed account of the four victims. He included everything he'd gleaned from the police reports about their domestic circumstances, employment history, reputation among friends and colleagues, habits, physical condition, personality, family relationships, hobbies and social behaviour. Next, he wrote a short résumé of the pathologist's report on each man, the nature of their injuries and a description of the crime scenes. Then he began the crucial process of organizing and arranging his information into meaningful patterns so he could start to draw his conclusions.

None of the four victims had any history of homosexual relationships, as far as can be ascertained. (We cannot exclude a secret homosexual/bisexual orientation, but there is no evidence in any of the four cases to suggest this.) Yet each body was dumped in an area known primarily for its use by the gay community. In particular, the bodies were dumped in spots which are notorious for the consummation of casual sexual encounters. What does this say about the killer?

1.   He is a man who is not comfortable with his own sexuality. He deliberately chooses men who are not openly gay-identified. It may well be that he has made a sexual approach to his victims in the past and has been rebuffed. The killer is almost certainly not an out gay; he probably represses his own sexuality at some personal cost. He probably grew up in an environment where masculinity was highly prized and praised and homosexuality condemned, possibly on religious grounds. If he is in a sexual/domestic relationship, it will be with a woman. And he will almost certainly have sexual problems within that relationship, probably ones of potency.

Tony stared bleakly at the screen. Sometimes he hated the way his job constantly forced him to confront his own problems. Did his own sexual failings mean he was really stuck on the road less travelled by? Was there going to be a night when some woman went too far, when her determination to translate his problem into a comment on her womanhood tipped him over the edge? For Tony, it was a scenario that was all too vivid. That's why Angelica was safe. When she drove him to distraction, he could slam the phone down, rather than slap her face. Or worse. Best stay out of risk, he thought. Don't even think about thinking about Carol Jordan. You've seen it in her eyes, she's interested in more than your mind. Don't even think about it, fuck-up. Get back to work.

2.   He despises those who express their homosexuality openly. At least part of his motivation in using these dumping grounds is to show his contempt for them, as well as to frighten them. He's also demonstrating his superiority; 'Look at me, I can come and

go among you and none of you know me. I can desecrate your places, and you can't stop me.'

3. He is nevertheless familiar with areas where gay men go to socialize and to pick up sexual partners. It may be that his job takes him into the Temple Fields area from time to time, perhaps to make deliveries or to provide some service to businesses. He is fascinated with the gay culture, to the extent that he has scouted out the specific area in Carlton Park where gay cruising goes on.

4. He has a high degree of self-control. He is driving into a populous area and dumping bodies without behaving in a way that draws attention to himself.

'Tell me about it,' Tony said bitterly. He got up and stalked a path from the window to the door. 'I could have written the manual.' Ever since the bullies had started to pick on him, the smallest boy in the street and in his class, he'd learned the harsh lessons of self-control. 'Never show you're hurt, it only encourages them. Never show they've hit the mark, it only reveals your weak points. Learn to be one of the lads. Learn the vocabulary, learn the body language, acquire the attitude. Mix it all together and what do you get? You get a man who hasn't got the remotest idea of who he is. You have a consummate actor, a human impostor who can take on local colour like a chameleon.' The miracle was that it fooled so many people. Brandon clearly thought he was a good bloke. Carol Jordan obviously fancied him. Claire, his secretary, thought he was the best boss she'd ever had. He was passing for human, all right. The only one he couldn't fool was his mother, who still treated him with the thinly disguised contempt which was all he'd ever known from her. His fault his father had left them, and no wonder, according to her. She'd have dumped him in some children's home if it hadn't been for her need to keep in with her parents, the ones who held the purse strings. As it was, she'd dived head first into a career as soon as she'd been able to persuade her mother to mind little Tony. He'd done his best to be good, as Granny had instructed him, but it wasn't always easy. She wasn't a bad woman, just constrained by her own upbringing into the belief that children should be seen and not heard. His grandfather's response to domestic tyranny was to escape to the betting shop, the bowling green and the Legion. Tony had swiftly learned self-control the hard way. Was that what had happened to Andy, too? Rubbing his hand across eyes surprisingly damp, Tony threw himself back into his chair and started typing frantically.

5. His domestic and work situation allows him to be free on Monday evenings, and he does not expect to be spotted in Temple Fields by anyone who knows him. This throws up several possibilities: he may have chosen Monday nights specifically because it's his night off work or because his wife/girlfriend is away from home on Monday nights; he may have decided to kill on Mondays because the first time was a Monday and it worked out for him and now has superstitious power; or he may have decided to keep on killing on Mondays in the hope that it will skew the investigation. He is obviously intelligent, and such careful planning should not be presumed to be beyond him.

Tony paused for thought, flicking through the pages of notes he'd made. He wasn't thinking like Handy Andy yet, but the elusive mind was getting closer and closer. He wondered again if his involvement in the twisted logic of killers was a surrogacy, the only thing that prevented him from joining their number. God knows, there were times when the inevitable drive that surged through their heads seemed attractive. And there were times enough when he'd felt murderous rage, though it was usually turned against himself rather than the person he was in bed with. 'Enough, already,' Tony said aloud, and returned to the glowing screen.

The offender is an organized serial killer, who is managing to maintain a constant eight-week gap between killings. This consistency is unusual in itself, since the normal pattern is that the space between murders decreases as they lose their power to satisfy the killer's fantasies. One reason for the maintenance of this gap may be that he spends so long stalking his victim before the kill. Thus the delights of anticipation, coupled with the savour of his previous kills, acts as a brake. I also believe that the killer is using his camcorder to record his activities and that this is also fuelling his fantasies between kills.

Tony stopped to consider what he had written. The stumbling block. His analysis probably looked good enough to convince the lay person, but he was far from satisfied with it. But no amount of dredging of his mind or his data could come up with a better explanation. With a sigh, he continued.

What is the primary intent of his killings? We can rule out killing in the course of criminal activity, such as armed robbery or burglary. We can also rule out emotional, selfish or cause-specific killings, such as self-defence, compassion, assassination or domestic disputes. This places the killings in the category of sexual homicides.

The chosen victims all fall into the low-risk category. In other words, they all had occupations and lifestyles that didn't make them vulnerable targets. The flip side of this is that the killer has to take high-level risks to capture and kill them. What does this tell us about the killer?

1. He is operating under extremely high stress levels.

2. He plans his kills very carefully. He cannot afford to make mistakes, because if he does, his victims will escape and put him at risk, both physically and legally. He is almost certainly a stalker. He chooses his victims carefully, and studies their lives in detail. Interestingly, so far he has not been thwarted in his choice of evening. Is this a result of careful planning, prearrangement or just luck? We know that the third victim, Gareth Finnegan, told his girlfriend he was going on a lads' night out, but none of his male friends or colleagues seemed to know anything about it, and it is not clear whether he was abducted from his home or if the contact took place at a prearranged point. It may be that the killer has had prior arrangements to meet each of his victims, either at their homes or elsewhere. He may even be posing as an insurance salesman or something similar, though I feel it's unlikely that he would have the people skills to do such a job successfully for a living.

3. He likes the extra excitement that walking out on the high wire gives him. He needs that buzz.

4. He must have some areas of emotional maturity in his make-up that allow him to hold himself under control in these highly stressful situations. This may also allow him to buck the poor work-history pattern so common among serial offenders. (See below.)

Most serial offences demonstrate a degree of escalation, indicating the killer's need for more thrills, better execution of his fantasies. Like a roller coaster, each high needs to be bigger to compensate for the inevitable low that has preceded . . .

Tony looked up, startled. What was that noise? It had sounded like the door to the open-plan outer office, but at this time of night, there shouldn't be anyone on this floor. Nervously, he pushed himself away from the computer desk, steering his chair across the carpet on silent castors till he was behind his desk and out of the pool of light shed by the lamp beside the computer. He held his breath and listened. Silence. The tension gradually began to ooze away. Then, abruptly, a line of light appeared under his office door.

The metallic taste of fear gripped Tony. The nearest thing to an offensive weapon on his desk was a chunk of agate he used as a paperweight. He snatched it up and moved stealthily out of his chair.

When Carol opened the door, she was taken aback to find Tony halfway across the room, hefting a rock in his hand. 'It's me,' she yelped.

Tony's arms dropped to his side. 'Oh shit,' he said.

Carol grinned. 'Who were you expecting? Burglars? Journalists? The bogeyman?'

Tony relaxed. 'I'm sorry,' he said. 'You spend all day trying to get inside some nutter's head and you end up as paranoid as he is.'

'Nutter,' Carol mused. 'Now would that be some technical term you psychologists use?'

'Only inside these four walls,' Tony said, walking back to his desk and putting the agate back where it belonged. 'To what do I owe the pleasure?'

'Since British Telecom don't seem to be able to connect us, I thought I'd better come round personally,' Carol replied, pulling up a chair. 'I left a message on your machine at home this morning. I assumed you'd already left for work, but you weren't here either. I tried again around four, but there was no reply from your extension. At least, I assume that's why the switchboard operator said, "I'm putting you through now," and I ended up in a black hole.

And, of course, now the switchboard have all gone home and I never thought to ask for your direct line.'

'And you a detective,' Tony teased.

'That's my excuse, anyway. Actually, I couldn't face another minute in Scargill Street.'

'Want to talk about it?'

'Only if I can talk with my mouth full,' Carol said. 'I'm starving. Could you go a quick curry?'

Tony glanced at his computer screen, then back at Carol's drawn face and tired eyes. He liked her, even though he didn't want to get close, and he needed her on his side. 'Just let me save this file, and I'm out of here. I can come back later and finish this.'

Twenty minutes later they were attacking onion bhajis and chicken pakora in an Asian café in Greenholm. The other customers were students and those of the terminally right-on tendency who hadn't quite adjusted to the fact they were no longer studying anything except political correctness. 'It's not exactly Good Food Guide, but it's cheap and cheerful, and the service is quick,' Tony apologized.

'Fine by me. I'm more egg on toast than Egon Ronay. My brother got the gourmet genes in our family,' Carol said. She glanced quickly around her. Their table for two was less than a foot away from the next. 'Did you bring me here deliberately so we couldn't talk about work? Some psychologist's ploy to refresh my mind?'

Tony's eyes widened. 'I didn't even think of that. You're right, of course, we can't talk about it in here.'

Carol's smile lit up her eyes. 'You can have no idea how much pleasure that gives me.'

They ate in silence for a few minutes. Tony broke the silence. That way, he stayed in control of the subject. 'What made you decide to be a copper?'

Carol raised her eyebrows. 'Because I like oppressing the underprivileged and hassling racial minorities?' she tried.

Tony smiled. 'I don't think so.'

She pushed her plate to one side and sighed. 'Youthful idealism,' she said. 'I had this crazy idea that the police should be there to serve and protect society from lawlessness and anarchy.'

'It's not such a crazy idea. Believe me, if you dealt with the people I used to handle, you'd feel relieved that they weren't on the streets.'

'Oh, the theory's fine. It's just the practice that's such a bummer. It all started when I read sociology at Manchester. I specialized in the sociology of organizations, and all my contemporaries despised the police force as a corrupt, racist, sexist organization whose sole role was to preserve the illusory comfort of the middle classes. To some extent, I agreed with them. The difference was that they wanted to attack institutions from the outside, whereas I've always believed that if you want fundamental change, it has to come from inside.'

Tony grinned. 'You little subversive, you!'

'Yeah, well, I guess I didn't realize what I was getting into. David knocking out Goliath was a piece of piss compared with trying to change things in the police.'

'Tell me about it,' Tony said with feeling. 'This national task force could revolutionize the clear-up rate on serious crimes, but the way some senior officers carry on, you'd think I was setting up a scheme to allow paedophiles to retrain as child minders.'

Carol giggled. 'You mean, you'd rather be back in the locked ward with your nutters?'

'Carol, sometimes I feel like I've never left. You've no idea what a refreshing change it is to work with people like you and John Brandon.'

Before Carol could reply, the waiter arrived with their main courses. As she spooned out lamb and spinach, chicken karahi and pilau rice, Carol said, 'Does your job create the same problems with having a private life as the police service does?'

Instantly defensive, Tony answered with a question. 'How do you mean?'

'Like you said earlier, you get obsessed with the job. You spend your time dealing with shitheads and animals –'

'And that's just your colleagues,' Tony butted in.

'Yeah, right. And you come home at night after dealing with broken bodies and fractured lives and you're expected to sit down and watch the soaps and act like normal people do.'

'And you can't because your head's still plugged into the horrors of the day,' Tony finished. 'And with *your* job, you have the added complication of shift work.'

'Exactly. So, do you get the same problems?'

Was she asking out of idle curiosity or was this an oblique way of finding out about his private life? Sometimes Tony wished he could just switch off the part of his head that had to analyse every statement, every gesture, every intricate piece of body language and just revel in the pleasure of eating dinner with someone who seemed to enjoy his company. Suddenly aware that he had left too long a pause between the question and the answer, Tony said, 'I'm probably even worse at switching off than you. Men generally seem to get much more obsessive than women. I mean, how many female train spotters, stamp collectors or football fanatics do you know?'

'And that interferes in your personal relationships?' Carol persisted.

'Well, none of them have ever gone the distance,' Tony said, struggling to keep his voice light. 'I don't know if that's down to the job, or to me. Mostly, the last thing they've screamed at me as they walked out the door hasn't been, "you and your bloody nutters", so I guess it must be me. How about you? How do you handle the problems of the job?'

Carol's fork continued its journey to her mouth and she chewed and swallowed her mouthful of curry before she answered. 'I've found that men aren't very sympathetic towards shifts unless they do them too. You know, you're never there with the tea on the table when they've got to rush out to that vital squash match. Add to that the difficulty of getting them to understand why the job drives you inside your head and what are you left with? Junior doctors, other coppers, fire fighters, ambulance drivers. And in my experience, there aren't many of them who want a relationship with an equal. I guess the job takes too much out of us for us to have much left over. The last guy I was involved with was a doctor, and all he wanted to do when he wasn't working was sleep, fuck and party.'

'And you wanted more?'

'I wanted the occasional conversation, maybe even a movie or a night out at the theatre. But I put up with it because I loved him.'

'So what made you end it?'

Carol stared down at her plate. 'Thanks for the compliment, but I didn't. When I moved up here, he decided that driving up and down the motorway was a waste of good shagging time, so he dumped me for a nurse. Now it's just me and the cat. He doesn't seem to mind the irregular hours.'

'Ah,' Tony said. He had heard the real pain under the surface, but for once, all his professional skills didn't seem adequate to the response.

'How about you? You involved with anyone?' Carol asked.

Tony shook his head and carried on eating.

'Nice bloke like you, I'd have thought you'd have been snapped up ages ago,' Carol said, the tease in her tone covering something Tony wished he was imagining.

'Ah, but you've only seen the charming side. When the moon's full, I sprout hair on the palms of my hands and bay at the moon.' Tony leered melodramatically at Carol. 'I am not what I appear to be, young woman,' he growled.

'Oh, Grandmamma, what big teeth you've got!' Carol said in falsetto.

'All the better to eat my curry with,' Tony laughed. He knew this was the point where he could have moved the relationship forward, but he had spent too long constructing his defences against precisely these moments of weakness to let them down that easily. Besides, he told himself, he had no need of a relationship with her. He had Angelica and bitter experience had taught him that was all he could handle and still function.

'So how did you get into this soul-destroying line of work?' Carol asked.

'I discovered while I was working on my DPhil that I hated getting up on my hind legs and talking to an audience, which kind of ruled out academic work. So I went into clinical practice,' Tony said, slipping easily into a flow of anecdotes about his work. He felt himself relax, like a man walking on a frozen lake who realizes he's back on dry land.

They spent the rest of the meal on the safer ground of their careers, and Carol asked the waiter for the bill when he came to clear off the table. 'I'm picking up the tab, OK? Nothing to do with feminism; you're a legitimate business expense,' Carol said.

As they walked back to Tony's office, he said, 'So, back to work. Tell me about your day.'

The swift switch away from the personal back to the case confirmed to Carol the need to play it cool with Tony. She'd never seen anyone back off so fast at gentle flirtation. It was puzzling, all the more since she sensed he liked her. And she had no doubts about her capacity to attract men. At least tracking Handy Andy with him gave her space and time to build a bridge between them. 'We got a break this morning. At least, that's what we're all hoping.'

Tony stopped abruptly and turned to face Carol. 'What kind of a break?' he demanded.

'Don't worry, you're not being ignored,' Carol said. 'It's something that would be a minor detail in most investigations, but because we've got so little to go on here, it's got everybody excited. There was a torn fragment of leather on a nail by the gate in the Queen of Hearts's yard. Forensic did a rush job on it, and it turns out that it's very unusual. It's deerskin, and it comes from Russia.'

'Oh, my good God,' Tony said softly. He turned away and took a couple of steps. 'Don't tell me, let me guess. You can't get it in this country, and you'd probably need to send someone to Russia to source it, it's so obscure. Am I right?'

'How the hell did you know that?' Carol asked, catching him up and grabbing his sleeve.

'I've been expecting something like this,' he said simply.

'Like what?'

'An outrageous red herring that'll have the entire police force running around like headless chickens.'

'You think this is a red herring?' Carol almost shouted. 'Why?'

Tony rubbed his hands over his face and ran them through his hair. 'Carol, this guy has been so careful. He's been almost clinical in his obsession with leaving no clues. Serial killers have typically got high IQs, and Handy Andy is certainly one of the cleverest I've ever come across, either personally or in the whole literature. Yet suddenly, out of nowhere we get not just any old clue, but a clue so obscure that it could only possibly be left by a tiny segment of the population. And you're standing here telling me you think this is for real? That's exactly what he's trying to achieve. I bet the lot of you have been running around like blue-tailed flies all day trying to suss out where this obscure piece of Russian leather came from, haven't you? Oh, and don't tell me, let me guess. I bet there's now a whole squad tracking back through Stevie McConnell's life trying to establish where the hell he got it from.'

Carol stared at him. It seemed so blindingly obvious when he explained it like that. Yet not one of them had questioned the validity of the leather scrap.

'Am I right?' Tony asked, more gently this time.

Carol pulled a face. 'Not a whole squad. Just me and Don Merrick and a couple of DCs. I've spent most of the day on the phone talking to governing bodies in weightlifting and body-building, trying to establish if McConnell's ever been on a national or regional team that either competed in Russia or competed against Russians. And Don and the lads have been grilling travel agencies trying to check if he's ever been on holiday there.'

'Oh, Christ,' Tony groaned. 'And?'

'Five years ago, he was one of a team of weightlifters from the North West who competed in an event in what was then Leningrad.'

Tony took a deep breath. 'The poor unlucky bastard,' he said. 'I don't expect the idea that this was deliberately planted to have occurred to any of you,' he added. 'I don't mean that patronizingly. I realize how much closer you are to all of this and how desperately you want to catch this bastard. I just wish someone had told me earlier, before it assumed this major significance for everyone.'

'I did *try* to phone you this morning,' Carol said. 'You still haven't said where you were.'

Tony held his hands up. 'I'm sorry. I'm overreacting. I was in bed, asleep, with the phones turned off. I was exhausted after last night, and I knew I couldn't concentrate on writing the profile unless I had some sleep. I should have checked my answering machine when I got up. Sorry, I shouldn't have had a go.'

Carol grinned. 'I'll let you off this time. Just save the fearsome bit for when we catch Handy Andy, huh?'

Tony pulled a face. 'Shouldn't that be "if"?'

He looked so vulnerable and fallible, his shoulders slumped, his head down, that Carol's impulses overrode the decision she'd taken only minutes before to play it cool. She stepped forward and pulled Tony into a tight hug. 'If anyone can do it, you can,' she whispered, rubbing the side of her head against his chin like a cat marking its territory.

Brandon stared at Tom Cross, his face a mask of horror. 'You did *what?*' he demanded.

'I searched McConnell's house,' Cross said belligerently.

'I thought I said categorically that we had no right to do that? No judge in the land is going to accept that arrest for common assault in the street gives sufficient grounds for suspicion of murder.'

Cross smiled. It was a rictus that would have raised a Rottweiler's hackles. 'With respect, sir, that was then. Once Inspector Jordan had established that McConnell had been to Russia, the picture changed. Not a lot of people have had access to obscure Russian leather jackets, after all. It puts him in the frame. And there's more than one JP around that owes me one.'

'You should have cleared it with me,' Brandon said. 'The last order I gave on the subject was no search.'

'I tried, sir, but you were in a meeting with the Chief,' Cross said sweetly. 'I thought I'd better strike while the iron was hot, being as how we don't have him banged up indefinitely.'

'So you wasted more time searching McConnell's house,' Brandon said bitterly. 'Don't you think you and your men could have been better employed?'

'I haven't told you yet what we found,' Cross said.

Brandon felt his chest constrict. He wasn't a man given to premonitions, but the sinking foreboding that gripped him now was as palpable as any solid fact he'd ever examined. 'Think very carefully about what you say next, Superintendent,' he said cautiously.

A momentary frown of puzzlement flashed over Cross's features, but he was too full of the message he bore to worry about the ACC's words. 'We've got him, sir,' he said. 'Bang to rights. We found one of Gareth Finnegan's firm's Christmas cards in McConnell's bedroom, and a sweater that's a dead ringer for the one Adam Scott's bird says was missing from his house. Plus a traffic ticket with Damien Connolly's badge number on it. Add that to the Russian connection, and I think it's time to charge the little arse bandit.'

Of course, the discovery that one has a natural bent for something does not necessarily mean one should pursue it blindly. While I was disposing of Paul's body, this time in a dark doorway in an alley in Temple Fields, I had already decided who my next target would be. But even after so magnificent an experience as the one I'd just shared with Paul, I had no intention of repeating it with Gareth.

It was going to be third time lucky. Gareth, I already knew, was a man of rich and fertile sexual imagination. Even as I was digitizing Paul's pathetic performance into the computer, I was mourning the fact that, thanks to Gareth, I would never have the opportunity to perfect the extraordinary talent I had discovered in myself. With the resources at my command, I've been making movies like I've never seen. The ultimate snuff stuff. If I could have marketed them, I would have made a fortune. I know there's a market out there. Plenty of people would pay a lot of money to watch Paul fuck me in his death spasms on the Judas chair. And as for what I've done with Adam ... Let's just say that no one's ever seen sixty-nine like it.

As a treat, I went to the cemetery where Adam had been buried a few weeks before. The funeral had featured on the local television news, which I'd video-taped and studied so I could be fairly sure where the grave was. After dark, I made my way through the graves, and found Adam's within twenty minutes. I opened the can of red spray paint

I'd brought with me and sprayed 'WANKER' on one side of the grey granite, and 'POOFTER' on the other side. That should give the police something to occupy their minds.

The following evening, while I was waiting for Gareth to emerge from the firm of solicitors where he was a salaried partner, I whiled away the time with the hyperbole of the Bradfield Evening Sentinel Times. This time, I'd made the front page.

GAY KILLER STRIKES AGAIN?

The mutilated body of a naked man was found this morning in Bradfield's gay village.

The murder victim had been dumped in the fire-exit doorway of the gay club Shadowlands in an alley off Canal Street in the notorious Temple Fields district.

This is the second time in two months that the body of a naked man has been discovered in the gay cruising area.

Now locals fear a perverted serial killer is stalking the city's large homosexual community.

Today's gruesome discovery was made by nightclub owner Danny Surtees, 37, as he arrived for a meeting with his accountant.

He said, 'I always go into the club through the fire door at the side. I park my car in the alley. This morning, the door was blocked by something covered by a couple of black bin bags.

'When I grabbed hold of the bags to try and pull them away from the door, they just came away in my hands and I saw there was a body under them.

'He was horribly injured. There was no way he was still alive. I'm going to have nightmares about this for the rest of my life.'

Mr Surtees said the doorway had been clear when

he locked up his club just after three this morning.

The victim, said to be in his early thirties, has not yet been identified. Police describe him as white, 5ft 11ins, slightly built, with dark-brown collar-length hair and hazel eyes. He has an old scar from an appendicectomy.

A police spokesman said, 'We believe the man was killed elsewhere and the body dumped in the alley between three and eight a.m.

'We would urge anyone who was in the Temple Fields area last night to come forward for the purpose of elimination. All information will be treated in the strictest confidence.

'At this stage of our enquiry, there is no evidence to connect this killing with the murder two months ago of Adam Scott.'

Carl Fellowes, the full-time worker at the Bradfield Gay and Lesbian Centre, said today, 'The police say that they don't think there's a connection between these two murders.

'I don't know what makes me more worried on behalf of the city's gay community – the thought that there's one nutter out there killing gay men, or the thought that there are two of them.'

I didn't know whether to laugh or cry. One thing was clear, though. PC Plod was a long way from covering himself in glory over this case. I'd obviously done a good job covering my tracks.

I folded up my newspaper, finished my cappuccino and signalled for my bill. Any minute now, Gareth would emerge from his office and walk through the rush-hour streets to the tram. I wanted to be ready for him. I had something really special planned for him tonight, and I wanted to make sure he was home alone to enjoy it.

10

> The world in general, gentlemen, are very bloody-minded; and all they want in a murder is a copious effusion of blood; gaudy display in this point is enough for them. But the enlightened connoisseur is more refined in his taste.

Penny Burgess topped up her glass of Californian Chardonnay from the bottle in the fridge and walked back through to her living room in time to hear the headlines on the BBC local news. Nothing fresh to worry about, she thought with relief. An armed robbery she could catch up with first thing in the morning. The police were still questioning a man in connection with the gay serial killings, but no charges had been laid yet. Penny sipped her wine and lit a cigarette.

They were going to have to move soon, she thought. By morning, they'd either have had to charge him with something or let him go. So far, no one had got a sniff of the suspect's identity, which was pretty remarkable. The whole pack had been leaning heavily on their personal police contacts, but for once, the reservoir of information had resolutely refused to leak. Penny decided she'd better take a look at the magistrates' court lists in the morning. There was an outside chance that the cops had something fairly innocuous to charge their suspect with so they could hang on to him while they dug around for the evidence they needed to make the serial killing charges stick.

As the news cut away to the weather forecast, the phone

rang. Penny reached over to the occasional table by the sofa and grabbed the receiver. 'Hello?' she said.

'Penny? It's Kevin.'

Hallelujah, Penny thought, sitting up and grinding out her cigarette. All she said, however, was, 'Kevin, my man. How's it hanging?' She raked in her handbag for a pencil and her notebook.

'Something's come up you might be interested in,' the police inspector said cautiously.

'It wouldn't be the first time,' Penny said suggestively. Her occasional sexual encounters with the very married Kevin Matthews had provided her with more than an inside track on Bradfield Metropolitan Police. He'd turned out to be one of the best lovers she'd ever had. She just wished he could overcome his Catholic guilt more often.

'This is serious,' Kevin protested.

'So was I, superstud.'

'Listen, do you want this info or not?'

'Definitely. Especially if it's the name of the guy you've got in custody for the Queer Killings.'

She heard the sharp intake of breath. 'You know I can't tell you that. There are limits.'

Penny sighed. It was the story of their relationship. 'OK, so what can you tell me?'

'Popeye's been suspended.'

'He's off the case?' Penny asked, her mind racing. Tom Cross? Suspended?

'He's off the *job*, Pen. He's been sent home pending disciplinary action.'

'Who by?' Jesus, this was a story and a half. Just what had Popeye Cross been up to this time? She felt a momentary panic. What if he'd been caught out giving the suspect's name to one of her rivals? She almost missed Kevin's reply.

'John Brandon.'

'What the hell for?'

'Nobody's saying,' Kevin said. 'But the last thing he did before he saw Brandon was to carry out a search of our suspect's house.'

'A legal search?' Penny probed.

'Far as I know he had grounds under PACE,' Kevin said cautiously.

'So what's going on, Kevin? Has Popeye been planting evidence, or what?'

'I don't know, Pen,' Kevin said plaintively. 'Look, I've got to go. If I hear anything else, I'll call you, OK?'

'OK. Thanks, Kev. You're a star, you know.'

'Yeah, well. I'll speak to you soon.'

The line went dead. Penny dumped the phone back on the base unit and jumped to her feet. She hurried through to her bedroom, pulling off her dressing gown on the way. Five minutes later, she was running down the two flights of stairs from her flat to the underground garage. In the car, she checked the address in her A–Z, then set off, mentally rehearsing what she was going to say on the doorstep.

It was Tony who had pulled away from the clinch first. His body withdrew from hers in a gesture that rendered four inches forty.

Trying to keep it light, to cover the awkwardness that had sprung up between them, Carol said, 'Sorry, you just looked like you needed a hug.'

'Nothing wrong with that,' Tony said stiffly. 'We use it all the time in group therapy.'

They stood for a moment, eyes not quite meeting. Then Carol moved to Tony's side, slipped a hand through his unyielding arm and steered him forwards across the university courtyard. 'So when do I get to look at this profile?'

The conversation was on safe ground again, but Carol was still too close for comfort. Tony could feel the tension inside him, like a cold hand squeezing his chest. He forced himself to speak in a calm, normal voice. 'I want to do another couple of hours' work now, and I'll get stuck into it again first thing in the morning. I should have a draft ready for you by early afternoon. How does three o'clock sound to you?'

'Fine. Look, do you mind if I stick around now while you're working? I could do with rereading some of those statements, and I'll get no peace if I go back to Scargill Street.'

Tony looked doubtful. 'I suppose.'

'I promise not to molest you, Dr Hill,' Carol teased.

'Damn,' Tony said, snapping his fingers in mock-disappointment. Look at you, he thought cynically. Passing for human, sure of all the moves. 'Actually, it's not that. I'm only hesitating because I'm not used to working with someone else in the room.'

'You won't know I'm there.'

'I doubt that very much,' Tony said. She might read that as a compliment, but he knew the truth.

Penny pressed the doorbell of the mock-Tudor detached house in one of south Bradfield's more select streets. Even on a superintendent's salary, it should have been beyond Tom Cross's reach. But Popeye's reputation for being lucky had been enhanced a few years back when he'd won a high five-figure sum on the pools. The subsequent party had passed into police mythology. Now, it looked like he'd dropped his lucky pixie somewhere along the road.

A light snapped on in the hallway and someone lumbered towards the door, turned into an amorphous lump by the stained glass. '*Friday the Thirteenth* meets *Hallowe'en*,' Penny muttered under her breath as she heard the lock turn. The door cracked open a suspicious few inches. Penny angled her head round to smile at the shape behind the door.

'Superintendent Cross,' she said, the white cloud of her

breath meeting the swirl of smoke issuing from the door. 'Penny Burgess, *Sentinel Times*.'

'I know who you are,' Cross snarled, the slur of drink evident in those few words. 'What the hell do you want, coming round here this time of night?'

'I hear you've had a bit of a problem at work,' Penny tried.

'You hear wrong then, madam. Now, bugger off.'

'Look, it'll be all over the media tomorrow. You're going to be under siege. The *Sentinel Times* has always supported you, Mr Cross. We've been on your side all through this investigation. I'm not some visiting fireman from London, up here to put the boot in. If you've been sidelined, our readers have got a right to hear your side of the story.' The door was still open. If she'd managed to say that much without him slamming it shut in her face, the chances were that she was going to get something usable out of him.

'What makes you think I'm off the case?' Cross asked defiantly.

'I heard you've been suspended. I don't know why, and that's the reason I wanted to hear your side of it, before we get fed the official line.'

Cross scowled, his gooseberry eyes seeming to pop even further out. 'I've got nothing to say,' he told her, grudging every syllable.

'Not even off the record? You're willing to stand by and let them trash your reputation after all you've done for the force?'

Cross opened the door wider and looked down his drive towards the street. 'You on your own?' he asked.

'Not even my newsdesk know I'm here. I only just heard.'

'You'd better come in a minute.'

Penny stepped across the threshold into a hall that looked like a Laura Ashley sample book. At the far end of the hall, a door was half open, the television voices distinct even at that distance. Cross steered her in the opposite direction, into a long sitting room. When he switched the lights on, Penny's eyes were assaulted by more patterns than a knitting shop. The only thing the curtains, carpets, rugs, wallpaper, frieze and scatter cushions had in common was that they were all shades of green and cream. 'What a lovely room,' she stammered.

'You think so? I reckon it's bloody hideous. The wife says it's the best money can buy, which is the only argument I've heard for staying potless,' Cross grumbled, heading for a cocktail cabinet. He poured himself a stiff drink from a decanter, then, as an afterthought, said, 'You'll not be wanting one, with you having the car.'

'That's right,' Penny said, forcing the warmth into her voice. 'Can't take chances with your lads out on the roads.'

'You want to know why them gutless bastards have suspended me?' he demanded belligerently, thrusting his head forward like a hungry tortoise.

Penny nodded, not daring to take out her notebook.

'Because they'd rather listen to some poncey bloody doctor than a proper copper, that's why.'

If Penny had been a dog, her ears would have been standing to attention. As it was, she settled for a polite raise of the eyebrows. 'A doctor?' she said.

'They've brought this wanker of a shrink in to do our job. And he says the arse bandit we've got banged up is innocent, so it's bollocks to the evidence. Now, I've been a copper for twenty-odd years, and I trust my instincts. We've got the bastard, I can feel it in my water. All I did was try to make sure he stayed behind bars till we nail down all the bloody loose ends.' Cross downed his drink and banged his empty tumbler on the cabinet. 'And they've got the fucking nerve to suspend *me*!'

Manufacturing evidence, then. Although she was desperate to know more about the mysterious doctor, Penny sensed that she'd better let Cross air his grievances first. 'What did they say you'd done?' she asked.

'I've done nothing wrong,' he said, pouring another massive slug from the decanter. 'Trouble with bloody Brandon is he's been flying a desk for so long, he's forgotten what the job's about. Instinct, that's what it's about. Instinct and hard bloody work. Not some fucking trick cyclist with a head full of daft bloody notions like a fucking social worker.'

'Who is this guy, then?' Penny asked.

'Dr Tony bloody Hill. From the fucking Home Office. Sits in his ivory tower and tells us how to catch villains. He's got no more idea of coppering than I have of nuclear bloody physics. But the good doctor says, let the poofter go, so Brandon says yes, sir, no, sir, three bags full, sir. And just because I don't agree, I'm out on my arse.' Cross swallowed more whisky, his face flushed with anger and drink. 'Anybody'd think we were dealing with bloody Mastermind here, not some fucking dumbshit arse bandit who's had a bit of luck so far. You don't need smartarses with bloody "doctor" in front of their name to catch scum like this. All you do is give the homicidal little fairy ideas above his station.'

'It's fair to say, then, that you don't agree with the line the investigation's taking?' Penny asked.

Cross snorted. 'That's one way of putting it. You mark my words, if they let this little fucker back on the streets, we'll be looking at another body.'

To Tony's surprise, Carol proved to be true to her word. She sat at his desk, working her way through the pile of statements while he carried on working at his computer. Far from distracting him, he found her presence curiously soothing. He had no trouble picking up the profile where he'd left off earlier.

Like a roller coaster, each high needs to be bigger to compensate for the inevitable low that has preceded it. In this instance, there are three principal signs of escalation. The wounds to the throat have become increasingly deep and assured. The sexual mutilation has developed from a few tentative cuts in the genital region to full-scale amputation. And the bites he inflicts then cuts away have increased in number and in depth. Yet he has managed to stay sufficiently in control to cover his tracks.

It is difficult to assess whether or not the level of torture he is administering is escalating, since he seems to be using different torture methods in each case. The fact that he needs the stimulus of these different methods is, however, in itself a form of escalation.

Judging by the pathologist's report, the sequence of events would seem to be:

1. Capture, using handcuffs and ligatures round the ankles.

2. Torture, including sexually motivated acts such as biting and sucking.

3. The fatal blow to the throat.

4. Postmortem genital mutilation.

What does this tell us about the killer?

1. He has sophisticated and highly developed fantasies, which he is exploring through his torture methods.

2. He has a killing place. The amounts of blood and other bodily fluids generated by his activities could not be readily cleaned away from a normal domestic environment; it would be taking far more of a chance than his other cautious behaviour indicates. It will almost certainly have facilities for him to clean himself up after his killings, and power so he can run lights and a camcorder. We should be looking for something like a lock-up garage, a building that is secure but probably has running water and electricity. It may also be in an isolated location, thus avoiding the possibility

of his victims' screams being overheard. (He will almost certainly remove any gags while he is torturing them; he will want to hear them scream and plead for mercy.)

3. He is obsessed with torture, and obviously has enough manual skills to construct his own engines of torture. He does not appear to have either medical or butchery skills, judging by the clumsy and tentative nature of the early throat-cutting and genital mutilation.

Tony turned away from the screen and glanced across at Carol. She was totally absorbed in her reading, the familiar frown line between her eyes. Was he being crazy to back off from what she appeared to be offering? More than anyone he'd ever been involved with she would understand the pressures of his job, the highs and lows that accompanied getting inside the head of a sociopath. She was intelligent and sensitive, and if she committed herself as thoroughly to a relationship as she did to her career, she might just be strong enough to work through his problems with him rather than use them as a stick to beat him with.

Suddenly aware of his eyes on her, Carol looked up and flashed him a tired smile. In that instant, Tony made his mind up. No way. He had enough problems dealing with the crap in his head without allowing anyone else to make it a hostage to fortune. Carol was just too sharp to let her any nearer. 'Going OK?' she asked.

'I'm starting to get a feel for him,' Tony admitted.

'That can't be a very pleasant place to be,' Carol said.

'No, but it's what I'm paid for.'

Carol nodded. 'And I guess it's satisfying. And exciting?'

Tony smiled wryly. 'You could say that. I sometimes wonder if that makes me as twisted as them.'

Carol laughed. 'You and me both. They say the best thief-takers are the ones who get inside the heads of the villains. So if I'm going to be the best at what I do, I have to think like a villain. That doesn't mean I want to do what they do, though.'

Strangely comforted by her words, Tony turned back to his screen.

The time the killer spends with his victims can also provide pointers. In three of the four cases, the killer appears to have made contact in the early evening and to have dumped the bodies in the early hours of the following morning. Interestingly, in the third case, he spent far longer with his victim, apparently keeping him alive for the greater part of two days. This was the killing that took place over Christmas.

It may be that he is normally unable to spend long with his victims because of the other demands of his life, demands which altered over the Christmas period. These are more likely to be work-related demands than domestic ones, though it is possible that he is in a relationship with someone who returned alone to their family at Christmas, thus giving him time to spend with his victim. Another possibility is that the extended time he spent with Gareth Finnegan was a bizarre Christmas present to himself, a reward for the good performance of his previous 'work'.

The short space of time that elapses between the killings and the dumping of the bodies suggests that he does not use drink or drugs to any significant degree during the torture and murders. He would not risk being stopped by the police for erratic driving while he has a body in the boot, whether alive or dead. Also, although he appears to have used his victims' cars on occasion, it is clear that he also has a vehicle of his own. The chances are that this is a reasonably new vehicle in good condition, since he can't afford to take the chance of being stopped in a routine police check.

Tony hit the 'save' key on his computer and sat back with a satisfied smile. This was as good a place to stop as any. Tomorrow morning, he'd complete the detailed checklist of characteristics he'd expect to find in Handy Andy, and outline proposals for potential courses of action by the police officers on the case.

'You done?' Carol asked.

He turned to see her leaning back in the chair, her pile of folders closed. 'I didn't realize you'd finished,' he said.

'Ten minutes ago. I didn't want to disturb the flying fingers.'

Tony hated others studying him the way he studied them. The idea of being a patient on the receiving end of his own probing was one of those nightmares that he woke from in a sweat. 'I've had it for tonight,' he said, making a copy of his file on a floppy disc which he then pocketed.

'I'll give you a lift home,' Carol said.

'Thanks,' Tony said, getting to his feet. 'I can never be bothered bringing the car into town. To tell you the truth, I don't much like driving.'

'Can't say I blame you. The city traffic's hell on wheels.'

When Carol pulled up outside Tony's house, she said, 'Any chance of a cup of tea? Not to mention a pee?'

While Tony put the kettle on, Carol slipped upstairs to the bathroom. She came downstairs to the sound of her own voice issuing from his answering machine. She paused at the foot of the stairs, spying on him as he leaned against his desk, pen and paper in hand, listening to his messages. She enjoyed her growing sense of familiarity with his face and the lines of his body. Her voice ended and the machine beeped. 'Hi Tony, it's Pete,' the next voice announced. 'I've got to be in Bradfield next Thursday. Any chance of a bed and a beer Wednesday night? Congratulations on getting on board the Queer Killer investigation, by the way. Hope you catch the bastard.' Beep. 'Anthony, my darling.

Wherever can you be? I'm lying here, longing for you. We've got some unfinished business, lover boy.'

At the sound of the voice, Tony straightened up and he turned to stare at the machine. The voice was husky, sexy, intimate. 'Don't think you can –' Tony's hand shot out and cut the voice off abruptly.

So much for not being involved with anyone, Carol thought bitterly. She stepped forward through the doorway. 'Let's just forget the tea. I'll see you tomorrow,' she said, her voice cold and brittle as ice on a winter puddle.

Tony whirled round, panic in his eyes. 'It's not what it seems,' he blurted out without thought. 'I've never even met the woman!'

Carol turned out of the doorway and walked down the hall. As she fumbled with the lock, Tony spoke coldly. 'I'm telling you the truth, Carol. Even though it's actually none of your business.'

She half turned, found a smile from somewhere and said, 'You're quite right. It *is* none of my business. Till tomorrow, Tony.'

The closing of the door reverberated through Tony's head like a jackhammer. 'Thank God you're a psychologist,' he said bitterly as he slumped against the wall. 'A layman might have really buggered that one up. You really believe in making the job a piece of piss, don't you, Hill?'

When Gareth half smiled at me on the tram, I was convinced that my dreams were on the point of fulfilment. Because of an unexpected crisis at work, and all the extra overtime that entailed, I hadn't been able to follow him for more than a week.

His image had lulled me to sleep when I came home at all hours from work, and his voice throbbed hungrily in my ears, but I needed to see him in the flesh. I'd set my alarm clock to give me plenty of time to be outside his house before he left for work, but I was so exhausted I slept right through it. When I started into wakefulness, I realized my only chance was to catch up with his tram a couple of stops further down the line.

The tram was pulling in as I ran on to the platform. I eagerly scanned the first section, but couldn't see him. Anxiety rose in my throat like bile. Then I saw his gleaming head, sitting right by the door of the second carriage. I pushed through the crowd and managed to stand right next to him, my knees brushing his. At the physical contact, he looked up. His grey eyes crinkled at the corners and a smile flickered on his mouth. I smiled back and said, 'Sorry.'

'No problem,' he said. 'This tram gets busier by the day.'

I wanted to continue the conversation, but for once I could think of nothing to say. He returned to the Guardian and I had to settle for watching him out of the corner of *my peripheral vision while I pretended to stare out at the passing cityscape. It wasn't much, I know, but it was a start. He had acknowledged me; he knew I existed. Now, it could be only a matter of time.*

Shakespeare got it right when he said, 'The first thing we do, let's kill all the lawyers.' That way at least there would be fewer liars at large. Even the words sound the same; lawyer, liar. I should have expected nothing else from a man who speaks one day for the plaintiff, the next for the defendant.

I'd parked just round the corner from Gareth's house, where I could watch him come home without being seen, thanks to the tinted windows of my jeep. His house had no hedge, so I could see right into his living room from my vantage point.

I knew his habits by now. He arrived home just after six, went through to the kitchen for a can of Grolsch, and returned to the living room where he drank his beer and watched TV. After about twenty minutes, he'd fetch some food from the kitchen – pizza, TV dinner, baked potato. Cooking clearly wasn't his forte. When we were together, I'd have to take over responsibility for that side of our life.

After the news, he'd leave the room, presumably to do some work in another room of the house. I imagined law books arrayed on pine shelves. Then, he'd either return to the TV later in the evening, or walk down to the pub on the corner for a couple of lagers.

Gareth needed someone to share his life, I thought as I waited for him to come home. I was just the person to do that. Gareth was going to be my Christmas present to me.

At a quarter past five, a white Volkswagen Golf slipped into a parking place just beyond Gareth's house and a woman got out. She leaned back into the car and picked up a briefcase bulging with files and a shoulder bag. I thought she looked vaguely familiar as she walked down the pavement. Petite, light-brown hair pulled back in a heavy plait, big tortoiseshell glasses, black suit, white blouse with a froth of lace at the throat.

When she turned in at Gareth's gate, I couldn't quite believe it. For the few seconds it took her to get to the door, I told myself she was his estate agent, his insurance agent, a colleague dropping off some papers. Anything. Anything.

Then she opened the flap of her bag and took out a key. My mind screamed 'No!' as she inserted the key into the lock and let herself in. The living-room door opened and she dumped her briefcase by the settee. Then she was gone again. Ten minutes later, she was back, wrapped in Gareth's big white towelling dressing gown.

Frankly, I was with Shakespeare all the way.

'Twas the season to be jolly, so I forced myself not to let my disappointment colour my mood. Instead, I concentrated on researching my next project. I wanted something appropriate to the season, some good old barbaric Christian symbolism. There's not really a lot you can do with a manger and swaddling clothes, so I allowed myself some artistic licence and went for the other end of the life.

Crucifixion as a form of punishment was probably borrowed by the Romans from the Carthaginians. (Interesting, isn't it, how the Romans referred to everyone else as the barbarians . . .) The Romans adopted it round about the time of the Punic Wars, and initially, it was a punishment reserved for slaves only. Which seems appropriate enough, since that was the only role I expected Gareth to be fit for now. Later in the days of empire, it became a more general punishment, meted out to any locals who had the temerity to misbehave after the Romans had kindly come along and conquered – sorry, civilized – them.

Traditionally, the felon was flagellated, then forced to carry the crossbeam through the streets to the place where *a tall stake had been driven into the ground. Then he was nailed to the crossbeam and hauled up by a system of pulleys. His feet were sometimes nailed, sometimes tied to the stake. On occasion, death by exhaustion was given a helping hand by the soldiers, who broke the legs of the victim, which must have allowed him a merciful lapse into unconsciousness. For my purposes, however, I decided to opt for the more decorative St Andrew's Cross. For one thing, it would place more interesting stresses on Gareth's muscles. For another, should he rise to the occasion, it would make access a lot easier.*

Interestingly, crucifixion was never used as a punishment for soldiers except for the crime of desertion. Maybe the Romans had the right idea after all.

11

But who meantime was the victim, to whose abode he was hurrying? For surely he could never be so indiscreet as to be sailing about on a roving cruise in search of some chance person to murder? Oh, no: he had suited himself with a victim some time before, viz., an old and very intimate friend.

Brandon stared bleakly at the sheet of paper in the typewriter. Tom Cross might have been a long way from the ACC's idea of the perfect copper, but he'd always appeared to be a good thief-taker. Antics like tonight's served only to raise a question mark over his whole career. Just how many other people had Cross fitted up over the years without anyone being any the wiser? If Brandon hadn't himself bent the rules and taken Tony on their illicit search, no one would have doubted the 'evidence' Tom Cross had turned up. No one except Stevie McConnell would have known that two of Cross's three 'finds' had arrived with him. The mere thought of the consequences of that was enough to send a prickle of cold sweat down Brandon's back.

Cross had left Brandon with no option but to suspend him. The disciplinary hearing that would inevitably follow would be painful for all concerned, but that was the least of Brandon's worries. He was far more troubled about the effect on the murder squad's morale. The only way to combat it was to take direct responsibility for the enquiry himself. Now, all he had to do was convince the Chief that he was right. With a sigh, Brandon pulled the last sheet of paper out of the machine and inserted another page.

His memo to the Chief Constable was brief and to the point. That only left one task before he could crawl home to bed. Sighing, Brandon glanced at the clock. Thirty minutes to midnight. He pushed the typewriter away from him and started writing on a sheet of his personal memo paper. 'To Detective Inspector Kevin Matthews. From John Brandon, ACC (Crime). Re: Steven McConnell. Following the suspension of Superintendent Cross, I will assume direct command of the murder squad. There are no grounds for charging McConnell with anything other than assault. McConnell should be released on bail pending a court date for the assault charge, and on separate bail to return to Scargill Street in a week so that we can question him further if more evidence arises. In view of his refusal to give us any information about his contacts, or any names of people he might have introduced to Gareth Finnegan and Adam Scott, we should pursue any contacts he does make. A warrant for a tap on his phone should also be obtained, on the basis of his connection to Scott and Finnegan, and the contact we now know he had with Damien Connolly in a professional capacity. Our enquiries into the four related murders should continue on a broad front, though I suggest that, following his release on bail, we maintain close surveillance of McConnell. There will be a case conference of senior officers tomorrow at noon.' He signed the memo and sealed it in an envelope. How to make friends and influence people, he thought as he walked downstairs to the desk sergeant. Brandon prayed that Tony Hill was right about Stevie McConnell. If Tom Cross had been right to follow his instinct, it would be more than the morale of the CID that would be at risk.

Carol slumped over the dining table, chin resting on her folded forearms, one hand tickling Nelson's belly. 'What do you think, boy? Is he just another lying bastard, or what?'

'Prrrt,' the cat said on a rising intonation, his eyes closed to slits.

'I thought you'd say that. I agree, I know how to pick them,' Carol sighed. 'You're right, I should have kept my distance. That's what happens when you make the running. You get the knockbacks. They don't usually come from that far out of left field, though. At least now I know why he kept backing off. Better off without him, cat. Life's tough enough without playing second fiddle.'

'Mrrr,' Nelson agreed.

'He must think I'm brain dead, expecting me to believe that a total stranger leaves messages like that on his answering machine.'

'Rowrr,' Nelson complained, rolling over on to his back, batting her fingers with his paws.

'All right, so you think it's ridiculous too. But the man's a psychologist. If he was going to make something up to explain the fact that he'd lied to me, he'd make it a damn sight more plausible than funny phone calls. All he had to say was that it was somebody he'd finished with who wouldn't take the message.' Carol rubbed the sleep out of her eyes, yawned and stood up in one languid movement.

The door to the boxroom Michael used as a study opened and he stood framed in the doorway. 'I thought I heard voices. You could talk to me, you know. At least I answer you.'

Carol gave a tired smile. 'So does Nelson. It's not his fault we don't speak cat. I didn't want to disturb you; I could see you were working.'

Michael walked over to the drinks cabinet and poured himself a small Scotch. 'I was only play-testing, trying to spot the glitches in what we've done so far. No big deal. How's your day been?'

'Don't ask. They've moved us over to Scargill Street. It's

a hellhole. Imagine going back to doing your calculations on an abacus, and you get the picture of my current working environment. The atmosphere's shit, and Tony Hill's spoken for. Apart from that, everything's magic.' Carol followed Michael's example and poured herself a drink.

'Want to talk about it?' he asked, perching on the arm of one of the sofas.

'Thanks, but no thanks.' Carol swallowed her drink in one, shuddered at the kick of the spirit and said, 'I've brought you a set of pictures, by the way. How soon can you take a look at them?'

'I've scrounged some computer time with the software tomorrow evening. That do you?'

Carol put her arms round Michael and gave him a hug. 'Thank you, bro,' she said.

'My pleasure,' he said, returning the embrace. 'You know how I love a challenge.'

'I'm going to bed,' she said. 'It's been a long one.'

No sooner had Carol turned out the light than she felt the familiar thud of Nelson landing on the foot of the bed. It was reassuring to feel his warmth against her legs, though it was no substitute for the body she'd hoped for earlier in the evening. Of course, as soon as her head hit the pillow, her sleepiness vanished. The exhaustion was still there, but her mind was racing. Please God, by tomorrow afternoon, the awkwardness between her and Tony would have evaporated. The sting of humiliation would still be there for her, but she was a grown-up and a professional. Now she knew he was off limits, she wouldn't place him in a difficult position again, and now he knew she knew, maybe he'd be able to relax. Either way, the profile should provide more than enough neutral ground between them. She could hardly wait to see what he'd come up with.

On the other side of the sleeping city, Tony too lay in bed, staring at the ceiling, tracing imaginary road maps in the cracks round the plaster rose. He knew there was no point in switching out his bedside lamp. Sleep would elude him, and in the darkness, he'd start to feel the slow choke of claustrophobia closing in on him. Counting sheep had never appealed; the slow watches of the night were when Tony Hill became his own therapist. 'Why did you have to ring tonight?' he murmured. 'I *like* Carol Jordan. I know I don't want her in my life, but I didn't want to hurt her either. Hearing your blandishments on the answering machine must have felt like a smack in the face, after me saying there wasn't anybody in my life.

'An outsider would say we hardly know each other, everything that happened tonight was an overreaction. But outsiders don't understand the bonding, the intimacy that springs out of nowhere when you're working closely together on a manhunt, when the clock's ticking the next victim's life away.'

He sighed. At least he hadn't blurted out the one thing that might have convinced Carol he wasn't lying, the truth he'd so carefully kept locked inside himself. What was it he told his patients? 'Let it out. It doesn't matter what it is, speaking it is the first step in taking away the pain.'

'What a load of crap that is,' he said bitterly. 'It's just another one of the tricks in my magic bag, designed to legitimize my prurient curiosity, tailored to unleash the twisted minds of the fuck-ups who are driven to act out their fantasies in a way society can't accommodate. If I'd told Carol the truth, said the i-word, it wouldn't have taken my pain away. It would only have made me feel even more of a worthless piece of shit. It's all very well for old men to be impotent. Men my age who can't get it up are a joke.'

The phone rang, startling him. He rolled over, scrambling for the receiver. 'Hello?' he said, his voice tentative.

'Anthony, at last. Oh, how I've missed you!'

His surge of anger at the languid, husky voice died as soon as it flared. What was the point in raging at her? She wasn't the problem. He was. 'I got your message,' he said, resigning himself. She hadn't caused the awkwardness with Carol; there would have been no grounds for awkwardness at all if he hadn't been such a pathetic excuse for a man. No point in even thinking about relationships with nice, normal women. He would have blown it with Carol, just as he'd always blown it with women as soon as they got close. The best he could hope for was telephone sex. At least it generated a kind of equality; it allowed men to fake not just orgasm but erection too.

Angelica chuckled. 'I thought I'd leave you something nice to come home to. I hope you're not too tired for some recreation.'

'I'm never too tired for your kind of recreation,' Tony said, swallowing the self-disgust that threatened to overwhelm him. Think of it as therapy, he told himself. Tony lay back and let the voice flow over him, his hand straying down his chest towards his groin.

The cleaners were gossiping by the lift as Penny Burgess emerged on the third floor of the *Bradfield Evening Sentinel Times* office. She walked down the newsroom, snapping on lights as she passed, humming tunelessly under her breath. She tossed her bag on the desk by her computer terminal and logged on. She executed the commands that took her into the library database, and pressed the key for 'search'. Five options were offered: 1. Subject; 2. Name; 3. By-line; 4. Date; and 5. Pictures. Penny hit 2. At the 'surname' prompt, she typed 'Hill'. At the 'forename' prompt, she keyed in 'Tony', and at the 'title' prompt, she entered, 'Dr'. Then she sat back and waited while the computer sorted through the gigabytes of information stored in its huge memory. Penny flipped open her cigarette packet and pulled out her first cigarette of the day. She was only a couple of drags into it when the screen flashed 'Found (6)'.

Penny retrieved the six items and called them up on her screen. They appeared in reverse order of date. The first was a two-month-old cutting from the *Sentinel Times*. It had been written by one of the news reporters. Although she'd read it at the time, she'd completely forgotten about it. As she read it, Penny whistled softly.

INSIDE THE MIND OF A KILLER

The man the Home Office have chosen to spearhead the hunt for serial killers spoke today about the latest slaying that has terrified the city's gay community.

Forensic psychologist Tony Hill is one year into a major study funded by the government which will lead to the setting up of a criminal profiling task force similar to the FBI unit featured in *The Silence of the Lambs*.

Dr Hill, 34, was formerly the chief clinical psychologist at Blamires Hospital, the maximum-security mental unit which houses Britain's most dangerous criminally insane offenders, including mass murderer David Harney and serial killer Keith Pond, the Motorway Madman.

Giving his verdict, Dr Hill said, 'I have not been called in by the police to consult on any of these cases, so I know no more than your readers do about them.'

Either Dr Hill had been lying to her colleague, or his formal involvement with the case came after the interview. If that was the case, Penny could see how to exploit it in a way that would appeal to her editor. She could picture the headline now. 'POLICE FOLLOW *BEST*'S LEAD IN MURDER HUNT.' She quickly flicked through the rest of the piece. It didn't tell her anything she didn't already know, although she was interested that Dr Hill had speculated that the discrepancies in the third killing might mean there were two killers out on the streets. That was an idea that seemed to have sunk without trace. It was something to ask Kevin about next time she managed to get him on the end of a phone.

The next cutting was from the *Guardian*, and announced the setting up of the Home Office programme for developing a national task force to deal with serial offenders. The project was to be based at Bradfield University. The article gave her more background on Dr Hill, and she jotted down his career details in her notebook. No dummy, this guy. She'd have to handle him carefully. She tapped her teeth with her pen and wondered why the *Sentinel Times* hadn't run a feature on the study, with a profile of Dr Hill. Maybe they tried and had been knocked back. She'd have to check with her colleagues on Features.

The next two cuttings were from a national tabloid, a two-part series on serial killers that had been timed to coincide with the general release of *The Silence of the Lambs*. Dr Hill was quoted in both articles, talking in general terms about the work of psychological profilers.

The last two cuttings dealt with one of his most prominent patients, Keith Pond, the so-called Motorway Madman. Pond had abducted five women from motorway service areas, then savagely raped and murdered them. At the time of his trial, only two of the bodies had been found. But after extensive therapy with Dr Hill, Pond had revealed the whereabouts of the other three bodies. Dr Hill had been hailed as a worker of miracles by the bereaved family of one of the victims. One of the two pieces had attempted a profile of Dr Hill, but they had scant information to go on. As usual, the journalist hadn't let that stand in the way of a good story.

Tony Hill, who has never married, is devoted to his work. A former colleague said, 'Tony's a workaholic. He's married to the job.

'He's totally driven by the desire to understand what makes his patients tick. There's probably not another psychologist in the country who has his knack of getting inside their twisted minds and working out what makes them do what they do.

'I sometimes thought he related better to mass murderers than he did to normal punters.'

The reclusive Dr Hill lives alone and is notorious for not mixing socially with colleagues. Apart from studying the minds of serial killers, the only hobby he apparently indulges in is hill-walking. On weekends off, he regularly drives to the Lakes or the Yorkshire Dales and tramps the fells.

'Sounds like a real barrel of laughs,' Penny said aloud, scribbling more notes on her pad. She returned to the main menu, where she selected the fifth option. Again, she entered Tony's name for a picture search. The data banks revealed there was one stock picture on file. Penny called it up and stared at the face that appeared on her screen. 'Gotcha!' she exclaimed. She had only seen him once before, but now she knew who Carol Jordan's new sidekick was.

Penny leaned back in her seat, savouring her third cigarette, and registered that the newsroom was starting to fill up. One quick phone call, then she could afford the time to treat herself to a fry-up in the canteen. Reaching for the phone, she dialled Kevin Matthews's home number. He picked up on the second ring. 'DI Matthews,' came the sleepy mumble.

'Hi, Kev, it's Penny,' she said, savouring the stunned silence that greeted her announcement. 'Sorry to bother you at home, but I thought you'd rather answer my questions there than in the office.'

'Wh-what?' he stuttered. Then, muffled, 'Yeah, it's work. Go back to sleep, love.'

'How long has Dr Tony Hill been on the team?'

'How did you hear about that? Shit, that's supposed to be top secret!' he exploded, his nervousness transforming itself into anger.

'Tut, tut. Kev, she'll never get back to sleep if you yell like that. Never mind how I know, just be grateful you can put your hand on your heart and deny it came from you. How long, Kev?'

He cleared his throat. 'Just a couple of days.'

'Was it Brandon's idea?'

'That's right. Look, I really can't talk about this. It's supposed to be kept under wraps.'

'He's doing a profile, right?'

'What do *you* think?'

'Working with Carol Jordan? Brandon's blue-eyed girl on this one, is she?'

'She's the liaison officer. Look, I've got to go. I'll talk to you about this later on, OK?' Kevin tried to sound menacing, but failed.

Penny smiled and slowly exhaled a mouthful of smoke. 'Thanks, Kev. I owe you a very special one.' She replaced the handset, cleared her screen and opened a story file.

'Exclusive. By Penny Jordan,' she typed. Never mind breakfast. She had far more interesting stuff to do.

Tony was back in front of his screen by half past eight. Instead of the guilt he'd expected to feel about his erotic encounter, he felt refreshed. Giving himself permission to indulge himself with Angelica had somehow released and relaxed him. Surprising though he found it under the circumstances, he'd actually become aroused as she'd talked him through an outrageous, imaginative sexual encounter. He hadn't actually managed to sustain his erection as far as orgasm, but because there was no one there to share his failure, it hadn't seemed to matter. Maybe a few more calls from Angelica would be all he needed to contemplate the reality with something less than abject panic.

But not at work. What he needed now was complete peace. He'd already instructed his secretary to hold all his calls, and he turned off the ringer on his direct line. Nothing and nobody was going to interrupt the flow of his thoughts. His feeling of satisfaction continued as he read through the work he'd done the day before. He was ready now to put himself on the line and commit his conclusions about Handy Andy to paper. Tony poured himself a cup of coffee from his Thermos and took a deep breath.

We are dealing with a serial killer who will certainly kill again unless he is caught. The next killing will take place on the eighth Monday following the death of Damien Connolly unless some trigger accelerates this. What might push him over the edge into extreme escalation could be some catastrophic event that causes him to lose whatever it is he is using to keep the fantasy alive. Since, for example, he is using videos, loss of or damage to his tapes could lead to loss of control. Another possible scenario is that an innocent person is charged with the killings. That would be such an affront to his sense of himself that he might commit his next murder ahead of schedule.

I believe it is likely that he has already selected his next victim and is familiarizing himself with that victim's movements and lifestyle. The chances are that the chosen victim is a man not known to the gay community. He will be, to all intents and purposes, a straight man living a heterosexual lifestyle.

The fact that his last victim was a police officer is disturbing. It is highly probable that this was choice, not accident or coincidence. The killer is sending a message to the investigation. He is demanding that we take notice of him, that we take him seriously. He is also telling us that he is the best; he can catch us but we can't catch him. There is a theory that such behaviour is a way of inviting capture, but I do not believe that is what is going on in this case.

It is possible that his next target may also be a police officer, perhaps even one who is working on the investigation. This alone will not be sufficient motive for the killer to choose them; they must also fit the victim criteria that he has drawn up in his own mind in order for the killing to assume its full meaning for him. I would strongly recommend that any officers who fit the victim profile employ extra vigilance at all times, noting any suspicious vehicles parked near their homes, and checking to see whether they are being followed to and from work and social events.

The stalking and preparation serves two main purposes for the killer: it cuts down on the potential surprise elements when he comes to carry out the killing, and it also fuels the fantasy that is the all-important area of the killer's life.

Our killer is probably a white male, aged between 25 and 35. He is likely to be at least 5ft 10ins tall, well muscled, with considerable upper-body strength. In spite of this, he probably has a poor body image. He may work out in a gym, but if he can afford it, he would prefer to use his own equipment in the privacy of his home. He is right-handed.

He won't look like a con. He'll look deeply, deeply average. He will have a demeanour that doesn't provoke suspicion. He's the sort of bloke you wouldn't look at twice, and certainly wouldn't suspect of being a multiple murderer. He may have tattoos and/or self-inflicted scars, but these are likely to be fairly discreet.

He is familiar with Bradfield, and his knowledge of Temple Fields is clearly current. This implies someone who lives and probably works in the city. I don't think he's a casual visitor, nor a former resident who simply comes back here to kill. There is no obvious geographical pattern to the homes or workplaces of his victims, except that they all lived in reasonably close proximity to a tram line. The first victim's home is most likely to be geographically closest to where the killer lives or works. Looking at the general background and style of the victims, and working on the principle that he's sticking to the kind of environment he knows and understands, I would suspect that the killer lives in privately owned property rather than rented, a house rather than a flat, in a suburban area of similar properties to those of the victims. The victims' houses are probably worth more than the killer's; these are men that in some way he aspires towards.

He is probably of above average intelligence, though I would not expect him to have a university degree. His school record is probably quite patchy, with poor attendance and highly variable marks. He will never have lived up to his potential or to other people's expectations of him. Most serial killers have a bad employment record, flitting from job to job, being sacked more often than resigning. But this man exhibits an extraordinary level of control in the commission of his murders, so I would expect him to be capable of holding down a steady job, possibly even one with some degree of responsibility and forward planning. However, I don't think his job will involve much contact with his fellow human beings, since his relationships with others will be characterized by their dysfunctional nature. His victims are all white-collar workers, with the marginal exception of Damien Connolly, which indicates to me that he probably operates in a similar working environment. I wouldn't be surprised to find him working in a technology-related area, possibly computers. This is an employment area where people can hold down good jobs without having significant people skills. People who don't fit in are accepted and acceptable in the weird world of software engineers; indeed, they are often highly prized since they are hard to replace. I doubt if our killer is a leading-edge creative person in the software world, but I wouldn't be surprised to find him as a systems manager or a program tester. He probably doesn't get on well with his bosses, being inclined to be insubordinate and argumentative.

He will be middle class in terms of his job, his aspirations, his clothes and his home, although he may be working class in background. He is good with his hands, but I am inclined to think he is not in a manual occupation, if only because of the high degree of planning involved in these murders.

Socially, he feels isolated. He may not necessarily be a loner, but he does not connect with people. He feels like an outsider. He probably has developed superficial social skills, but somehow his behaviour always strikes the wrong note. He's the one who laughs too loudly, the one who thinks he's making jokes when he's actually being deeply offensive, the one who sometimes seems to have drifted off in a daydream all of his own. He's the one who doesn't really have any friends, who will join in with the group but never pair off with one buddy in particular. He has little insight into his social failings. He prefers to be alone with his fantasies, because when others are involved socially, he can't fully control what's happening around him.

It's entirely possible that he does not live alone. If he lives with someone, it will be a woman rather than a man. Because he is sexually attracted to men and cannot accept that, he will not under any circumstances be living with a man, not even in a platonic relationship. His relationships with women may well be sexual, but he will not be an enthusiastic or successful lover. His performance will be barely adequate, and he may regularly experience problems in achieving and/or sustaining an erection. However, he will not be impotent during the commission of his crime, and will almost certainly be able to complete a full sexual act of some sort with his victims.

Tony paused and stared out of the window. Sometimes it felt like the chicken and the egg. Did he empathize with his patients because he too knew the frustrations and anger of impotence, or had his sexual problems increased precisely so that he could do his job better? 'Does it matter?' he said impatiently. He ran a hand through his hair and concentrated once again on the screen.

If he is living with someone, she will almost certainly have no suspicion whatsoever that her partner is the killer. It's therefore quite likely that her first instinct will be to alibi him, since in her heart, she knows it couldn't possibly be him. Any suspects solely alibied by girlfriends or wives should therefore not be eliminated on those grounds alone.

He is mobile, with his own car, which is in good condition (see above). And on Monday nights, he's free to roam without hindrance or obligation to be somewhere.

He is a highly structured personality, a control freak. The sort who has a tantrum because his girlfriend has forgotten to buy his favourite cereal. He believes he's absolutely justified; he thinks that in his crimes, all he is doing is actually committing the actions that everybody else wants to but lacks the bottle for. He has a big chip on his shoulder and feels that the world has conspired against him; how come, since he's so bright and talented, he's not running the company instead of doing this poxy job? How come, since he's so charming, he's not going out with some supermodel? The answer is, the world is out to do him down. He has the egocentric world view of the spoiled child, and has no insight into the impact of his behaviour on others. All he sees is the way events affect him.

He is a persistent fantasist and daydreamer. His fantasies are elaborately constructed and seem more significant to him than reality. His fantasy world is where he retreats both from choice and also whenever he faces any kind of setback or obstacle in his day-to-day life. The fantasies are likely to involve violence as well as sex and may also be fetishistic. These fantasies don't remain static; they lose their power and have to be developed further.

He is certain that he can act out his violent fantasies without anyone being able to stop him. He has supreme confidence that he is smarter than the police. He is not planning for the day he will be caught. He thinks he's too clever for that. He has been very careful to erase forensic traces, which is why, as I have already outlined to Inspector Jordan, I am convinced that the fragment of Russian deerskin left at the scene of the fourth killing is a red herring of the grossest kind. He is almost certainly keeping a close eye on the investigation, and will doubtless be laughing his socks off as we run round trying to source the leather. Even if the police do trace it, I suspect that when we find the killer there will be nothing among his possessions that will remotely connect to it.

If he has any criminal record at all, it is likely to be a juvenile one. Possible offences include: vandalism, minor arson, stealing, cruelty to younger children or animals, assault on teachers. However, somewhere along the line, our killer has learned enormous self-control, and he's unlikely to have an adult record.

He will keep abreast of the investigation as much as possible, and will thrive on publicity as long as it appears to accord him the glamour and respect he craves. It is interesting that Adam Scott's grave was desecrated shortly after the second murder. This may have been an attempt to raise the profile of his crimes. He is possibly someone who has contacts with police officers, and if he does, he will endeavour to use this to gain information about the progress of the investigation. Any officer who feels they are being pumped in this way should be encouraged to report it to senior officers in the murder squad.

Tony saved his file and read the whole thing through again. Some of the psychologists he'd worked with incorporated great slabs of background about the likely childhood background of the killer, as well as a checklist of behaviours that the killer would possibly have exhibited when he was growing up. Not Tony. There was time enough for that sort of information once there was a suspect ripe for interrogation. Tony never forgot that he was dealing with coppers who were out there at the sharp end. Men like Tom Cross, who didn't give a toss what kind of hideous childhood their suspect had endured.

Thinking of Tom Cross sharpened Tony's critical eye. Convincing him of the value of the profile was going to be a nightmare.

The first edition of the *Bradfield Evening Sentinel Times* hit the street just before noon. The eager searchers after flats, jobs and bargains snatched the first copies from the street vendors without even looking at the front page. They turned straight to the section of small ads that they hoped would meet their needs, holding the front and back pages up to the advantage of passers-by. Anyone curious enough to glance at the banner headlines on the front page would have discovered 'MURDER HUNT BOSS DUMPED. Exclusive, by our Crime Correspondent, Penny Burgess.' Further down the page, the bottom right-hand quarter was taken up with a photograph of Tony, saying, 'MURDER COPS FOLLOW *BEST* LEAD. Exclusive by Penny Burgess.' If they'd been intrigued enough to buy their own copy, they could have read a sub-headline saying, 'Top shrink we chose joins Queer Killer hunt, see story p. 3.'

In an office high above the bustling streets of Bradfield, a murderer stared at the paper, excitement churning inside. Things were working out beautifully. It was as if the police were acting out the killer's own fantasies, proving that wishes do come true.

The world was out in the city streets, buying Christmas presents they'd still be paying for at Easter, the fools. I was in my dungeon, making sure I would have a Christmas I'd never forget. Even though it was to be Gareth's last on this earth, I was sure every detail of it would be as clearly etched on his memory as it was going to be on my video tape.

I'd arranged our meeting with all the care and precision I could. The advent of the bitch meant I couldn't take the chance of capturing him at home as I'd done with Adam and Paul. I'd had to make alternative plans.

I sent him an invitation. I reasoned that Christmas Eve would be spoken for, either by family or by the bitch, so I chose December 23rd. I couched it in terms I knew he wouldn't be able to resist and that he'd never dare show the bitch. The final sentence read, 'Admission by invitation only.' A clever touch, that. It meant he'd have to bring with him the only evidence of contact between us.

The directions on the back led, if he cared to check it out in advance, to an isolated holiday cottage high up on the moors between Bradfield and the Yorkshire Dales; the opposite side of the city to Start Hill Farm and my dungeon. I anticipated that the cottage would be let over Christmas. But I had no intention of allowing Gareth to get that far.

* * *

It was a Christmas-cliché sort of night; bone-white crescent moon, stars twinkling like diamond chips on a cocktail watch, grass and hedgerows heavy with rime. I pulled over on to the verge of the single-track moorland road that led up to the holiday cottage and a couple of farms. In the distance, I could see the dual carriageway leading into Bradfield like a ribbon of fairy lights strung across the Pennines.

I turned on my hazard lights, got out of the jeep and opened the bonnet. I placed what I needed near at hand, then I leaned against the front wing and waited. It was freezing, but I didn't care. I'd calculated well. I'd only been waiting for about five minutes when I heard the sound of an engine straining up the steep incline. The lights swung round the bend below me and I stepped out, waving furiously, looking frozen and worried.

Gareth's elderly Escort stopped abruptly in front of the jeep. I took a couple of hesitant steps towards him as he opened the door and got out. 'Some kind of a problem?' he asked. 'I'm afraid I know next to nothing about cars, but if I can maybe give you a lift . . . ?'

I smiled. 'Thanks for stopping,' I said. There was no flicker of recognition in his face as he drew nearer. I hated him for that.

I stepped back towards the jeep, gesturing under the bonnet. 'It's not a big problem,' I said. 'Only, I need three hands. If you can just hold this part in place so I can get a spanner on this nut . . .' I pointed into the engine. Gareth leaned over the bonnet. I picked up the spanner and let him have it.

Within five minutes, he was trussed tighter than a turkey in the boot of his own car. I had his car keys, his wallet and the invitation I'd sent him. I drove back down through the city to the farm, where I dumped the unconscious body unceremoniously down the cellar steps. I didn't have time to do any more then, not if I was going to get back to the jeep.

I drove Gareth's car into the centre of Bradfield, leaving it in Temple Fields in a back alley off Crompton Gardens. Nobody noticed me; they were all too busy partying. It was a mere ten minutes' walk across town to the railway station.

A twenty-minute train ride and a brisk fifteen-minute walk brought me back to the jeep. Cautiously, I approached. There was no sign of life, no suggestion that anyone had been poking around. I drove back to Start Hill Farm whistling 'Hark The Herald Angels Sing'.

When I switched the cellar light on, Gareth's dark-grey eyes flashed angry fire at me. I liked that. After the pathetic terror of Adam and Paul, it was refreshing to see a man who had some guts. The muffled sound that came from behind the tape on his mouth was more like an angry grunt than a plea.

I stooped over him and stroked his hair back from his forehead. At first, he jerked away from me, then he became calm and still, calculation in his eyes. 'That's more like it,' I said. 'No need to fight, no need to resist.'

He nodded, then grunted, signalling down towards his gag with his eyes. I kneeled beside him and picked at one corner of the surgical tape. Once I had a good grip, I ripped it free in one swift movement. It's kinder than doing it gradually.

Gareth worked his jaw, licking his dry lips. He glared at me. 'Some fucking party,' he snarled, his voice a little shaky.

'It's exactly what you deserve,' I said.

'How the fuck do you work that out?' he demanded.

'You were meant for me. But you took up with that slag. And you tried to keep it a secret.'

Light dawned in his eyes. 'You're . . .' he started.

'That's right,' I interrupted. 'So now you know why

242

you're here.' My voice was as cold as the stone floor. I stood up abruptly and walked over to the bench where I'd laid out my equipment.

Gareth was talking again, but I shut out the sound of his voice. I know how persuasive lawyers can be, and I wasn't about to be deflected from my course by any amount of sweet talking. I opened the ziplock bag and took out the chloroform pad. I turned back to Gareth and kneeled beside him. With one hand, I gripped his hair and with the other I applied the pad to his mouth and nose. He struggled so convulsively that I ended up with a clump of hair in my hand before he subsided into unconsciousness. Just as well I was wearing my latex gloves, otherwise his hair would have cut me. The last thing I needed was my blood mingling with his.

When he was out cold, I cut his clothes off. I took the strap from the Judas chair and fastened it round his chest, under the armpits. I'd fixed a rudimentary pulley and hoist to one of the ceiling beams, and I attached the hook to the strap. I raised Gareth's body with the hoist till he swung like mistletoe in a draught. Once he was up in the air, it was the work of moments to undo the handcuffs and fasten him to my Christmas tree.

I'd bolted two planks to the wall in the shape of a St Andrew's Cross, and covered them thickly with prickly boughs of blue Norwegian spruce. To each arm of the cross, I'd attached leather straps, which I fastened around his wrists and ankles. I opened up Gareth's curled fists and taped his hands open to the cross. Finally, I removed the hook and let the wrist straps take the strain. His body slumped alarmingly, and for a moment I was concerned that I hadn't fitted strong enough straps. There was a brief creaking of leather on wood, then silence. He hung like a martyred apostle on the dungeon wall.

I laid out my club hammer and the sharpened cold chisels

I'd chosen for the job. We'd be together now till Christmas night. I intended to savour every minute of our forty-eight hours.

12

Very few men commit murder upon philanthropic or patriotic principles ... As to the majority of murderers, they are very incorrect characters.

The four detective inspectors sat stony-faced in what had been Tom Cross's office as John Brandon gave them the official version of the superintendent's suspension. Sometimes, Brandon wished he was one of the lads again, able to explain his reasons without appearing to undermine his own position by doing so. 'What we've got to do is put this behind us and move this enquiry forward,' he said briskly. 'Now, what's the score with McConnell?'

Kevin leaned forward in his seat. 'I did as you instructed, sir. He left our custody just before midnight, and I've had a team on him ever since. He hasn't put so much as a toe out of line so far. He went straight home, seemed to go to bed, judging by the lights. He was up at eight this morning, and he's gone off to work. I've got one lad in the gym, posing as a new member, and another one out on the street.'

'Stick with it, Kevin. Anything else? Dave, anything interesting coming out of the computer yet?'

'We're following up a lot of car numbers and blokes with previous for any gay-related offences, both on the gay-bashing and the gross indecency side. We're also about to cross-check those lists with the ones Don Merrick's been getting from travel agents of people who have booked holidays in Russia. Once we get the profile, we might be able to develop some suspects, but it's uphill at the moment, sir.'

Carol chipped in. 'Some of the weightlifting associations said they'd supply us with lists of their members who'd either been to Russia or competed against Russian teams.'

Dave pulled a face. 'Oh goody, more bloody lists,' he said.

'I've got a contact in the leather business,' Stansfield said. 'Biggest importer in the UK. I asked him about the leather scrap and he said that with it being deerskin, it's probably not your common-or-garden labourer's jacket. He said it was likely to be someone with a bit of clout but not real power. You know. Somebody like a DI,' he grinned. 'Or a town-hall official halfway up the greasy pole. A deputy stationmaster. The second mate on a ship. That sort of thing.'

Dave grinned. 'I'll tell HOLMES to keep an eye out for ex-KGB men.'

Brandon started to say something, but he was cut off by the peal of the telephone. He grabbed it and said, 'Brandon here . . .' His face lost all expression, turning as wooden as the coffins he looked as if he should be carrying. 'Yes, sir. I'll be there right away.' He put the phone down gently and stood up. 'The Chief Constable is interested in hearing how this evening's paper came to look the way it does.' He crossed the room and paused by the door, one hand on the handle. 'I'm sure the person who washed our dirty linen in Ms Burgess's sink will be hoping I can persuade him not to make an example of him.' He gave Carol a frosty smile. 'Or her, come to that.'

Tony locked his office door behind him and gave the project secretary a happy wave and smile. 'I'm going out for a bite of lunch, Claire. I'll probably go to Café Genet in Temple Fields. Inspector Jordan's due at three, but I'll be back by then. OK?'

'You're sure you don't want to return one of these calls from the journalists?' Claire called after him.

Tony swung round, continuing to walk backwards across the office. 'What journalists?' he asked.

'First off, that Penny Burgess from the *Sentinel Times*. She's been trying every half-hour since I came in. Then, in the last hour, they've been on from all the national newspapers, and Radio Bradfield.'

Tony frowned, baffled. 'Why?' he asked. 'Did they say what they wanted?'

Claire held up the copy of the *Sentinel Times* she'd nipped out to buy from the campus newsagent. 'I'm no psychologist, Tony, but I think it might have something to do with this.'

Tony stopped in his tracks. Even across the office he could read the headlines and make out his own photograph splashed across the front page of the paper. Like an iron filing pulled by a magnet, Tony moved closer to the paper till he could read Penny Burgess's name on both stories. 'May I?' he said hoarsely, reaching out for the paper.

Claire relinquished it and watched his reaction. She liked her boss, but she was human enough to relish his discomfort at being exposed in the evening paper. Tony hastily flicked the front page over, hunting for the full story about himself. With a mounting sense of horror, he read:

Dr Hill is well equipped to enter the twisted mind of the Queer Killer. As well as his two university degrees and a wealth of experience in dealing directly with the criminal perverts who have terrorized society, he has a reputation for dogged determination.

A colleague said, 'He's married to the job. It's all he lives for. If anyone can catch the Queer Killer, it's Tony Hill.

'It's only a matter of time now, I'm convinced. Tony

is relentless. He won't give up till this bastard is nailed down tight.

'Let's face it, Tony's got a top-class brain. These serial killers might have high IQs, but they're never very smart when it comes to staying out of custody.'

'Dear Christ,' Tony groaned. Apart from the fact that no self-respecting colleague would ever have given quotes like that, the article was tantamount to throwing down the gauntlet to Handy Andy. It read like a challenge. He felt sure Handy Andy would find a way to respond to that. Tony threw the paper down on the desk and scowled at it.

'It is a bit over the top,' his secretary said sympathetically.

'It's bloody irresponsible, never mind over the top,' Tony raged. 'Oh, bollocks to it. I'm going for lunch. If the Chief Constable rings, tell him I've left for the day.' He walked off again towards the door.

'What about Inspector Jordan? What if she rings?'

'You can tell her I've left the country.' With the door open, he paused. 'No, only joking. Tell her I'll be here for our meeting.'

As he stood waiting for the lift, Tony realized nothing in his experience had prepared him for a direct confrontational challenge with a killer. This was one he'd have to fly by the seat of his pants.

Kevin Matthews drained his pint glass and waved it at the barmaid. 'Even if it is a red herring, he's still got to have had access to this bloody obscure bit of leather in the first place, hasn't he?' he demanded stubbornly of Carol and Merrick. 'Same again?'

Merrick nodded. 'I'll have a coffee this time, Kevin,' Carol said. 'And chuck us a menu, would you? I've got a feeling I'm in for a long session with the doc, and he's got a nasty habit of forgetting about food.'

Kevin ordered the drinks then turned back to Carol. With the persistence that had won him promotion, he said, 'I'm right though, aren't I? To plant the leather like that, not only has he had access to it, he also knows how unusual it is.'

'Agreed,' Carol said.

'So it's not a waste of time trying to source it, is it?'

'I never said it was,' Carol said patiently. 'Now, are you going to fill me in on what happened with Tom Cross, or do I have to copy our murderer and bring out the torture gear?'

While Kevin explained what had happened, Merrick's attention drifted. He'd already heard the tale more times than enough. He leaned against the bar and surveyed the clientele. The Sackville Arms wasn't the nearest pub to the Scargill Street station, but it sold draught Tetleys from Yorkshire and Boddingtons from Manchester, which inevitably made it the police local. The pub was on the outer fringes of Temple Fields, which had given it an added attraction for the local officers when Scargill Street had still been open. The location had meant that hookers or petty villains who wanted to drop a word in the ear of their personal contact on the force could manage it unobtrusively. However, in the few months that Scargill Street had been mothballed, the pub had subtly changed. The regulars had got used to having the place to themselves, and there was a clearly discernible distance between the coppers and the rest of the customers. The officers who'd been using the pub in an attempt to recruit new sources from the community's underbelly had met with a chilly reception. Even with a serial killer on the loose, no one wanted to get back into the habit of informing now they'd kicked it.

With his policeman's eyes, Merrick slowly scanned the room, classifying the drinkers. Hooker, dealer, rent boy, pimp, rich man, poor man, beggar man, wimp. He was jolted out of his scrutiny by Carol's voice. 'What do you think, Don?' he caught.

'Sorry, ma'am, miles away. What do I think about what?'

'That it's about time we developed some of our own snouts among the toms, instead of having to rely on the Vice Squad's girls. They've been round the houses so many times, I'd go outside to check if they told me it was raining.'

'Never mind the hookers,' Merrick said. 'We need to know a damn sight more about how the gay community works. I don't mean the lads that are out of the closet and down the Hell Hole. I mean the secretive ones. The ones that don't flaunt it. They're the ones who might have come across this guy before. I mean, from all I've ever read about serial killers, sometimes they don't actually kill the first time, they just have a go. Like the Yorkshire Ripper did. So maybe there's some frightened little guy in the closet who's been on the receiving end of a bit of violence that got out of hand. That might be the road to a break.'

'And God knows we need a break,' Kevin said. 'But if we don't know how the connections are made, how do we connect?'

Carol said thoughtfully, 'When in doubt, ask a policeman.'

'Do what?' Kevin asked.

'There are gay officers in the Job. More than most, they must know about keeping a low profile. They'd be able to tell us.'

'That doesn't answer the question,' Kevin protested doggedly. 'If they're so busy keeping it quiet, how do we know who they are?'

'The Met has an association of gay and lesbian police officers. Why don't we get in touch with them, in confidence, and ask for their help? Somebody must have some contacts in Bradfield.'

Merrick stared at Carol with admiration, Kevin with

frustration, both wondering silently how it was that Inspector Jordan always had an answer.

Tom Cross glanced down at the front page of the *Sentinel Times*, a smirk of satisfaction twitching his cigarette up and down. Ms Burgess might have thought she was in control of their little encounter the night before, but Tom Cross knew different. He'd played the spider to her fly, and she'd done exactly what he expected of her. No, credit where it's due. She'd done better than he'd expected. That line about the police staggering lamely in the wake of the *Sentinel Times* when it came to seeking out Dr bloody Hill was a corker.

There were going to be a lot of angry men in Bradfield police today. That was the revenge element of Tom Cross's game with Penny Burgess. But someone else was going to be angry too. When he read tonight's paper, the killer was going to be more than a little put out.

Tom Cross stubbed out his cigarette and slurped from his mug of tea. He folded his paper and placed it on the table in front of him and stared out of the café window. He lit another cigarette. He'd set out to provoke the Queer Killer. Provoked, he'd start to get careless, to make mistakes. And when Stevie McConnell did that, Tom Cross would be ready and waiting. He'd show those sorry bastards in command how to catch a killer.

Tony was back in the office by ten to three. Even so, he wasn't early enough to beat Carol. 'Inspector Jordan's here,' Claire said as soon as he opened the outer office door. She gestured with her head towards his office. 'She's in there waiting. I told her you'd be back.'

Tony's responding smile was strained. As he gripped the door handle, he clenched his eyes tightly and took a deep breath. Nailing what he hoped was a welcoming smile on his face, Tony opened the door and stepped into his office.

At the sound of the door, Carol turned away from the window she'd been staring out of and gave him a cool, appraising look. Tony closed the door behind him and leaned against it.

'You look like a man who's just stepped in a puddle that's deeper than his shoe,' Carol remarked.

'That's an improvement, then,' Tony said with more than a trace of irony. 'Usually I feel like I've stepped in a puddle that's deeper than my head.'

Carol took a step towards him. She'd rehearsed what she was going to say. 'There's no need to feel like that with me. Last night ... well, you were less than candid and I misread the signals. So can we please forget the whole thing and concentrate on what's important between us?'

'Which is?' Tony sounded impersonal as a therapist, his question conversational rather than challenging.

'Working together to nail this killer.'

Tony pushed himself away from the door and made for the safety of his seat, careful to keep the desk between them at all times. 'That's fine by me.' He gave a crooked smile. 'Believe me, I'm far better at professional relationships than the other kind. Think of it as a lucky escape.'

Carol walked round to the opposite side of the desk and pulled up a chair. She crossed her trouser-clad legs and folded her hands in her lap. 'So let's have a look at this profile.'

'We don't have to behave as if we're strangers,' Tony said quietly. 'I respect you, and I admire the way you're so open to learning new aspects of the job. Look, before ... before what happened last night, we seemed to be moving towards a friendship that went beyond work. Was that such a bad thing? Couldn't we settle for that?'

Carol shrugged. 'It's not easy making friends after you've exposed your weaknesses.'

'I don't think showing someone you're attracted to them is necessarily a weakness.'

'I feel foolish,' Carol said, not quite sure why she was opening up like this. 'I had no right to expect anything from you. Now, I'm angry with myself.'

'And with me too, I expect,' Tony said. This was proving less traumatic than he had imagined. His counselling techniques hadn't rusted over from lack of use, he thought with relief.

'Mostly with myself,' Carol said. 'But I can deal with that. The important thing for me is that we get the job done.'

'Me too. It's pretty rare for me to find a police officer who seems to have a grasp of what I'm trying to do.' He picked up the papers on his desk. 'Carol ... This isn't about you, you know. It's about me. I have problems of my own that I need to deal with.'

Carol stared at him long and hard. He felt a quick twitch of panic as he realized he could not read her eyes. He had no idea what she was feeling. 'I hear what you're saying,' she replied, her voice cold. 'Speaking of problems,' she added, 'haven't we got some work to do?'

Carol sat alone in Tony's office with his profile of the serial killer. He had left her to read it while he worked next door with his secretary, catching up on the correspondence that had piled up since Brandon had hijacked him only a handful of days before. She couldn't remember ever having been so fascinated by a report in her entire career. If this was the future of policing, she desperately wanted to be part of it. At last, she came to the end of the main body of text and turned to a separate sheet.

Points to pursue:
1. Had any of the victims ever mentioned to a friend/relative that they had been the subject of an unwanted homosexual approach? If so, when, where and from whom?

2. The killer is a stalker. His first encounter with his victims probably takes place quite a long time before he kills – weeks rather than days. Where is he encountering them? It may be something as banal as where they take their dry-cleaning, where they have their shoes heeled, where they buy sandwiches, where they have tyres or exhausts put on their cars. Given that they all lived close to the tram network, I think we should check whether the victims regularly used the trams to go to and from work, or to go out in the evenings. I suggest that in-depth background checks are done, going through bank accounts, credit-card statements and anecdotal evidence from colleagues, girlfriends and family members. This may help develop suspects.

3. Is there any indication that the victims were keeping the night in question free for any particular purpose? Gareth Finnegan lied to his girlfriend about it – did any of the others?

4. Where is he doing his killing? It's unlikely to be in his home, since he will have calculated the possibility of being arrested, and will have taken pains to avoid leaving forensic traces there. It's also got to be big enough for him to build and use the torture engines we are assuming in these cases. It may be an isolated lock-up garage, or a unit on an industrial estate which is deserted at night. Bearing in mind that he almost certainly lives in Bradfield, it's possible that there exists an isolated rural property that he has undisturbed access to.

5. He must have found out about instruments of torture somewhere so that he could construct his own. It might be worth checking with bookshops and libraries to see if any of their customers has enquired about or ordered books on torture.

Carol flicked back a few pages, rereading a couple of paragraphs which had particularly struck her first time through. She found it hard to credit how quickly Tony had assimilated the stacks of files she'd delivered. Not only that, but he'd drawn out of them the key points that created for the first time in Carol's mind a picture, albeit shadowy, of the man she was hunting.

But the profile raised questions in her mind. At least one of those questions didn't seem to have occurred to Tony. She wondered if it wasn't referred to because he had dismissed it out of hand. Either way, she had to know. And she had to find a way of asking that didn't sound like an attack.

I hated to keep Gareth hanging on, but I had to leave him for one little errand. In his car, I'd found a few of the Christmas cards his company sent out to favoured clients, already signed by all the partners. Inside one, with a fountain pen, a stencil set and Gareth's blood, I'd written in block capitals, 'A MERRY CHRISTMAS TO ALL YOUR READERS; YOUR EXCLUSIVE CHRISTMAS GIFT IS WAITING IN THE SHRUBBERY OF CARLTON PARK BEHIND THE BANDSTAND. COMPLIMENTS OF THE SEASON FROM SANTA CLAWS.' It wasn't easy to write with the blood; it kept congealing on the nib, which I had to clean every few letters. Luckily, there was no shortage of ink.

I addressed a Jiffy bag to the editor of the Bradfield Evening Sentinel Times *and put the card in it, along with a video I'd made a couple of weeks before, when I'd started to plan what to do with Gareth. I'd already decided to change my modus operandi slightly. Temple Fields was bound to be risky now; even if the queens were too drunk or stoned to be vigilant, the police would be keeping an eye open for more than the occasional cottaging poof. But the nature trail through the shrubbery of Carlton Park is almost as notorious a pick-up area.*

Early on a rainy Sunday morning, when there was nobody about, I'd driven out to Carlton Park with my camcorder. I started off by the wrought-iron bandstand. I walked around it, filming it from every angle. It wouldn't take long before somebody in the BEST office recognized the landmark. After all, Carlton Park is the biggest park within the city boundaries, and there's a brass-band concert there every Sunday from April to September. I deliberately kept the camcorder at chest level rather than on my shoulder; I've read of instances where correct estimates of height have been made simply from the angle photographs have been taken from. If some forensic scientist was going to draw any conclusions from this video, I wanted to be sure they would be the wrong ones.

Leaving the bandstand behind, I walked down the nature trail towards the shrubbery. I panned across the general area where I thought I'd dump the body, then stopped filming. I passed nobody on my way back to the jeep. That was probably just as well, since I was grinning from ear to ear at the thought of the news editor puzzling over my Christmas message.

The message would also serve two other functions. It would minimize the time it took to identify Gareth's body, which meant the publicity machine would have plenty of fodder to keep it going through what was always a slack news period. Secondly, it would send the police on a wild goose chase, working out who could have had access to the Christmas cards.

The police might even decide that someone connected with Gareth through work had decided to bump him off and make it look like a copycat killing by dumping the body in a gay cruising area. Just the sort of thing a deranged and disillusioned client would do. If I got really lucky, they might even give the bitch a hard time, too.

I drove into the city centre to post the packet at the main post office. There were enough last-minute panicking gift-givers for me to be unremarkable. I stopped at an off licence on the way back to buy a bottle of champagne. I don't normally drink when I'm working, but this was a special occasion.

When I got back, Gareth was semi-conscious, mumbling incomprehensibly. 'Santa's here,' I said cheerfully as I came down the stairs. I popped the cork on the champagne and poured two glasses. I took one over to Gareth and, standing on tiptoe, I gently lifted his lolling head. I held the glass to his lips and tilted it. 'You'll enjoy this,' I said. 'It's vintage Dom Perignon.'

His eyes snapped wide open. For a moment, he looked bewildered, then he remembered and he fixed me with a look of pure hatred. But he was parched, and couldn't resist the champagne. He swallowed it greedily, not savouring it at all. Then he belched in my face, a look of strange satisfaction in his eyes.

'Wasted on you,' I said angrily. 'Like all the fine things in life.' I stepped back and slashed the glass across his face. It shattered against his nose, cutting his cheek to ribbons. I was glad Auntie Doris wouldn't be coming back. She'd had that set of six fragile crystal glasses as a silver-wedding present, and she'd never used them, terrified that someone would break one. She'd been right to be concerned.

Gareth shook his head. 'You're evil,' he slurred. 'Pure evil.'

'No, I'm not,' I said softly. 'I'm justice. Remember justice? It's what you're supposed to stand for.'

'Twisted, evil bastard,' he replied.

I couldn't believe he still had the stamina for bravado. It was time to show him who was boss. I'd already pinned his hands to the cross with a couple of cold chisels. The blood had congealed around them, black and hard. Now it was the turn of his feet.

When he saw me pick up my tools from the workbench, he finally cracked. 'There's no need for this,' he said desperately. 'Please. You could still let me go. They'd never find you. I've no idea where we are. I don't know who you are, where you live, what you do for a living. You could move away from Bradfield and they'd never find you.'

I took a step closer. Tears welled up in his eyes and spilled over, trickling through the blood on his cheek. They must have stung, but he never flinched. 'Please,' he whispered. 'It's not too late. Even if you killed those other men. Was it you who killed them?'

He was smart, I had to give him that. Too smart for his own good. He'd just earned himself some more suffering. I turned away and dropped the chisel and club hammer on the workbench. Let him think I was having second thoughts. Let him spend the night convinced I was going to have mercy. That would make Christmas Day all the sweeter.

I shut the cellar door behind me and went upstairs to bed, armed with my videos and the best part of a bottle of vintage champagne. I was having the best Christmas I'd ever had. I remembered all those years of desperate hope, praying that this would be the year my mother would buy me presents like other children got. But all she'd ever done was let me down. Now I'd worked out that the only person who could give me what I craved was myself; I knew that for the first time in my life, I could look forward to the kind of Christmas other people have, filled with surprises, satisfaction and sex.

13

Reading his acts by the light of such mute traces as he left behind him, the police became aware that latterly he must have loitered. And the reason which governed him is striking; because at once it records – that murder was not pursued by him simply as a means to an end, but also as an end for itself.

The Wunch of Bankers was one of the few city-centre watering holes where Kevin Matthews felt safe meeting Penny Burgess. A fun pub with blaring rap music and decor modelled on soap operas – the Rover's Return Snug, the Woolpack Eaterie, the Queen Vic Lounge, and the Cheers Beer Bar – was the last place he was likely to see another copper or Penny another journalist.

Kevin made a face as his taste buds clenched on the strong bitter coffee that lurked under a swirl of foam that looked more like industrial effluent than a cappuccino. Where the hell was she? He glanced at his watch for the twentieth time. She'd promised she'd be here by four at the latest, and now it was ten past. He pushed the half-empty cup away from him and grabbed his fashionable raincoat from the banquette beside him. He was about to stand up when the pub's revolving door hissed round and disgorged Penny. She waved and headed straight over to his table.

'You said four o'clock,' Kevin greeted her.

'God, Kevin, you're getting really anal in your old age,' Penny complained, giving him a peck on the cheek as she subsided on to the seat beside him. 'Get me one of those mineral waters with a hint of fruits of the forest, there's a love,' she said, her voice mocking the pretensions of her chosen drink.

When Kevin returned with a glass already sweating with condensation, Penny immediately put a proprietorial hand on the inside of his thigh. 'Mmm, thanks,' she said, sipping her drink. 'So what's new? Why the urgent meeting?'

'Today's paper,' he said tonelessly. 'The shit's really hit the fan.'

'Oh, good,' Penny said. 'Maybe we'll get some positive action. Like a suspect you've got some evidence against.'

'You're not understanding. They're hunting for the mole. The Chief had Brandon on the carpet this morning, and the upshot is that Internal Affairs have mounted a leak enquiry. Penny, you've got to cover my back,' Kevin said desperately. Penny took her time lighting a cigarette. 'Are you listening to me?' Kevin demanded.

'Of course I am, sweetheart,' Penny soothed automatically, her mind already planning her story for the morrow. 'I just don't understand why you're getting so worked up. You know a good journalist never reveals her sources. What's the problem? You think I'm not a good enough journalist?' With an effort, Penny forced herself to listen to Kevin's reply rather than the voice in her head reeling off headlines.

'It's not that I don't trust you,' Kevin said impatiently. 'It's inside the force I'm worried about. Everybody will be desperate to put themselves in the clear, so anybody that knows about us will be falling over themselves to tell Internal Affairs. And once they know that we're, well, you know? That'll be it. I'll have had it.'

'But nobody knows about us. Or not from me, they don't,' Penny said calmly.

'I thought nobody knew too. Then Carol Jordan said something that made me think she does.'

'And you think Carol's going to shop you to Internal Affairs?' Penny said, failing to hide the incredulity she felt. She hadn't had many dealings with the CID's most glamorous officer, but what she knew of the inspector didn't incline her to cast her in the role of grass.

'You don't know her. She's totally bloody ruthless. She wants to go all the way, that one, and she'd drop me in it soon as look at me if she thought it would take her a rung up the ladder.'

Penny shook her head in exasperation. 'You're overreacting. Even if Carol Jordan has mysteriously discovered that we're seeing each other, I'm sure she's too busy covering herself with glory from her liaison with Dr Hill to be bothered with shopping you. Besides, if you think about it rationally, she's got nothing to gain from getting herself a reputation with the lads as a grass.'

Kevin shook his head dubiously. 'I don't know. Penny, you've no idea what it's like on this job. We're all working eighteen-hour days, and we're getting nowhere.'

Penny stroked the inside of his thigh. 'Sweetheart, you're under a lot of pressure. Look, tell you what. If it all comes on top and somebody fingers you, Internal Affairs are bound to come to us and front us up. They'll be looking for corroboration. If that happens, I'll make it look like Carol Jordan's my source, OK? That should muddy the waters.'

Kevin's smile was worth the flannel, she decided. That, and one or two other things about him. Reassured, he bounced to his feet. 'Thanks, Pen. Listen, I've got to be a place. I'll call you soon so we can get together, OK?' He leaned over and kissed her deep and hard.

'Keep me posted, lover boy,' Penny said softly to his retreating back. Before he even reached the doors, her intro was taking shape. Oh yes, she could see it now.

Bradfield police are devoting new resources to the hunt for the serial killer who has claimed four victims and placed men in jeopardy as never before.

But the extra officers will not be joining the search for the monstrous Queer Killer. Their job will be to police the police themselves.

Top brass in the force are so alarmed by the accuracy of the *Sentinel Times*'s stories on the killings that they have set up a full-scale mole hunt to uncover the source of our stories. Instead of catching the killer, the mole-catchers will be tracking down fellow officers who subscribe to the view that the terrified public have a right to know what's going on.

Carol opened the door to the outer office and said, 'I'm all done. Can we talk?'

Tony looked up from the computer screen absently, held up one finger and said, 'Yeah, sure, give me a minute,' and finished what he was doing.

Carol retreated and took a deep breath. No matter how professional she tried to be, she couldn't help the surge of attraction she felt for this man. Ignoring it was easier said than done. Moments later, Tony joined her. He perched on the edge of his desk, his hair standing on end like Dennis the Menace from thrusting his fingers through it while he concentrated. 'So,' he said. 'What's the verdict?'

'I'm impressed,' she said. 'It really pulls everything together. There were a couple of things, though.'

'Only a couple?' Tony asked, his voice close to a chuckle.

'You talk a lot about how he must be strong, to overpower his victims and move them around. Also, you speculate about how he gets them into a vulnerable position in the first place. I was wondering if maybe there were two of them.'

'Go on,' Tony said, no hint of frost in his voice.

'I don't mean two men. I mean a man and someone else

who appears vulnerable. Maybe an adolescent boy or, more likely, a woman. I don't know, maybe even a person in a wheelchair. A partner in crime. Like Ian Brady and Myra Hindley.' Carol shuffled the papers, putting them back in order. Still Tony said nothing. After a few moments watching his expressionless face, she added, 'I know you've probably thought about it already, I just wondered if it was a possibility we should still bear in mind.'

'Sorry, I didn't mean to look like I was ignoring you,' Tony said hurriedly. 'I was reviewing the thought, weighing it against what we know and against the profile. One of the first things I considered was whether or not it was a solo. On the balance of overwhelming probability, I decided it was. Cases like the Moors Murders where you have two people acting in tandem to carry out atrocities are incredibly rare, for a kick off. Also, I'd expect to find more variation in the methodology and the pathology if there were two people involved; it's hard to believe their fantasies would coincide so exactly. But it's interesting that you've come up with it. You're right in one respect. If he's working with a woman it does explain how he gets close to his victims without them putting up a fight.' Tony sat staring straight ahead, brows lowered in thought.

Carol stayed motionless in her seat. Eventually, Tony turned to face her and said, 'I'm going to stick with my soloist. Yours is an interesting idea, but I can't see evidence that convinces me I should shift from the most highly probable scenario.'

'OK, point taken,' Carol said calmly. 'Moving on from that, have you considered the possibility of a transvestite? Like you just said, a woman could get close without them putting up a fight. What about if the woman was a man in drag? Wouldn't that have the same effect?'

Tony looked startled for a moment. 'Maybe you should think about applying to join the national task force when it's set up,' he stalled.

Carol grinned. 'Flattery will get you nowhere.'

'I mean it. I think you've got what it takes to do this kind of work. You see, I'm not infallible. I hadn't actually considered a transvestite. Now, why did I ignore that possibility?' he mused, thinking aloud. 'There must be some subconscious reason why I rejected it before it even got to the front of my mind . . .' Carol opened her mouth to speak, but he said, 'No, wait a minute, please, let me work this out.' His hands ran through his hair again, rearranging the dark spikes.

She subsided, telling herself he was just as arrogant as all the rest, unable to accept he might just have missed something. Stop kidding yourself he's different, she told herself sternly.

'Right,' Tony said, his voice rich with satisfaction. 'We're dealing with a sexual sadist, agreed?'

'Agreed.'

'Sado-masochism is the power trip of sexual fetishes. But transvestism is the diametric opposite of that. TVs want to assume the supposedly weaker role that women have in society. What underpins transvestism is the belief that women have a subtle power, the power of their gender. It couldn't be further removed from the brute transaction of pain and power that sado-masochists crave. That's not part of a TV's fantasy at all. To convince the victims that they're dealing with a woman and not a man in drag, the killer would have to be an accomplished cross-dresser. But, uniquely in my experience of clinical psychology, he'd also have to be a sexual sadist. The two just don't go together,' Tony explained with an air of finality. 'The same goes for a transsexual. Probably more so, in fact, because of the counselling they have to go through before they're accepted for treatment.'

'So you're ruling it out, then,' Carol said, feeling unreasonably crushed.

'I never rule anything out. That's asking to make a fool

of yourself in this game. What I think is that it's so unlikely that I would be loath to include it in a profile because its very inclusion might push people in the wrong direction. But by all means keep it in mind. You're thinking along the right lines.' He smiled, unexpectedly, taking the sting of patronage out of his words. 'Like I said at the start, Carol, together we can crack it.'

'And you're absolutely convinced that it isn't a woman?' she asked.

'The psychology's all wrong. Taking the most obvious point, this killer's an obsessive, and that tends to be a male trait. How many women do you know who hang about station platforms in the rain in anoraks writing down train numbers?'

'But what about that syndrome, what's it called, where people get obsessed with someone else to the point where they make their lives a misery? I thought it was mainly women who suffer from that?'

'De Clerambault's Syndrome,' Tony said. 'And yes, it is principally women who suffer from it. But they only focus on one person, and the only person who's likely to get dead as a result is the sufferer, who sometimes commits suicide. The thing is that women's obsessions and compulsions are different from men's. Men's obsessions are about control; they collect stamps and catalogue them, they collect a pair of knickers from every woman they've slept with. They need trophies. Women's obsessions are about submission; in eating disorders, it's the obsession that takes them over and controls them rather than the other way about. A sufferer from de Clerambault's Syndrome who married the object of her desire would probably be the chauvinist's ideal of the perfect wife. That pattern doesn't fit our killer.'

'I see what you mean,' Carol said, loath to give up the one fresh idea she felt she'd contributed to the profiling process.

'Add to that the sheer physical strength involved here,' Tony continued, seeing her reluctance. 'You're fit. You're probably quite strong for your height. I'm only a couple of inches taller than you. But how far do you think you could carry me? How long would it take you to pick my body up from the boot of a car and dump it over a wall? Could you throw me over your shoulder and carry me through Carlton Park to the shrubbery? Now bear in mind that all the victims have been taller and heavier than me.'

Carol gave a rueful smile. 'OK, you win. I'm convinced. There was one other thing that occurred to me.'

'Let's hear it.'

'Reading your profile, it seems to me that the reason you advance for the maintenance of the gaps between the killings just isn't strong enough,' she started tentatively.

'You noticed that too,' he said wryly. 'It didn't convince me either. But I couldn't think of anything else to explain it. I've never encountered anything quite like it, either face to face or in the literature. All the serial offenders I know about go through escalation.'

'I've got a theory that might cover the problem,' Carol said.

Tony leaned forward, his expression absorbed. 'Speak to me, Carol,' he said.

Feeling like a goldfish in a bowl, Carol took a deep breath. She'd wanted his attention, but she wasn't quite sure if she liked it now she had it. 'I remember what you said to me a couple of days ago about the intervals.' She closed her eyes and recited, ' "With most serial killers, the gap between the killings tends to decrease quite dramatically. It's their fantasies that trigger off the killings in the first place, and the reality never quite matches up to the fantasy, no matter how much they refine their killing procedures. But the more extreme they get, the more blunted their sensibilities become and the more stimulus they need to get the sexual buzz that killing provides. So the kills have to become more frequent. Shakespeare said it. 'As if increase of appetite had grown by what it fed on.'" Am I right?'

'Remarkable,' Tony breathed. 'Can you do that with visuals as well, or is it only auditory?'

Exasperated, Carol cast her eyes upwards. 'Auditory only, I'm afraid. Anyway, when I read the bit in the profile where you suggest he might work with computers, something clicked. The question you didn't actually put but is obviously bothering you is, why isn't he getting desensitized to the videos faster as time goes by?'

Tony nodded. The point she'd raised was powerful, and it was precisely what was troubling him. He searched to find an answer that would satisfy them both. Groping for the solution as he went along, he said, 'Suppose, for the sake of argument, that the first video had the potential to keep him stable for twelve weeks. But he'd already set in train the process of capturing his second victim, and the opportune moment came along before he was actually compelled to kill again. He just couldn't resist the chance when it presented itself so perfectly. Afterwards, he realizes he's left eight weeks between the killings and he decides that eight weeks is going to be his pattern. So far, the videos have allowed him to maintain that. Maybe that is going to change now.'

Carol shook her head. 'It's plausible, but I'm not convinced.'

Tony grinned. 'Thank God for that. Neither am I. There's got to be a better explanation, but I don't know what it is.'

'How much do you know about computers?' she asked.

'I know where the on/off switch is and I know how to use the software I need to work with. Other than that, I'm a moron.'

'Well, that makes two of us. My brother, however, is a computer whizz kid. He's a partner in a games software house. The stuff he works on is leading-edge technology. Right now, he and his partner are developing a low-cost system that will allow games players to put images of themselves in the games that they're playing. In other words, instead of it being Arnie kicking the shit out of the bad guys on the screen in *Terminator 2*, it would be Tony Hill. Or Carol Jordan. The point is that there's already the hardware and software around that allows you to scan video tape and import the images into a computer. I think they call it digitized images. Anyway, once you've got that into the computer, you can manipulate it exactly how you want to. You can incorporate still photographs, or bits from other videos. You can superimpose things. When they first got the original hardware about six months ago, Michael showed me this sequence he'd made up himself. He'd taped some of the Tory Party conference and he'd also imported a video sex guide. He'd selected all these government ministers' faces while they were giving their speeches and superimposed them on the sex video.' Carol snorted with laughter at the memory. 'It was a bit choppy, but believe me, you've never seen John Major and Margaret Thatcher getting on so well! It gave a whole new meaning to the word "gobbledegook"!'

Tony stared at Carol in stunned silence. 'You're kidding me,' he said.

'It's the perfect explanation of why the videos manage to keep him under control.'

'Wouldn't that mean he'd have to be a real boffin, like your brother?'

'I don't think so,' Carol said. 'From what I gathered, the actual techniques involved are fairly simple. But the software and the peripherals that you need to do it are incredibly expensive. You could be talking two or three grand just for one piece of software. So he's either working for a company where he has that sort of equipment on tap and the privacy to work on his own stuff, or else he's a computer hobbyist with a lot of disposable income.'

'Or a thief,' Tony added, only half joking.

'Or a thief,' Carol agreed.

'I don't know,' Tony said dubiously. 'It does answer the problem, but it's totally off the wall.'

'And Handy Andy isn't?' Carol said belligerently.

'Oh, he's off the wall, all right, but I'm not sure he's that together.'

'He builds torture machines. That would be a lot easier with a computer design program. Tony, something's keeping him stable on his eight-week cycle. Why not this?'

'It's a *possibility*, Carol, no more than that at this stage. Look, why don't you make some preliminary enquiries, see how feasible what you're suggesting would be in practice?'

'You don't want to include it in the profile?' Carol asked, bitterly disappointed.

'I don't want to undermine the things I feel are strongly probable by including something that's really only a bit of kite-flying at this stage. You said yourself, it was triggered off by one of the few bits in the profile that is little more than speculation. Don't get me wrong, I'm not knocking the idea. I think it's brilliant. But we're going to have to work bloody hard as it is to overcome the resistance in some quarters to the profile as a whole. Even people who are broadly in support of the idea aren't necessarily going to agree with some parts of it. So let's not give them any easy targets. Let's bottom it, present it to them gift-wrapped so the snipers can't just knock it straight off the perch. OK?'

'Fine,' she said, knowing in her heart he was right. She picked up a sheet of paper and a pen. 'Check out software manufacturers and consultancies in Bradfield area,' she muttered to herself as she wrote. 'Check with Michael about manufacturers of necessary hardware/software then check sales records. Check recent thefts.'

'Computer clubs,' Tony added.

'Thanks, yes,' Carol said, adding that to her list. 'And bulletin boards. Oh boy, I'm going to be really popular with the HOLMES team.' She got to her feet. 'It's going to be a long job. I'd better get cracking. I'll take this down to Scargill Street now and give it to Mr Brandon. We'll need you to come in and go through it.'

'No problem,' Tony said.

'I'm glad something isn't.'

Tony stared out of the window of the tram, watching the city lights pass in a blur of rain. There was something cocoon-like about the gleaming white interior of the tram. Graffiti-free, warm, clean; it felt like a safe place to be. As the driver approached traffic lights, he gave a blast on the breathy horn. It sounded like a noise from childhood, the sort of hooting that a cartoon train would produce, he decided.

He turned away from the window and covertly studied the half-dozen other passengers on the tram. Anything to take his mind off the curious emptiness he felt now he had delivered his profile. It wasn't as if this would be the end of his involvement with the case. Brandon had told Carol that she was to have a daily briefing with him.

He wished he could have been more encouraging about her computer theory, but years of training and practice had rendered the habit of caution ingrained. The idea itself was brilliant. Once she had done some research into the practicability of what she was suggesting, he'd be only too happy to endorse it with her fellow officers. But for the sake of his profile's credibility, he had to keep his distance from ideas that the average copper would dismiss as science fiction.

He wondered how the police were faring that evening. Carol had called him to say that teams were going out in Temple Fields, trawling the area's regulars, trying to see if the profile suggestions produced any recognition. With luck, they might get some names that would cross-reference to data already in HOLMES, either from previous criminal records or from the car index numbers whose registered keepers had been fed into the system.

'The next stop will be Bank Vale station. Bank Vale station next stop,' the electronic voice from the speakers announced. With a start, Tony realized they had left the city centre far behind and were emerging on the far side of Carlton Park, less than a mile from his home. Bank Vale came and went, and Tony swung round in his seat, ready to make for the exit doors when the next stop was announced.

He walked briskly through the neat suburban streets, past the school playing fields, skirting the small copse that was all that remained of the plantation that had given the Woodside area its name. Tony glanced at the trees as he hurried past, thinking wryly that the path cutting diagonally through the wood would almost certainly be completely deserted. First it was the women walking home alone who had abandoned it. Then it was the children, kept away by anxious parents. Now, in Bradfield, it was the men who were learning the bitter lessons of life in jeopardy.

Tony turned into his street, relishing the quiet of the cul-de-sac. He'd get through the evening somehow. Maybe drive down to the supermarket and buy the ingredients for a chicken biryani. Pick up a video. Catch up on his reading.

As he turned the key in the lock, the phone started ringing. Dropping his briefcase, Tony ran for the phone, kicking the door to behind him. He picked up the phone, but before he could say anything, her voice trickled into his ear like warm olive oil soothing an earache. 'Anthony, darling, you sound like you're panting for me.'

He'd managed to avoid thinking about it all the way home, but he knew this was what he'd been hoping for.

Brandon had turned out the bedside light less than a minute before the phone rang. 'You should have known better,'

Maggie murmured as he dragged himself away from her complaisant warmth and reached for the receiver.

'Brandon,' he growled.

'Sir, it's Inspector Matthews,' the tired voice said. 'We've just picked up Stevie McConnell. The lads have just lifted him at the ferry port in Seaford. He was about to get on a ship for Rotterdam.'

Brandon sat up in a tangle of duvet, ignoring Maggie's protests. 'What have they done?'

'Well, sir, they didn't think there was a lot they could do, being as how he's on police bail and there's no conditions for him to breach.'

'Are they holding him?' Brandon was out of bed and reaching for his underwear drawer.

'Yes, sir. They've got him in the Customs lads' office.'

'What on?'

'Assaulting a police officer.' Kevin's voice somehow summoned up the image of a smirk as disembodied as the Cheshire Cat's smile. 'They rang me to ask what they should do next, and since you've taken such a personal interest in the case, I thought I should ask you first.'

Don't push it, Brandon thought savagely. All he said, however, was, 'I'd have thought it was pretty obvious. Arrest him for attempting to pervert the course of justice and bring him back to Bradfield.' He wrestled into a pair of boxer shorts and leaned over to pick up his trousers from the back of a chair.

'I take it we show him to the magistrates this time and ask that they refuse bail?' Kevin's voice was so sweet it was on the border of costing him his teeth, and not from decay.

'That's what we normally do when we have grounds, Inspector. Thanks for keeping me informed.'

'One other thing, sir,' Kevin said unctuously.

'What?' Brandon growled.

'The lads have also had to make another arrest.'

'*Another* arrest? Who the hell else have they had to arrest.'

'Superintendent Cross, sir. Apparently, he was trying rather forcibly to prevent McConnell from boarding the ferry.'

Brandon closed his eyes and counted to ten. 'Is McConnell hurt?'

'Apparently not, sir, just a bit shaken up. The super has a black eye, though.'

'Fine. Tell them to let Cross go home. And tell them to ask him to call me tomorrow, OK, Inspector?' Brandon replaced the phone and leaned over to kiss his wife, who had reclaimed the duvet and was rolled up tight as a hibernating dormouse.

'Mmm,' Maggie murmured. 'Are you sure you have to go in?'

'It's not my idea of a good time, believe me, but I want to be there when they bring this prisoner in. He's just the sort of bloke who might fall downstairs.'

'A problem with his balance?'

Brandon shook his head grimly. 'Not *his* balance. Other people sometimes get a bit unbalanced, love. We've already had one maverick on the prowl tonight. I'm not taking any more chances. I'll see you when I see you.'

Fifteen minutes later, Brandon walked into the murder squad room. Kevin Matthews was slumped over a desk at the far end of the room, his head cradled in his arms. As Brandon approached, he heard the soft snore of Kevin's breathing. He wondered when any of the squad had last had a straight night's sleep. It was when officers got tired and edgy at the lack of results that the serious mistakes happened. Brandon desperately wanted to avoid his name in lights ten years down the road as the man who masterminded a sensational miscarriage of justice, and he'd go to any lengths to avoid it. There was only one problem with that, he wryly acknowledged to himself as he sat down opposite Kevin. In order to keep his finger on the pulse of the investigation, he had to work the same kind of ridiculous hours that led to the very misjudgements he wanted to avoid. *Catch 22*. He'd read that, a few years back now, when Maggie had decided to go to evening classes and take the A Levels she'd never got round to at school. She'd said it was a wonderful book, funny, savage, sharply satirical. He'd found it almost too painful. It reminded him too strongly of the Job. Especially on nights like tonight when previously sane men turned desperado.

The phone rang. Kevin stirred, but didn't wake. Pulling a sympathetic face, Brandon reached over and lifted it. 'CID. Brandon speaking.'

There was a momentary, confused silence. Then a strained voice said, 'Sir? Sergeant Merrick here. Sir, we've copped for another body.'

Getting Gareth to Carlton Park was less easy than I'd anticipated. I'd done my reconnaissance carefully, I thought, and I'd counted on being able to drive down the access road used by the gardeners. What I hadn't taken into account was the long Christmas break. The road was blocked off by two metal posts slotted into the asphalt and locked in place with heavy padlocks. I could probably have squeezed through on the verge, since the jeep would have had no problem flattening the small shrubs that lined the road. But I would inevitably have left tyre tracks and probably tiny traces of paint. I had no intention of allowing Gareth to deprive me of my liberty, so that option was closed to me.

I parked the jeep round the back of the storage shed where the park staff kept their equipment. At least there I was out of sight both from the road and the park. There weren't many people around at two o'clock on Boxing Day morning, but success is all about taking pains.

I got out of the jeep and scouted around. The shed was out; it had a burglar alarm. But the gods were smiling on me now. Around the side of the shed, there was a low wooden trolley, the kind that porters used to wheel along station platforms in the days when there were railway porters who didn't think shifting luggage was beneath them. The gardeners probably used it to transport plants round the park. I pushed it back to the jeep and tipped Gareth's naked body on to it. I tucked a couple of black plastic bin liners round the body and sprayed the axles with a quick blast of lubricating oil to cure a nasty squeak, then stealthily I set off towards the shrubbery.

Again, I was lucky. I saw no one. I steered the trolley round to the rear of the bandstand towards the shrubs that covered the steep slope behind. At the edge of the path, I pushed the trolley on to the grass verge and into the edge of the shrubs. Then, wary of leaving footprints on the soft ground, I clambered on to the trolley and rolled Gareth's body off the end and into the bushes. I stepped back and jumped down, pulling the trolley after me. The bushes looked a little battered, but there was no sign of Gareth. With luck, he'd remain undiscovered until the postman delivered my Christmas message to the BEST.

Ten minutes later, the trolley was back in place and I was nosing out of the park's rear entrance on to a quiet lane opposite the churchyard. Even though the chances of being spotted were slim, I waited until the main road was in sight before I turned my lights on. Unlike Temple Fields, this was exactly the sort of area where some nosy insomniac would notice a strange vehicle in the early hours.

I drove home and slept for twelve hours, waking up in time for an interesting couple of hours on my computer before I went in to work. Luckily, it was a busy night, so I had plenty of complex problems to take my mind off the anticipation of the following day's Sentinel Times.

They'd done me proud, in spite of the short time they'd had to deal with my message. They'd obviously got on to the plod right away, and managed to persuade them to take it seriously. They'd given me the front page, complete with a photograph of my message, though without anything that would identify who the card had come from.

KILLER ALERTS BEST!

The naked and mutilated victim of a twisted killer has been discovered in a city park following a bizarre message sent to the Sentinel Times.

The killer, who signed himself 'Santa Claws', revealed in a grisly Christmas message that he had dumped the body in Carlton Park.

The sick communiqué appeared to be written in blood. It was scrawled on the company Christmas card of one of the city's leading firms of solicitors.

It was accompanied by a home video of the body's location, which BEST staff immediately recognized from the distinctive bandstand on Park Hill.

Alerted by BEST reporters, police dispatched a squad of uniformed and plain-clothes officers to the area of the park mentioned in the Christmas card.

After a short search among bushes off the nature trail near the bandstand, as indicated in the video, a uniformed constable discovered the body of a man.

According to police sources, the body was naked. The man's throat had been cut and his body mutilated.

It is believed that he may have been tortured before his death.

Although this area of Carlton Park is known as a pick-up area for predatory homosexuals, police are not presently connecting this killing with the murders earlier this year of two young men whose bodies were dumped in the Temple Fields 'gay village' area of the city.

The body has not yet been identified, and police have not released a description of the victim, who is believed to be in his late twenties or early thirties.

The package, which had been posted on Christmas Eve in Bradfield, arrived at the offices of the Sentinel Times in this morning's post, addressed to the news editor, Matt Smethwick.

Mr Smethwick said, 'My first thought was that someone was playing a sick joke, especially since I know one of the solicitors in the firm concerned.

'Then I realized my friend was out of the country on a skiing holiday, so it couldn't have been him who posted the package.

'I rang the police right away, and luckily they took it seriously.'

I should think they did. I'd never been more serious in my life. In spite of what the police were saying, the thought that Gareth was the third in a series must have made the short journey across their minds. It had certainly not escaped the attention of the journalists, who used the latest discovery as an excuse to rehash the killings of Adam and Paul. By the time the City Final edition hit the streets, they'd even found a rent-a-quote academic to spout forth.

INSIDE THE MIND OF A KILLER

The man the Home Office have chosen to spearhead the hunt for serial killers spoke today about the latest slaying that has terrified the city's gay community.

Forensic psychologist Tony Hill is one year into a major study funded by the government which will lead to the setting up of a criminal profiling task force similar to the FBI unit featured in The Silence of the Lambs.

Dr Hill, 34, was formerly the chief clinical psychologist at Blamires Hospital, the maximum-security mental unit which houses Britain's most dangerous criminally insane offenders, including mass murderer David Harney and serial killer Keith Pond, the Motorway Madman.

Giving his verdict, Dr Hill said, 'I have not been called in by the police to consult on any of these cases, so I know no more than your readers do about them.

'I'm reluctant to make a snap judgement, but if pushed, I'd say it was certainly possible, and possibly likely that the murders of Adam Scott and Paul Gibbs were committed by the same person.

'On the surface, this latest killing looks similar, but there are certain crucial differences. For a start, the body has turned up in a very different sort of location. Even though Carlton Park is also known as a gay cruising area, it's got a very different ambience from the urbanized Temple Fields.

'Also, the sending of the message to the Sentinel Times is a significant variation. Nothing similar happened in the earlier cases, and the killer makes no reference to previous killings.

'That inclines me to think we may be dealing with at least two separate individuals here.'

And so on and so forth, all of it in much the same vein. All of it saying in neon lights, 'We haven't got the faintest idea where to start looking.' I didn't think that worrying about Dr Tony Hill was going to keep me awake at nights. I decided it was time to teach the powers that be a couple of lessons they wouldn't forget in a hurry.

14

A man is not bound to put his eyes, his ears, and understanding into his breeches pocket when he meets with a murder. If he is not in a downright comatose state, I suppose he must see that one murder is better or worse than another, in point of good taste. Murders have their little differences and shades of merit, as well as statues, pictures, oratorios, cameos, intaglios or what not.

Tony lay sprawled in his bath, a snifter of brandy close at hand. Languid, relaxed, spent, he couldn't remember the last time he'd felt this comfortable, this optimistic. His experiences on the phone with Angelica, coupled with his conviction that he'd done a good job on the profile, had given him fresh hope. Maybe he didn't have to be dysfunctional. Maybe he could join the rest of the world, the ones who handled things, who assimilated the past and shaped their world according to what they wanted to see. 'I can change my life,' he announced.

The cordless phone rang. In a slow, flowing movement, Tony reached for it. It held no terrors for him now. Strange how he had grown to welcome rather than fear Angelica's calls. 'Hello,' he said cheerfully.

'Tony, it's John Brandon. I'm sending a car round for you. We've got another one.'

Tony sat up, the water swilling up and down like an experiment in a marine laboratory. 'You're sure?'

'Carol Jordan and Don Merrick were at the scene within five minutes of the shout.'

Tony squeezed his eyes shut. 'Oh God,' he groaned. 'Where is it?'

'The public toilets in Clifton Street. Temple Fields.'

Tony stood up and stepped out of the bath. 'I'll see you there,' he said heavily.

'OK, Tony. The car should be with you in five minutes or thereabouts.'

'I'll be ready.' Tony cut off the connection and walked out of the bathroom, towelling himself dry as he went. His mind racing, he pulled on jeans, T-shirt, shirt, sweater and leather jacket, adding an extra pair of socks as he remembered how bitter the night had been earlier. The doorbell rang just as he was tying the laces of his boots.

In the squad car, the atmosphere of tension wrecked any possibility of constructive thought as they sped through the night streets, blue light strobing against the unearthly orange of the streetlights. His escort, a pair of macho traffic cops, maintained a taciturn pose of absolute control that didn't lend itself to conversation. Tyres squealing, they swept into Clifton Street, the driver slamming on the anti-lock brakes at the sight of the police tapes that cut off access to the central section of the street.

The tape was lifted for Tony, who headed for the middle of the street where a cluster of police vehicles and an ambulance were parked at seemingly random angles. As he drew closer, he could see the sign for the public toilets, lit up against the looming dark of the building. By the ambulance, he spotted the conspicuous figure of Don Merrick, unmistakable with his bandaged head. Ignored by the milling officers, Tony pushed his way through to Merrick, who was deep in conversation on a mobile phone. He gave Tony a quick wave to signal he'd spotted him, and wound up his phone conversation with, 'All right, thanks, sorry to have bothered you.'

'Sergeant,' Tony said. 'I'm looking for Mr Brandon. Or Inspector Jordan.'

Merrick nodded. 'They're both inside. You'll be wanting a look too, I suppose.'

'Who found the body?'

'One of the street girls. She claims all the ladies loos were full, and that's why she went into the disabled cubicle. Me, I'd lay money she was with a client. He'll have legged it at the first sight of trouble.'

Out of the corner of his eye, Tony saw Carol emerge from the toilets. She made straight for the pair of them. 'Thanks for turning out,' she said as Merrick moved away and continued making his phone calls.

'If I said I wouldn't have missed it for the world, someone would almost certainly take it the wrong way,' Tony replied wryly. 'What makes you think it's Handy Andy?'

'The victim's naked, and his throat's been cut. He'd obviously been brought there in a wheelchair, but he'd been tipped out on to the floor. And lying on top of him, there was a copy of last night's *Sentinel Times* front page,' Carol replied, her voice strained, her eyes haggard. 'We provoked him, didn't we?'

'We didn't. The newspaper might have, but we didn't,' Tony said bleakly. 'I didn't expect him to react this fast, though.'

Merrick approached again and said cheerfully, 'Looks like I've tracked down the wheelchair. One went walkabout from the maternity hospital reception earlier on tonight. With a bit of luck, somebody might have seen it.'

'Good work, Don,' Carol said. 'Shall we take a look, then?' she asked Tony. He nodded and followed her as she shouldered her way through the milling officers towards the toilet entrance. Tony slowly walked into the lavatories, making a mental inventory as he looked around him, conscious of the black rubber tiled floor with its raised circles, the apparently random pattern of the grey and black tiles on the wall, the defiant graffiti, the raw dank air, the smell of disinfectant barely masking the piss. Inside the entrance, the toilets split in two, men to the left, women to the right. The disabled toilet was to the right, just by the entrance to the women's toilets. Brandon and Kevin Matthews stood by the door, looking in through the wide doorway. Tony walked up and joined their glum and silent communion. A photographer was standing just inside the door, off to one side, recording a scene that would shake some jury to the core, provided Brandon's men could deliver Handy Andy to them. Every few seconds, the stark white light of the flash etched the scene on the retinas of the watching men.

Tony stared intently at the body lying sprawled on the floor. It was, as Carol had said, naked, but it was not clean. There were smears of some sort of dark, oily substance on knees, elbows and one ankle. And there were bloodstains on the body too. The cut to the throat was wide, but not, Tony suspected, deep enough to have caused death. As far as he could see, the sexual organs themselves were undamaged, but the man's rectum and anus and the soft flesh around there had been savagely removed with deep cuts from a sharp blade. A warm surge of relief flowed through him, forcing him to recognize what he'd been refusing to think about. Like Carol, he too had been afraid that somehow his activities had provoked Handy Andy to break his cycle and to strike again. Ever since Brandon's phone call, that horror had been sitting on his shoulder like a malevolent bird of prey.

Tony turned to Brandon and said bluntly, 'It's not him. You've got a copycat.'

From the shadows at the far end of Clifton Street, coat collar turned up, Tom Cross joined the ghouls who seemed to spring from under the pavement itself and watched the familiar ritual dance of a murder-scene investigation. His lips pursed in a tight smile and he moved further back into the shadows. He took his diary out of his inside pocket and ripped out a page for notes. In the dim light from a streetlamp, he wrote, 'Dear Kevin; I bet you a bob to a gold clock that the Queer Killer didn't do this one. All the best, Tom.'

Seaford had been embarrassing as well as painful, but Tom Cross was not a man who allowed humiliation to stand in the way of his purpose. He folded the note in four and wrote, 'Detective Inspector Kevin Matthews. Personal', on it. He pushed his way through the crowd till he caught the eye of one of the constables behind the tape. 'You know who I am, don't you, lad?' Cross demanded.

The constable nodded hesitantly, casting a quick glance to either side, to see who was watching his encounter with the force's current leper.

Cross proffered the note. 'See that Inspector Matthews gets this, there's a good lad.'

'Yes, sir,' the constable said smartly, enclosing the note in his gloved fist, finding a moment to wonder who'd had the bottle to give Popeye Cross a shiner like that.

'I'll remember you when I'm back in harness,' Cross said over his shoulder as he pushed back through the spectators.

Cross cut back through an alley to the Volvo, parked in front of a nightclub's fire exit. The day had been far from satisfactory, and the morning held no promises of improvement. But the conviction that his message to Kevin Matthews was the truth made Tom Cross feel there had been some point to his activities.

'The postmortem will back me up,' Tony said stubbornly. 'Whoever killed this guy, it wasn't our serial killer.'

Bob Stansfield scowled. 'I don't see how you can be so sure, just because of a few oil stains.'

'It's not just that the body wasn't clean.' Tony ticked the points off on his fingers. 'He's the wrong age group. He's barely twenty, if that. Far from being in the closet, he was well known on the gay scene. You'd identified him by three this morning.'

Kevin Matthews nodded. 'Well known to Vice. Chaz Collins. An ex-rent boy who worked in a bar and liked rough sex.'

'Exactly,' Tony said. 'Also, there's not a mark on his penis or his testicles, whereas our killer has been progressively violent with those organs. All the press have been told so far is that the victims have been sexually mutilated. We haven't indicated how or where. This killer has interpreted that as a justification for getting rid of the whole anal area. I suspect he's done that because he buggered the victim before he killed him and he wanted to make sure Forensic didn't pick up any semen.' Tony paused to collect his thoughts, and to pour another cup of coffee from the pot that the canteen had sent up with the breakfast trolley John Brandon had ordered for their morning conference.

'The wheelchair,' Carol said. 'He took a big risk stealing that from the maternity hospital. I don't think that fits with the cautious behaviour the serial killer has always displayed so far.'

'And he's not been tortured,' Kevin added, through a mouthful of sausage-and-egg roll. 'Or not obviously, anyway.' He had a note in his pocket that would determine his view as much as anything that was said inside this room. Popeye might be off the job, but Kevin would back his instinct against anyone's.

But Bob Stansfield wasn't giving up. 'OK, what if he's doing it differently to make us think it's a copycat? What if he's deliberately trying to confuse us? After all, you can't ignore the newspaper lying there. And Dr Hill's profile warned us that the stress of inaccurate newspaper coverage might throw his pattern out.'

Tony carried on meticulously building a bacon-and-egg roll. He squirted an aureole of brown sauce round the yolk, closed the lid, squashed it so the yolk broke, then said,

'There's nothing wrong with that as a theory. It's perfectly feasible that he might kill just to flaunt his skills. It wouldn't be planned so far ahead as the others, so his choice of victim might well be very different. But the underlying pattern would be the same.'

'But it is,' Stansfield insisted. 'This kid had his throat cut, same as the other ones. And this bastard had made a right mess of him. How can you say he wasn't tortured when you look at the state of his arse?'

'If I was a betting man, I'd lay you a hundred to one that Chaz Collins didn't die from having his throat cut. I'd bet he was manually strangled and his throat cut afterwards to make it look like he's one of the serial-killer victims. I think what happened here is that some rough sex got a bit out of hand. Chaz was struggling while he was being sodomized, and his sex partner grabs him round the throat to get him to calm down. In the frenzy of orgasm, he squeezes too tight and he has a corpse on his hands. He figures his only chance of getting away with it is making it look like the serial killer's handiwork, and just in case we don't get the message, he dumps last night's paper on the body.'

'It's certainly plausible,' Brandon said, fastidiously wiping his greasy fingers on a paper tissue from a pack in his pocket.

'I think Tony's right,' Carol said decisively. 'My first reaction was that this was the fifth victim, but the more I think about it, the more I think I was wrong. You know what really clinches it for me?' Four pairs of eyes looked quizzically at her. She felt under as much pressure as she ever had in the witness box. 'Last night wasn't Monday.'

Tony grinned. Stansfield cast his eyes upwards. Kevin nodded reluctantly, and Brandon said, 'You think the night of the week's that important to him?'

Carol nodded. 'There's obviously some very strong reason why he goes for Monday, whether it's practical or superstitious. And whatever it is, it means a lot to him. I don't think he'd break it just to stick two fingers up to us.'

'I agree with Carol,' Kevin chipped in. 'Not just because of the night of the week. The other stuff, too.'

Stansfield looked surprised. 'Well, I'm obviously out-voted here,' he said good-naturedly. 'Separate job it is. Who's going to handle it, then?'

Brandon sighed. 'I'll have a word with Chief Superinten-dent Sharples at Central, pass the buck on to him. If it's not one of ours, it'll be down to their chief inspector.'

'He's off sick,' Kevin reminded him absently.

'So he is. Well, it'll be passed on to whichever inspector drops unlucky this morning. Now, I know the events of last night deprived us of the chance to give Dr Hill's profile the attention it demands, but I think we should –' Brandon was cut short by a knock at the door. 'Come in,' he said, trying to keep the irritation out of his voice.

The uniformed desk sergeant came in with a couple of envelopes. 'These have just come in, sir. One from Forensic, one from the path lab,' he said, laying them on the desk in front of Brandon. He was gone by the time Brandon had taken a sheaf of papers from each.

The others hid their impatience as Brandon skimmed through the pathologist's preliminary findings. ' "Dear John",' he read out, ' "I know you'll be screaming for some-thing on this one, since on the face of it, it looks like your serial killer has finally left some forensic traces. The bad news is, I don't think this is your man's handiwork. The victim was already dead from asphyxiation before his throat was cut. He was probably strangled manually. Also, I don't think he was cut with the same blade as your four earlier victims. From the look of it, this was a longer and thicker blade, more like a chef's vegetable chopping knife. Whereas, as you know, I reckon the earlier ones were done with something more like a filleting knife. Time of death I'd put between eight and ten p.m. last night. I'll let you have a full report as soon as . . ." blah, blah, blah. Well, looks like you were right, Tony.'

'Just as well I'd agreed to go along with you in time, otherwise I'd have looked a right prat,' Bob Stansfield said, extending a hand to Tony. 'Nice one, Doc.' Carol smiled secretly. Thank God the rest of the team were finally starting to accept Tony had something worth saying. It was amazing how different the atmosphere was now that Cross had gone.

Kevin shifted uncomfortably in his chair and said, 'What have Forensic got to say? Anything about our cases, or is it all preliminary stuff on Chaz Collins?'

Brandon flicked through the other papers. 'Prelims . . . prelims . . . prelims . . .' He drew his breath in sharply. 'Jesus Christ,' he said, baffled disgust in his voice.

'What is it, sir?' Carol asked.

Brandon rubbed a hand over his long face and stared at the paper again, as if checking that he hadn't misread it. 'They've been looking at the burns on Damien Connolly's body. Trying to work out what caused them.'

Tony stopped moving, the last bite of his sandwich halfway to his mouth. 'So what's the verdict?' Bob Stansfield demanded bluntly.

'This is totally bloody mental,' Brandon said. 'The only thing the lads in Forensic can come up with is the attachments for a cake-icing kit.'

'Of course,' Tony breathed dreamily, a distant smile lighting up his eyes. 'All the different star shapes. It's obvious, once it's pointed out.' He was suddenly aware that the other four were staring at him. Carol alone looked concerned. On the other faces, he saw expressions he'd seen before. Wariness, repugnance, disgust, incomprehension.

'Twenty-four-carat head banger,' Stansfield said bitterly. No one was quite certain whether he meant the killer or Tony.

*   *   *

The day Penny Burgess took over the *Bradfield Evening Sentinel Times*'s crime beat, she resolved that she was going to have better contacts than any of her male predecessors had managed. She realized that the male rituals of the masonic lodge and the smoker were going to remain closed worlds to her, but she determined that nothing was going to happen of any significance even there without her knowledge.

It wasn't surprising, then, that her home phone had rung twice between six and seven that morning. Both calls were from police officers, telling her that the man who'd been questioned earlier in connection with the Queer Killings had been arrested trying to skip the country. No names, no pack drill, but the anonymous suspect would be up before the magistrates that morning to be remanded in custody on a charge of attempting to pervert the course of justice. Following on from the discovery of a fifth body that had kept Penny out of her bed till gone two that morning, the connection was obvious.

Penny smiled dreamily to herself over her second cup of strong Earl Grey. It would be another front page for her tonight. Provided the editor and the lawyer didn't lose their bottle. She dumped her cup and cereal bowl in the sink and picked up her coat. Either way, it was going to be an interesting day.

Carol had drawn the short straw when it came to going to court to make sure everything went according to plan before the magistrates. Stansfield and Kevin had a backlog of routine enquiries to pursue, and Tony had gone to Leeds to keep a long-standing appointment with a Canadian academic psychologist who was attending a conference in the city. They needed, said Tony, to discuss some esoteric aspect of his task-force study. 'Conceptual mapping,' he'd told her as they'd snatched a few moments together after the group briefing.

He might as well have said 'quantum mechanics,' she thought ironically as she ran up the steps of the court building, her collar turned up against an east wind that promised sleet before dinner. She was going to have to learn a lot if she was going to get anyone to consider her seriously for this task force, that much was clear.

Any thoughts of the task force vanished as soon as she cleared the security check and turned into the long corridor that housed half of the dozen magistrates' courts. Instead of the usual disgruntled and defiant knots of low-level law breakers and their depressed families, she came face to face with a milling mob of journalists. She'd never seen that kind of media turnout at a Saturday-morning court, normally the quietest of the week. At the heart of the crowd, she could see Don Merrick, his back to the courtroom door, looked harassed.

Carol immediately wheeled round on her heel. But she was too late. She'd not only been spotted but also recognized by one of the handful of journalists who weren't visiting firefighters sent up by the national media networks at the sniff of a good tale. As she rounded the corner, they shot after her. All except Penny Burgess, who leaned against the wall and gave Don Merrick a tired smile.

'You weren't the only one that got the early-morning phone call, then,' he said cynically.

'Unfortunately not, Sergeant. At least the lads seem more interested in your guv'nor than they do in you.'

'She's better looking,' Merrick said.

'Oh, I wouldn't say that.'

'So I've heard,' Merrick said drily.

Penny's eyebrows climbed. 'You must let me buy you a drink sometime, Don. Then you can find out for yourself if the gossip's true.'

Merrick shook his head. 'I don't think so, pet. The wife wouldn't like it.'

Penny grinned. 'Not to mention the guv'nor. Well, Don,

now the pack's gone off in full cry after Inspector Jordan, are you going to let me exercise my democratic right to report the proceedings of the magistrates?'

Don Merrick stood clear of the door and waved her in. 'Be my guest,' he said. 'Just remember, Ms Burgess, the facts, and nothing but the facts. We don't want innocent people put at risk, do we?'

'You mean, like the Queer Killer's been doing?' Penny asked sweetly as she slipped past him and into the court.

Brandon stared in disbelief at Tom Cross. His face was knit in an expression of deep complacency, his multi-coloured eye socket the only disruption to a picture of smug self-satisfaction. 'Just between ourselves, John,' he was saying, 'you have to admit I was bang on the button about McConnell. That stiff last night – it wasn't down to the Queer Killer at all, was it? Well, it couldn't have been, could it, on account of you had me laddo banged up down-stairs.' Ignoring the absence of ashtrays in the ACC's office, Cross lit a cigarette and puffed a happy cloud of smoke into the air.

Brandon struggled, but he couldn't find the words. For once, he was speechless.

Cross looked around vaguely for somewhere to flick his ash, and settled for the floor, rubbing it into the carpet with the toe of his shoe. 'So when do you want me to start back on the job?' he asked.

Brandon leaned back in his chair and stared at the ceiling. 'If it was up to me, you'd never work in this town again,' he said pleasantly.

Cross choked on a mouthful of smoke. Brandon looked back down and savoured the moment. 'By heck, you like your joke, John,' Cross spluttered.

'I've never been more serious in my life,' Brandon said coldly. 'I called you here this morning to warn you off. What you did to Steven McConnell yesterday afternoon was assault. The file stays open, Superintendent. If you come anywhere near this investigation again, I'll have no hesitation in charging you. In fact, I'll enjoy it. I will not have this force brought into disrepute by any officer, serving or under suspension.' As Brandon's words sank in, Cross paled, then turned puce with anger and humiliation. Brandon stood up. 'Now get out of my office and my station.'

Cross got to his feet like a man concussed. 'You'll regret this, Brandon,' he stuttered furiously.

'Don't make me, Tom. For your own sake, don't make me.'

Thinking on her feet, Carol led the journalists round to the small lounge outside the lawyers' cafeteria. 'OK, OK,' she said, trying to damp down their baying with exaggerated hand movements. 'Look, if you'll just give me two minutes, I'll come right back and answer your questions, OK?'

They looked uncertain, one or two at the back showing a tendency to drift back towards the courts. 'Look, people,' she said, gently massaging her jaw, 'I'm in agony. I've got raging toothache, and if I don't ring my dentist before ten, I've got no chance of him fitting me in today. Please? Give me a break? Then I'm all yours, promise!' Carol forced a pained smile and slipped through to the cafeteria. There was a phone on the far wall, which she picked up. She made great play of taking out her diary and looking up a page, while dialling the familiar number of the court. 'Court one, please.' She waited for the connection, then said to the clerk, 'This is Inspector Jordan here. Can I speak to the CPS solicitor?'

Moments later, she was talking to the Crown Prosecution Service lawyer. 'Eddie? Carol Jordan. I've got about thirty hacks here waiting for Steven McConnell to come up. They're dying to jump to all the wrong conclusions, and I think you might prefer to get him on now while I've got them tied up at an impromptu press conference. Can you swing it with the clerk?' She waited while the solicitor muttered with the court clerk.

'Can do, Carol,' he said. 'Thanks.'

Keeping up the pretence, Carol put the phone down and scribbled something in her diary. Then she took a deep breath and headed back towards the pack.

Damien Connolly, the ultimate PC Plod. I couldn't have found a better person to teach the police a lesson if I'd searched for a year. But he was already there, on my list, one of my own personal Top Ten. He was harder to stalk than the others, because his shift pattern was often in conflict with the hours I work. But, as my grandmother always used to say, nothing worth having comes easy.

I trapped him in the usual way. 'I'm sorry to trouble you, but my car's broken down and I don't know where the nearest call box is. Can I use your phone to ring the AA?' It's almost laughably easy to get across the threshold of their homes. Three men dead, and still they fail to take the most elementary precautions. I almost felt sorry for Damien, since of all of them, he is the only one who had not betrayed me. But I needed to make an example of him, to show the police how pathetically useless they are. It was galling to find myself in agreement with the so-called 'gay community', but they were one hundred per cent correct when they said that while supposedly gay men were being killed, the police would do nothing. Killing one of their own would be the one thing that would make them sit up and notice. At last, they'd be forced to give me the recognition and respect I deserve.

To mark this, I had devised something a bit special for Damien. An unusual method of punishment, used occasionally to act as a terrible example pour discourager *les autres. It seems to have been most commonly used in cases of high treason, where men had plotted to kill the king. Appropriate, I thought. For what was Damien if not an integral part of the group that would bring me down if only they could?*

The earliest record of this treatment in England was in 1238, when some minor nobleman broke into the royal lodge at Woodstock intent on killing Henry III, there on a hunting trip. To demonstrate to any other potential traitors that the king was serious about attempts on his life, the man was sentenced to be torn limb from limb by horses then beheaded.

Another would-be royal assassin met the same fate in the mid eighteenth century. The aspiring assassin's name just had to be an omen. François Damiens stabbed King Louis XV at Versailles. His sentence read that 'his chest, arms, thighs and calves be burned with pincers; his right hand, holding the knife with which he committed the said attack, burned in sulphur; that boiling oil, melted lead, and rosin and wax mixed with sulphur be poured into his wounds; and after that his body be pulled and dismembered by four horses.'

According to reports of the execution, Damiens's dark-brown hair turned white during the torture. Casanova, that other great lover, reported in his memoirs, 'I watched the dreadful scene for four hours, but was several times obliged to turn my face away and to close my ears as I heard his piercing shrieks, half the body having been torn away from him.'

Obviously, I couldn't get a team of horses down into the cellar, so I'd had to come up with my own arrangement. I'd built a system of ropes and pulleys, attached to floor and ceiling and linked with one of those powered winches that are used on yachts. Each rope ended in a steel shackle that would fasten round wrist or ankle. By adjusting the lengths and tensions on the ropes, I had suspended Damien in midair, his limbs spread in a massive, human X, his pathetic genitals dangling in the middle like something in a butcher's shop.

The chloroform had a worse effect on him than it did on any of the others. As soon as he came round, he vomited violently, not an easy thing to achieve when you're hanging upright four feet above the floor. It was just as well I'd removed his gag, or he'd have choked on his own vomit, which would have cheated me out of my satisfaction in his punishment.

He was completely bewildered. He had no idea why he was there. 'Because I chose you,' I told him. 'You were just unlucky enough to choose the wrong job. Now I'm going to question you the way you question your suspects.'

While I'd been poking around in Auntie Doris's kitchen, vaguely looking to see if she had anything I might find useful, I'd come across her icing set. I remembered that icing set. Every year, her Christmas cakes were a miracle of artistry that any of Bradfield's bakers would have been hard pressed to equal. Once, she'd been called away by Uncle Henry while she was doing the big cake, and I'd picked up the icing bag, determined to help. I can't have been more than six.

When she came back from whatever disgusting farmyard task she'd been helping with and saw my efforts, she went berserk. She grabbed the weighted leather strop that Uncle Henry used to keep his cut-throat razors sharp and beat me so hard she tore my shirt. Then she locked me in my room without any supper, leaving me there for the best part of twenty-four hours with nothing but a bucket to piss in. I knew I had to find an appropriate use for her treasured icing set.

There was a blowlamp in the cellar which I used to heat up the icing attachments so I could leave my mark on Damien, just as the executioner had on his namesake Damiens two hundred and forty years before. There was something quite beautiful about the way his skin blossomed into scarlet starbursts as the red-hot piping rosettes came into contact with his pale flesh. It was also astonishingly effective. He told me everything I wanted to know and lots of rubbish I didn't give a damn about. I was just sorry he wasn't directly involved in the investigation into my previous work. I could have confirmed at first hand how hopelessly at sea the police are.

I decided to deposit the remains in Temple Fields again. I'd used the time since Gareth to find additional safe sites for the disposition of my handiwork. The back yard of the Queen of Hearts was perfect for my purpose; secluded and isolated at night. But it would come alive the next day, ensuring Damien wouldn't be left out in the cold for too long.

The time was ripe for a new game. In preparation for this, shortly after Adam, I went up into the loft and opened the trunk that contains those parts of my past I have retained. One of the things I'd kept as a souvenir was a leather jacket that was given to me by the engineer on a Soviet factory ship, in lieu of payment for a night he won't forget in a hurry. It looks and feels different from anything I've ever seen in this country. I ripped strips of leather from the sleeve until I was satisfied that I'd got something that could have been snagged on a nail or the sharp corner of a lock. I tucked the scrap in a drawer, then I chopped the rest of the jacket into shreds, stuck it in a plastic bag with eggshells and vegetable peelings, and drove into town until I found a skip to dump it in. By the time I needed to use the red herring, the remains of the jacket would be long buried in some anonymous landfill.

I couldn't help feeling a thrill at the thought of how many man-hours the police would waste trying to track down where this strange little piece of leather had come from, but they'd never tie it in to me. Apart from anything else, no one in Bradfield has ever seen me wear it.

This time, the publicity outshone everything I'd achieved so far. At last, the police admitted that one mind was behind all four killings. Finally, they had realized it was time to take me seriously.

With Damien off the planet and in my computer, I still had one more person to deal with before I could return to my original project. I couldn't settle to the task of finding a man worthy of me, a man to share my life as an equal and respectful partner, not until I had punished the man who had publicly treated me with such contempt.

Dr Tony Hill, the fool who hadn't even realized that Gareth Finnegan was one of my bodies, was the target. He had insulted me. He had poured scorn on me, refusing to acknowledge the extent of my achievements. He had no idea of the calibre of the mind he was up against. He was going to have to pay for his arrogance.

I couldn't help but see his disposal as a challenge. Wouldn't anyone?

15

Can they not keep to the old honest way of cutting throats, without introducing such abominable innovations . . . ?

The sound of a roaring crowd greeted Carol as she closed the door of the flat behind her. Michael, sprawled on one of the sofas, didn't even take his eyes off the rugby match on the television. 'Hi, sis,' he said. 'Needle match. Ten minutes, and I'm all yours.'

Carol glanced at the screen where muddy giants in England and Scotland's colours were sprawled across the turf in a collapsed scrum. 'Very hi-tech,' she muttered. 'I need a shower.'

Fifteen minutes later, brother and sister were sharing a celebratory bottle of cava. 'I have some print-out for you,' Michael said.

Carol perked up. 'Anything significant?'

Michael shrugged. 'I don't know what's significant to you. Your killer used five different-shaped objects to make the marks. I separated them out into five separate patterns. You've got what looks like a heart and some rudimentary letters. A, D, G and P. Mean anything to you?'

Carol shivered involuntarily. 'Oh, yes. Plenty. You got the print-out here?'

Michael nodded. 'It's in my briefcase.'

'I'll look at it in a bit. Meanwhile, can I pick your brains again?'

Michael drained his glass and refilled it. 'I don't know. Can you afford me?'

'Dinner, bed and breakfast at the country-house hotel of your choice, first weekend I have off,' Carol offered.

Michael pulled a face. 'At this rate, I could be collecting my pension before I collect on that one. How about you do my ironing for a month?'

'A fortnight.'

'Three weeks.'

'Consider it a done deal.' She offered her hand and Michael shook it.

'So, what do you want to know, sis?'

Carol outlined her theory about the computer manipulation of the killer's videos. 'What do you think?' she asked anxiously.

'It's a can-do,' he said. 'No question about that. The technology's available, and it's not difficult software to use. I could do it standing on my head. But you're talking serious money. Say three hundred for a video capture card, four hundred for a ReelMagic card, another three to five for a decent video digitizer, plus at least a grand for a state-of-the-art scanner. The real killer is the software, though. There's only one package that will do what you're talking about to any real quality. Vicom 3D Commander. We've got it, and it set us back nearly four grand, and that was six months ago. The last upgrade cost us another eight hundred. Manual thick as a house brick.'

'So it's not a piece of software that many people would have?'

Michael snorted. 'Damn right it isn't. It's a serious bit of kit, that. Professionals like us, video production studios and very serious hobbyists only.'

'How readily available is it? Could you buy it over the counter?' Carol asked.

'Not really. We dealt directly with Vicom, because we wanted them to run us a full demo before we committed ourselves to laying out that much dosh. Obviously, some specialist business suppliers sell it, but they wouldn't be shifting it in bulk. That would be mail order, anyway. Most computer stuff is.'

'The other stuff you mentioned – are they things that lots of people would have?' Carol asked.

'They're not uncommon. Off the top of my head, say two or three per cent market penetration on the video stuff, maybe fifteen per cent on the scanner. But if you're thinking of tracking down your man, I'd start with the Vicom end,' Michael advised.

'How do you think they'd be about letting us look at their sales records?'

Michael pulled a face. 'Your guess is as good as mine. You're not a competitor, and this is a murder investigation. You never know, they might be happy to cooperate. After all, if this guy is using their stuff, it'd be bad PR if they didn't. I can dig out the name of the guy we dealt with. He was their sales director. Scottish bloke. One of those names you can't tell which is the Christian name. You know, Grant Cameron, Campbell Elliott . . . It'll come to me . . .'

While Michael searched through his contacts book, Carol refilled her glass and savoured the prickle of bubbles against her palate. Lately, pleasure seemed to have been in short supply. But if she could come up with some leads on her theory, all of that might change.

'Got it!' Michael exclaimed. 'Fraser Duncan. Give him a ring Monday morning and mention my name. Time you got a break, sis.'

'You're not wrong,' Carol said with feeling. 'Believe me, I deserve it.'

Kevin Matthews lay sprawled across the rumpled king-sized bed, smiling up at the woman straddling him. 'Mmm,' he murmured. 'That was a bit nice.'

'Better than home cooking,' Penny Burgess said, running

her fingers through the dark auburn hair that curled across Kevin's chest.

Kevin chuckled. 'Just a bit.' He reached for the remains of the hefty vodka and coke Penny had poured for him earlier.

'I'm surprised you could get away tonight,' Penny said, moving forward languidly so her nipples brushed his.

'We've had so much overtime lately she's given up expecting me home for anything except for a bit of kip.'

Penny let her upper body fall heavily on Kevin, thrusting the breath out of his body. 'I didn't mean Lynn,' she said, 'I meant work.'

Kevin grabbed her wrists and wrestled her off him. When they subsided, lying side by side, giggling breathlessly, he finally said, 'There wasn't much to do, tell you the truth.'

Penny snorted incredulously. 'Oh yeah? Last night Carol Jordan finds body number five, the suspect is arrested trying to leave the country and you tell me there's nothing much doing? Come on, Kevin, this is me you're talking to.'

'You've got it all wrong, darling,' Kevin said magnanimously. 'You and all the rest of your media cronies.' It wasn't often he got the chance to put Penny right and he intended to make the most of it.

'What do you mean?' Penny propped herself up on one elbow, unconsciously covering her body with the duvet. This wasn't a bit of fun any more; this was work.

'Number one. The body Carol found last night wasn't one of the serial killer's victims. It was a copycat job. The postmortem proved that beyond reasonable doubt. It was just another seedy little sex murder. Central should clear it up in a few days with a bit of help from Vice,' Kevin said, the self-satisfaction obvious in his voice.

Penny bit on the bullet and said sweetly through clenched teeth, 'And?'

'And what, darling?'

'If that was number one, there must be a number two.'

Kevin smiled, so smug that Penny made the instant decision that he was on the out just as soon as she had an acceptable alternative lined up. 'Oh yes, number two. Stevie McConnell isn't the killer.'

For once, Penny ran out of words. The information was shocking in itself. But more shocking was the fact that, knowing this, Kevin had said nothing. He had remained silent and let her paper run a story that was eventually going to make her look an ill-informed pillock. 'Really?' she said, in the superior accent she hadn't used since the day she'd gratefully quit boarding school and made the decision to go vocally downmarket.

'That's right. We knew that before he legged it.' Kevin lay back on the pillows, blissfully unaware of the look of distilled hatred that Penny was beaming in his direction.

'So what exactly was that pantomime at court this morning in aid of?' she demanded in tones her elocution mistress would have been proud of.

Kevin smirked. 'Well, most of us had already decided that McConnell wasn't our man. But Brandon had put a tail on him, so when he tried to skip the country, we were more or less obliged to pull him in. By that time, it was starting to look definite that McConnell isn't the Queer Killer. Plus, he doesn't fit the profile that Tony Hill came up with.'

'I don't believe I'm hearing this,' Penny said sharply.

Kevin finally registered that all was not well. 'What? You got a problem, darling?'

'Just a fucking bit,' said Penny, enunciating each syllable crisply. 'You mean to tell me you've not only put an innocent man on remand, you've also let the world's press broadcast the assumption that this man is quite probably the Queer Killer?'

Kevin propped himself up and took another swig of his drink, reaching out to rumple Penny's hair with his other hand. She pulled away with a jerk. 'It's no big deal,' he said patronizingly. 'Nobody can get a lynch mob together and go round his house while he's inside. And we reckon that telling the world between the lines that we've got the killer banged up might just provoke the real killer into getting in touch with us to make sure we know he's still out there.'

'You mean you want to drive him to kill again?' Penny demanded, her voice rising.

'Of course not,' Kevin said indignantly. 'I mean, to get in touch. Like he did after he'd killed Gareth Finnegan.'

'My God,' Penny said wonderingly. 'Kevin, how can you sit there and tell me that nothing bad can happen to Stevie McConnell while he's locked up in prison?'

While Penny Burgess and Kevin Matthews were arguing the morality of Stevie McConnell's remand, in C Wing of Her Majesty's Prison Barleigh, three men were taking turns to show Stevie McConnell what happens to sex cases in prison. At the end of the landing, a warden stood impassively, appearing as oblivious to McConnell's screams and entreaties as a deaf man with his hearing aid switched off. And on the moors above Bradfield, a ruthless killer put the finishing touches to the torture instrument that would help show the world that the man in prison was not the person responsible for four perfectly executed serial punishments.

The HOLMES room was a quiet hum of activity, operators staring into screens and tapping keys. Carol found Dave Woolcott sitting in his office picking listlessly at fish and chips. He looked up when she entered and managed a wan smile. 'Thought you were having a night off,' he said.

'I'm still hoping to. My brother promised to buy me a bucket of popcorn all to myself if I make it to the multiscreen before the film begins. I just wanted to swing by and run something past you.' She dumped two plastic bags on Dave's desk. Glossy computer magazines spilled out.

'I've got this theory,' she said. 'Well, more of a hunch.' For the third time, Carol outlined her idea about the killer importing videos and transforming them into supports for his fantasies.

Dave listened carefully, nodding as Carol's ideas sank in. 'I like it,' he said simply. 'I've read that profile a couple of times now, and I really can't accept what Dr Hill says about keeping stable just by using videos of the killings. It doesn't make sense. Your idea does. So what do you want from me?'

'Michael reckons that tracing the buyers of Vicom 3D Commander might lead us to him if we're right. I'm not so sure. It's possible that the company the killer works for has the software, and he does the manipulation work there. To be on the safe side, though, he'd need to do all the scanning and digitizing at home. So I thought it would also be worthwhile doing a trawl of the suppliers of video digitizers and video capture cards. We can find suppliers via the ads in these magazines, since virtually all computer stuff comes mail order. We should also contact local computer clubs too. If you've got any bodies to spare, that is.'

Dave sighed. 'Dream on, Carol.' He picked up a magazine and flicked through the pages. 'I suppose I could draw up a list tonight and tomorrow, and first thing Monday morning we could get a couple of DCs to do a ring-round. When my operators will have time to input the data, I don't know, but I will see that it gets done. OK?'

Carol grinned. 'You're a star, Dave.'

'I'm a bloody martyr, Carol. My youngest's cut two teeth that I haven't even seen yet.'

'I could stay and help you go through the magazines,' Carol said reluctantly.

'Oh, bugger off. Go and enjoy yourself. It's about time one of us did. What are you going to see?'

Carol pulled a face. 'It's a Saturday Special double bill – *Manhunter* and *The Silence of the Lambs*.'

Dave's laughter echoed in her ears all the way to the car.

The long howl seemed to come from the pit of his stomach. As his orgasm shuddered through him like a runaway train, Tony felt a glorious sense of release. 'Oh, God,' he groaned.

'Oh, yeah, yeah,' Angelica gasped. 'I'm coming again, again, oh, Tony, Tony . . .' Her voice faded in a gulping sob.

Tony lay back on his bed, chest heaving, the smell of sweat and sex heavy around him. He felt as if he'd been suddenly detached from a burden he had been carrying for so long he had ceased to notice its weight. Was this what being cured felt like, this sense of light and colour, this sensation of having dumped the past like sacks of coal in a bunker? Was this how his patients felt when they'd unloaded their mess on him?

In his ear, he could hear the ragged sound of her breathing. After a few moments, she said, 'Wow. Just wow. That was the best ever. I just love the way you love me.'

'It was good for me, too,' Tony said, meaning it for once. For the first time since they had started this strange combination of therapy and sexual gameplaying, he'd had no trouble with his erection. Right from the start, he'd been hard as a rock. No fading, no wilting, no shame. Just the first problem-free sex he'd had for years. OK, so Angelica wasn't actually in the room with him, but it was a giant step in the right direction.

'We make the sweetest music,' Angelica said. 'Nobody's ever turned me on like you do.'

'Do you do this often?' Tony asked languidly.

Angelica chuckled, a husky, sexy gurgle of laughter. 'You're not the first.'

'I could tell that. You're far too much of an expert,' Tony flattered, not entirely insincerely. She'd been the perfect therapist for him, that much was certainly true.

'I'm very choosy about the men I allow to share with me,' Angelica said. 'It's not everyone who appreciates what I have to offer,' she added.

'They'd have to be very strange not to enjoy it. I know I do.'

'I'm glad, Anthony. You'll never know how glad. I have to go now,' she said, her tone changing abruptly to the businesslike one Tony had come to associate with the end of their calls. 'Tonight has been really special. We'll talk soon.'

The line went dead. Tony switched off the phone and stretched out. Tonight, with Angelica, for the first time in his life, Tony had felt a protective care that succoured without smothering. His grandmother, he knew intellectually, had loved him and cared for him, but theirs had never been a demonstrative family, and her love had been brusque and practical, meeting her needs rather than his. The women he'd been involved with in the past had, he now realized, been her emotional doppelgangers. Thanks to Angelica, he dared hope the pattern had been broken. It had caused him enough pain over the years.

His sexual life had started later than most of his contemporaries, in part because his body had been reluctant to mature. Until his seventeenth year, he'd been by far the smallest boy in his class, condemned to dating the thirteen- and fourteen-year-olds who were even more scared of sex than he was. Then, suddenly, he'd shot up five inches in as many months. By the time he'd gone to university, he'd lost his virginity in a clumsy fumble on a single bed, the candlewick bedspread leaving him with uncomfortable friction burns for days afterwards. His girlfriend, relieved to be rid at last of the encumbrance of her virginity, had dumped him days later.

At university, he'd been too shy and hard-working to improve his experience by much. Then, when he'd started work on his doctorate, he'd fallen head over heels with a young philosophy tutor in his college. Because he was bright and interesting, he captured her interest. Patricia made no secret of the fact that she was a woman of the world, just as she made no secret of the fact that she had ended their relationship because of his lacklustre performance between the sheets. 'Face it, sweetheart,' she'd told him, 'your brain might be DPhil material, but your fucking wouldn't earn you an O level.'

It had been downhill from then. The last couple of women Tony had been involved with had thought he was a perfect gentleman, never pressurizing them into bed. Until they got him there and discovered how seldom he could actually deliver. He had long ago discovered how hard it was to convince a woman that the fact that he couldn't get it up had nothing whatsoever to do with her. 'They just got fed up with having their egos bashed,' he said aloud.

Maybe now he had finally found a way to confront the past and move forward. A few more nights like tonight with Angelica and maybe, just maybe, he'd be ready to try the real thing. He wondered if her services extended to that. Perhaps he should start thinking about dropping a few hints.

Brandon read the sheet of paper on his desk and rubbed the grit of sleep from his eyes. He and Dave Woolcott had spent the evening going through the dozens of reports that had flowed in from the actions Dave had ordered in response to the correlations thrown out by the HOLMES computer. In spite of their determined efforts to find some slender thread of evidence to unravel back to the killer, there was nothing that either of them could identify as a lead.

'Maybe this idea of Carol's will do the business for us,' Dave yawned.

'We've tried everything else,' Brandon said, his voice as depressed as his face. 'It can't hurt to run with it.'

'She's a smart operator, that one,' Dave remarked. 'She'll be running the shop one of these days.' There was no bitterness in his tone, only a tired admiration. Another yawn split his face.

'Go home, Dave. When was the last time you saw Marion awake?'

Dave groaned. 'Don't you start, sir. I was going to knock off anyway, there's not a lot doing. I'll be in tomorrow, finish off listing these computer suppliers.'

'OK, but not too early, you hear? Give your family a treat. Eat breakfast with them.' Before he took his own advice, Brandon wanted to go through the witness statements and officers' impressions once more, unable to believe that there wasn't something lurking in there that would give them their first serious break. By the time he was halfway through he was finding it almost impossible to motivate himself to get through the rest of the pile. The prospect of tucking himself round Maggie's warm body was overwhelmingly appealing.

Brandon sighed and focused on the next sheet of paper. His scrutiny was interrupted by the insistent trill of his telephone. 'Brandon,' he sighed.

'Sergeant Murray here, front desk. Sorry to interrupt you, sir, but none of the inspectors are in the station at the moment. Thing is, there's a gentleman down here I think you'll want to talk to. He's a neighbour of Damien Connolly's, sir.'

Brandon was already out of his chair. 'I'm on my way,' he said.

The man at the front desk was sitting on the wooden bench that ran along the wall, head down, the rough blur of stubble dark along his jaw. As Brandon came round from behind the counter, he looked up. Late twenties, Brandon estimated. Sun-bed tan, bruised circles under his eyes. Some sort of businessman, judging by the expensive but sombre suit and the silk tie hanging askew under the open top button of the shirt. He had the rumpled, red-eyed look of someone who's been travelling so long they've forgotten which day or which city it is. Seeing someone more tired than himself seemed to inject Brandon with fresh energy. 'Mr Harding?' he said cheerfully. 'I'm John Brandon, the Assistant Chief Constable in charge of the investigation into Damien Connolly's death.'

The man nodded. 'Terry Harding. I live a couple of doors down from Damien.'

'My sergeant tells me you might have some information for us.'

'That's right,' Terry Harding said, his voice thick with exhaustion. 'I saw a stranger driving out of Damien's garage the night he was killed.'

I had already started work on Dr Tony Hill even before I
had dispatched Damien Connolly. It seemed poetic justice
to me that, like Damien, his name was already on my
list as a potential partner. If I had needed any kind of
reinforcement that I was doing the right thing by punishing
him, that was it.

So, I already knew where he lived, where he worked and
what he looked like. I knew what time he left the house
in the morning, what tram he caught to work, and how
long he stayed in his little office in the university.

I only realized how smoothly everything had gone up
till now when things started to move in directions I hadn't
predicted and didn't like. I suppose I'd made the mistake
of underestimating the stupidity of the forces opposed to
me. I'd never thought there was much brain power shared
out among the officers of Bradfield police, but the latest
developments shook even me. They arrested the wrong
man!

Their incredible lack of intelligence and perception was
matched only by the media, following uncritically like
sheep. I couldn't believe it when I picked up the Sentinel
Times to read that a man was in custody helping police
enquiries into my killings. The arrest came after a street
assault involving a police officer. How on earth could they
imagine that someone who had taken as much care as I
had would end up in some street brawl in Temple Fields?

It was an insult to my intelligence. Did they really think I was some out-of-control street yob?

I read and reread the article, unable to credit the depths of their foolishness. Anger burned inside me. I could feel it in my guts like indigestion and wind cramps rolled into a spiky ball. I wanted to do something vicious and dramatic, something that would prove to them how wrong they were.

I worked out with my weights till my muscles were trembling from effort and my kit was saturated with sweat, but still the anger refused to abate. I stormed upstairs to my computer and worked on the videos of Damien that I'd imported into my system. By the time I'd finished, we'd performed sexual gymnastics that the Russian national team would have been proud of. But nothing satisfied me. Nothing took the anger away.

Luckily, unlike them I'm not stupid. I know how dangerous uncontrolled anger could be for me. I needed to harness my anger, to be creative with it and make it work for me. I forced myself to channel my rage into constructive pathways. I planned in meticulous detail how I would capture Dr Tony Hill, and what I would do with him when I got him. I'd be keeping him in suspense – literally.

Squassation and strappado. The Spanish Inquisition knew exactly how to make the most of what was available. They simply harnessed the most powerful force on the planet, the force of gravity. All you need is a winch, a pulley, a few ropes and a lump of stone. You fasten the victim's hands behind his back and run a rope from them through the pulley. Then you tie the stone to his feet.

In his book The Horrid Cruelties of the Inquisition, published in 1770, John Marchant described this efficient torture most eloquently:

He is then drawn up on high, till his head reaches the pulley. He is kept hanging in this manner for some time, that by the greatness of the weight hanging at his feet, all his joints and limbs may be dreadfully stretched, and on a sudden he is let down with a jerk, by the slacking of the rope, but is kept from coming quite to the ground, by which terrible shake, his arms and legs are disjointed, whereby he is put to the most exquisite pain; the shock which he receives by the sudden stop of his fall, and the weight at his feet stretching his whole body more intensely and cruelly.

The Germans added a refinement that attracted me. Behind the victim, they placed a spiked roller, so that as he descended, the rollers cut into and excoriated his back, leaving his body a bloody, dislocated mass. I considered reproducing this effect, but even after a lot of juggling with the layout, I couldn't come up with a design on the computer that I was satisfied would work smoothly, unless I cuffed his hands in front of him, which makes the squassation and strappado far less effective. Keep it simple, that's my motto.

While I was planning and constructing, I took steps to draw my web even tighter around Dr Hill. He might think he could climb inside my head, but he'd got things the wrong way round.

I couldn't wait to get started. I was counting the hours.

16

'Now, Miss R., supposing that I should appear at about
midnight at your bedside, armed with a carving knife, what
would you say?' To which the confiding girl had replied,
'Oh, Mr Williams, if it was anybody else, I should be frightened. But as soon as I heard your voice, I should be tran-
quil.' Poor girl; had this outline sketch of Mr Williams been
filled in and realized, she would have seen something in the
corpse-like face, and heard something in the sinister voice,
that would have unsettled her tranquillity forever.

When the phone rang, Carol's first reaction was outrage.
Ten past eight on a Sunday morning could only mean work.
She stirred, a long, low growl of discontent making Nelson's ears prick. Carol's arm appeared from under the
covers, groping around on the bedside table. She connected
with the phone and grunted, 'Jordan,' into it.

'This is your early-morning alarm call.' The voice was
far too cheerful, Carol decided, before the identity of her
caller registered.

'Kevin,' she said. 'This better be good.'

'It's better than good. What would you say to a witness
who saw the killer drive away from Damien Connolly's
house?'

'Say again?' she mumbled. Kevin repeated his announcement. The second time round, his voice catapulted Carol
into a sitting position, on the edge of the bed. 'When?' she
demanded.

'The guy walked in late last night. He's been out of the

country on business. Brandon interviewed him. He's called a meeting for nine,' Kevin said, excited as a Christmas child.

'Kevin, you bastard, you might have called me before now . . .'

He chuckled. 'I thought you needed your beauty sleep.'

'Bollocks to beauty sleep . . .'

'No, I've only been in five minutes myself. Can you bring the doc in with you? I just tried calling him, but there was no reply.'

'OK, I'll swing round by his place and see if I can raise him. He seems to have a habit of switching the phones off. Fancy thinking he could get away with a decent night's sleep. You can tell he's not a copper,' she added. Carol replaced the phone abruptly and headed for the shower. The thought that Tony might have switched off his phone because he was with the woman on the answering machine crossed her mind. The idea made her stomach hurt. 'Silly bitch,' she muttered to herself as the water cascaded over her.

By twenty to nine, she was leaning on Tony's doorbell. After a couple of minutes, the door opened. Bleary eyed, struggling with the belt of his dressing gown, Tony peered out at her. 'Carol?'

'Sorry to wake you,' she said formally. 'You weren't answering your phone. Mr Brandon asked me to pick you up. There's a meeting at nine. We've got a witness.'

Tony rubbed his eyes, looking bemused. 'You better come in.' He walked down the hall, leaving Carol to close the door behind her. 'Sorry about the phones. I was late getting to sleep, so I switched them off.' He shook his head. 'Can you hang on while I have a shower and a shave? Otherwise, I'll make my own way in. I don't want you to be late on my account.'

'I'll wait,' Carol said. She picked the paper off the mat and flicked through it, leaning against the wall, alert for the telltale signs of a third person's presence. She felt unreasonably pleased when she heard none. Even though she knew her reaction was childish, it didn't mean these responses were going to stop overnight. She was just going to have to learn to disguise them until they died away, as she felt sure they would eventually, starved out of existence by Tony's lack of interest.

Ten minutes later, Tony reappeared in jeans and rugby shirt, hair damp and neatly brushed. 'Sorry about that,' he said. 'My brain doesn't work until I've had a shower. Now, what's all this about a witness?'

Carol told him the little she knew on the way to the car.

'That's great news,' Tony enthused. 'First big breakthrough, isn't it?'

Carol shrugged. 'It depends how much he can tell us. If the guy was driving a red Ford Escort, it doesn't take us a lot further forward. We'd need something solid to cross-match. Maybe something like the computer angle.'

'Oh yes, the computer theory. How goes that?'

'I discussed it with my brother. He reckons it's perfectly feasible,' Carol said coldly, feeling patronized.

'Great!' Tony enthused. 'I really hope that works out. I wasn't trying to pour cold water on it, you know. I have to work with the balance of probabilities, and your idea's way beyond my parameters. But it's the kind of investigative brainwave that we're going to need on the national task force. I really think you should seriously consider signing up when we get the show on the road.'

'I didn't think you'd be comfortable with the idea of working with me after this,' Carol said, eyes firmly fixed on the road.

Tony took a deep breath. 'I've never met a police officer I'd rather work with.'

'Even if I do trespass on your personal space?' she asked bitterly, hating herself for picking at the hurt like an old scab.

Tony sighed. 'I thought we'd agreed we could be friends? I know I . . .'

'Fine,' she interrupted, wishing she'd never opened up the conversation. 'I can do friends. What do you think of Bradfield Victoria's chances in the Cup?'

Startled, Tony twisted in his seat and stared at Carol. He saw a smile twitching at the corner of her mouth. Suddenly, they were both laughing.

The latest government threats to the prison service meant the officers at HM Prison Barleigh had started to work to rule. That in turn meant that prisoners were banged up for twenty-three hours in every twenty-four. Stevie McConnell lay on his side on his bunk bed in the cell he had to himself. Following the attack that had left him with two black eyes, a couple of cracked ribs, more bruises than he could count, and the kind of sexual damage that made sitting down an option too painful to contemplate readily, he had asked for and been granted solitary confinement.

It didn't matter how much he protested that he wasn't the Queer Killer. Nobody cared, neither cons nor screws. He'd realized that the warders held him in as much contempt as his fellow prisoners when he'd heard the sounds of slopping-out all along the wing. But no officer had unlocked his cell door to allow him to empty the stinking bucket of his sewage that sat in the corner, its smell insistent and somehow more disgusting than any of the dozens of public toilets where Stevie had picked up strangers for sex.

As far as he could see, his prospects were bleak. The very fact that he was behind bars was enough to condemn him in most people's eyes. Probably the whole world was convinced that the Queer Killer had taken his last victim now that Stevie McConnell was in jail. After he'd been released following his first stretch of questioning, he'd been painfully aware that everyone at work, staff and clients, were giving him a wide berth, refusing to meet his eyes.

One drink in a Temple Fields bar where he'd been a regular for years had been enough to show him that gay solidarity had mysteriously deserted him too. The police and the press clearly thought he was their psychopath. And until they caught the Queer Killer, Bradfield wasn't going to be a welcoming place for Stevie McConnell. The decision to move out to Amsterdam where an ex-lover ran a gym had seemed to make sense at the time. It hadn't occurred to him that they'd be tailing him.

The irony that this had all happened to him because he'd rushed to the defence of a police officer in the first place was not lost on Stevie. He gave a bitter bark of laughter. That big Geordie sergeant was probably counting his blessings that he'd been smacked with a half-brick, figuring that that was the only thing that had saved him from being the Queer Killer's next victim. The reality was that Stevie McConnell was the only victim around that night. And it wasn't going to get any better. Even his shocked family didn't want to know, according to his solicitor.

Lying there, examining his future dispassionately, he came to a decision. Grimacing with pain, Stevie rolled off the bunk and took off his shirt, wincing at the stab of pain from his ribs. With his teeth and nails, painstakingly he unpicked the seams that held the denim together. On the sharp end of a bed spring, he ripped the edges of the material so he could tear it into thin strips, which he plaited together for extra strength. He tied one end of the make-shift ligature round his neck in a tight noose, then climbed on to the top bunk. He fastened the other end of his short rope to the bottom rail of the upper berth.

Then, at seventeen minutes past nine on a sunny Sunday morning, he threw himself head first over the edge.

Like an ailing company which has won a life-saving tender against all odds, Scargill Street was buzzing with excited activity. At the heart of it all was the HOLMES room, where officers stared into screens, manipulating the new information, evaluating the new correspondences the system was throwing out.

In his office, Brandon held a council of war with his four inspectors and Tony, all of them clutching a photocopy of Brandon's notes on his interview with Terry Harding. The ACC had only had five hours' sleep, but the prospect of movement on the enquiry had given him a new energy, betrayed only by the heavy shadows around his deep-set eyes. 'To recap, then,' Brandon said. 'At about quarter past seven the night Damien Connolly was killed, a man drove out of his garage in some kind of big four-wheel drive jeep, dark in colour. He got out of the jeep to close the garage door, and that's when our witness got his best look at him. The description we've got is white, five ten to six feet, aged between twenty and forty-five, possibly with his hair tied back in a ponytail. Wearing white trainers, jeans and a long waxed coat. Overnight, the HOLMES team have been going through the vehicles clocked in Temple Fields that fit the description. Most of these drivers have already been interviewed, but they're all going to be followed up and questioned more thoroughly now we've got Terry Harding's evidence. Bob, I want you to take charge of that, and I want alibis checking too.'

'Right, boss,' Stansfield said, flicking the ash off his cigarette with a determined motion.

'Oh, and Bob? Can you get someone to check that Harding really has been in Japan all week on a business trip? I want to make sure we cover all the bases on this one.' Stansfield nodded.

'I'm sending a car round for Harding at eleven o'clock,' Brandon went on, checking the list he'd made in the kitchen at seven. 'Carol, I want you to do the interview. Check what taxi firm Harding used to take him to the airport; let's see if we can get that time narrowed down a bit more. Tony, I'd like you to sit in on it. Maybe you can help us with strategies to improve his recollection, see if we can get any firm description of what this character looks like.'

'I'll do my best,' he said. 'At least I can probably distinguish between what he really remembers and what he thinks he remembers.'

Brandon gave him an odd look, but carried on regardless. 'Kevin, I want you to organize a team to hit the car showrooms, get as many brochures and posters as you can of four-wheel drive jeeps, so we can show them to Mr Harding and see if he can give us a positive ID.'

'Will do, sir. Do you want us to go back to the neighbours in the earlier cases, see if anyone noticed the same vehicle there?' Kevin asked eagerly.

Brandon considered for a moment. 'Let's see how we go on today,' he said after a few moments. 'It'll take a lot of bodies and time to go over the old ground again, and we might not need it. It's probably worth having a word with the rest of the neighbours in Connolly's street, though. Now we've got something positive to hit them with. Good idea, Kevin. Now, Dave. What can you do for us?'

Woolcott outlined the actions the HOLMES team were already carrying out. 'With it being Sunday, I'm holding back on contacting Swansea until we've tried to get the vehicle narrowed down. The more information we can give them, the fewer possibilities we'll have to deal with. If this Harding bloke can give us make, model and year, or at least eliminate some models, we can ask DVLC to let us have a list of all the matches throughout the UK. Then we can start interviewing registered keepers, starting with Bradfield and moving out from there. It's a helluva big job, but we should get there in the end.'

Brandon nodded his acknowledgement. 'Anybody got anything else?'

Tony lifted a hand. 'If you're questioning neighbours anyway, it might be worth extending the enquiries slightly.'

All eyes were on him, but he was only aware of Carol's. What had happened between them had sharpened his desire to be instrumental in capturing Handy Andy. 'This guy is a stalker, I don't think anyone would dispute that now. I think he'd been watching Damien Connolly for a while. Given that we're in the middle of winter and it's not the ideal weather for standing around in the open, chances are he did the bulk of his spying from his car. He probably didn't park up in the close itself, since he'd be too noticeable in such a short street. I'd guess he parked on the street that runs along the bottom, somewhere that he had the house in his line of sight. Maybe someone there noticed an unfamiliar vehicle parked outside for long stretches.'

'Good thinking,' Brandon said. 'Kevin, can you cover that?'

'Will do, sir. I'll get the lads on to it.'

'And the lasses,' Carol said sweetly. 'And maybe we should ask them not to concentrate on the four-wheel drive motor. If this guy's as careful as we think he is, he might only use the jeep for the actual snatches and go for something different when he's doing the stalking, just in case a nosy neighbour has clocked him.'

'What do you think, Tony?' Brandon asked.

'It wouldn't surprise me,' he said. 'It's important we don't forget how competent this killer is. He might even be using hired cars.'

Dave Woolcott groaned. 'Oh God, don't do this to me.'

Bob Stansfield looked up from the pad where he'd been scribbling the names of his team. 'I take it that the other lines of enquiry that Dr Hill suggested are on the back burner for now?'

Brandon pursed his lips grimly. The euphoria had died somewhere during the briefing. The weight of the work ahead seemed unbearable, the idea of finding the killer almost as distant as it had before Terry Harding walked into the station. 'That's right. No disrespect, Tony, but your suggestions are hypotheses, and what we've got now is our first solid set of facts.'

'No problem,' Tony said. 'Hard evidence always comes first.'

'And Carol's idea about the computer stuff? Should we still pursue that?' Dave asked.

'Same thing applies,' Brandon said. 'It's a hunch, not a fact, so yes, it goes on the back burner.'

'With respect, sir,' Carol chipped in, determined not to be sidelined. 'Even if Terry Harding gives us a positive ID on the make and model of the vehicle, we might be no further forward. We need other elimination factors before we can narrow things down. If I'm right about the computer, we'd be looking at such a small segment of the population that it would be significant if we did get a cross-match.'

Brandon considered for a moment. Then he said, 'Point taken, Carol. OK, we can pursue it, Dave, but not as a priority. Only as and when we have bodies freed up from the main enquiry. Right, are we all clear what we've got to do?' He looked around expectantly, registering the series of nods. 'OK, team,' Brandon said, his voice stern. 'Let's go for it.'

'And may the force be with you,' Kevin said under his breath to Carol as they emerged from the office.

'I'd rather have the force than the gutter press,' she said drily, turning her back on him. 'Tony, can we find a quiet corner and plan our strategy for this interview?'

'The only way you're going to get more out of him is by hypnosis,' Tony told Carol as they talked in the corridor after an hour with Terry Harding.

'Can you do that?' Carol asked.

'I've got the basic technique. Judging by his eye movements and body language, he was telling the truth about what he saw, not making anything up or exaggerating, so he might come across with more detail under hypnosis, particularly if we have pictures to show him.'

Ten minutes later, Carol was back with a sheaf of car brochures that Kevin's team had scavenged from city dealerships. 'This what we need?'

Tony nodded. 'Perfect. You sure you want me to give this a go?'

'It's got to be worth a try,' Carol said.

They walked back into the interview room, where Terry Harding was finishing a mug of coffee. 'Can I go now?' he said plaintively. 'Only I'm due to fly out to Brussels tomorrow and I haven't even unpacked my bag.'

'Not much longer, sir,' Carol said, sitting down to one side of the table. 'Dr Hill would like to try something with you.'

Tony smiled reassuringly. 'We've got some pictures of the kind of jeep you saw leaving Damien's garage. What I'd like to do, if you're agreeable, is to put you in a light hypnotic trance and ask you to look at them.'

Harding frowned. 'Why can't I just look at them as I am?'

'The chances are better that you'd recognize the particular model,' Tony explained soothingly. 'Thing is, Mr Harding, you're obviously a very busy man. Since you saw the incident, you've travelled to the other side of the world, you've had a series of important business meetings, and you've probably not had enough sleep. All of that means your conscious mind has probably filed away the details of what you saw last Sunday. Using hypnosis, I can help you retrieve that information.'

Harding looked dubious. 'I don't know. Always supposing you could get me to go under, you could make me say anything.'

'Unfortunately, that's not the case. If it was, hypnotists would all be millionaires,' Tony joked. 'Like I said, all it does is free up the stuff you've buried because it's not important.'

'What do I have to do?' Harding said suspiciously.

'Just listen to my voice and follow what I tell you,' Tony said. 'You'll feel a little strange, a little spaced out, but you'll be in control at all times. I use a technique called neuro-linguistic programming. It's very relaxing, I promise you.'

'Do I have to lie down, or what?'

'Nothing like that. And I'm not going to wave a watch in front of you. Are you prepared to give it a try?'

Carol held her breath, watching Harding as an assortment of expressions chased each other across his face. Finally, he nodded. 'I doubt you'll be able to get me under,' he said. 'I'm a man who knows his own mind. But I'm willing to try.'

'OK,' said Tony. 'I want you to relax. Close your eyes if it feels more comfortable. Now, I want you to go deep down inside yourself . . .'

Elated with their success, Tony and Carol bounced into the murder squad room. Bob Stansfield was standing by the window, staring out at the rain-drenched street below, his shoulders slumped, a cigarette burning unheeded in his hand. He glanced round and Carol called, 'Cheer up, it might never happen.'

Stansfield swung round and said bitterly, 'You obviously haven't heard the news.'

'What news?' Carol asked, walking over to him.

'Stevie McConnell topped himself.'

Carol rocked on her heels and stumbled against a desk. Her ears were ringing and she thought she was going to faint. Instinctively, Tony moved forward and steered her into a chair. 'Deep breaths, Carol. Deep and slow,' he said softly, leaning over her, staring intently at her white face.

She closed her eyes, dug her nails into her palms and

obeyed. 'Sorry,' Stansfield said. 'It knocked me for six too.'

Carol looked up and pushed her hair away from a forehead suddenly clammy. 'What happened?'

'Apparently he took a beating yesterday. A sex-case special, by all accounts. So, this morning he tore up his shirt and hung himself. The fucking warders never noticed, on account of they're playing at work to rule,' he added savagely.

'The poor bastard,' Carol said.

'There's going to be hell to pay,' Stansfield predicted. 'I'm glad it was fuck all to do with me. At least it won't be my arse in the fire. I mean, Brandon's bombproof, so it's going to be some poor fucker of an inspector who's going to carry the can.'

Carol looked at him as if she'd like to hit him. 'Sometimes, Bob, you really fuck me off,' she said coldly. 'Where's Brandon?'

'Down in the HOLMES room. Probably hiding from the Chief.'

They found Brandon and Dave Woolcott closeted in the inspector's cubby hole off the main room. 'We've got a positive make, sir,' Carol said, her initial exuberance flattened by Stansfield's news. 'We know what car he was driving.'

Penny Burgess turned off the main road on to the Forestry Commission track that led deep into the heart of the woodland. She was aiming for a car park and picnic area in the middle of the woods. It was one of her favourite spots from which to strike off through the trees and up on to the bare gritstone edges where the wind could blow away all the accumulated dross of the week. She certainly needed it after the last few days of hard graft, big stories and not enough sleep.

The record on the radio finished and the announcer said,

'And now, over to the newsroom for the headlines on the hour.' The news ident followed, then a woman said in a voice altogether too bright for her subject matter, 'Northern Sound news on the hour. A man who was questioned by Bradfield police in connection with the serial killings that have terrorized the city was found dead this morning in his cell at Barleigh jail.'

In her shock, Penny took her foot off the accelerator and pitched forward as the car stalled. 'Shit!' she exclaimed, her hand shooting out to twist the volume higher.

'Steven McConnell is thought to have committed suicide by hanging himself with a noose made from his own clothes. McConnell, the manager of a body-building gym in the city, was arrested last week after a street brawl involving an undercover police officer in the city's gay village,' the newsreader continued, sounding for all the world as if she were announcing the results of the Eurovision Song Contest. 'He was released on bail, but rearrested after attempting to flee the country. A Home Office spokesman said there would be a full enquiry into the circumstances of his death.

'The economy has never been in a better position, the Prime Minister said today . . .' Penny turned the key in the ignition and did a perilous five-point turn in the narrow lane before stamping on the gas and shooting back towards the road. It was just as well, she thought, that she'd already decided to dump Kevin. After the story she was about to write, she couldn't imagine him ever wanting to see her again anyway.

Tony drummed his fingers on the back of the cab's seat, a curious restlessness possessing him. Leaving Scargill Street hadn't been easy, but he knew he had no role while the police worked on their one piece of solid evidence. The last thing they needed in that maelstrom of reproach and driven activity was for him to sit around reminding them of all the reasons why he'd never been convinced that Stevie McConnell was their man.

His consolation was that he felt certain that Angelica would phone tonight. As the taxi hissed through the wet and empty streets, Tony rehearsed the conversation. He felt a new confidence, a certainty that tonight he would have no problems, that he had finally wrestled his demon into submission thanks to her strange erotic therapy. He would tell her she had no idea how much her phone calls had meant to him. That she had helped him more than she could know. Satisfied that he had things under control, Tony sighed comfortably and cleared his mind of Handy Andy.

Penny Burgess popped the top on a can of Guinness, lit a cigarette and switched on her computer. After making a handful of phone calls to firm up the version of events she'd heard on the radio, she was fired with the self-righteous enthusiasm that only politicians, journalists and fundamentalist preachers seem capable of harnessing for professional advancement.

She inhaled a long stream of smoke, thought for a moment, then started to hammer the keys.

Bradfield's serial killer claimed his fifth victim yesterday (Sunday) when gay body-builder Stevie McConnell killed himself in a prison cell.

Police had implied that McConnell was himself the Queer Killer in a cynical bid to force the real killer's hand.

But their twisted exercise ended in tragedy when McConnell, 32, hung himself with a makeshift rope woven from his own torn shirt. He tied it to the top bunk in his solitary-confinement cell at Barleigh prison and threw himself off, strangling himself.

And last night, a police officer involved in the

Queer Killer investigation admitted, 'We've known for several days that Stevie McConnell wasn't the killer.'

McConnell had pleaded with prison staff to put him in solitary after a barbaric attack by fellow inmates the previous day.

A source inside Barleigh prison said, 'He took a real beating. The word on the grapevine when he arrived was that he was the Queer Killer, only the police didn't have enough evidence to charge him yet.

'Prisoners don't like sex killers, and they tend to make their feelings known. McConnell got a brutal hammering. He was badly beaten up, and sexually assaulted too.'

Warders are said to have turned a blind eye to McConnell's savage battering. Then yesterday (Sunday) because of a prison officers' work to rule, he was left unattended in his cell for long enough to end his life. A Home Office spokesman said there would be a full enquiry into the incident.

McConnell managed Bodies gym in the city centre, where the killer's third victim, solicitor Gareth Finnegan, was a member.

McConnell faced a minor assault charge after coming to the rescue of an undercover police sergeant who was attacked by a third man in the Temple Fields gay village.

He then tried to flee the country while he was out on bail. Police rearrested him as he was about to board a ferry for Holland, and persuaded magistrates to remand him in custody.

A police source revealed, 'What we did made people think that McConnell was the killer, and that's what we wanted.

'Serial killers are very vain, and we thought that the killer would be so outraged that we had pointed the finger at the wrong person that he would break cover and make contact.

'It's all gone horribly wrong.'

A friend of McConnell's said last night, 'Bradfield police are murderers. As far as I'm concerned, they killed Stevie.

'The police really grilled him about the serial killings. They put him under all kinds of pressure.

'Even though they let him go afterwards, mud like that sticks. He got the cold shoulder at work, and out in the gay bars.

'That's why he decided to leg it. It's a tragedy. Worse than that, it's a pointless tragedy.

'This hasn't taken the police an inch closer to finding the killer.'

Penny lit another cigarette and read through her copy. 'Pick the bones out of that, Kevin,' she said softly, hitting the keys that would save the file and transmit it via her modem to the office computer. Then, as an afterthought, she typed:

Memo to newsdesk.
From Penny Burgess, Crime Desk.
I am taking tomorrow (Monday) as time off in lieu of working extra hours last week and today. Hope this doesn't pose too many problems!

'A Land Rover Discovery, metallic grey or dark blue?' Dave Woolcott confirmed, making a note on a pad.

'That's what the man said,' Carol agreed.

'Right. With it being Sunday, I can't get a full run-down from Swansea on every vehicle like that on our patch,' Dave said.

'What we could do, though, is get a team going round

the main dealerships and the quality second-hand dealers asking for their records of anyone who's bought one,' Kevin suggested. Like all of them, he was fired with an excitement only slightly tempered by the tragic news from Barleigh.

'No,' Brandon said. 'That's a waste of time and personnel. There's no guarantee that the killer bought his vehicle locally. We wait until tomorrow morning. Then we go flat out.'

Everyone looked disappointed, even though they recognized the force of Brandon's argument. 'In that case, sir,' Carol said, 'I'd like to work with Dave compiling lists of computer hardware and software suppliers so we're ready to roll with that as soon as there are some spare bodies to hit the phones.'

Brandon nodded. 'Good thinking, Carol. Now, why don't the rest of us go home and rediscover what our houses look like?'

Tony was stretched out on the sofa, trying to persuade himself he was enjoying the luxury of watching TV when the doorbell rang. The hope of company come to rescue him from his restless boredom catapulted him to his feet and down the hall. He opened the door, a smile already spreading across his face.

The smile died halfway as he registered that he was out of luck. There was a woman on the doorstep, but she wasn't one of his friends or colleagues. She was tall, big-boned, with heavy, blunt features and a strong, square jaw. She pushed her long dark hair away from her face and said, 'I'm really sorry to trouble you, only my car's broken down and I don't know where there's a pay phone. I wondered if I might use your phone to call the AA? I'll pay for the call, of course . . .' Her voice trailed off and she smiled apologetically.

When I clocked Sergeant Merrick in the Sackville Arms, I thought I was going to pass out. I'd only gone there because I knew the detectives from Scargill Street use it. I wanted to hear what the gossip was among the murder squad. I wanted to hear them talk about me and my accomplishments. The last thing I expected was to see so familiar a face staring out at me.

I was sitting unobtrusively in the corner when I saw Merrick come in. I debated whether to leave, but I decided that might make me noticeable. The last thing I wanted was for him to recognize me and follow me for whatever reasons of his own. Besides, why should I let a policeman drive me away from my lunch break?

But I couldn't stop the churning in my stomach in case he caught sight of me and moved across to speak to me. I wasn't afraid of him, but I just didn't want to draw attention to myself. Luckily, he was with two of his colleagues, and they were too busy discussing something – me, probably, had they but known it – to pay much attention to anybody else. I recognized the woman from the papers. Inspector Carol Jordan. She looks better in the flesh than in print, probably because her hair's a lovely shade of blonde. The other man I hadn't seen before, but I filed his face away for future reference. Carroty-red hair, pale skin, freckles, boyish features. And of course, Merrick, head and shoulders above the others, some kind of dressing on his head. I wondered how he'd come by that.

I'd never hated Merrick the way I hated some of the others, even though he'd taken me into custody a couple of times. He'd never treated me with the contempt they had. He'd never sneered at me when he arrested me. But I could see he still saw me as an object, someone not worthy of respect. He never understood that when I sold my body to sailors it was for a purpose. But whatever I did then is irrelevant now. I am different now, I am a changed person. What happened back in Seaford feels as irrelevant and remote as something I'd seen at the cinema.

In a strange way, being in the presence of the very officers who are trying to track me down was quite exciting. I got a real buzz out of being only feet away from my hunters, who didn't sense their prey. They didn't even have enough sixth sense to realize there was something extraordinary happening, not even Carol Jordan. So much for women's intuition. I see it as a sort of test, a measure of my ability to delude my pursuers. The notion that they can catch me is so absurd, it's unthinkable.

I felt so strong after that encounter that the next day's paper hit me like a blow with a sandbag. I was walking through the main computer room when I saw an early edition of the Sentinel Times lying on some junior engineer's desk. FIFTH BODY IN QUEER KILLER'S RAMPAGE screamed out at me.

I wanted to rage and shout, to throw things through windows. How dare they? My handiwork is so individual, how could they mistake some blundering copycat's body for one of mine?

I was trembling with suppressed fury when I made it back to my own office. I'd wanted to ask the engineer if I could have a look at his paper, but I didn't trust myself to speak. I wanted to rush out of the office to the nearest newsagent's and snatch a copy off the counter. But that *would have been unforgivable weakness. The secret of success, I told myself, was to behave normally. To do nothing that would make my colleagues think there was something peculiar going on in my life.*

'Patience,' I told myself, 'is the cardinal virtue.' So I sat at my desk, fiddling with the intricacies of a piece of software that needed rewriting. But my heart wasn't in it, and I know I wasn't justifying my salary that afternoon. By four o'clock, I could stand it no longer. I grabbed my phone and dialled the special number that broadcasts Bradfield Sound to callers.

The story was the lead item on the news bulletin, as it ought to have been. 'The body of a man found in the Temple Fields area in the early hours of the morning is not the fifth victim of the serial killer who has brought terror to Bradfield's gay community, police revealed this afternoon.' As the newsreader's words sank in, I felt my anger depart, the hollowness inside me whole once more.

Without waiting for more, I slammed the phone down. They'd got something right at last. But I'd gone through four hours of hell because of their mistake. Every hour I'd suffered would be an hour added on to the agonies of Dr Tony Hill, I vowed.

Because the Bradfield police have now committed the ultimate absurdity. Dr Tony Hill, the stupid man who hadn't even recognized that all my crimes belonged to me, has been appointed the official police consultant to the serial-killer enquiry. The poor, deluded fools. If that's their best hope, then they clearly have no hope.

17

In a murder of pure voluptuousness, entirely disinterested, where no hostile witness was to be removed, no extra booty to be gained and no revenge to be gratified, it is clear that to hurry would be altogether to ruin.

The agony was so extreme Tony wanted to believe he was in a nightmare. He had never understood before how many different kinds of pain there were. The dull throb in his head; the harsh rasp in his throat; the screaming, wrenching rip in his shoulders; and the knives of cramps in his thighs and calves. At first, the pain blocked all his other senses. His eyes screwed up tight, all he knew was suffering so stark it made the sweat pop out on his forehead.

Gradually, he learned to bear the extremes of his pain, realizing that if he took his weight on his feet, the cramps would slowly subside and the excruciating tearing in his shoulders grow less. As the torment became more tolerable, he grew aware that he felt nauseous, a deep queasiness that sat in his stomach and threatened to spill over at any moment. God alone knew how long he'd been hanging here.

Slowly, fearfully, he opened his eyes and raised his head, a movement which sent a spasm of agony through his neck and shoulders. Tony looked around. Instantly, he wished he hadn't. He knew immediately where he was. The room was brightly lit, spotlights mounted on the ceiling and walls revealing a whitewashed room, its rough stone floor marked with dark stains that he knew without examination were the visible remains of the blood that had pooled and splashed there. Facing him was the blind eye of a camcorder on a tripod, a red light on the side indicating that his scrutiny was not going unrecorded. Fixed to the far wall was a magnetic strip with a selection of knives hanging neatly on it. In one corner of the room, he saw the unmistakable implements of torture. A rack; a strange contraption like a chair which he recognized but could not name at first. Something religious? Something vaguely Christian? Something treacherous, not what it seemed? A Judas chair, that was it. And on the wall, a huge wooden saltire, like some hideously perverted holy relic. A soft moan escaped from his dry lips.

Now he knew the worst, he took stock of his own position. He was naked, his skin gooseflesh in the chill of the cellar. His hands were fastened behind his back; judging by the hard edges cutting into his wrists, by handcuffs, held taut in their turn by a rope or chain or something that was obviously fastened to the ceiling. This hawser was tight enough to force his upper body forward, leaving him doubled over at the waist. Tony managed to push himself on to the tips of his toes and twist his body sideways. Out of the corner of his eye, he could see a strong nylon rope leading from behind him, through a pulley, along the ceiling, through another pulley on to a winch.

'Jesus Christ,' he croaked. He was afraid to look at his feet, lest his worst fears should be confirmed, but he forced his eyes downwards nevertheless. As he had feared, each ankle was encased in a leather strap. The straps in their turn were attached to a rope cradle that held a heavy stone flag. An involuntary shudder of fear rippled through him, stressing his tortured muscles even further. He knew about torture; to treat his patients he'd had to study the history of sadism. Not even in his worst moments had he imagined he would face so inhuman a fate.

His mind was already racing ahead. He would be

winched up till he reached the ceiling. His muscles would wrench and tear, his joints strain to their utmost limit. Then the winch would be released, letting him drop a few feet before the brake was applied. The weight of the stone flag, still hurtling downwards accelerating at thirty-two feet per second, would finish the job, ripping his joints apart, leaving him dangling in a jumble of dislocated limbs. If he was lucky, the shock and pain would thrust him into unconsciousness. Strappado, brought to a fine art by the Spanish Inquisition. No need for high tech in torture.

In a bid to escape the blind panic his knowledge had brought him to, he forced himself to cast his mind back to what had happened. The woman at the door, that was where it had started. As he had let her into the house, Tony had felt a niggle of familiarity. He felt sure he'd seen her somewhere, but he couldn't imagine having seen someone so distinctively ugly and not remembering. He'd walked ahead of her down the hall and into his study. Then, the faintest whiff of a strangely medicinal, chemical smell, before a hand had sneaked round his neck and clamped a cold, disgusting pad on his face. A kick behind his knee to buckle his legs and bring him down. He'd struggled, but with her weight on top of him, it had only lasted for moment before he had lost consciousness.

Then he had drifted in and out of a half-world of light and dark, aware only of the pad that seemed constantly to send him out as soon as he struggled into consciousness. Until, finally, he had come round. In Handy Andy's torture chamber. Out of nowhere, a quotation sprang into his mind. 'Depend upon it, sir, when a man knows he is to be hanged in a fortnight, it concentrates his mind wonderfully.' Somewhere, he knew there was a clue in what had happened that might just allow him to escape what seemed inevitable. All he had to do was to find it.

Had he been completely wrong in his profile? Was the woman who had kidnapped him Handy Andy? Was she the one? Or was she just the decoy, the willing accomplice who got off on her master's vice? Again, he replayed what his memory would allow him to snatch back. He summoned up the woman's image again. Clothes first. Beige mac, cut continental style, just like Carol's, swinging open to reveal a white shirt, enough buttons undone to reveal the swell of full breasts and a deep cleavage. Jeans, trainers. Trainers. They were the same make and model as his own. But none of this was significant, Tony told himself. They were only outward symbols of the care Handy Andy took not to be caught. The woman's garb had been chosen so that if she did leave any stray fibres, they wouldn't show up as having any significance, being identifiable as having come from either Carol's clothes or his. And Carol had been in his house often enough now for her to have left stray fibres.

The woman's face didn't really ring any bells either. She was tall for a woman, at least five feet ten, with chunky bone structure to match. Not even her mother could have called her attractive, with her heavy jaw, slightly bulbous nose, wide mouth and eyes set curiously far apart. Even though she was skilfully, if heavily, made up, there wasn't a lot she could do with the basic building materials. He was sure they'd never been in a room together, though he couldn't rule out having passed her in the street, at the tram station or on campus.

The trainers. For some reason he kept coming back to the trainers. If only the pain would stop long enough for him to focus properly. Tony locked his legs straight, trying to relieve the agonizing strain on his shoulders. The fraction of an inch he gained wasn't nearly enough. Again, visceral fear gripped him and he blinked away a tear.

What was it about the trainers? Tony summoned every ounce of concentration he could master, and called up the image of the woman again. With a slow gasp of understanding, he realized what it was. The feet were too big.

Even for a woman of that height, the feet were too big. As soon as he grasped that, he remembered the hands too. First, black leather, later thin latex gloves covering big hands, fingers thick and strong. The person who had brought him here had not always been a woman.

Carol pressed the doorbell again. Where the hell was he? The lights were on, the curtains drawn. Maybe he'd nipped out to pick up a pizza, post a letter, buy a bottle of wine, rent a video? With a frustrated sigh, she turned away and walked down to the end of the street, turning into the ginnel that ran between Tony's street and the houses behind. She walked down to his back yard, where a previous owner had demolished the wall and concreted half the area to provide the hard standing where Tony had told her he always kept his car.

The car was in place, exactly where it should have been. 'Oh, bloody hell,' Carol complained. Edging past the car, she walked up to the house and peered through the kitchen window. The light from the open door into the hall cast a pale glow over the room. No sign of life. No dirty dishes, no empty bottles.

On the off chance, Carol tried the back door. No joy. 'Bloody men,' she grumbled as she strode back to her car. 'Five minutes, pal, then I'm off,' she said, throwing herself into the driver's seat. Ten minutes crawled by, but no one appeared.

Carol started the engine and drove off. At the end of the street, she glanced across at the pub on the other side of the main road. It was worth a try, she supposed. It took less than three minutes to check the smoky, crowded rooms and discover that wherever Tony Hill was, it wasn't in the Farewell to Arms.

Where else could he be within walking distance at nine o'clock on a Sunday night? 'Anywhere,' she told herself. 'You can't be his only friend in the world. He wasn't expecting you; you only called round to arrange a meeting for tomorrow.'

Giving up, Carol drove home. The flat was empty. Michael, she remembered, was out to dinner with some woman he'd met at a trade fair. She decided to give up on the world and go to bed. But first, she'd better leave a message on Tony's machine. If she turned up two mornings running without warning, he might start to get twitchy. The answering machine checked in after a couple of rings, but there was no outgoing message, just a series of clicks followed by the tone. 'Hi, Tony,' she said. 'I don't know if your machine's working properly, so I don't know if you'll get this message. It's twenty past nine, and I'm about to have an early night. I'll be in the office first thing, working on the computer supplies stuff. Mr Brandon's called a case conference for tomorrow at three. If you want to get together before then, give me a call. I'll be in the HOLMES room if I'm not in the squad room.'

Sitting down with Nelson on her lap and a stiff drink by her side, Carol thought about the job that lay ahead. The list of computer supplies companies who sold the peripherals and hardware Handy Andy would need to construct his own images was depressingly long. She had told Dave not to start work on it until she'd had a chance to check out the software company. Their list of customers would be shorter, and they would have the Discovery to cross-reference that list with. Only if that came up blank would she set Dave's team loose on the dozens of numbers she'd painstakingly compiled that evening. 'We'll get there, Nelson,' she told the cat. 'It just better be worth the trip.'

The clatter of high heels on stone cut through the delirium of pain like a wire through cheese. So everyday a sound, translated by its location into a threat. He had no idea whether it was day or night, or how long had passed since he had been snatched from his life. Tony forced himself into alertness as the sound approached him from behind. She was coming downstairs. At the foot of the stairs, the clicking ended. He heard a low chuckle. Slowly, one step at a time, the footsteps crossed behind him. He could sense the scrutiny he was under.

She took her time, skirting round his trussed body until she moved into his line of vision. Tony was momentarily taken aback by the magnificence of her body. From the neck down, she could have been a model for a soft-porn magazine. She stood with legs apart, arms akimbo. She wore a loose red silk kimono, which fell open to reveal an extraordinary red leather basque with peephole nipples and a split crotch. Black stockings sheathed shapely, muscular legs which ended in black stilettoes. Even under the kimono, he could see the clear outline of strong, well-muscled arms and shoulders. From where he was hanging, she was as erotic as a kaolin poultice.

'Worked it out yet, *Anthony*?' she drawled, the warmth of suppressed laughter evident in her voice.

The stressing of his full name was the last turn in the Rubik's cube of his memory. His mind racing, Tony said, 'I suppose a couple of paracetamol would be out of the question, Angelica?'

The low chuckle again. 'Glad to see you haven't lost your sense of humour.'

'No, only my dignity. I wasn't expecting this, Angelica. Nothing in our phone conversations led me to imagine this is what you had in mind for me.'

'You had no idea who I was, did you?' Angelica said, pride unmistakable in her tones.

'Yes and no. I didn't know you were the person who killed those men. But I did know you were the woman for me.'

Angelica frowned, as if uncertain how to respond. She turned away and checked the camcorder. 'You took long enough to get that far. Do you have any idea how many times you slammed the phone down on me?' Her voice was angry, not hurt.

Tony sensed the danger and tried to find emollient words. 'That was because I had a problem, not because of you.'

'You had a problem with me,' she said, moving over to the stone benches that ran along one wall. She picked up another cassette and walked back to the camera.

Tony tried again. 'Quite the opposite,' he said. 'I've always had trouble with relationships with women. That's why I didn't know how to treat you in the beginning. But it got so much better. You know it did. You know we were wonderful together. Thanks to you, I feel like all my problems are behind me.' He hoped she wasn't alive to the unintentional irony in his words.

But Angelica was no fool. 'I think you can safely say that, Anthony,' she said with a wry smile.

'You outsmarted me, you know. I was convinced the killer was a man. I should have known better.'

With her back to him, Angelica swapped the cassettes in the camcorder. Then she wheeled round and said, 'You'd never have caught me. And with you out of the way, no one else will either.'

Ignoring the threat, Tony continued to chat, straining to keep his voice warm and even. 'I should have realized you were a woman. The subtlety, the attention to detail, the care you took to clear up after yourself. It was stupid of me not to grasp that those were the hallmarks of a woman's mind, not a man's.'

Angelica smirked. 'You're all the same, you psychologists.' She spat the word out as though it were an obscenity. 'You've got no imagination.'

'But I'm not like them, Angelica. OK, I made that one crucial mistake, but I bet I know more about you than any of them ever did. Because you've shown me the inside of your mind. And not just through the killings. You've shown me the real woman, the woman who comprehends love. But I guess they didn't understand you, did they? They didn't believe you when you told them you had a woman's spirit trapped in a man's body. Oh, I expect they pretended to, I expect they patronized you and talked down to you. But deep down, they wrote you off as a freak, didn't they? Believe me, I've never done that.' Tony's voice cracked as he reached the end of his speech, his mouth dry with a mixture of fear and chloroform. At least the adrenaline coursing through his veins seemed to be acting as an analgesic.

'What do you know about me?' she said roughly, the pain on her face a strange contrast with the coquettish pose she had adopted.

'I need a drink if we're going to talk,' Tony said, gambling that her narcissism would demand that she share her exploits, that she needed to hear his version of herself. If he was to have any chance of escaping with his life, he needed to build up a relationship with her. A drink would be the first brick in the wall. The more he could get her to see him as an individual, not as a cipher, the higher his chances rose.

Angelica scowled suspiciously. Then, with a toss of her head that sent her long hair swirling, she turned away and walked to a slop sink set against the wall. She turned on the tap and looked around vaguely for a drinking vessel of some kind. 'I'll get a glass,' she muttered, passing him and clattering up the steps again.

Tony felt a surge of relief at his small victory. Angelica was gone for less than thirty seconds, returning with a thick white mug. Kitchen above, Tony deduced as she walked back to the sink. She moved well in the heels, her stride measured and feminine. It was interesting, since she had obviously reverted to more masculine movements under the stress of kidnapping and killing. That was the only way to account for Terry Harding's conviction that he'd seen a man driving off from Damien Connolly's.

Angelica filled the mug and approached Tony cautiously. She gripped his hair, pulled his head back agonizingly and tipped freezing water into his mouth. As much went down his chin as his throat, but the relief was palpable. 'Thanks,' he gasped as she withdrew.

'One should always be hospitable to one's guests,' she said sardonically.

'I hope to remain one for some time,' Tony replied. 'You know, I admire you. You've got style.'

She frowned again. 'Don't bullshit me, Anthony. You won't get round me with stupid flattery.'

'It's not bullshit,' he protested. 'I've spent days and nights poring over the details of what you've achieved. I'm so deep inside your head, how could I not admire you? How could I not be impressed? The other ones you brought here, they didn't have a clue about who you are, what you can do.'

'That's true, I'll grant you that. They were like babies, frightened, stupid babies,' Angelica said contemptuously. 'They didn't appreciate what a woman like me could do for them. They were treacherous. lecherous fools.'

'That's because they didn't know you like I know you.'

'You keep saying that. Prove it. Prove you know anything about me.'

The gauntlet was well and truly down now, Tony thought. Never mind singing for your supper, talk for your life. This was the proving ground, the place where he would discover if his psychology was indeed a science or just bullshit.

'Fraser Duncan? Hello, this is Detective Inspector Carol Jordan of Bradfield police,' she said. Carol had never grown used to referring to herself by her full title. She felt as if, any moment, someone was going to jump out and shout,

'Oh no, you're not! We found you out at last.' Luckily, that didn't seem to be happening today.

'Yes?' The voice was cautious, the single syllable drawn out in a question.

'Actually, it was my brother, Michael Jordan, who suggested you might be able to help me with an enquiry we're pursuing.'

'Oh, yes?' The climate was getting warmer. 'How is Michael? Is he enjoying the software?'

'I think it's absolutely his favourite toy,' Carol replied.

Fraser Duncan laughed. 'An expensive toy, Inspector. Now, what can I do for you?'

'It's the Vicom 3D Commander I wanted to talk to you about. In strictest confidence, you understand. We're pursuing a major murder investigation, and one of the theories I'm looking at is that our killer might be using your software to edit his own videos, maybe even to import other material into them. That would be possible, wouldn't it?'

'More than possible. It would be perfectly straightforward.'

'So, do you keep records of all your customers?' Carol asked.

'We do. We don't sell all the packages direct, obviously, but anyone who buys the Commander should register their purchase with us since that gives them access to a free customer helpline and also means they get priority mailings when we develop upgrades.' Duncan was positively expansive now. 'Do I detect a request for access to our customer database, Inspector?'

'You do indeed, sir. This is a murder enquiry and the information could be crucial to us. Can I stress too that it would be completely confidential? I would personally undertake to ensure that your data is removed from our system as soon as we have finished with it,' Carol said, trying not to sound as if she was begging.

'I don't know,' Duncan said hesitantly. 'I'm not sure I like the idea of you and your colleagues hammering on the doors of my customers.'

'It wouldn't be like that, Mr Duncan. No way. What we would do is input the list into our Home Office Major Large Enquiry System and cross-match it against existing data. We would only act on any correlations that came up with people who are already in there.'

'Is this the serial killer you're after?' Duncan asked abruptly.

What did he want to hear, Carol wondered momentarily. 'Yes,' she said, taking a gamble.

'Let me call you back, Inspector. Just to make sure you are who you say you are.'

'No problem.' She gave him the main police switchboard number. 'Ask them to put you through to me in the HOLMES room at Scargill Street.'

The next five minutes passed in a fever of impatience. The phone barely chirruped before Carol had it to her ear. 'Inspector Jordan?'

'You owe me, sis.'

'Michael!'

'I've just been telling Fraser Duncan what an honourable little person you are and despite what he's heard about the police, he can trust you.'

'I love you, bro. Now get off the phone and let the man talk to me!'

Within the hour, Vicom's data was inside the HOLMES computer network, thanks to Dave Woolcott and the miracles of modern technology. Carol had passed Fraser Duncan on to him after they had agreed the ground rules for the data use, and Carol had listened uncomprehendingly to Dave's end of a conversation which consisted of alien expressions like 'baud rate' and 'ASCII files'.

Carol sat by Dave's side as he worked on one of the terminals. 'OK,' he said. 'We've got the list from Swansea of everyone within a twenty-mile radius of Bradfield who has one of these Discoveries. We've also got the list of names from Vicom of people who have bought their software. I hit this key, and go down this menu to this option, wild-card match, and now we sit back and let the machine talk to itself.'

For an agonizing minute, nothing happened. Then the screen cleared and a message flashed up. '[2] matches found. List matches?' Dave hit the 'y' key and two names and addresses appeared on the screen.

1: *Philip Crozier, 23 Broughton Crag, Sheffield Road, Bradfield BX4 6JB*
2: *Christopher Thorpe [sort criterion 1]/Angelica Thorpe [sort criterion 2], 14 Gregory Street, Moorside, Bradfield BX6 4LR*

'What does that mean?' Carol asked, pointing to the second option.

'The Discovery is registered to Christopher Thorpe and the software was bought by Angelica,' Dave explained. 'Using the wild-card option means that the machine sorted by address as well as by name. Well, Carol, you've got something. Whether it means anything or not, we'll have to see.'

Penny Burgess strode over the rough, fissured limestone of Malham Pavement. The sky was the bright blue of early spring, the rough moorland grasses starting to look more green than brown. From time to time, larks shot out into the air and poured their songs into her ears. There were two occasions when Penny really came alive. One was on the trail of a hot story. The other was up on the high moorlands of the Yorkshire Dales and the Derbyshire Peak District. Out in the open air, she felt free as the skylarks, all pressure gone. No newsdesk demanding copy by an hour ago, no contacts to be appeased, no looking over her shoulder to be sure of staying ahead of her rivals. Just the sky, the moors, the extraordinary limestone landscape, and her.

For no reason, Stevie McConnell burst into her thoughts. He'd never see the sky again, never walk a moor and watch the turning of the seasons. Thank God she had the power to make sure that someone would pay for that inhuman deprivation.

Philip Crozier's house was a narrow, terraced three-storey modern town house, the ground floor consisting mainly of an integral garage. Carol sat in the car, eyeing it up and down. 'We going in, ma'am?' the young detective constable in the driving seat asked.

Carol thought for a moment. Ideally, she'd wanted Tony to be with her when she interviewed the people whose names the computer had spat out. She'd tried ringing him at home. No reply. Claire said he hadn't come into the office yet, which surprised her since he'd had a nine-thirty appointment. Carol had swung round by the house, but it looked exactly the same as it had the night before. Off having fun with his lady friend, she'd decided. Serves him right if he misses out on the showdown with Handy Andy, she thought maliciously, then immediately regretted her childishness. Failing Tony, she'd have liked to have had Don Merrick with her. But he was out pursuing other lines of enquiry that had flowed from the identification of the Discovery. The only person she could find who wasn't urgently involved with something else was DC Morris, on the third month of his secondment to CID.

'We might as well see if he's in,' Carol said. 'Though he's probably at work.'

They walked up the path, Carol taking in the details of the neatly trimmed lawn and the smart paintwork. The house didn't really fit Tony's profile. It was more like the victims' houses in terms of value and status, rather than the home of someone who aspired to their lifestyles. Carol pressed the bell and stepped back. They were about to give up and return to the car when Carol heard feet pounding downstairs. The door swung open to reveal a stocky black man dressed in grey sweat pants and a scarlet T-shirt, his feet bare. He couldn't have looked more different from Terry Harding's description. Carol's heart sank momentarily, then she reminded herself that Crozier might not be the only person with access to his software and his Discovery. He was still worth interviewing. 'Yeah?' he said.

'Mr Crozier?'

''S right. Who wants to know?' His voice was relaxed, the Bradfield accent strong.

Carol produced her warrant card and introduced herself. 'I wonder if we could come in and have a word, sir?'

'What about?'

'Your name has cropped up in some routine enquiries and I'd like to ask you some questions for the purposes of elimination.'

Crozier's brows furrowed. 'What sort of enquiries?'

'If we could just come in, sir?'

'No, hang on, what's all this about? I'm trying to get some work done here.'

Morris stepped to Carol's side. 'There's no need to be difficult, sir, it's just routine.'

'Mr Crozier isn't being difficult, Constable,' Carol said coolly. 'I'd feel just the same in your shoes, sir. A car answering the description of yours has been involved in an incident, and we need to eliminate you from our investigation. We're speaking to several other people in connection with this enquiry, sir. It won't take long.'

'All right then,' Crozier sighed. 'You'd better come in.'

They followed him up stairs carpeted in functional cord carpet into an open-plan living room-cum-kitchen. It was furnished in expensive but minimalist style. He waved them to two leather and wood armchairs and dropped into a leather bean bag on the polished wood floor. Morris pulled out his notebook and ostentatiously opened it to a fresh page.

'You work from home, then?' Carol asked.

''S right. I'm a freelance animator.'

'Cartoons?' Carol said.

'I do mostly science animations. You want something for your Open University course that shows how atoms collide, I'm your man. So what's all this about?'

'You drive a Land Rover Discovery?'

''S right. It's in the garage.'

'Can you tell me if you were driving it last Monday night?' Carol asked. God, was it only a week ago?

'I can. I wasn't. I was in Boston, Massachusetts.'

She went through the routine questions that established precisely what Crozier had been doing, and who she could check the information with. Then she stood up. Time for the key question, but it was important to keep it looking casual. 'Thanks for you help, Mr Crozier. One more thing – is there anyone else who has access to your house while you're away? Someone who could have borrowed your car?'

Crozier shook his head. 'I live on my own. I don't even have a cat or plants, so nobody has to come in when I'm away. I'm the only one with keys.'

'You're sure of that? No cleaning lady, no colleague who drops in to use your system?'

'Sure, I'm sure. I do my own cleaning, I work alone. I split up with my girlfriend a couple of months back and I changed the locks, OK? Nobody's got keys except me.' Crozier was starting to sound tetchy.

Carol persisted. 'And no one could have borrowed your keys without your knowledge and had them copied?'

'I don't see how. I'm not in the habit of leaving them lying around. And the car's only insured for me, so nobody else has ever driven it,' Crozier said, his irritation clearly mounting. 'Look, if somebody did anything criminal in a car with my number on, they were using faked-up plates, OK?'

'I accept what you're saying, Mr Crozier. I can assure you that if the information you've given me checks out, you won't be hearing from us again. Thanks very much for your time.'

Back at the car, Carol said, 'Find me a phone. I want to try Dr Hill again. I can't believe he's gone AWOL the one time we really need him.'

It's laughable. They pick a man who can't even tell whether I've carried out a particular punishment or not and they employ him to help them catch me. They could at least have shown me the respect of employing someone who has some reputation, an opponent worthy of my skills, not some idiot who has never encountered someone of my calibre.

Instead, they insult me. Dr Tony Hill is supposed to be producing a profile of me, based on his analysis of my killings. When this account is published, years hence, after my death in my bed from natural causes, historians will be able to compare his profile with the reality and laugh at the gross inaccuracies of his pseudo-science.

He will never come close to the truth. For the record, I set down that truth.

I was born in the Yorkshire port of Seaford, one of the busiest fishing and commercial docks in the country. My father was a merchant seaman, the first officer on oil tankers. He went all over the world, then he would come home to us. But my mother was as bad a wife as she was a mother. I can see now that the house was always in chaos, the meals irregular and unappetizing. The only thing she was good at, the only thing they could share, was the drinking. If there was an Olympic pairs event for pissheads, they'd have walked off with the gold.

When I was seven, my father stopped coming home. Of

course, my mother blamed me for not being a good enough son. She said I'd driven him away. She told me I was the man of the house now. But I could never live up to her expectations. She always wanted more from me than I was capable of, and ruled me by blame rather than praise. I spent more time locked in the cupboard than most people's coats do.

Without my father's pay cheque, she was thrown on the resources of the welfare system, which was barely enough to live on, never mind get drunk on. When the building society repossessed the house, we went to live with relatives in Bradfield for a while, but she couldn't handle their disapproval, so we moved back to Seaford, when she turned to the town's other boom industry, prostitution. I grew accustomed to the procession of disgusting, drunken sailors traipsing through the succession of grubby flats and bedsits where we lived. We were always behind with the rent, usually doing a moonlight flit just before the bailiffs got really heavy.

I grew to hate the ugly, grunting copulation that I was a constant witness to, and stayed out of the house as much as I possibly could, often sleeping rough down by the docks. I used to pick on kids that were younger than me to get their money off them so I could afford to eat. I moved schools almost as often as we moved house, so I never did too well there, in spite of the fact that I knew I could run rings round most of the other kids, who were just stupid.

As soon as I was 16, I left Seaford. It wasn't a wrench; it wasn't as if I'd ever managed to make many friends, what with moving all the time. I'd seen enough of men to know that I didn't want to grow up like them, and I felt different inside. I thought if I moved back to a big city like Bradfield I'd find it easier to work out what I wanted. One of my mother's cousins got me a job at the electronics firm where he worked.

About that time, I discovered that dressing in women's

clothes made me feel good about myself. I got my own bedsit so I could do it whenever I wanted to, and that calmed me down a lot. I started studying computer science at evening classes, and eventually got some proper qualifications. About that time, my mother got left a house in Seaford in her brother's will.

I got the chance of a job back in Seaford, working in computer systems for the local private phone company. I didn't really want to go back there, but the job was too good to turn down. I never went near my mother. I don't think she even knew I was there.

One of the few good things about Seaford is that it's handy for the ferry to Holland. I used to go there every other weekend, because in Amsterdam I could go out dressed as a woman and nobody batted an eyelid. Over there, I met a lot of transsexuals as well as transvestites, and the more I talked to them, the more I realized that I was just like them. I was a woman trapped in a man's body. That explained why I'd never had much sexual interest in girls. And although I found men attractive, I knew I wasn't a poof. They disgust me, with their pretence at normal relationships when everybody knows that it's only men and women that can fit together properly.

I went to see the doctors at Jimmy's in Leeds, where they do all the sex-change operations in the north, and they turned me down. Their psychologists were as stupid and blinkered as all the rest of their brotherhood. But I managed to find a private doctor in London who prescribed the hormone treatment I needed. Of course, I couldn't go on working while this was going on, but I spoke to the boss and he said he'd give me a good reference for another job when I'd had the operation and I was a woman.

I had to go abroad for the operation, and it was all much more expensive than I expected. I went to my mother and asked her if she'd mortgage the house to lend me the money and she just laughed at me.

So I did what I'd learned from her. I sold myself on the docks. It's amazing how much money sailors will pay for a travesti. They get out of their heads with excitement at the thought of someone who has breasts and a cock. I wasn't like the other hookers either; I didn't blow it all on drink or drugs or a pimp. I stashed it all away till I could afford the operation.

When I came to Seaford, not even my own mother recognized me at first. I'd only been back a few days when she took that tragic accidental overdose of drink and pills. Nobody was surprised. Yes, Doctor, you can add her to the list.

With my qualifications, experience and reference, I had no trouble getting a job as a senior systems analyst with the phone company in Bradfield. The money I made from the sale of the house in Seaford bought me my home in Bradfield, and I started the task of finding a worthy man to share my life.

And Dr Tony Hill presumes to understand me, without knowing any of this? Well, in a very short time, I'll share it all with him. Such a shame he won't have the chance to write it down for himself.

18

The truth is, I am a very particular man in everything relating to murder; and perhaps I carry my delicacy too far.

Don Merrick walked into the HOLMES room munching a two-inch-thick double cheese and Bar-B-Q bacon burger. 'How do you do it?' Dave Woolcott asked. 'How do you get those slack Alices down the canteen to cook you edible food? They could burn a cup of tea, that lot, but you always manage to twist them round your little finger.'

Merrick winked. 'It's my natural Geordie charm,' he said. 'I just pick on the ugliest one and tell her she reminds me of my mother when she was in her prime.' He sat down and stretched his long legs. 'I've checked out the half-dozen Discoveries your sergeant gave me. They're all in the clear. Two of them are women, two of them have got rock-solid alibis for at least two of the nights in question, one's got multiple sclerosis, so he couldn't have done the jobs, and the sixth sold his to a dealership in the Midlands three weeks ago.'

'Great,' Dave said heavily. 'Give the list to one of the operators so we can update the file.'

'Where's the guv?'

'Carol or Kevin?'

Merrick shrugged. 'I still think of Inspector Jordan as my guv'nor.'

'She's off chasing wild geese,' Dave said.

'She got a result, then?' Merrick asked.

'Two cross-matches.'

'Let's have a look,' Merrick said.

Dave rummaged among his papers and found three sheets of paper stapled together. The first listed the two correlations. Merrick frowned and flicked over a page. The second was a print-out of the result of a criminal records search on Philip Crozier. Nothing known. Hurriedly, he turned to the third page, which listed two Christopher Thorpes. One had a last-known address in Devon and several convictions for burglary. The second had a last-known address in Seaford. There were a string of juvenile convictions; assaulting a football referee, breaking windows at a school, shoplifting. There were half a dozen adult convictions, all for soliciting prostitution. Merrick sucked in his breath sharply and turned back to the front page. 'Fuck,' he said.

'What is it?' Dave asked, suddenly alert.

'This here. Christopher Thorpe, the Seaford one?'

'Yeah? Carol reckoned it wasn't the same one as ours. I mean, he's got convictions for being a male prostitute, but this one in Bradfield looks to be married, because the woman at the same address has his surname. And let's face it, you don't get dockland rent boys driving around in serious motors like the Discovery.'

Merrick shook his head. 'No, you've got it all wrong. I know this Christopher Thorpe from Seaford. I worked on Vice in Seaford before I came here, remember? I was the arresting officer on two of these charges in soliciting. Christopher Thorpe was halfway to a sex change at the time. He had the tits and everything, he was trying to earn enough money to get the operation. Guess what his working name was? Dave, Christopher Thorpe isn't *married* to Angelica Thorpe, he *is* Angelica Thorpe.'

'Fuck,' Dave echoed.

'Dave, where the hell is Carol?'

*   *   *

Angelica stood in front of him, hands on hips, chewing one corner of her mouth. 'You can't, can you? You can't prove it because you know nothing about my life.'

'In one sense you're absolutely right, Angelica. I don't know the facts of your life,' Tony said carefully, 'but I think I know a bit about the shape of it. Your mother didn't do a very good job of loving you. Maybe she had a problem with drink or with drugs, or maybe she just didn't understand what a little kid needed. Either way, she didn't make you feel loved when you were little. Am I right?'

Angelica scowled. 'Go on. Dig yourself a hole.'

Tony felt a prickle of fear tingle at the base of his skull. What if he'd got it wrong? What if this woman was the exception to every statistical near certainty Tony had held at the front of his mind during the whole enquiry? What if she was the one serial killer who had come from a happy, loving family? Dismissing his doubts as a luxury he couldn't afford right now, Tony ploughed on. 'Your father wasn't around much when you were growing up, and he never showed you he was proud of his son, even though you did everything you knew how to make him feel that pride. Your mother expected too much of you, kept telling you you were the man of the house, and giving you a bad time when you behaved like the child you were instead of the man she wanted to pretend you were.' Angelica's face twitched in a spasm of recognition. Tony paused.

'Go on,' she grated between clenched teeth.

'It's not easy for me to talk, doubled over like this. Can't you slacken the rope a bit, let me stand upright?'

She shook her head, her mouth sulky as a child's.

'I can't look at you properly like this,' Tony tried. 'You've got a fabulous body, you must know that. If it's going to be the last thing I see, at least let me appreciate it.'

She cocked her head to one side, as if replaying his words to check them for truth or trickery. 'All right,' she conceded. 'It doesn't mean anything's changed, though,' she added as she moved to the winch and released it. She let out about a foot of slack.

Tony couldn't bite back the scream of pain that shot through his shoulders as the muscles were released from the strain that had stretched them to their limit. 'It'll wear off,' Angelica said roughly as she returned to her station by the camcorder. 'Keep talking,' she instructed him. 'I've always enjoyed fantasy fiction.'

He eased himself upright, struggling against the pain. 'You were a bright kid,' he gasped. 'Brighter than the rest of them. It's never easy making friends when you're so much smarter than the other kids. And maybe you moved around a bit. Different neighbours, maybe even different schools.'

Angelica was back in control of herself, her face impassive as he continued. 'It wasn't easy to make friends. You knew you were different from everybody else, special, but you couldn't work out why at first. Then as you grew up, you realized what it was. You weren't the same as the other boys because you weren't a boy at all. You had no interest in girls sexually, but it wasn't because you were gay. No way. It was because you were really a girl yourself. What you discovered was that dressing up in women's clothes made you feel like you'd come home, like this was how you were meant to be.' He paused and gave her a crooked smile. 'How am I doing so far?'

'Very impressive, Doctor,' she said coldly. 'I'm fascinated. Carry on.'

Tony flexed his shoulder muscles, relieved to discover that the damage so far seemed to be only temporary. The pins and needles that raged across his back seemed no more than a minor irritation after what he'd been through. He took a deep breath and carried on. 'You decided to become the person you were inside, the woman you knew you really were. God, Angelica, I've got so much respect for you, putting yourself through that. I know how hard it is to get the medical profession to take the idea seriously. All the hormone therapy, the electrolysis, living as a half-man, half-woman while you waited for the operations, and then all the pain of the surgery.' He shook his head, wonderingly. 'I know I wouldn't have the courage to put myself through all that.'

'It wasn't easy.' The words escaped from Angelica's lips, almost against her will.

'I believe you,' Tony said sympathetically. 'And after all that, to find yourself wondering if it had been worth it after all, when you realized that the stupidity, the insensitivity, the lack of insight you'd identified in men didn't just disappear because you were a woman. They were still the same old bunch of bastards, incapable of recognizing an exceptional woman when they were offered her love and affection on a plate.' He paused, studying her face, deciding if the time was right for the big gamble. The coldness had left her eyes, replaced by a look almost of misery. He softened his voice and lowered the volume. Please God, let his training pay off.

'They rejected you, didn't they? Adam Scott, Paul Gibbs, Gareth Finnegan, Damien Connolly. They turned you down.'

Angelica shook her head violently, as if by activity she could deny the past. 'They *let* me down. They *let* me down, they didn't turn me down. They betrayed me.'

'Tell me about it,' Tony said softly, praying that his hard-earned techniques weren't going to fail him now. 'Tell me about it.'

'Why should I?' she shouted, stepping forward and slapping him so hard he tasted blood as his cheek impacted against his teeth. 'You're no better than them. What about that slag? That blonde bitch, that fucking plonk you've been giving one to?'

Tony swallowed the warm salty blood that filled his

mouth. 'You mean Carol Jordan?' he said, playing for time. How should he play this? Should he lie or tell the truth?

'You know full well who I mean. I know you've been with her, don't fucking try lying to me,' she hissed, raising her hand again. 'You treacherous, faithless bastard.' Her hand cracked him across the face again, so hard he heard his neck crick under the force of it.

Tears sprang to his eyes involuntarily. The truth wasn't going to work. It would only earn him more punishment. Praying he could lie with conviction, Tony pleaded, 'Angelica, she was just a fuck, just someone to scratch the itch. You'd got me so horny with your phone calls. I didn't know when you were going to call again, or even if you were.' He allowed anger to creep into his voice. 'I wanted you and you didn't tell me how I could get hold of you. Angelica, it's like you with the other ones. I was filling in time, waiting for my equal. You can't believe that a mere cop would answer my fantasies, do you? You should know, you've had one too.'

Angelica stepped back, shock on her face. Sensing he had made some kind of a breakthrough, Tony pursued her with his words. 'We were different, you and me. They weren't worthy of you. But we were special. You must know that, from our phone calls. Didn't you sense that we had something extraordinary? That this time it would be different? Isn't that what you really want? You don't want the killing. Not really. The killing only happened because they weren't worthy, because they let you down. What you really want is a worthy partner. What you want is love. Angelica, what you want is me.'

For a long moment she stared at him, eyes wide, mouth open. Then confusion took over, as obvious to Tony as a hooker's come-on. 'Don't use that word to me, you worthless scumbag,' she stuttered. 'Don't fucking say it!' Her voice was a low, throaty scream. Suddenly, she turned on her heel and ran from the room, her heels clattering up the stairs.

'I love you, Angelica,' Tony shouted desperately after her retreating footsteps. 'I love you.'

Carol and DC Morris stood on the doorstep of the small terraced house in Gregory Street. She didn't need to be a psychologist to read his body language. Morris was fed up at trailing round pursuing Carol's daft hunch. 'They must be out at work,' he remarked after their fourth assault on the doorbell.

'Looks that way,' Carol agreed.

'Shall we come back later?'

'Let's go on the knocker,' Carol suggested. 'See if any of the neighbours are around. Maybe they can tell us when the Thorpes get back from work.'

Morris looked as if he'd rather be on crowd control at a student demo. 'Yes, ma'am,' he said in a bored voice.

'You take across the street, I'll go for this side.' Carol watched him trudge across the street as wearily as a miner at the end of his shift, shook her head with a sigh and turned her attention to number twelve. This was much more the kind of territory Tony had suggested for their killer. Thinking of Tony just made Carol cross again. Where the hell was he? She really needed his input today, not to mention a bit of support for an idea that everybody else seemed to think was a complete waste of time. He couldn't have picked a worse moment to go on the missing list. It was unforgivable. At least he could have phoned his secretary and not left her having to field his calls and make excuses for him.

There was no bell on the door of number twelve, so Carol bruised her knuckles on the solid wood. The woman who opened it looked like a caricature from a soap opera. In her forties, her make-up would have been over the top for dinner in LA, never mind mid-afternoon in a Bradfield back street. Her dyed platinum blonde hair was piled high in a lopsided beehive. She wore a tight black sweater with a scoop neck revealing a cleavage the texture of crumpled tissue, shiny blue skin-tight leggings, white stilettoes and a thin gold ankle chain. A cigarette dangled from a corner of her mouth. 'What is it, love?' she said nasally.

'Sorry to trouble you,' Carol said, flashing her warrant card. 'Detective Inspector Carol Jordan, Bradfield police. I'm trying to get in touch with your next-door neighbours at number fourteen, the Thorpes, but there doesn't seem to be anybody home. I wonder if you happen to know what time they get in from work.'

The woman shrugged. 'Search me, love. That cow comes and goes at all hours.'

'What about Mr Thorpe?' Carol asked.

'What Mr Thorpe? There's no Mr Thorpe next door, love.' She gave a croak of laughter. 'It's easy seen you've never clapped eyes on her. Any man that married that ugly cow would have to be blind and bloody hard up. So what've you got her for?'

'It's just routine enquiries,' Carol said.

The woman snorted. 'Don't give me that fanny,' she said. 'I've watched enough episodes of *The Bill* to know they don't send inspectors out on routine enquiries. It's about time you put that cow behind bars, if you want my opinion.'

'Why is that, Mrs . . . ?'

'Goodison, Bette Goodison. As in Bette Davis. Because she's an ugly, anti-social cow, that's why.'

Carol smiled. 'I'm afraid that's not a crime, Mrs Goodison.'

'No, but murder is, isn't it?' Bette Goodison crowed triumphantly.

Carol swallowed, hoping the effect of the word wasn't as visible as it was palpable. 'That's a very serious accusation.'

Bette Goodison took a final drag of her cigarette and

expertly flipped the dog end across the narrow pavement and into the gutter. 'I'm glad you think so. It's more than your mates at Moorside nick did.'

'I'm sorry you feel you've not been well served by my colleagues,' Carol said in a concerned tone. 'Perhaps you could tell me what you're talking about?' Please God, let this not be a rerun of the Yorkshire Ripper case, where the killer's best friend told the police they suspected he was the Ripper and the police paid no attention.

'Prince, that's who we're talking about.'

For one wild moment, Carol had a vision of the diminutive American rock star buried in the back yard of a Bradfield terrace. Pulling herself together, she said, 'Prince?'

'Our German shepherd. Always complaining about him, that Angelica Thorpe was. And she had no grounds. That dog was doing her a service. Anybody so much as walked down our ginnel and that dog let you know about it. She'd have paid a fortune for a burglar alarm as efficient as that dog. Any road up, a few months back . . . August, it were, weekend before Bank Holiday, we come home from work, Col and me, and Prince is gone. Now, there's no way he could have got out of that yard, and he'd have gone for anybody that came in. There's only one way he could have disappeared, and that's if he was murdered,' Mrs Goodison said, stabbing Carol in the chest with her finger for emphasis. 'She poisoned him and then she got rid of the body so there would be no proof. She's a murderer!'

Normally, Carol would have walked a mile barefoot to avoid this conversation, but she was in pursuit of Handy Andy, and any oddity was something to be grasped eagerly. 'How can you be so sure it was Mrs Thorpe?' she asked.

'Stands to reason. She were the only one that ever complained about him. And the day he went missing, me and Col were out at work, but she were home all day. I know that for a fact, because she were on nights that week. And when we knocked on her door to ask did she know anything about him going missing, she just smiled all over that ugly gob of hers. I could have put her face in for her,' Mrs Goodison said emphatically. 'So what are you going to do about it?'

'I'm afraid that without evidence, there's not much we can do,' Carol said sympathetically. 'You're sure, are you, that Mrs Thorpe lives alone?'

'Nobody'd want to live with an ugly cow like that. She never even has visitors. Not surprising, mind, she looks like a brick shithouse in drag.'

'Do you happen to know what kind of car she drives?' Carol asked.

'One of them bloody yuppie jeep things. I ask you, who needs a bloody great jeep in the middle of Bradfield? It's not like we live up some farm track, is it?'

'And do you know where she works?'

'I don't know and I don't care.' She glanced at her watch. 'Now, if you don't mind, my serial's starting.'

Carol watched the door close behind Bette Goodison, an unpleasant suspicion starting to form in her mind. Before she could try number ten, her pager bleeped insistently. 'Phone Don at Scargill Street. Double urgent,' she read.

'Morris!' Carol shouted. 'Get me to a phone. Pronto monto.' Whatever was going on in Gregory Street could wait. Don clearly couldn't.

Exhausted, Tony had slipped into some nightmare delirium doze. A gout of freezing water thrown in his face smacked him straight to agonized attention, his head snapping back painfully. 'Augh,' he groaned.

'Wakey, wakey,' Angelica said roughly.

'I was right, wasn't I?' Tony said through swollen lips. 'You've had time to think about it, and you know I'm right. You want the killing to stop. They had to die, they deserved to die. They let you down, they betrayed you, they didn't deserve you. But all that can change now. It can be different with me, because I love you.'

The rigid mask of her face crumpled before his eyes, becoming softer, more tender. She smiled at him. 'It's never been about sex, you know. I could always have sex. Men paid me for sex. They paid me a lot of money for sex. That's how I paid for the surgery, you know. They always wanted me.' Her voice was filled with a strange mixture of pride and anger.

'I can see why,' Tony lied, arranging his face in what he hoped was an expression of hunger and admiration. 'But what you really wanted was love, wasn't it? You wanted more than loveless sex on the streets or faceless sex down the phone. You deserve that. God, you deserve it. That's what I can give you, Angelica. Love isn't just physical attraction, though God knows you're attractive. But love's about respect, admiration, fascination, and I feel all of that for you. Angelica, you can have what you want. You can have it with me.'

Her warring emotions were written plainly on her face. He could see that part of her desperately wanted to believe him, wanted to escape into the normal world of relationships. But that part had to contend with a level of self-esteem that was so low she couldn't imagine anyone worth loving wanting to love her. And, underlying it all, suspicion that he was trying to entrap her. 'How can we?' she demanded harshly. 'You've been trying to hunt me down. You're with the police. You're on their side.'

Tony shook his head. 'That was before I realized you were the same woman I'd fallen in love with on the phone. Angelica, love is the one emotion that overrides duty. Yeah, I've worked with the police, but I'm not one of them.'

'You lie down with dogs, you get up with fleas,' she sneered. 'You've been trying to put me away, Anthony. You expect me to believe you? You must think I'm really stupid.'

'Quite the opposite. If you want to talk about stupid, talk about the police. Mostly, they're one-dimensional, boring bigots who couldn't keep a psychologist interested for more than five minutes. I don't have anything in common with them,' he argued desperately.

She shook her head, more in sorrow than in anger. 'You work for the Home Office. Your whole career, you've spent catching serial offenders and treating them. And you expect me to believe you'd suddenly change sides and stay loyal to me? Come on, Anthony, I'm not going to fall for crap like that.'

Tony felt his powers flagging. His brain just wasn't fast enough any longer to keep her at bay. Wretchedly, he said, 'I've not made a career of catching people, only treating them. I had to do that, don't you understand? Inside the places where I've worked is the only place where I can find minds that are complex enough to be interesting. It's like going to see animals at the zoo. You want to watch them in their natural habitat, but if the only way you are ever going to see them is at the zoo, you go. I've always had to wait till they were in captivity before I could study them. But you, you're still in the wild, still the way you want to be, perfected in your craft. And compared to them, you're the cream of the crop. You're exceptional. I want to spend the rest of my life being excited by your mind. I can't imagine ever finding you boring.' Terrifying, maybe, but never boring.

Her lower lip thrust out, bringing an expression of calculating petulance to her face. She nodded in the direction of his groin, where his penis hung limp. 'So if you find me that attractive, how come it doesn't show?'

It was the one question to which Tony had no answer at all.

'What have we actually got, Carol?' Brandon challenged.

Carol paced the floor of Brandon's office, ticking off

her points on her fingers. 'We've got a transsexual. Not a transsexual who went through the controlled, counselled National Health Service process, but one who, according to Don, was turned down for a sex change here and had to finance an operation abroad by selling sex. So right from the start, we know we've got someone who has been examined by psychiatrists and found to be unstable. We've got this transsexual driving a vehicle identical to the one driven by a suspect in Damien Connolly's murder. We've got a neighbour who's convinced that Angelica Thorpe offed her dog. The dog was killed a fortnight before the first murder. Angelica Thorpe bought software that would allow her to manipulate videos in her computer system, which fits a theory of the killer's behaviour developed by me and endorsed by our psychological profiler. She even lives in the kind of house Tony said she would,' Carol argued vehemently.

'When she was Christopher, she was definitely a few butties short of a picnic,' Don chipped in.

'I wish we could ask Tony about this,' Brandon said, stalling.

'So do I,' Carol said through her teeth. 'But he's obviously found something more important to do today.' A sudden thought hit Carol like a sandbag to the neck. Her knees started to buckle and she collapsed into the nearest chair. 'Oh, my God,' she gasped.

'What is it?' Brandon asked, concerned.

'Tony. He hasn't been in touch with anybody since he left here yesterday. He had two task-force meetings arranged for today, according to his secretary, but he hasn't shown up at work, and he hasn't phoned in. He wasn't home last night, and he's not there now.' Carol's words hung in the air like a cloud of poisonous smoke. A wave of nausea lurched up from her stomach, almost choking her. Somehow, she maintained her composure under Brandon's concentrated stare.

368

With fingers that trembled, Carol picked up Brandon's copy of the profile from his desk. Urgently, she flicked through the pages till she found what she was looking for. '"It is possible that his next target may also be a police officer, perhaps even one who is working on the investigation. This alone will not be sufficient motive for the killer to choose them; they must also fit the victim criteria that he has drawn up in his own mind in order for the killing to assume its full meaning for him. I would strongly recommend that any officers who fit the victim profile employ extra vigilance at all times, noting any suspicious vehicles parked near their homes, and checking to see whether they are being followed to and from work and social events." Think about it, sir. Think about the victim profile. Sir, Tony fits it perfectly.'

Not wanting to believe what Carol was suggesting, Brandon said, 'But it's not eight weeks. It's not time!'

'But it *is* a Monday. Don't forget, Tony also pointed out that his timetable could be accelerated if something happened to traumatize him. Stevie McConnell, sir. Think of all the publicity. Someone else was getting the credit for his crimes. Look, it's in here, sir: "Another possible scenario is that an innocent person is charged with the killings. That would be such an affront to his sense of himself that he might commit his next murder ahead of schedule." Sir, we've got to move on this now!'

Brandon's hand was on the phone before she'd even started her last sentence.

The front door opened directly into the house. Downstairs couldn't have looked more normal. The small living room was furnished inexpensively but comfortably with a two-seater sofa and matching chair upholstered in moss-green Dralon. There was a TV, video, mid-priced stereo system and a coffee table complete with a copy of *Elle*. A pair of framed posters of whales in the ocean hung on the walls.

The single bookshelf contained a selection of science-fiction classics, a couple of Stephen King novels and a trio of Jackie Collins bonkbusters. Carol, Merrick and Brandon moved cautiously through the room, past the stairs and into the kitchen diner. It was surgically neat as a showroom, work surfaces clean and uncluttered. On the drainer, one mug, one plate, one fork, one knife.

With Brandon leading the way, they climbed the narrow stairs built between the two downstairs rooms. The front bedroom was pink and frothy as a strawberry milkshake. Even the kidney-shaped dressing table, with its skirt of lace, was pink. 'Barbara Cartland, eat your heart out,' Merrick muttered. Brandon opened the wardrobe and flicked through the array of women's clothes. Carol headed for the drawers in a pink tallboy and worked her way down. They contained nothing more disturbing than a selection of tacky underwear, much of it in red satin.

It was Merrick who first broached the back bedroom. As soon as he opened the door, he knew no one was going to be screaming to the papers about magistrates granting warrants on non-existent evidence. 'Sir?' he shouted. 'I think we've cracked it.'

The room was arranged as an office. A large desk held a computer and assorted peripherals that none of them could identify. To one side was a telephone linked to a sophisticated tape recorder. A small video-editing desk was in one corner, next to a filing cabinet. A wheeled trolley carried a television and video, both state of the art and top of the range. Shelves lined two walls, filled with computer games, videos, cassettes and computer disks, each box labelled neatly in firm capitals. The only alien object in the room was a leather recliner, the material slung hammock-like on a steel frame.

'Bingo,' Brandon breathed. 'Well done, Carol.'

'Where the fuck do we start?' Merrick said.

'Do either of you know how to work the computer?' Brandon asked.

'I think we should leave that to the experts,' Carol said. 'It might be programmed to crash the data if someone else tries to log on.'

'OK. Don, you take the filing cabinet, I'll take the videos, and Carol, you take the cassettes.'

Carol moved across to the shelves of cassettes. The first couple of dozen seemed to be music tapes, ranging from Liza Minnelli to U2. Next were a dozen marked 'AS' and numbered from one to twelve. Fourteen marked 'PG' followed, then fifteen with 'GF', eight with 'DC' and six with 'AH'. The concatenation of initials was far beyond the boundaries of coincidence. Carol picked the first 'AH' tape and, heart heavy with misgivings, slotted it into the cassette player. She picked up the headphones plugged into the machine and gingerly pushed them into her ears. She heard the sound of a telephone ringing, then a voice so familiar she could have wept. 'Hello?' Tony said, his voice reduced by the telephone line.

'Hello, Anthony,' a voice not entirely strange to her said.

'Who is this?' Tony asked.

A chuckle, low and sexy. 'You'll never guess. Not in a million years.' Got it, thought Carol, grim foreboding gripping her. The voice on the answering machine.

'OK, so tell me,' Tony said, his voice curious, friendly, joining in the game.

'Who would you like me to be? If I could be anyone in the world?'

'Is this some kind of wind-up?' Tony demanded.

'I've never been more serious in my life. I'm here to make your dreams come true. I'm the woman of your fantasies, Anthony. I am your telephone lover.'

There was a moment's silence, then the phone slammed down at Tony's end. Over the dialling tone, Carol heard the strange woman say, '*Hasta la vista*, Anthony.'

She stabbed the stop button and violently pulled out the headphones. She turned round to see Brandon transfixed by the image of Adam Scott stretched out on a rack, naked and apparently unconscious. Part of her mind could not comprehend what she was seeing. Evil, she thought, should be drenched in blood, not prosaically displayed on a suburban television screen.

'Sir,' she forced out. 'The tapes. She's been stalking Tony.'

Tony tried a laugh. It came out more like a sob, but he carried on regardless. 'You expect me to get an erection? Trussed up like this? Angelica, you chloroformed me, kidnapped me and left me to come round alone in a torture chamber. I'm sorry to disappoint you, but I've got no experience of bondage. I'm too bloody scared to get a hard-on.'

'I'm not letting you go, you know. Not to run straight back to them.'

'I'm not asking you to let me go. Believe me, I'm happy to be your prisoner if that's the only way I can spend time with you. I want to get to know you, Angelica. I want to prove my feelings to you, I want to show you what love feels like. I want to show you whose side I'm really on here.' Tony tried to turn on the kind of smile he'd learned that women responded to.

'So show me,' Angelica challenged, letting one hand run caressingly down her body, lingering over her nipples and edging towards her crotch.

'I'm going to need your help. Just like I needed you on the phone. You made me feel so good, like a real man. Please, help me now,' Tony pleaded.

She took a step towards him, moving sinuously as a stripper. 'You want me to turn you on?' she drawled in a ghastly parody of seduction.

'I don't think I can do it like this,' Tony said. 'Not with my arms pinned behind me like this.'

Angelica stopped dead and scowled. 'I said, I'm not letting you go.'

'And I said I'm not asking you to. All I'm asking is that you cuff my hands in front of me. So I can touch you.' Again, he forced the gentle smile.

She looked at him consideringly. 'How do I know I can trust you? I'd have to set your hands free so I could cuff them in front of you. Maybe you're trying to double-cross me.'

'I won't. I give you my word. If it makes you feel safer, chloroform me again. Do it while I'm unconscious,' Tony said, gambling again. Her reaction would tell him all he needed to know about his chances.

Angelica moved behind him. An exultant voice in his head screamed 'Yes!' He felt the warmth of her hand between his as she gripped the cuffs and painfully jerked them up. 'Shit!' Tony yelled as new arrows of pain shot up his arms and through his shoulders. He heard a click of metal as the shackle connecting the rope to the handcuffs snapped free. Angelica released the handcuffs and Tony collapsed to his knees, his legs buckling under him. 'Jesus Christ!' he swore as he crashed forwards on to his face, feeling the rough stone graze his cheek.

Moving swiftly, Angelica unlocked one side of the handcuffs, seized the back of his hair and pulled him upwards. Still holding the arm with the handcuffs attached, she stepped in front of him and roughly gripped his other arm just below the bicep, dragging it across his body. Seconds later, his hands were cuffed again, this time in front of him. He knelt like a supplicant, his discomfort doubled by the tight leather straps round his ankles. 'You see?' he gasped. 'I told you I wouldn't try anything.'

Panting slightly, Angelica stood in front of him, legs apart. 'So show me,' she demanded.

'You'll have to help me up. I can't do it by myself,' he protested weakly.

She bent down and grabbed his hair again, hauling him up on to legs whose muscles trembled with the effort of staying upright. They stood, inches apart, the silk of her kimono brushing his hands. He could feel the warmth of her breath on the raw flesh of his grazed cheek. 'Kiss me,' he said softly. Whores never get to kiss, he told himself. This'll make it different.

Something flickered in Angelica's eyes, but she leaned over him, releasing his hair and pulling his face to hers. It took every ounce of his willpower not to flinch as her lips met his, her tongue invading his mouth, exploring his teeth and tongue. Your life depends on it, he told himself. You've got a plan. Tony forced himself to kiss her back, thrusting his tongue into her mouth, telling himself there were worse things in the world, and this woman had made her previous victims endure some of them.

After what felt like the longest kiss of his life, Angelica pulled away, looking critically down to his groin. 'I'm going to need some help here,' Tony said. 'It's not been an easy day.'

'What kind of help?' Angelica asked, panting slightly through parted lips. It was clear that she was having no difficulty with the sexual arousal that was beyond him.

'Give me head. That's the one thing that always works when I'm having trouble. I've felt your mouth now; I just know you'll be terrific. Please, I really want to make love to you.'

Almost before he'd finished speaking, she was on her knees, hands flickering over his balls. Tenderly, she lifted his flaccid penis and slipped it into her mouth, not taking her eyes from his face. Tony reached out and began to stroke her hair. Then, with what felt like infinite slowness, he pulled her head forward on to him, forcing her head down, her eyes away from him.

Then, summoning up what remained of his strength,

Tony raised his hands and brought the handcuffs crashing down on the back of Angelica's head.

The blow caught her completely off guard and she went crashing forward between his legs, her teeth snagging agonizingly on him. Tony let himself fall backwards, feeling a tearing in his ankles as they protested against a movement they were never designed to make. As he hit the ground, he doubled forwards and grabbed Angelica's head, banging it hard on the stone floor till her body stopped thrashing.

He dragged himself over her prone figure till his numb fingers could reach the ankle straps. With maddening clumsiness, he struggled to unfasten the sets of buckles that fixed him to the stone slab. After what felt like hours, he was finally free. As he tried to stand, his ankles refused the challenge, turning over and catapulting him to the floor again, sending excruciating daggers of pain up his legs. Moaning, he dragged himself across the floor towards the steps. He had barely travelled a couple of yards when the body on the floor groaned. Angelica lifted her head, blood and mucus turning her face into a grisly Hallowe'en mask. When she saw him, she roared like a wounded animal and started scrambling to her feet.

The search for a clue to Angelica's killing ground was growing more desperate as their fear and concern for Tony grew. They had emptied out the contents of the filing cabinet on to the floor. Every scrap of paper was scrutinized for any hint of the location of the cellar revealed in the video. Invoices, guarantees, bills and receipts all got the treatment. Carol was wading through a file of official correspondence, hoping to come across some lease or mortgage details, anything that related to another property. Merrick was ploughing through the files relating to Thorpe's sex change. Brandon had already had one false alarm, coming across a stack of solicitor's letters relating to a property in Seaford. It soon became clear, however, that they concerned the sale of Thorpe's late mother's home in the town.

It was Merrick who found the key. He'd finished with the sex-change files and started on a bundle of assorted letters, filed under 'Tax'. When he came across the letter, he had to read it twice to make sure wishful thinking wasn't making him imagine things.

'Sir,' he said cautiously. 'I think this might be what we're looking for.'

He handed the letter to Brandon, who read the letterhead of Pennant, Taylor, Bailey and Co., Solicitors. 'Dear Christopher Thorpe,' it said. 'We have received a letter from your aunt, Mrs Doris Makins, in New Zealand, authorizing us to pass on to you the keys for Start Hill Farm, Upper Tontine Moor, by Bradfield, W. Yorkshire. As her agents, we are empowered to allow you access to said property for the purposes of maintenance and security. Please make arrangements with this office to collect the keys at your convenience . . .'

'Access to an isolated rural property,' Carol said, looking over Brandon's shoulder. 'Tony said that's what the killer might have. And now she's got him there.' A wave of anger poured through her, displacing the slow burn of fear that had been eating through her from the moment they'd unlocked the macabre secrets of that superficially normal office.

Brandon closed his eyes momentarily then said tightly, 'We don't know that, Carol.'

'And even if she has got him, he's a clever bloke. If anyone can keep himself out of trouble with his gob, it's Tony Hill,' Don chipped in.

'Never mind whistling in the bloody dark,' Carol said sharply. 'Where the hell is Start Hill Farm? And how soon can we get there?'

Tony looked around in desperation. The rack of knives was over to his left, impossibly high up. As Angelica got to her knees, he clawed at the stone bench and hauled himself upright. His hand closed on the haft of the knife as she staggered to her feet and threw herself at him, still bellowing like a cow bereft of its calf.

Her weight and the momentum of her charge bent Tony backwards over the bench. Her hands scrabbled for his throat, gripping his windpipe so tightly that white lights started to dance in front of his eyes. Just when he thought he could hold on no longer, he felt the warm, sticky gush of blood against his stomach and Angelica's grasp became flabby as a wet newspaper.

Before he could take it all in, he heard footsteps crashing down the stone steps. Like a mad vision of paradise, Don Merrick crashed downstairs, rapidly followed by John Brandon, his jaw dropping at the tableau in front of him.

'Fucking hell,' Brandon breathed.

Carol pushed past the two men and stared uncomprehendingly at the carnage before her.

'You lot took your time,' Tony gasped. As he passed out, the last thing he heard was his own hysterical laughter.

Epilogue

Carol pushed open the door of the side ward. Tony was propped up on a pile of pillows, the left side of his face swollen and bruised.

'Hi,' Tony said, a wan half-smile the best he could manage without too much pain. 'Come on in.'

Carol closed the door behind her and sat down on a chair by the bed. 'I brought you some bits and pieces,' she said, dumping a plastic bag and a padded envelope on the coverlet.

Tony reached out for the bag. Carol winced inside as she saw the bracelet of bruises round his inflamed wrists. He took out a copy of *Esquire*, a can of Aqua Libra, a tin of pistachio nuts and a Dashiel Hammett omnibus. 'Thanks,' he said, surprised by how her choice touched him.

'I wasn't sure what you liked,' she said defensively.

'Then you're obviously a good guesser. The perfect task-force officer.'

'If a little slow on the uptake,' Carol said bitterly.

Tony shook his head. 'John Brandon was here earlier. He told me how you worked it all out. I don't see how you could have got there any quicker.'

'I should have realized sooner that you wouldn't have done a disappearing act at such a crucial time. Come to that, I should have realized as soon as I saw that profile that you could be a target and taken steps to protect you.'

'Bollocks, Carol. If anyone should have realized that, it was me. You did a bloody good job.'

'No. If I'd been on the ball, we'd have got there in time to save you having to ... to do what you did.'

Tony sighed. 'You mean, you'd have saved Angelica's life? For what? Years in a secure mental hospital? Look on the bright side, Carol. You've saved the state a fortune. No expensive trial, no years of incarceration and treatment to pay for. Shit, they'll probably give you a medal.'

'That's not what I meant, Tony,' Carol said. 'I meant you wouldn't have to live with the knowledge that you've killed someone.'

'Yes, well, I can't pretend it was the perfect outcome, but I'll learn to live with it.' He forced a smile. 'Don't take this the wrong way, but the first thing I'm going to do when I can walk again is go out and buy you a new mac,' he said. 'Every time I look at that coat of yours, I get the urge to scream.'

'Why?' Carol frowned in puzzlement.

'Didn't you know? She was wearing the identical mac when she turned up on the doorstep. That way, if she left any fibres at the scene, Forensic would assume they'd come from you.'

'Terrific,' Carol said ironically. 'How are the ankles, by the way?'

Tony pulled a face. 'I don't think I'll ever play the violin again. I managed to make it to the loo on crutches, but I had to sit on the edge of the bath to pee. They're saying there probably won't be any permanent damage, but it'll take a while for the torn ligaments to heal. How was your day?'

Carol pulled a face. 'Grisly. I suspect you'd have been in your element. You were right about keeping the fantasy alive. She, he, it, had tapes of all the telephone-sex conversations she'd had with her victims, and she'd stolen the outgoing message tapes from the men who had answering machines.

'It took the boffins a little while to crack the computer stuff. We didn't have anybody who really knew what they were doing, but my brother Michael came in and sorted it out for us.'

Tony gave a twisted smile. 'I didn't want to say anything at the time, but for a wild moment, I actually wondered about your brother.'

'Michael? You're kidding!'

Embarrassed, Tony nodded. 'It was when you posited the idea of the computer manipulation of the videos. Michael had the expertise to do that, no question. He's in the right age group, he lives with a woman but not in a sexual relationship, he's got access to all the information the killer needed about the way the police and forensic scientists work, his job is in the general area where I'd expect the killer to work, and he was in a position to know exactly what the police were up to and be involved in the investigation. If we hadn't caught Angelica when we did, I'd have been scrounging an invitation to dinner to check him out.'

Carol shook her head. 'See what I mean about being slow on the uptake? I had access to all the same information as you, and Michael never even crossed my mind as a possibility.'

'Not so surprising. You know him well enough to know he's not a psychopath.'

Carol shrugged. 'Do I, though? It wouldn't be the first time a close family member, a wife even, has made the same mistake.'

'Usually, they're either deluding themselves or they're emotionally unstable and dependent on the killer in some way. Neither of which would have applied in this case.' He gave a tired smile. 'Anyway, tell me about what your Michael uncovered.'

'The computer was a total goldmine. She'd kept her own diary of the stalking and the murders. It even says that she wanted it published after her death. Can you beat that?'

'Easily,' Tony said. 'Remind me to show you some of the academic papers I've got on the subject of serial killers.'

Carol shivered. 'Thanks, but no thanks. I got a print-out

of the diary for you. I figured you'd be interested.' She gestured to the envelope. 'It's in there. Also, as you'd surmised, she had video-taped the killings, and as I suggested, she'd imported them into her computer and manipulated the images to keep the fantasy alive. It was absolutely gruesome, Tony. It went way beyond nightmare.'

Tony nodded. 'I won't say you get used to it, because you never do if you're going to be any use at this job. But you do get to the stage where you can lock it away, so it doesn't jump out and wreck your head unawares.'

'Oh, yeah?'

'That's the theory. Ask me again in a few weeks,' he said grimly. 'Was there anything in there about how she chose her victims?'

'Just a fucking bit,' Carol said bitterly. 'She'd been at this for months before she even picked out the first victim. She worked for the phone company, a computer systems manager. Apparently, she used to work for a small private phone company back in Seaford, which gave her the experience to get the job in Bradfield. She was what they call a super-user of the computer system, so she had access to every piece of data in there. She used the phone company's computer to extract all the residential numbers who had made regular calls to sex chatlines in the past year.' Carol paused, letting the obvious question hang in the air.

'It was research,' Tony said wearily. 'I published a paper on the role of chatlines in the development of fantasies among serial offenders. Someone should have told Angelica not to jump to conclusions.'

Reading his remark as a veiled reproach, Carol moved on. 'She cross-referenced that against the electoral roll and came up with men who lived alone. Then she just checked them out by watching their houses. She had a clear picture of the physical type she wanted, and she wanted one with his own house, a decent income and good career prospects. Can you believe it?'

'Only too well,' Tony said grimly. 'Her rationale was that she never wanted to kill them, she only wanted to love them. But they made her murder because they betrayed her. She kept telling herself that what she really wanted was a man who would love her and live with her.'

Don't we all, Carol thought but didn't say. 'Anyway, once she'd decided on the likely candidate, she paved the way with the dirty phone calls. She got them on the hook that way, on account of all you sleazy men can't resist anonymous sex.'

'Ouch,' Tony said, wincing. 'In my defence, I'd have to say that a large part of my interest was purely academic. I was interested in the psychology of a woman who would do what she did on the phone.'

Carol smiled tightly. 'At least I know now that you were telling the truth when you said you didn't know the woman who was leaving the sexy messages on your answering machine.'

Tony looked away. 'And the discovery that a man you were attracted to was getting his rocks off in kinky telephone sex with a stranger must have been delightful for you.'

Carol was silent, unsure what to say. 'I've heard the tapes now,' she admitted. 'Yours are very different from the others. You were clearly uncomfortable a lot of the time. Not that it's any of my business.'

Still unable to meet her eyes, Tony spoke, his voice clipped and clinical. 'I have a problem with sex. To be precise, I have problems with achieving and maintaining an erection. The honest truth is that only part of me was treating the calls with professional interest. The other part of me was trying to use them as a kind of therapy. I know that makes me sound like a pervert, but part of the trouble with doing the job I do is that it's virtually impossible to find a therapist I can respect and trust who isn't connected in some way to the world I work in. And however much they verbally espouse the principle of client confidentiality, I've always been reluctant to expose myself to the risk.'

Realizing the difficulty Tony had had in making his confession, Carol reached out for his hand and covered it lightly with hers. 'Thank you for telling me that. It won't go any further. And if it makes you feel any better, the only people who have heard the tapes in full are me and John Brandon. You don't have to worry about what people are saying about you behind your back within the force.'

'That's something, I suppose. So, go on. Tell me about Angelica's phone calls to the other victims.'

'It was obvious that the men thought this was sex without any commitment or comeback. Angelica's analysis was completely different. She'd convinced herself that their responses meant they were falling in love with her. Unfortunately for the guys, they decided otherwise. As soon as they showed any interest in another woman, they signed their death warrants. Apart from Damien, that is. She killed him to teach us a lesson. You were going to be the other lesson.'

Tony shuddered. 'No wonder she had to go abroad for the sex-change operation. The NHS psychologists she saw must have had a field day with her attitudes and aspirations.'

'Apparently, they decided she was not an appropriate candidate for a sex change because of her lack of insight into her sexuality. They concluded that she was a gay man who couldn't cope with his sexuality because of cultural and family conditioning. They recommended counselling with a sex therapist rather than a sex change. There was an ugly scene at the time. He threw one of the psychologists through a glass door,' Carol revealed.

'Pity they didn't press charges,' Tony said.

'Yes. And you'll be pleased to hear they're definitely not going to charge you.'

'I should think not! Like I said, think of the taxpayers'

money I've saved. Maybe we should have dinner to cele-
brate when I get out of here?' he asked tentatively.

'I'd like that. There is one other good thing that came
out of all of this,' Carol said.

'What's that?'

'Penny Burgess took the day off yesterday to go walking
in the dales. Apparently, her car broke down and she got
stranded in the middle of a forest all night. She missed
the whole shooting match. There's a dozen by-lines in the
Sentinel Times tonight, and not a single one of them is
hers!'

Tony lay back and stared at the ceiling. Papering over
the cracks, that's what they were doing. He suspected Carol
knew that as well as he did, and he wasn't sorry for the
effort she was making. But he'd had enough for now. He
closed his eyes and sighed.

'Oh God, I'm sorry,' Carol said, getting to her feet. 'I
wasn't thinking. You must still be exhausted. Look, I'm
out of here. I'll leave you this stuff to read when you feel
up to it. I could drop in tomorrow if you like . . .'

'I think I'd like that,' Tony said wearily. 'It just comes
over me in waves sometimes.'

He heard her feet cross the floor and the click of the
door opening. 'Take care,' Carol said.

The door closed behind her and Tony pushed himself
back up till he was leaning against the pillows. He reached
for the padded envelope. While he couldn't cope with conversation, his curiosity wouldn't let him ignore Angelica's
diary. He pulled out a thick wedge of A4 paper. 'Let's see
what you were really made of,' he said softly. 'What's the
story? How did you justify, what did you hide behind?'
Hungrily, he began to read.

Wading through the outpourings of the psychologically
damaged was normally a routine exploratory experience
for Tony. But this was different, he realized after only a
few paragraphs. At first, he couldn't pin down what it was.

The writing was more literate, more controlled and more immediate than most of their ramblings, but that didn't explain why his response was so different. He moved on a few pages, fascinated and repelled equally. It was no more or less self-obsessed than other things he'd read, but there was a chilling relish here that was unusual. Most killers whose writings he'd read had gloried far more in their own bloody role, reflecting less on what they'd done to their victims and its effect on them, but here was someone who identified herself as much in terms of them. But even that couldn't entirely explain why he felt so unsettled by what he was reading. Whatever it was, it was making him more reluctant to continue the more he read, the opposite to his normal response. He'd been so obsessively keen to get inside the head of the killer he'd dubbed Handy Andy, but now it was laid out before him, it was as if he didn't want to know.

As he forced himself to read on, mentally chalking up the correct assumptions he'd made in his profile, it eventually dawned on him that what he was feeling was personal. These words were touching him in ways he'd never experienced before because the life outlined in these pages had touched him with a directness he'd never known before. These were the footsteps of his own personal nemesis that he was tracing, and it was an uncomfortable journey.

He tossed the papers to one side, unable to keep going, seeing his own fate mirrored in the broken bodies Angelica had meticulously described. The trouble with being a psychologist was that he knew exactly what was happening to him. He knew he was still in shock, still deep in denial. Although he couldn't get the events in the cellar out of his mind, there was still a distance between him and the memory, as if he were watching them from a long way off. One day the horror of the previous night was going to come roaring back in stereo, splashed across his inner eye in Cinemascope. Knowing that, this numbness was a blessing.

Already, he knew, his answering machine would be crammed with lucrative offers for the story of how the hunter turned killer. One day, he was going to have to tell that story. He hoped he'd have the strength to save it for a psychiatrist.

It was no comfort to rationalize that having been the target of one serial killer, he was statistically unlikely ever to find himself in that position again. All he could think of was the hours in the cellar, dredging his experience and knowledge for the magic words that would give him a few minutes longer to try for the key to his freedom.

Then that kiss. The whore's kiss, the killer's kiss, the lover's kiss, the saviour's kiss, all rolled into one. A kiss from the mouth that had been seducing him for weeks, the mouth whose words had given him hope for his future, only to leave him finally stranded in this place. He had spent his working life worming his way into the heads of those who kill, only to end up one of them, thanks to a Judas kiss.

'You've won, haven't you, Angelica?' he said softly. 'You wanted me, and now you've got me.'